My darling Brother -
with all my love -
Nello

SULEIMAN'S GOLD

SULEIMAN'S GOLD

Alistair Graham

Then shalt thou lay up gold as dust,
And the gold of Ophir as stones of the brooks.
Job xxii, 24

Book Guild Publishing
Sussex, England

First published in Great Britain in 2010 by
The Book Guild Ltd
Pavilion View
19 New Road
Brighton, BN1 1UF

Typesetting in Baskerville by
SetSystems Ltd, Saffron Walden, Essex

Printed in Great Britain by
CPI Antony Rowe

A catalogue record for this book is
available from the British Library

ISBN 978 1 84624 386 8

Thanks, Jane, for ideas, criticism and encouragement

Contents

Maps   ix

Photos   xi

Book One

1 Ssshlooop!   3

2 Sharp Horns and Quatermains   12

3 Ophir and the Land of Punt   21

4 Luoniek   30

5 Into the Madbet   43

6 Unholy Deeds in the Holy City   60

7 The Course of True Love   91

8 Even the Tightest Knot Comes Undone   109

Book Two

9   The Ancient Eldorado of all the Old Fools   135

10 Flashman's Gold   143

11 Sweat of the Sun and Tears of the Moon   153

12 A Snake Story   167

13 Scotching the Snake   189

14 The Unreliability of Men's Memories   202

15 Solomon's Triangle   211

Book Three

16 The Geologist   229

17 The Tsetse Fly   245

18 The Bobejaan   255

19 Shifta   260

20 My Life as a Brigand   274

21 I Do my Florence Nightingale Impression   291

22 A Proposition from Hell   309

23 Eldorado and How to Get There   330

24 On the Hollowness of Baobabs   344

25 Do Not Remove Thorns from Lions' Feet   367

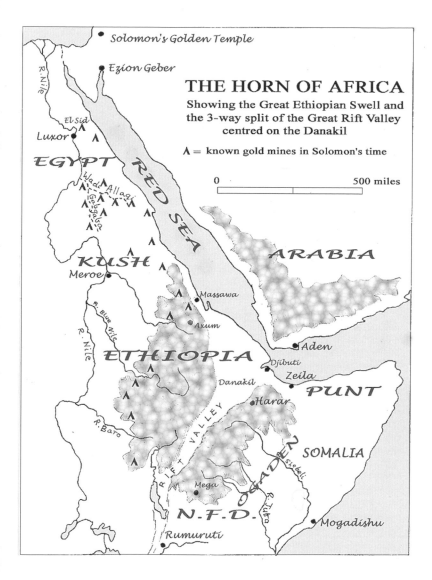

Solomon's Golden Temple

Ezion Geber

R. Nile

El Sid

Luxor

EGYPT

THE HORN OF AFRICA

Showing the Great Ethiopian Swell and
the 3-way split of the Great Rift Valley
centred on the Danakil

Λ = known gold mines in Solomon's time

0   500 miles

RED SEA

Wadi Allaqi

Gebeyt

KUSH

Meroe

ARABIA

Massawa

R. Blue Nile

R. Nile

Axum

ETHIOPIA

Aden

Djibuti

Zeila

Danakil

PUNT

Harar

R. Baro

RIFT VALLEY

OGADEN

R. Shebeli

SOMALIA

Mega

R. Juba

N.F.D.

Rumuruti

Mogadishu

ix

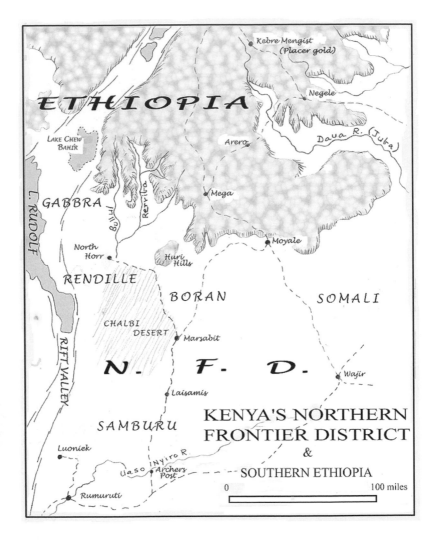

KENYA'S NORTHERN
FRONTIER DISTRICT
&
SOUTHERN ETHIOPIA

x

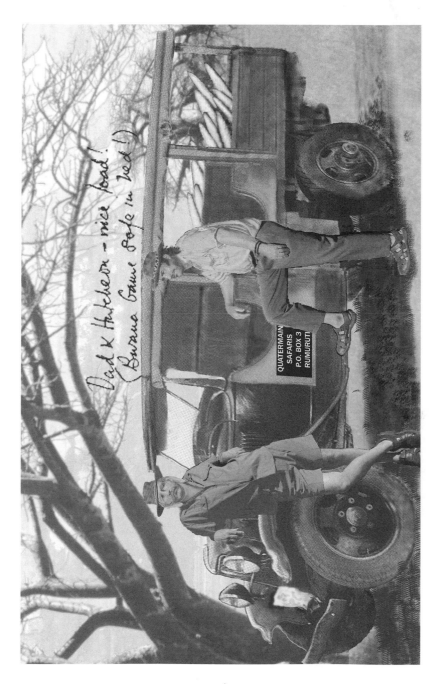

Dad & Hutchear — nice load!
(Bwana Game safe in bed!)

The only surviving photo of my mother, Amina, taken in 1926

My father, Rider Quatermain, in 1929

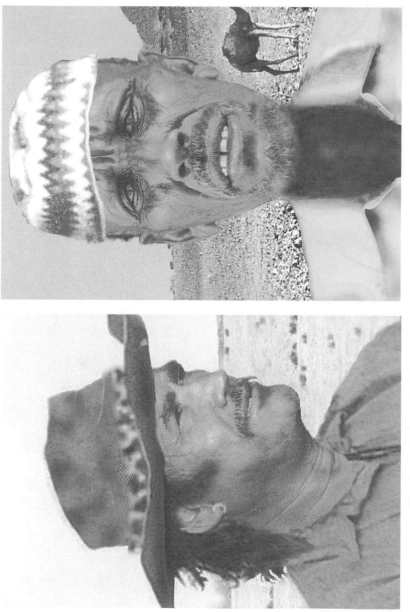

Hutcheon Graham (ca 1932), and Abdullahi's attempt to smile for a photo

xiii

Ndarakwa 1933
The buffalo that killed
the Boran woman

BOOK ONE

1

Ssshlooop!

No, no – not on the exhalation. You have to say it while sucking in your breath. *Ssschlooop!* And as you suck in the word pitch the sound lower towards the end. And not too fast – draw it out a bit. It's the noise your leg makes when you pull it out of black cotton mud as you stagger from your bogged truck to hard ground. A liquid, soggy *shloop* ending in a bit of a pop, even. It's virtually identical to the sound of a buffalo's horn being pulled out of your guts. You'll have to take my word for that, because it's unlikely that you or almost anyone else in the whole world has ever heard the awful shlooping gurgle of a buffalo's horn being withdrawn from deep inside your belly. One or two matadors may have lived to describe it; but in general, it's as rare an experience as hearing a baboon sing 'Red River Valley' in the evening up on the krans as he gets ready for bed. It's a sound that'll haunt me the rest of my life; and not because of black cotton mud or stranded trucks, but because I stuffed things up badly, very badly – so badly that I used up about three of my nine lives all in one go. Maybe four.

I'm writing this from a hospital bed where a longish spell of convalescence following my business with the buffalo had me reviewing my life, wondering, as one does after passing closer to the Pearly Gates than one would've had one not lost it on a slippery corner and skidded off into the rhubarb, how many of the standard issue nine lives are left. Shlooping the buffalo's horn chews up lives like a locust chews up mealies: very, very quickly. But I'll come back to that. Takes a bit of explaining.

In fact, in *point* of fact as Dad used to say, there's a bundle of stuff needs explaining, so much so that it's hard to know where to start. Some of you might say I'd led an extraordinary life, what with solving the mystery of King Solomon's mines and the adventures I had in the process. Getting impaled on a buffalo's horn isn't the half of it. How many sons in this day and age are *suriama* as the Swahili say, born of a slave girl? A small minority, though perhaps not as small as you might suppose, depending on what part of the world you live in. All the same, it's a distinction. No, it's not everyone whose destiny it is to be embroiled in one of history's most tantalising and romantic legends. And the legend of King Solomon's mines is one such, as captivating as any of the great stories of gold and bonanzas that the human mind is so easily hypnotised by. Ever since old Rider Haggard recounted my great-grandfather's alleged rediscovery of King Solomon's mines back in 1884 in his famous book of the same name, all sorts of people have picked up the tale where he left off. As they soon variously found out there was only one problem with Sir Rider's great story: it was pure bullshit.

That of course didn't stop anyone, bullshit never does. Hollywood made movies about it, the book sold like tickets to eternity and the legend went from strength to strength. Actually, it's not all flannel, not by a long shot. The mines are real enough and great-grandfather Allan Quatermain did set off in 1884 to find them. And Sir Henry Rider Haggard started out quite seriously to tell the tale. But old Allan was way off track (he realised his mistake, but not in time to do anything about it on that safari), leaving his friend Rider with a dilemma. Which he solved, as writers do, by making up a lot of flapdoodle and passing it off as the real thing. In the late 1800s, few people knew Africa well enough to question what Rider Haggard wrote. Quite the contrary, in fact, the great Victorian explorers were in the midst of describing Africa as full of thrilling adventure, astonishing people, blood-curdling practices and grand romance. So his story fitted the popular image well. Nowadays, he couldn't have pulled it off, as the tale he told just doesn't fit the geography or the time-scale or such history as there is.

Dad told me that in fact – in point of fact – his grandad, Allan Quatermain, had arranged with Rider Haggard, at that time secretary to the governor of Natal, Sir Theophilus Shepstone, that even if they found King Solomon's mines he wouldn't give their location away in the book he planned to write about it. They weren't stupid, however absurdly dreamy they were. No point in striking gold and then encouraging every other bugger to help themselves. There's just not that much of it about. So the story was always going to be a furphy in so far as the location of the mines was concerned.

What had fired up Allan Quatermain and his offsiders to trek off in search of King Solomon's mines in the first place was the discovery (by white men, that is: for the locals there was of course nothing new) in 1868 of the ruins of Great Zimbabwe, near the Mtilikwe River, one hundred and fifty miles east of Bulawayo in Matabeleland. Three years later the celebrated explorer Thomas Baines published his famous *The Gold Regions of Southeast Africa* and helped create one of the great fairytales of nineteenth-century Africa.

Now, Great Zimbabwe was an Iron Age settlement that flourished in the fifteenth century, collapsing shortly after for reasons unknown, but one or all of locusts, smallpox and all sorts of other scourges could have been implicated. Probably, though, the inhabitants simply exhausted the soil, grazed the pasture flat and burnt all the trees, scorching themselves out of business in a time when you simply moved on to vacant ground once you'd wiped out what you had around you. Not, you might say, that anything's really changed in that regard: but enough of that. The Iron Age in southern Africa was a time of very large human populations who built stone walls and other stone structures in many of their settlements. Great Zimbabwe was the biggest of them all, but would not have stirred so many idle imaginations had it not been for the simple fact that in those days it wasn't realised that these were late Iron Age relics only a few centuries old. Not knowing that, people naturally sought a more venerable and romantic explanation for them, particularly as southern Africa was otherwise quite devoid of any ruins or signs of ancient civilisations. Here at last was hard evidence of a former civilisation, the first such find in an otherwise historically bleak landscape. For what a man would like to be true, that he more readily believes, as the old saying rightly has it.

It wasn't long before someone, his imagination stoked perhaps by whisky, or, more likely, lost in the wonderland of a dagga blue, realised that, *jussus*, man, the round tower in the wall at Great Zimbabwe looked just like the towers the Phoenicians used to build thousands of years ago in the Mediterranean. The Phoenicians were here! *Nou dars 'n ding, ay*, now there's a thing! Phoenician ruins all the way down here, south of the Zambezi! These *okes*[1] must have sailed the length of the east coast of Africa – the fabled Land of Zinj – up the Sabi River from its estuary south of the port of Beira and then along its tributary the Mtilikwe to Great Zimbabwe. The overland leg was only three hundred miles along easily traversed, fertile river valleys. There, they traded for the principal consumer goods of their day,

---

[1] Corruption of *outjies* (pronounced okies), diminutive of *ou*, a chap, guy, fellow (Afrikaans).

gold, ivory and slaves, which, on their return to the Middle East, they said they'd got from Ophir, the legendary location of King Solomon's mines. *Krars,* man, it's so obvious, *ay.*

The pong of gold draws men as surely as the stench of rotting flesh pulls hyenas.

Now, *'n Boer maak altyd 'n plan,* as they used to say in the old Transvaal republics, a Boer always makes a plan. Many Boers, and rooineks too, made many plans as soon as the story of the link between Great Zimbabwe and King Solomon's mines was put about. Most of these plans consisted of nothing more creative than mining claims staked out all over the country around Great Zimbabwe. The mind boggles at all the contorted reasoning that must have been laboriously worked through round so many campfires by all those dreamers trying to choose exactly where to peg their claims. Fourteen years later, and taking into account that none of these claims had struck much gold, the famous South African hunter Allan Quatermain made his plan – to trek into the country around Great Zimbabwe and have a look for King Solomon's mines himself.

Allan Quatermain, my great-grandfather, was fifty-five in 1884 when he set off with Henry Rider Haggard (who masquerades in the story as the tall, bearded aristocrat with Danish antecedents, Sir Henry Curtis) and Captain John Good, to find the fabled Suleiman's mines. Well, you can read all about it in what became one of the best known books of its age, a book that has scarcely ever been out of print and which remains almost as popular now as it ever was. Although they didn't actually find King Solomon's mines they had a good safari and Rider Haggard wrote a great story about what they would've looked like had they indeed found them. It left my great grandad with a powerful urge to keep on searching and led to his death only seven years later, in 1891, on his second safari to look for King

Solomon's mines in the Northern Frontier District of the then British East African Protectorate that was to become in 1920 the Colony and Protectorate of Kenya.

Quatermains it seems aren't good at living to great ages. As Rider Haggard told it, Allan had one child, a son, Harry, born in 1862, whom he sent to England to study medicine. He qualified in 1885 and married early in the following year. Apparently, he chose to launch his medical career by working in a smallpox hospital where he contracted the disease and died within six months of his marriage. Allan had gone to England for the wedding and also, it seems, to discuss with his friends Haggard and Good the idea of making a second safari to look for King Solomon's mines, which, after reading the various historical accounts of the fabled gold of Ophir, they now realised were in all probability somewhere in the Horn of Africa. One of Rider Haggard's brothers, Jack Haggard, happened to have been posted in 1884 as the first British vice-consul to Lamu, the old Arab trading port on the northern coast of the newly proclaimed British East African Protectorate. He wrote to his brother Rider about the country and the romantic tales he'd heard of the then unknown hinterland. Lamu is situated a bit north of the mouth of a big river, the Tana, that drains the south-eastern slopes of Mount Kenya some three hundred miles or so inland. The Tana was an obvious route into the interior that would take them to the edge of the Kenya highlands from where they could then turn north towards the part of the world in which, they were sure, the fabled mines were located.

The abrupt death of his young son had shaken Allan and it was as much to help get over it as it was to go looking for fabulous gold mines that determined him to set off without delay on the expedition to East Africa late in 1886. Not much is known with certainty as to what happened on that last safari of Allan Quatermain's. Once again, it was agreed that Allan would keep a journal, as he had on their first safari, from which Rider Haggard would be able to put together a book. Rider was now a full-time author and depended on such material for his living. And once again, just as had happened on the first safari to look for King Solomon's mines, Rider Haggard had to fall back on his imagination when Allan failed to find the mines. The resulting book, *Allan Quatermain,* subtitled *Being an Account of his Further Adventures and Discoveries,* tells us that they disembarked in Lamu, spent a bit of time with the British Consul there from whom they gleaned what little was known in those days of travelling up the Tana River, put together a caravan and journeyed up the river to the foothills of Mount Kenya. They then set off north and never reappeared. However, a manuscript and Allan's diaries were eventually forwarded to Rider Haggard, postmarked Aden, by a Frenchman who had spent some time with them. Clearly, they had got to Ethiopia for the material to have been sent via Aden, because foreigners trading in Ethiopia often based themselves in Aden. It was widely rumoured that Allan and his friends had become *bougnoulisé* as the French say, gone native. For all that anyone knows they'd abandoned their quest and settled down to die of old age in some pleasant corner of Africa, all interest in King Solomon's mines forgotten. If they did, it didn't pan out too well for Allan Quatermain, because, according to the documents forwarded to Haggard, he got the spear in some scuffle or other, and died. Where, it simply isn't known.

Great-grandfather Allan, before leaving for East Africa on his last safari, had arranged for my widowed grandmother to move to South Africa to live on the family estate outside Grahamstown in the Eastern Cape. She named her son Rider Quatermain, in memory of the old family friend, Rider Haggard, and in 1892 married Richie Graham, the story of whose connection with the Quatermain family in

Grahamstown I'll come to later. As I've already said, elderly Quatermains are rare and my grandmother was no exception. She and Richie came to a sticky end in 1906, not yet forty years old, bushwhacked on a lonely drift across a river in Griqualand West.

The year following his mother and stepfather's murders my father, Rider Quatermain, turned his back on South Africa forever and moved north to British East Africa. It wasn't only the deaths of his parents that spurred him into a change of scene. It was, he said, the obvious moment to put into practice something he'd long contemplated. His mother and stepfather had told him all about Allan Quatermain's attempts to find King Solomon's mines and he was never happier than when reviewing the legend and trying to piece together what all the various references to it might mean.

Dad inherited old Allan Quatermain's willingness to believe in a good romantic story and he made up his mind at an early age that he'd pick up the scent where old Allan had left off and continue the search. He was convinced that the legendary gold of Ophir – King Solomon's mines – could be relocated. So persistent a legend could not possibly have imbedded itself in history so deeply without a good deal of substance. Short-lived events create equally short-lived memories. Real events have to be either spectacularly unique or persist for generations to create lasting legends. So for Dad there was only one question to be answered: where were they? He admitted that one possible explanation for the undoubted fact that mankind's collective memory had let slip their location was that all the gold had long ago been dug out and the holes in the ground abandoned like aardvark's burrows. But he preferred the alternative explanation, namely that something had happened that broke the continuity of working the mines, disrupting the knowledge of where they were. Something

SSSHLOOOP!

like a famine or an epidemic or some other cataclysmic
event. He regarded this as far more plausible, because, he
said, it had to be sudden and catastrophic. The location of
old ruins doesn't get forgotten simply because they are not
used any more.

Well, these sorts of explanations can be argued inter-
minably and that's exactly what Dad and I and his lifelong
friend Hutcheon Graham have done ever since I was old
enough to imagine what it was all about. We never tired
of it and it kept us going like a drug. Each new bit of
information or so-called revelation would lift our spirits,
sometimes to absurd levels of euphoria, only to be followed
as inevitably as a crap follows a feast by disconsolation as
each new lead dried up like a seasonal waterhole. But, as
with drugs, the appetite for a new fix of information never
flagged and to the last year of his life Dad was as hooked
on finding Suleiman's mines as any addict to his opiate.
And I with him.

11

2

Sharp Horns and Quatermains

April Fool's Day 1946 and I'm being washed in my hospital bed by Nurse Houlihan, a rather serious-looking girl I guessed to be much my age, twenty-five or so. Probably not what you'd normally call good-looking, being short, muscly and a bit too hairy – at least her legs were. I was reminded of how King Solomon when visited all those centuries ago by the Queen of Sheba had looked her over and found her quite pleasing except for her legs. Solomon had a thing about women with hairy legs and before acceding to the main purpose of her visit had ordered them shaved by the royal barbers. Not that Nurse Houlihan would find that little story as interesting as I did. She's quite rough and my wound hurts as she swabs my abdomen around the dressings. She sees me wince and says, 'Your father says it was your own fault you got hurt. What happened?'

'I collided with a buffalo by mistake, that's what happened.'

'So you weren't looking where you were going, was it?'

'No, I was looking all right.'

'Then why didn't you get out of the way?'

'Have you ever done any buffalo hunting?' I rather pointlessly asked her.

'No,' she said, quite sharply, 'and sure I won't be asking you to show me how. Seems like you need a bit more practice, wouldn't you say? Anyway,' she went on, 'you're a typical man. Either killing other men or being nasty to animals. Serves you right, if you ask me.'

'I'm not asking you. Your job is to make me better without hurting me even more in the process. I didn't ask you to be a nurse, either.'

A particularly sharp twinge of pain in my abdomen reminded me why I was lying pondering my predicament in Nairobi General Hospital in the first place. It was nearly three weeks ago that I'd shlooped the buffalo horn as Hutcheon put it, rather wittily he thought. The day had started ordinarily enough back home at Luoniek, Dad's *plaas* up past Mugi Springs, some fifty miles north of Rumuruti. Then two Samburu men from a kraal a day's walk away had come complaining that a buffalo had taken to charging at the women and children when they went out collecting firewood, and would I come and shoot the beast. This was a common enough request. The Game Department was theoretically responsible for keeping the peace between man and wild beast in the Colony, but was still short-staffed after the War and in any case chronically short of energy when it came to attending to ill-tempered buffalo and the like. Had Hutcheon been there he'd have been sure to remark that even if there had been a game warden anywhere in the area there would always have been the problem of getting him out of bed. The Samburu much preferred to get us to do any hit jobs they didn't feel like handling themselves, rather than waste their time knocking on the game warden's door. In those days the government didn't allow the Samburu to carry firearms and, armed only with a spear, disputing the right of way with a buffalo was something you would only encourage your worst enemy to do. In any event, we didn't mind. We always needed meat and liked to keep on good terms with the people with whom we traded cattle. They said the buffalo in question was so bold it would be easy to hunt and not take up a lot of time.

Dad and Hutcheon were otherwise occupied so I detailed Dad's ace hunter, Ndaragus, to accompany me and after a rough drive through the bush we arrived at the kraal. An hour or so later we found ourselves in a dense thicket of thorns in which, we were assured, the *nyati mbaya*, the bad buffalo, was holed up. I had armed myself with one of Dad's beloved doubles, his Boss .577, and Ndaragus was carrying the ancient .500 that he had been inseparable from since Dad gave it to him some forty years back when he was a skinny little squirt of an Ndorobo youth. Greying now, his face deeply lined and gaunt he was if anything even skinnier. He wasn't strong enough to heft the massive rifle up to shoulder height and aim it for more than a second or so, which meant that taking long and careful aim wasn't in Ndaragus's *Weltanschauung*. He simply swung the gun up and fired where he was looking. The technique had served him well, as he never fired unless he was too close to miss. As far as hunters went it would be hard to better Ndaragus' pedigree. He'd been taught his craft by none other than the legendary Arthur Neumann who had hunted elephant in the country where we lived for many years at the turn of the century. Neumann had taken an Ndorobo woman as his bush wife who brought her younger brother, Ndaragus, with her to his camp. From the beginning, the skinny little boy with the eyesight of a vulture had showed great aptitude and by the time Neumann gave up ivory hunting in 1906 Ndaragus was on his way to becoming a true ace hunter.

In the company of such a man, armed as we were, my mission should have been straightforward enough. A single shot from either rifle, fired from any conceivable angle, would instantly immobilise a buffalo – provided that the shot was at least approximately aimed at a vital spot. Off the mark and it would have practically no effect at all. In thick cover such as we were in, we would not be seeing our quarry at distances of more than a few yards. Shooting at close

14

range means, on the one hand, that your aim can be a lot less precise than it would have to be at long range; but on the other hand, there's not much time in which to correct mistakes should the target wish to take retaliatory action. The compromise is further unbalanced if the animal you're after has backup.

It was now getting on for two o'clock, and stinking hot. There was no wind and the sweat was oozing continuously down my face. Your eyebrows deflect rain and sweat to either side a bit; but on a boiling, humid day the sweat running down your forehead spills sideways into the corners of your eyes, carrying with it the dust and debris that settles on you constantly as you move through the thick vegetation. Long before we got to the buffalo my eyes were stinging and causing me to blink and wipe them repeatedly. The men who'd brought us here had alluded all the time to a single buffalo and when I'd asked if it was really alone they assured me that it was. *Peke yake, bwana, peke yake.* We'd believed them, because ever since picking up the animal's tracks near where the men said the women had been attacked early that morning we had not seen any other fresh tracks. Plenty of old buffalo spoor; but only one set of fresh tracks. As soon as the tracks entered the thicket the men had left us to it and Ndaragus and I had followed the spoor as quietly as we could through the dense vegetation. We'd gone perhaps seventy yards into the thicket when we started to smell the musky odour of an animal. We couldn't hear anything, but the smell told us we were getting very close. Just ahead were a few taller trees growing close together that cast some shade over the lower thicket. Almost certainly, this was where the buffalo had meant to spend the heat of the day. We looked at each other and moved slowly forward about three yards apart, Ndaragus on my right. It really was thick as hell, and the dense undergrowth forced us to crouch down repeatedly to ease ourselves under the higher, more horizontal branches. It's hard to shoot crouched down; you have to rock back onto your haunches to get the gun up. It's easy in such a position to be knocked over backwards by the recoil if you happen to get caught with your feet together rather than one foot behind the other.

Several things combined that day to take me on that detour past the Pearly Gates, closer I think than I'd ever been before. Close enough to make St Peter look up from his register to see who was making the commotion outside. Both Ndaragus and I happened to be almost lying down to slide ourselves under a fallen branch of one of the trees we'd noticed and had now reached. Our quarry was, as we'd rightly surmised, lying down just ahead. Not sleeping, though, or letting his mind wander, but listening and hearing sounds much fainter than we humans can discern. Like the sounds we were making for all that we tried not to. With a sudden, tremendous crashing of branches and a grunt he got to his feet and made straight for us. Instinctively we both pulled ourselves back out from under the branch to get into a position to fire. But it took a second or two to draw back far enough to get the space to raise the rifle barrels high enough. Squatting on your heels means you have to aim appreciably upwards when an animal as large as a buffalo is right upon you. All I saw was a buffalo coming straight at me, his head high as he squinted forward to see where I was. I remember that as I swung my rifle up the muzzles hit a branch that kept them at least a foot lower than I needed them to be. I tried to force the branch up, but couldn't. Already on my heels, I couldn't move further back. Nothing for it, but to lower the gun a bit and aim for a leg. Good idea – if you have a clear view. All I remember seeing, though, was the beast's head; its lower body was obscured by vegetation. I fired the right barrel blindly,

16

partly lost my balance and fired the left barrel even more blindly at the animal's body, still unable to raise the rifle towards the huge head that was at this point only about six feet away. Perhaps the strongest recollection I have is the sensation I got at that moment of impending doom. I was out of time, out of step, out of luck.

Though I didn't know it then the other complicating circumstance that day was that the buffalo was not alone. As I was struggling to get a clear shot at the animal charging me Ndaragus was dealing with a second that came just behind the leading one. It came directly at him, but being a little behind gave him a second or so's extra time. He got a clear shot and the buffalo went down, but not dead. He, being the experienced hunter he was, stood and carefully fired the second barrel to despatch the animal as it tried to regain its feet. At that point, he turned and was just in time to see the first buffalo swing its head and horns round and down right to the ground so as to hook the curved tip of the left-hand horn under me. The huge, massively muscled neck and shoulders then rotated the horn straight, and up, in an incredibly swift and powerful flick that sank the horn tip deep in my abdomen and raised me seven or eight feet off the ground. Instinctively I grasped the horn boss with both hands and hung on. The beast backed up a couple of steps, shook its head, lowered it and flicked up again to dislodge me. But I hung onto the boss with the desperate grip of a baby baboon clutching its mother's guts as she races up a tree. The efforts of the buffalo to get rid of me gave Ndaragus the time he needed to reload his gun, and fire. His first shot was good and the beast dropped in its tracks and me with it. For a few moments I just lay there, still clutching the horn boss. Ndaragus struggled over to me through the tangled branches and took hold of my shoulders to drag me clear. He yelled at me to let go, let go, and I relaxed my grip. With him pulling, I then pushed down on the horn boss and with a terrible, long-drawn-out schloooop my body slid off the horn.

It was otherwise absolutely dead quiet after the noise and commotion of a few seconds back, and the shloop seemed incredibly loud to both of us. I can't say I'd felt anything up to that point, or had any clear idea of what was going on, so that the awful gurgle was the first thing that really settled itself in my mind. I lay on my side holding my belly and looked up at Ndaragus. He caught my gaze and for what seemed like ages we just stared at one another. He of course thought I was done for. All the other people he knew who'd been gored by buffalos – and he knew a fair few – were dead. He knew the score and he was a realist. He figured he was looking into the eyes of a dying man. For my part, I didn't know what to think. I was beginning to hurt now, and there was quite a bit of blood oozing from between my fingers where I held my belly. Gingerly, I partially let go so that we could examine the wound. My fingers spanned a huge hole in my lower abdomen with the intestines pushing up through the gore. I began to regain my senses and got Ndaragus to remove my shirt and make a large pad to cover the wound. His shirt he tore into strips to bind round me and hold the dressing in place. I then sent him off to get help.

It was well into the night before I was back home being examined by Dad. A lifetime's practical medicine had made him a competent bush doctor. He gave me a shot of morphine and after listening carefully to Ndaragus's account of the incident, complete with an uncannily accurate rendering of the shloop phase, Dad slid his hand into the hole in my belly and carefully palpated my internal organs. He spoke as he did so, to himself really, saying that there was so little bleeding it seemed the liver, spleen and

18

kidneys had not been ruptured; neither had the intestines or stomach been punctured. There was no sign of any gut contents; only blood. The diaphragm was obviously intact. The horn had punctured the abdomen and then slid between the organs and the abdominal wall without piercing anything else. An amazing outcome to a normally much more horrific event. The internal organs press up against the abdominal wall quite firmly and for a sharp object to penetrate one but not the other requires a most fortunate juxtaposition of angles and pressures. But it happened that day and neatly cancelled out the bad luck, or misjudgement, immediately preceding it.

Dad irrigated the abdominal cavity with a saline solution to wash out as much blood and dirt as he could and then closed up the wound. It was obvious to both of us that a peritoneal infection was inevitable and we both knew just how dangerous and difficult to treat that would be. So Dad decided to leave immediately for Nairobi to get me into hospital as quickly as possible. The rains hadn't broken yet that year so at least the roads were dry. But it was a rough drive of around twenty hours non-stop, with Dad and Hutcheon spelling each other at the wheel. We were right about peritonitis and I was pretty ill for the next twelve days with high fever and considerable pain. But a combination of medicine helped by youth, fitness and a vigorous immune system won the day and gradually the infection subsided and the wound healed.

So it was that I reviewed the events of April Fool's Day 1946 and the weeks preceding it, trying to work out what lessons I should have learnt and what I should be doing to make sure I didn't spend any more Fool's days feeling so foolish. Naturally, I had no way of knowing that my tripping over a buffalo was to be overshadowed by something far more profound later that year. To put these events into perspective, though, I'll have to tell you about a lot of other things first to give you some idea of why we Quatermains do what many think are such imprudent not to say idiotic things.

3

Ophir and the Land of Punt

It was a hot summer's day in Port Elizabeth back in 1907 when Dad boarded one of the old Union Castle boats and left his home country of South Africa forever. The cold-blooded murder of his parents was the precipitating event that decided him; day-dreaming about Suleiman's gold was what was pushing him. As the coil of his life unwound it became ever more obvious that Dad was born not only with a Conradian romantic conscience, but with a sense that life itself is a romance so it was hardly surprising that the glittering tale of the fabled gold of Ophir should have lodged itself so firmly in his mind. Dad could no more ignore such things than a mongoose a snake. There were interludes caused by the two world wars – and many other things, too, as I shall presently relate – during which Dad thought little and did nothing about the legend of the mines; but the fascination never faded. I'm sure it was as tantalizing an image in the last year of his life as it was back then in his early twenties.

He himself never brought it up – probably it never occurred to him – but I often thought that his grandfather, Allan 'Hunter' Quatermain, must have had that same susceptibility to romance that Dad had. Although they never met, the pattern of their lives was very similar, which of course would hardly be surprising; children often repeat their parents' lives. Never knowing his father, who effectively missed out most of his life, could have led Dad to unconsciously pick up on the image of his grandfather. Both were hunter-traders, both were esteemed by their contemporaries for their skill and integrity in a calling answered mainly by rogues and chancers. And both had left their home countries for East Africa after the death of someone close, ostensibly to search for forgotten gold mines whose location was apocryphal even when they were in production three millennia ago.

I could be forgiven, I think, for wondering sometimes if my Quatermain forebears weren't as crazy as baboons on fermented doum palm nuts. Had there ever really been such a thing as King Solomon's mines? Had old Hunter Quatermain and his friend Rider Haggard just been trying to catch dust-devils? As time went on I heard not a few people opine that my father was. Don't know how a switched-on *oke* like him can believe in such *twak*, someone would say and everyone round the camp table would laugh and echo the sentiment. Dad, though, never cared about that sort of talk. If the ignorant toerags would bother to read their history they'd realise it's no fairytale, he'd say. I'll grant you history hasn't much to say, he'd add, but what it does is undeniable.

It would've been around 1933 when I was about twelve that Dad first showed me his grandfather's diaries. I found them pretty awesome on that first occasion, and still do after reading them I don't know how many times. Wonderful old, worn books, gnawed by silverfish and white ants, and chock-full of fascinating stories and arcane information. Dad kept each one tied with a little, thin *riempie*, a turn lengthways then a turn sideways that, for me, gave them a really special cachet. He was a good writer, old Hunter Quatermain, with a neat hand that made it easy to get into the sense of what he was saying. You can see how his friend Rider Haggard had been able to spin such yarns after reading these diaries; they're very evocative.

I'll always remember the first occasion Dad said it was time I read my great-grandfather's diaries for myself and learned a bit about the story of King Solomon's mines. It was the rains and I was home on school holidays, hoping, as did everyone, that the weather would let up so we could get out of camp into the bush. Dad thought it was a good moment to let me see Oom Allan's diaries. I can still see him untying the *riempie* from one of them, opening it at a page with a marker and telling me to read. The date was 1866 and Oom Allan had headed a series of jottings *Ophir and the Hebrew Kings*. The first bit read:

The legend of Ophir seems to begin with King David and Queen Bathsheba. David planned a really big temple in Jerusalem to house the Ark of the Covenant. Bought a piece of land for it on Mount Zion (where his ancestor Abraham was to have sacrificed Isaac). Drew up plans but never started. Ordered his son Solomon to build it. A good choice for the job as he seems to have been a megalomaniac like his father and spent most of his taxes on self-aggrandisement. Nothing changes, ay! But this temple was going to cost more than taxes could finance so David had been hoarding gold and silver. He had amassed, so the Old Testament says, '. . . three thousand talents of gold, of the gold of Ophir, and seven thousand talents of refined silver . . .' Taking a talent as about seventy-five pounds that comes to a hundred tons of gold. Plus two hundred and thirty tons of silver – one moerava *lot! Also says that Solomon annually imported six hundred and sixty talents of gold. (Annoyingly, doesn't say over how many years.)*

'So you see,' said Dad, 'there's no mistaking that King Solomon had access to one yelluva lot of gold considering the age. You have to remember that in those days people didn't have dynamite and bloody great mechanical hammers and fancy smelting furnaces. Most gold was simply

23

picked up. Once they'd found all the easy stuff the ancient Egyptians started chipping away at exposed ore bodies and pounding the chips into dust so they could melt out the gold. But it had to be rich ore for this to be worthwhile when you consider that the average *good* ore only contains an ounce or two of gold per ton. What miners call bonanza ores, the really lip-smacking stuff, still only contains pounds of gold per ton. Get through a lot of slaves smashing it all up into dust.'

'So where was this place Ophir?' I asked Dad.

'Read on, Alan,' he said, 'see what your great-grandfather had to say about that.'

Where was Ophir? To the O.T. authors it was presumably well known, by repute at least, because they never elaborate. Of course, they weren't interested, as apart from its gold Ophir had no bearing on their concerns. No native gold in the Middle East. How about Egypt? Pharaohs as crazy about gold as Hebrew kings. If it was Egypt they'd have said so. Solomon had trade agreement with Egypt, no mysteries there. Egypt had many gold mines but was a net importer of gold (from Kush) and not in a position to supply it. Some small gold mines in north-west Arabia at Midian.

Dad interrupted here, saying that in later diaries Allan mentioned that scholars such as Sir Richard Burton have shown that the Midian mines could not have been Solomon's source. I read on.

There are no other gold mines in Arabia. Solomon's gold must've come from much further afield. As it says in O.T.: 'And they came to Ophir, and fetched from thence gold, four hundred and twenty talents, and brought it to King Solomon.' Always Ophir, never mentioned any other place.

24

'So where do you think Ophir is?' I asked Dad.

'The answer's either dead simple or virtually impossible.'

Seeing my puzzlement, he said, 'Could be it's staring us in the face, if you like simple, boring explanations. I looked up what these etymologist chappies say, the *okes* that think they know which words other words come from. They dress it all up but basically they go by what word in another language the word in question sounds like. They say that Africa derives from the Latin, *afer*. Or maybe the Greek, *Aphriké*. On the other hand, maybe the Latin and Greek 'roots' derive from *Africa*, which predates them. But whatever the true etymology – and it looks like staying a veld secret – it's hard not to see the Hebrew *ophir* as just one of the many ancient words for *afer*, what we pronounce as *Africa*.

'Their Ophir was simply whatever lay beyond the world they knew, Egypt, the Middle East, Arabia. Maybe. Always sounds a bit trite to me.'

'So what's the other explanation?' I asked, 'the impossible one.'

'Well, some say Ophir was India. But that's inconsistent with history, because in Solomon's day it was Persia that dealt with India. Can't see the Persians allowing valuable trade goods to bypass them, nor would that've been sensible for the Indians, as Persia was just next door. Moreover, the oldest gold mines in India are thought to be only two thousand years or so. That's old, sure, but *after* old Suleiman's day. It definitely wasn't India.'

Dad went on. 'The likeliest place by far was the Land of Punt. Solomon had a navy based at Ezion-Geber in the Gulf of Aqaba. The Bible says these ships brought gold, and other stuff like ivory and incense, from Ophir. Even before his time the Egyptians prefabricated boats on the Nile, transported the bits across the desert and reassembled them in the Red Sea. They then sailed to Pun as they called it and brought back the usual gold, ivory, slaves, incense and

25

so on. Pun and Ophir were one and the same place. The complication is unravelling just where the Land of Punt was and where in Punt they found the gold. Where the punt is it? you might say!'

It's a romantic tale, no getting away from it. From the very first time I read Hunter Quatermain's diaries and listened to Dad's stories I conjured images of Ophir peopled by exotic kings and queens and pharaohs; ships full of ivory and myrrh, leopard skins and slaves and of course piles of gold that gleamed even at night. Seems like long ago but actually it was only twelve or so years back and though lots has happened since then nothing's happened to tone those images down. With luck, nothing ever will.

But to get back to my story. After we'd talked about Ophir I asked Dad, 'So, did King Solomon ever build his dad's temple?'

He paged through the same diary and handed it back to me.

Solomon . . . built a huge stone and timber temple. Walls extensively overlaid with gold. Lot of gold-plated furniture (including the Ark of the Covenant, subsequently stolen and taken to Ethiopia, they say). Altogether thought to have used at least twenty tons of gold to ornament the temple. Stood for centuries, but eventually knocked down and rebuilt several times, most recently (689) as a mosque, the Dome on the Rock, still standing.

'So you see,' said Dad, 'there's no question that old Suleiman built his golden temple using some of the many tons of gold he and his dad got from Ophir. Although it's often called a legend it isn't, really. It's a true story. The more these swotty *okes* delve into these Old Testament tales the more accurate they turn out to be. Remarkably so when you consider the opportunities for distortion over the millennia. The only legendary bit is the precise source of the gold of Ophir, the so-called King Solomon's mines. No one's ever found any mines that could unequivocally be those of Ophir. Serious mines they must've been, that yielded hundreds of tons. Sure, when it comes to statistics the old prophets weren't above puffing things up here and there, so the number of talents should probably be regarded as tentative. But the story itself – no reason to doubt that; not a one-off bible story. And there's one really interesting little fact that neither the old prophets nor Oom Allan could've known. Archaeologists in Jerusalem recently dug up a tablet on which is written "gold from Ophir". This tablet was made nearly *six hundred* years after old Suleiman died. Which means that gold was coming from Ophir for many, many centuries. Altogether, it *had* to be a huge amount.

'Then something happened,' Dad said, 'that really stoked everyone up like rockapes in the moonlight when a cloud shadow scuds by.' He untied another of Hunter Quatermain's diaries, riffled through it until he found the place he wanted, and handed it to me. The date was 1868 and old Allan was referring to the discovery of the ruins of Great Zimbabwe near the Mtilikwe river.

Everybody's saying King Solomon's mines have been found, the mystery's solved, etc. This oke Adam Render has stubbed his toes on a ruined stone city and imaginations are firing up like tamboekie *grass in the dry season because apparently there are ancient gold mines in the area. They all think he's found Ophir; maybe he has!*

Dad took the diary back and gave me another for the year 1884:

. . . and met up with Rider [he is referring to Rider Haggard] *who is all caught up in this Great Zimbabwe and*

27

Ophir twak. Says that now the archaeologists have had a good look at Great Zimbabwe they're certain it was built by Phoenicians. King Solomon employed Phoenician artisans for his temple and Phoenician sailors for his navy. Thinks the connection too remarkable to be coincidence; Zimbabwe is Ophir. Rider's imagination always boiling over, maybe he smokes dagga! Now he wants us to trek off and search for the Big One, the real King Solomon's mines. Says all the ones found so far are too small to have supplied Solomon's gold.

'Well, you know what all that led to,' said Dad.

I did, and it was fun reading Rider Haggard's book about King Solomon's mines and comparing it with what Oom Allan had written in his diary recording their epic safari. Hard to believe they related to the same event. What was clear from the diary was that early on old Hunter Quatermain had given up thinking that Great Zimbabwe had any connection with Ophir. One passage written in 1885 soon after their safari records one of the reasons why he'd abandoned the theory.

Young Fred Selous[2] spent a couple of nights in my camp. Well read feller, and a thinking sort of oke. Doesn't say much until he's got his facts straight, unlike most of us Bushveld denizens! Told me something very intriguing. Seems he'd come across an unusually deep, old mineshaft, which he went down on a rope. Found an old bucket at the bottom made of rawhide. As he said, obviously didn't date back to old Suleiman's day! A century or two maybe, but not more.

Dad then explained to me that once the archaeologists got a grip of themselves and took a closer look at Great Zimbabwe and all the old gold mines round it they realised none of it was more than a few centuries old. They were

---

[2] Frederick Courteney Selous, the renowned big game hunter (Ed)

Iron Age relics from long, long after Solomon's time. So old Hunter Quatermain was right to think he'd be better off in the Land of Punt, though he didn't live to hear his scepticism corroborated.

4

Luoniek

Like his grandfather, Dad was convinced when he disembarked from the *Llangibby Castle* in Mombasa in July 1907 that the mysterious lands to the north of Kenya – the Ogaden and Ethiopia – concealed the secret of King Solomon's mines. He was determined to get to know these alluring places and eventually to discover – perhaps – a clue to the riddle of Ophir and the legendary mines from which King Solomon had obtained his gold. He knew enough to understand that his task was an enormous one, perhaps a ridiculous one. At the turn of the century the interior of the Horn of Africa remained one of the least known and inaccessible parts of Africa, ungoverned and in the opinion of many ungovernable.

From the outset, he had a partner – Hutcheon Graham. They were lifelong friends – actually distant cousins – who'd grown up together in Grahamstown, and gone to the same school there, St Andrews. Hutcheon was a descendent of the notorious Scottish tribe of Grahams who, along with other infamous clans of border reivers, had made the Anglo-Scottish border of the fifteenth and sixteenth centuries an unremitting hell for the English. Lord Scrope, one-time English West March warden, noted in a report about the 'awful' Grahams that although he had hanged five or six of them it would 'probably only make the rest of the family worse.' Dad never tired of remarking that Scrope

had been dead right about that. One of Hutcheon's ancestors it seems had used the money got from selling stolen
English cattle to purchase a commission in the British Army,
which needed people like him, who knew all about border
skirmishing, to help secure the north-eastern border of
Cape Colony. The delicious pirates' irony of paying the
victim with his own money must have given the Graham
clan immense pleasure. In any event, Colonel John Graham
never returned to Scotland – quite possibly there were
compelling reasons for that – and the border garrison he
established in the Eastern Cape eventually became the town
of Grahamstown.

Dad and Hutcheon were a perfect match when it came
to the sort of enterprises Dad had in mind. Where Dad was
a dreamer, a romantic who always thought he saw admirable
traits in people, Hutcheon was not given to day-dreams and
always thought he saw the devil in people. Without him,
Dad would never have tempered his dreams as much as he
did; without Dad, Hutcheon would simply have ended up
where so many of his ancestors had – in an early, disreputable grave. Or so each told me of the other. At any rate,
they were lifelong friends and Hutcheon was in so many
ways a second father to me and my sister, whom we loved as
we did our real father.

Both were tall, lean men, good-looking or at least inter-
esting-looking according to many women and certainly
much lusted-after by not a few, though looks I suppose were
not necessarily the draw-card. But, whereas Dad was blond
with grey eyes, Hutcheon was black-haired, with a dark,
brooding look. With his heavy black eyebrows, black eyes
and swarthy complexion he could appear quite forbidding,
even sinister, an impression that the large gold earring in
his left ear probably strengthened. After school, Hutcheon
had done what he'd always dreamt of doing, which was to
emulate the sort of life their friend and neighbour, William

Finaughty,[3] had lived. Old Bill Finaughty, who'd grown up in Grahamstown with my great-grandfather, Allan Quatermain, had been an ivory hunter and trader – not to mention something of a rogue – and knew all the other hunters in the business. He arranged for Hutcheon to accompany the sons of Oom Jan Viljoen, one of the foremost Afrikaner hunters of his day, who still pursued their father's way of life. During the dry season they would leave their Groot Marico farms and head off north to hunt elephant, returning to sell their ivory when it got too wet for their trek oxen. One result of this experience was that, having spoken only the *Taal* for several years, he spoke English with a strong *japie*[4] accent. Another, according to Dad, was to add to his Scottish reivers' repertoire of rascality such additional knavery as the Afrikaner tribe could teach him.

Hutcheon was more powerfully built than Dad, and extraordinarily strong. Dad told me that once, as boys at school, he and Hutcheon had quarrelled over whether or not American guns such as were made by Winchester or Remington were as good as English guns. Not, of course, that either of them would've had a clue. Dad told me that he got completely carried away by his anger at Hutcheon's stupid obstinacy – and I can vouch for the man's capacity to be as stubborn as a camel – and told him he would thrash him, man, if he didn't belt up. 'Well,' Dad said, 'Hutcheon gave me one *moerava*[5] hiding for that. I'd never realised what an incredibly strong bastard he was until then. He ended up lifting me right off the ground and throwing me down like a dead steenbok. Didn't affect how we got along with each other – just eliminated one possibility from

---

[3] See *The Recollections of William Finaughty, Elephant Hunter*, by G.L. Harrison, 1916
[4] Slang for Afrikaner. From *plaasjapie*, a crude or ignorant person; bumpkin (Afrikaans)
[5] Expletive. Corruption of *jou ma se moer*, your mother's womb (Afrikaans)

my repertoire and taught me always to size up the other dog properly before I started barking at it.'

Dad had inherited a considerable amount from his parents' estate. The proceeds from the diamonds that old Allan Quatermain sold in England after his safari into Matabeleland in 1884 had been put into a trust fund for his son, Harry, then at medical school. Soon after qualifying, Harry went to work in a smallpox hospital and within a year was himself dead of the pox. Allan was devastated by his son's untimely death and it was as he recounts one of the reasons he returned to Africa. There was an awkward detail, though, that neither Allan nor Rider Haggard, in keeping with the Victorian mores of their day, was prepared to include in the story of Allan's life and that was that shortly before his death his son Harry had married a girl whom he'd got pregnant. Now Allan was left with an awkward widow and prospective grandchild who would have to be officially born prematurely. To help conceal the scandal he arranged for his son's widow, Emily, to emigrate to South Africa well before her baby was born. So it was that my father, Rider Quatermain, was born in Grahamstown in 1887, at nine pounds an embarrassing baby to arrive two months early.

In 1892 the young widow Emily, now living on the Quatermain estate outside Grahamstown in South Africa's Cape Colony, married Richie Graham, but chose to keep her first husband's name, which is why Dad grew up as Rider Quatermain. Richie's mother was officially a young divorcee, Harriet Flashman, when she married Cathcart Graham soon after coming to South Africa in 1858, and brought to the marriage a son, Buckley, by her alleged first husband. The truth was, however, that Cathcart was her first husband. Just how she came to be impregnated by the famous (though some hold infamous) Victorian soldier, Harry Flashman, is an interesting tale and one that has some relevance to the whole saga of King Solomon's mines. But I will come to the story of Buckley's bastardy anon.

The lives of the Quatermains and the Grahams had been entangled from the early days of Grahamstown. The marriage in 1862 of the Quatermain cousin Harriet to Cathcart Graham and then Emily's later marriage to Richie Graham reinforced the two families' long-standing connections. In the light of this, it was perhaps not surprising that Buckley, who went by the family name of Graham though he was not in fact a Graham by blood, fell in love with one of the many Graham girls of the town, Alice, whom he'd grown up with. He married her in 1886 and they had one son, Hutcheon, born in the same year – 1887 – as my father. The two boys were to become lifelong friends.

Emily's marriage to Richie was a happy and prosperous one and the couple substantially increased the already large estate they'd inherited on Allan's death. Then, in 1906, Richie and Emily were bushwhacked. They had for some years been illicit diamond buyers, IDB-*ies* as they were known, an activity they conducted under cover of their legitimate business of general trading. They owned several stores in remote parts of Griqualand West, which they serviced by ox wagon. One day, they were ambushed on the Riet River drift, and were both shot dead off their horses. Their murderers were never brought to book. The police regarded it as internecine warfare among IDB-*ies* and took little interest, soon abandoning the case.

My father, then nineteen, was deeply affected by the sudden and violent death of his parents of whom he was very fond. Richie had apparently been an exceptional step-father and Dad often said how much he missed them both. He became very depressed and was advised by the family doctor to get away from Grahamstown and the reminders of his parents and get himself involved in something altogether different. If he didn't make a drastic change in his life, the doctor said, his melancholia could become serious. He reminded Dad that he was extremely well off, having inherited what had become a substantial family fortune. Find something to occupy yourself with, the doctor had said, turn the money you have into even more. You're lucky to have the means to do pretty well whatever you fancy. That advice sealed Dad's decision to pick up on his grandfather Allan's pursuit of the legendary King Solomon's mines and leave Grahamstown and its memories behind.

Melancholia as it happened was to stalk Dad all his life like a jackal in the shadows, always there, sometimes obvious, sometimes not, sometimes bold as brass snapping at his peace of mind. Most of the time he was fine, an energetic, companionable man, witty, imaginative, extraordinarily well-read and a natural leader whom people were always happy to follow. Every now and then, though, he would quite suddenly clam up, become withdrawn and listless and avoid us all. These black moods didn't often last long, a few days at most, but they always returned at intervals. I inherited the trait, but my sister Leila didn't, in which respect, according to Hutcheon, she took after our mother.

Hutcheon and Dad stayed in touch after school and when Dad decided to bale out of South Africa and head for British East Africa he got hold of Hutcheon and asked him to go into the venture with him. Hutcheon didn't have any money to speak of, but observed that if Dad wanted to piss all his up against the British East African wall he would be happy to help him.

That's how my dad, Rider Quatermain, and his friend Hutcheon Graham got to outspanning in the *gramadoelas*[6] of British East Africa at Luoniek, north of Rumuruti, in 1908, to search for mythical gold mines whose existence

---

[6] Back of beyond, the sticks, the cow's guts (Afrikaans)

could only be inferred from tall tales written thousands of years ago by people who somehow always managed to avoid giving away their location. As Hutcheon facetiously said, 'Your dad had the same fanciful imagination as his namesake, the gallant knight Sir Henry Rider Haggard, and I saw it as my duty, ay, to prevent him from going belly-up in the first week. Not easy, man, he's a complete *dikkop*[7] when he gets to dreaming about this Hebrew Suleiman's imaginary gold mines.'

Leaving Mombasa, they made their way up-country to Nairobi, then a small, shambolic town populated by a *mélange* of officials, traders, soldiers, railwaymen, farmers, whores, hunters, dudes, crooks and a curiously large number of disreputable European aristocrats dissipating their inheritances. They took rooms in the House of Lords, as the Norfolk Hotel was known from the number of titled reprobates who kept its barmen busy, and set about learning something of the country.

'It was a very wonderful place in those days, ay, this *dorp* Nairobi,' said Hutcheon, talking to me years later. 'Reckon I never saw so many *skellums* per square mile, even considering all those *takhaar* Boers of the Groot Marico. Heard more *kak* talked and idiotic plans made as what I heard in the rest of my life put together. *Jussus*, man, your Dad's wildest dreams were nursery rhymes compared to what you heard in the House of Lords, ay. Some of them, though, were on the level and making steady money out of all the others busy wasting it. One of the first such *ous* we got to know was Les Tarlton, who'd started a safari hunting outfit with a friend of his – first of its kind I believe. Rich Yanks and the like were already eager to "go on safari" in East Africa, still are, as you know, and Tarlton figured he was on

---

[7] Stone curlew (literally fathead, Afrikaans). Has the foolish-looking habit of bobbing its very large head.

to a good thing laying on safaris for them. Struck us both as a *moer-on* easy way to make a living and we soon signed up with Tarlton to get to know the ropes. Did a couple of short safaris for him; then, after moving north for good, we set up on our own.

I loved to talk to Dad and Hutcheon about those early days in British East Africa and how they came to settle at Luoniek on the edge of the N.F.D., as the Northern Frontier District was universally known. They both liked to reminisce about those times, which must have been golden days for two young men of means eager to find adventure and possibly more in one of the most romantic corners of all Africa.

'The hunters who worked for Tarlton,' Dad recalled, '*ous* like Bill Judd, Cunninghame, Alan Black, Schindelar and all the rest of the toerags were a wild bunch, but they knew the country and we learnt a lot from them. But we soon bumped into some real rascals, let me tell you, ay. There were two in particular who had a lot to do with our coming up to Luoniek in the first place – Flash Jack Riddell and that stroppy little bastard, John Boyes. It was in the bar of the House of Lords one evening that these two *ous* started fighting, ay. Flash Jack was bigger than Boyes, but he had his time cut out getting the better of him because Boyes really wanted to *moera* him and what he lacked in size he made up for in meanness – and swear words; never heard such foul cursing. I asked what they were fighting over and was told they always had the hell in with each other over business – if what they did could be called that. What caught my interest was when I learnt that they made trading forays into the N.F.D., mainly for ivory. As both Hutcheon and I figured the N.F.D. was where we should be going we decided to meet up with these two rascals. We didn't have to wait long. Flash Jack turned up one Sunday, pissed, and jumped his horse over the tables in the House of Lords' dining-room. Seems he pulled this stunt quite often and everybody except the manager cheered him on. We got to talking and learnt he was an ex-Lancers officer, from the same regiment I think as Sir Harry Flashman who old Allan Quatermain had known. Birds of a feather they were at any rate, from what I heard. Flash was a hunter-trader who'd set up a business, the Boma Trading Company, with a branch in the N.F.D., one at Marsabit and another at Moyale on the Abyssinian border. He talked of the killing to be made buying horses in Abyssinia and selling them on in Kenya where the demand was very high. I said I'd heard there was still a lot of ivory to be had in the N.F.D. and I remember well the smile on Flash Jack's face at that remark. "When I take an ox wagon of trade goods up north I don't drive it back empty," he said. "Always looking for a bit of ballast, ay."

'Hutcheon was all for throwing in his lot with Flash Jack right away, and heading for the N.F.D. Must say I liked the *ou*, and I found his scorn for the law and authority very refreshing. He had style, I'll give him that, but he struck me as a bit too much of a chancer and I urged Hutcheon not to get too enthusiastic too soon. I tackled Flash about John Boyes and he got quite worked up, saying Boyes was always trying to outsmart him smuggling horses (the Emperor Menelik had forbidden them from buying horses in Abyssinia), that he was a crook, that we should watch our steps with him, and so on.

'We didn't have to seek Boyes out, because he came looking for us. He said he'd heard my name was Quatermain and was I related to Allan Quatermain? Hearing that I was he got really excited and told us how some years before he'd tried to trace old Hunter Quatermain's route through the N.F.D. into Abyssinia. Well, that set us off and we talked for hours with the 'King of the waKikuyu', as Boyes had crowned himself some years before. There is nothing, as you know, that more infuriates His Britannic Majesty and his flunkeys than commoners setting themselves up as kings, and they really had it in for Boyes. Even charged him with *dacoity* over it, though in the end the judge threw the case out. I took my hat off to Boyes for coming up with that one! He was of course *bougnoulisé* and a complete rogue from top to bottom, but we got on really well and always stayed friends. He tried like hell to get us to join him smuggling horses out of Abyssinia and I don't know what other devilry, but we could see that his real interest was only to stab Flash Jack in the back. For all his big mouth and shady deals he was a good bush operator, though. He and some Scandahooligan whose name I forget actually did bring a huge bunch of horses out of Abyssinia and sell them in Kenya, a truly remarkable achievement.

'After a few months hunting for Tarlton out of Nairobi we decided it was time to make our move. Hutcheon had got to know some *kaburu*[8] transport riders who had the government contract to carry supplies by ox wagon from Archer's Post on the Uaso Nyiro river to Marsabit. Two of these *ous*, Prinsloo and Klopper as I recall, gave us some valuable advice. "*Pasop kerêls*," they said, "stay away from the track we use. Too many bloody government officials on that road, always trying to sniff out what every *oke* is doing. You're better off over to the west a bit where they never go." Apart from that sound advice we were lucky to meet up with another *ou* in the bar of the House of Lords one evening by name of Henry Darley.[9] Said he was an ivory hunter – as did every second *ou* you met in those days – and we got talking about the N.F.D., which he said he knew well. He seemed nervous, looking closely at every newcomer to the bar. I asked him if he was expecting someone and he

---

[8] Corruption of Boer (Swahili)
[9] See *Slaves and Ivory* by Major Henry Darley, 1925

looked quite startled. He calmed down after a few drinks and said that he was always dreading to see some government official walk in who recognised him. "You, see," he said, "I'm wanted for hunting in the Closed Areas of Uganda and the Sudan without a permit. Can't afford to get caught. The longer I stay here the more dangerous it gets."

'I didn't pay that much attention; we'd heard plenty of stories like that since coming to BEA. All the same, he had great tales to tell of the extraordinary goings on in respect of gold and ivory and slaves in the wild country where BEA abutted on Abyssinia, and when he heard we were planning to go north he invited us to accompany him to his camp. "I've got an excellent camp at Mugi Springs," he said "that I won't be using again after this trip. Things are just too hot for me in BEA and it's time I moved to Abyssinia for good. My camp's just the location you need if you're planning to operate in the N.F.D. It's on the Loroghi plateau about fifty miles north of the new government outpost at Rumuruti on the Uaso Nyiro river."

'Well, we took up his offer and rode with him to Mugi Springs. The rest you know.'

That was how Dad and Hutcheon came to settle at Luoniek, a few miles west of Mugi Springs, on land they bought many years later when it was demarcated for cattle ranching. At the time, though, the authorities were none too enthusiastic about Dad's intention to live permanently on the edge of what was then the Closed Area of the N.F.D. They had some justification for their attitude since just about everyone who'd preceded Dad and Hutcheon had turned out to be a scoundrel. Like Dr Atkinson, a sidekick of Lord Delamere, who'd notoriously blown up several Rendille men with a keg of gunpowder in order to steal a pile of ivory he'd been trying to buy from them. Then there'd been the famous ivory hunter Arthur Neumann who'd committed suicide shortly after leaving the N.F.D., and about whom some said it was surprising his conscience had stuck it out that long. More recently, John Boyes and Flash Jack Riddell had been smuggling horses and ivory, and there'd been plenty of others doing the same. To get over this problem, Dad called on the Quatermains' old family friend, Rider Haggard, to pull a few strings back in Whitehall where he was well connected,[10] a move whose success predictably infuriated the local officials.

To begin with they got to know the country and its people by trading cattle. They bought stock from the Samburu and Boran, fattened them up at Luoniek and sold them on. It was good business and it took them all over the district, which they soon got to know well. Hutcheon especially enjoyed buying ivory on the side and smuggling it out under the noses of such authorities as existed in those days, a pastime he was a master at. The Great War then interrupted things. In 1914 Dad and Hutcheon volunteered for the irregular Bowker's Horse and with their knowledge of the bush were assigned to the campaign to see the Germans off from German East Africa, now Tanganyika. They were both with old Fred Selous, who'd hunted in Southern Africa with old Allan Quatermain, when Selous got the bullet in 1917 in a skirmish with the Germans near the Rufiji River. They had many other fascinating stories to tell – but I must get on with the real story, which is to say the story of how I came to be part of the Quatermain quest to find the gold mines of Ophir that history connects with the great Hebrew king, Solomon, and the dazzling temple he built in Jerusalem. I say the real story, because Dad and Hutcheon's early safaris didn't get them any information about Suleiman's gold mines other than that they were not

---

[10] In 1919 Rider Haggard was knighted for his public service on the Empire Settlement Commission and many others

41

in the N.F.D., which nobody really thought they were in the first place.

No, the real story only begins with the strange tale of how my father came by my mother. The romance of it makes me wince and, as an Abyssinian woman once said to me, aches my heart and tears my eye.

5

Into the Madbet

The fourth holiest city of al-Islam is Harar, the little walled town perched high on the Chercher Mountains on the eastern ramparts of the Great Rift Valley just before they peter out to the line of low hills that fringe the coast of the ancient Land of Punt. In Dad and Hutcheon's time it was already a somewhat tatty place for its glory days were long past. For many centuries it had been the capital of the Arab Zeila empire, but that itself had crumbled away in medieval times. The town lingered on as a Moslem citadel until, in 1887, the Emperor Menelik II fulfilled the age-old Abyssinian dream of incorporating the town and surrounding country into the Abyssinian empire. The slaughter of the last emir by the conquering Abyssinians put paid forever to its status as a purely Moslem enclave.

You can get a taste of the more recent history of Harar and the people of Punt from Sir Richard Burton's engrossing book *First Footsteps in East Africa* that I, like my dad before me, never tire of reading. In it Burton recounts his epic penetration of Harar in 1854, sixty-five years before Dad visited the place and some thirty years before Menelik sacked the town. Ostensibly, His Britannic Majesty's government had sent Burton on this risky, not to say hare-brained, expedition to investigate the trade possibilities of the coast of Punt. In reality, it was all Burton's idea and his purpose was exploration to satisfy his obsession with peering into the more exotic and obscure corners of the earth. Official sanction could only be obtained if it was suitably dressed up in political and economic terms. Burton had not yet blotted his official copybook, at least not irrevocably, so was able to wangle the official sanction he needed. He had planned to enter the city clandestinely, disguised as an Arab nobleman, as he had famously done in Mecca and Medina. However, at the last moment, he changed his mind and chanced his arm as an undisguised *faranj*.[11] Harar's emir, dying of tuberculosis, and chary of riling the British, let him get away with it and Burton spent ten days in Harar as the emir's 'guest'. In those days entry to the town by infidels was forbidden on pain of death. Burton defied this decree and got away with it – though his knowledge of and enthusiasm for al-Islam was so much greater than that of most Moslems that he was widely regarded as more of a Moslem than an infidel. He openly claimed, for example, the honorific *haji* as a result of his previous visits to Mecca and Medina and could lead prayers as well as most mullahs. By 1919, half a century on from Burton, the emirs of Harar were forgotten, the walls of the city were crumbling and infidels came and went freely.

This was enough in itself to attract Dad to the place, but there is something else about Harar that made his going there inevitable. You see, it isn't just a high, cool, well-watered spot in the lofty Chercher Mountains that rise ten thousand feet above sea level. It's also a relic of the true glory days of the Land of Punt, long, long before the time of the Prophet and the Zeila empire. That Harar came to play such a role in history was a consequence of the region's unique geography of which the two outstanding features are the Abyssinian swell and the Great Rift Valley. The valley

---

[11] Foreigner, primarily a white foreigner (Arabic). Corruption of Frank (Frenchman). Adopted by most Horn of Africa and Indian languages.

is a three-way rupture of the swell whose southern arm – the Great Rift Valley proper – is all above sea level. The other two arms, one filled by the Red Sea and the other by the Gulf of Aden, mark the swinging away to the north-east of the Arabian peninsula from its parent land mass of Africa. Harar lies near the hub, just east of the main valley, which separates the bulk of the Abyssinian highland swell from the rest of the Horn – Punt, Somalia and the Ogaden. The valley was also a cultural barrier that marked the border between the Arab peoples of the Arabian peninsula and the African peoples of the Abyssinian swell. Harar was the gateway in this barrier through which trade goods – mainly slaves, ivory and gold – passed from the African hinterland to Arabia and itinerant Red Sea traders. As Dad liked to say, it was highly probable that the very first coffee beans to be exported to the world beyond Africa passed through Harar, as may also have been the case with the first *chat*[12] to, as the Arabs say, 'feed the minds of the pious.'

All this meant that it was only a matter of time before Dad made his way north to Harar to find out what he could about its role, if any, in the legend of Ophir and King Solomon's mines. Dad was convinced that some at least of the gold of Ophir must have passed through Harar – perhaps a very large part of it. Not long after the end of the Great War when Dad and Hutcheon had returned to Luoniek and civilian life he reckoned the time had come to go and see for himself this place beyond the N.F.D. that conjured such a romantic image in his mind. The great Emperor Menelik was dead, but Abyssinia was still run along the lines the formidable warrior had set up. The country was split into provinces akin to the baronies of mediaeval Europe, governed by army generals who effectively owned

---

[12] Mild amphetamine-like drug from leaves and shoots of *Catta edulis*, chewed all over the Horn of Africa and exported to Arabia

them. Travel through a province required two passports, one bearing the emperor's or a minister's seal and the other the governor's seal. Either one by itself would not suffice, for Ethiopians are the quintessential bureaucrats, surpassing even the French in the making of bureaucracy an end in itself. Present only the emperor's passport and the provincial governor will ask rhetorically who is the emperor to go over his, the governor's, head in such arrogant fashion; present only the governor's passport and he will ask how he could possibly allow one to pass without the emperor's prior authority. A substantial consideration would always resolve the conundrum, naturally, but Dad abhorred that. So he spent the considerable time it took – the best part of a year – to assemble the complete range of properly sealed passports for the journey. He was considerably aided by the fact that His Britannic Majesty's government had recently established consulates at several places around western, southern and eastern Abyssinia. If you went now in 1946, after all the changes wrought by the Second World War, to Mega in the Sidamo province of Southern Ethiopia you would find it hard to believe that in 1914 the British opened a consulate there. Mega is an extraordinarily remote and forgotten spot from anyone's point of view, a tiny market in the *gramadoelas* on the road to nowhere with nothing happening or likely to. True, His Britannic Majesty's consulate at Mega was only a single mud *pondokie* with a grass roof, staffed by a lone functionary, the consul; but it was all the same HBM's Consulate for Southern Abyssinia and was to play a part in Dad's search for King Solomon's mines.

All this of course was long before I was born or saw the country for myself. What I know of Dad and Hutcheon's memorable safari to Harar is gleaned from listening to them tell various parts of the tale to their friends and safari clients, or to me and my sister in answer to the many questions we two had about our own origins and place in the scheme of things Quatermain. I will recount these tales as best I can, though I could never truly recreate the vivid impressions they made on me, for Dad and Hutcheon were wonderful storytellers. I would only be exaggerating a bit if I said that sometimes they were almost as good as Herman Bosman's immortal Oom Schalk Lourens, surely the greatest storyteller of them all. As best I can tell it Dad's story went as follows.

'We'd been instructed by the Nairobi legation during the extraordinarily tedious process of getting the passports to travel to Harar via Moyale, where there was a border post for both countries. From Moyale we were to proceed to Mega and report to the consul who would facilitate our onward journey. Shortly before we set off we got a terse telegram from Addis Ababa on behalf of the consul in Mega stating that we must take him a bag of golf clubs. Bloody hell, we thought, these Pongo Pooh-Bahs certainly know how to get everyone running around on damn-fool errands for them. Why can't they get their own blasted golf clubs? And what on earth did the consul for southern Ethiopia want golf clubs for? If they'd instructed us to bring a dozen cases of malt whisky or Dom Pérignon I'd have thought nothing of it. I took plenty of good booze anyway.

'Well, I had a bag of clubs sent up from Nairobi, plus a box of nyacks, and you can imagine the comments from all the *watu*[13] along the way concerning the mysterious load one of our camels was carrying. We put together a caravan of five camels and detailed Abdullahi, Ndaragus and three Boran men to accompany us and did the three hundred or so miles to Moyale in a little over three weeks. Sodding lions gave us stick at two places on the way and succeeded in mauling one of our camels just before dawn one morning

---

[13] People (Swahili)

when they caught us napping. Both the two sims[14] in question got the bullet before they could kill the camel, but it reminded us just how easy it is to get jumped by the notorious N.F.D. lions.

'We got to Moyale and checked in at the DC's boma[15] to give our *salaams* to Harold Kittermaster, a huge, rugged-looking bloke who'd already made his mark in the N.F.D.'s folklore. His officious predecessor, "Faras al" Glenday, showed up while we were there and reminded us just how damned stuffy these administrators could be when expressing their views on our operations in "their" N.F.D. They saw us as the next wave of freebooting villains, indistinguishable from the likes of Flash Jack Riddell, Dr Atkinson, John Boyes, Henry Darley and all the others who it has to be admitted had given them cause to be wary. They knew that we bought illicit ivory from the locals and sold it on the coast, but they'd never been able to catch us at it. I would point to the astonishingly large stashes of ivory HBM's minions regularly accumulated – destined for General Revenue, of course, of course – and ask what it was that gave the Crown first rights over Nature's loose goods. That would set them twittering like masked weavers round a boomslang; but at the clink of a free whisky bottle the scolding would die down, their beaks would gape like nightjars and it was all what-can-I-do-to-help-you-on-your-way-old-chap. Not that I held that against them. Plain water can go only so far towards quenching the kind of thirst you get in the N.F.D.'s more remote and arid outposts. Moyale's on the first rise of the Abyssinian highlands, but it's still the N.F.D. – hot, sandy and dusty with the seemingly never-ending dry easterly wind whirling your brains around inside your head like dry goat shit in a dust-devil. To protect HBM's interests they

---

[14] Slang for lions. Corruption of *simba* (Swahili)
[15] District Commissioner's compound (Swahili)

had a small detachment of King's African Rifles and to protect their own interests they had a large cellar stacked with the various lubricants essential to the smooth running of an empire's machinery. We'd included a camel in our caravan loaded exclusively with quality liquor to ensure our bona fides with the many officials we would have to pretend to be in awe of along the way, so all in all we were made welcome in Moyale. We bedded down several suns in good form with Kitters' mob, who had some great – and useful – stories to tell of life on the Ethiopian border. They'd have kept us there until the aforementioned camel felt like he was treading on air if they could've.

'We eventually moved on with Kitters warning us to keep our eyes peeled for brigands and did the sixty miles to Mega in three and a bit days. Fantastic country. The path winds up the escarpment to Deka Roba and by the time you reach Mega you're more than five thousand feet above sea level. It's cool and green – well, greenish – and without that bloody desert wind. At Mega, which is just a small, ragged Boran market, we finally met HBM's consul, Arnold Hodson, with whom we'd been corresponding over the last year or so. A small, wiry *oke* in a pith helmet and long riding boots, with huge, soft eyes is how I remember him. He was delighted to see us and we camped beside his consulate for the next few days to find out something about southern Abyssinia from the man who knew more about that part of the world than any other *faranj* before him and probably since.'

'The first surprise was when he declined our offer to take his pick of good drink from our ambulant cellar. Turned out he was teetotal. *Nou dar's 'n ding,* Hutcheon remarked upon learning that Arnold scorned booze and you'd have to admit that abstemious government officials are as rare as Nandi bears.[16] If you totted up how many gallons of grog a

---

[16] Fabulous animal of the Kenya highlands, occasionally seen, never captured

day it took to run an empire you'd come up with a spectacular figure, that's for sure. Enough to work Victoria Falls for a spell. On the other hand, you have to agree that HBM's consuls were a singular breed of men not cast from the general mould. Furthermore, as Hutcheon also noted (trust Hutcheon), there was no sign of any young Boran handmaidens curtseying demurely in the background so that we were constrained to ask what the hell he did when not consulating.

'"I see you brought them," he said, pointing to the camel carrying the bag of golf clubs. "Tomorrow's Sunday – we'll tee off straight after breakfast."

'"Tee off?" I said, not getting it.

'"Golf," he said. "You do play, don't you?"

'"Golf? Where in hell would we play golf?" I asked, looking round the Boran countryside. As far as one could see there were rolling hills and valleys falling away to the south, mostly scrubby woodland with some grassy patches broken up by many south-heading watercourses. Here and there were large herds of white Boran cattle, flocks of sheep, plenty of camels and many horses, donkeys and mules. Hardly any fields – the Boran believe themselves to be ordained herders and scorn cultivation even here where crops were quite feasible.

'"Afraid we can't play eighteen holes – I've only put in nine so far. Of course, we can play those nine twice or three . . ."

'He wasn't kidding. This was a British consulate and with all three of the regulation soothers of wine, women and song apparently inadmissible what would a solo British consul do after a day's diplomacy in the *gramadoelas* of Abyssinia? Why, play golf, old man, wouldn't want to go troppo, what? And that's exactly what Arnold had done. He'd put in a golf course. Looming over the market was Mega Mountain, its summit another three and a half thousand feet above us.

Between the peaks and us was an extensive flat, open *amba*, the grass kept short by cattle and sheep. Up here with the lammergeyers, HBM's representative for southern Abyssinia had superimposed a nine-hole golf course on the Boran grazing lands. Holes with flags being impractical among free-ranging livestock he'd positioned sun-bleached cow skulls as surrogate holes, with players deemed to have holed out once the ball was within a yard of the skull. None among the cook, the scullion, the butler, the equerry, the *dhobi*, the footmen, the *syces*[17] or the Boran had progressed beyond caddie so that he was eager to find someone other than himself to play against. Well, neither Hutcheon nor I were exactly low handicap players, but we agreed to give it a go – for the sake of the empire, old chap – and spent a considerable part of the next few days being tutored in the elements of the game. It got quite difficult to remember that we were searching for King Solomon's mines.

'The mystery of the golf clubs having been dispelled I turned to the more interesting question of what had possessed His Britannic Majesty to establish a consulate in this particular corner of the Horn of Africa in the first place. Pooh-Bahs in offices thousands of miles removed from the action do damn-fool things; but this seemed downright bizarre, especially as Abyssinia was not part of the empire nor had Britain any intention of making it so. I asked Arnold what the hell he was supposed to be doing here – when not playing golf, that is. Or reading about it. The man not only played, but had a huge collection of books on golf, which, he assured us, he loved to read to the moths at night by the light of a smoky Dietz lamp.

' "The post was created in 1914 at the outbreak of war," he said. "That's when I came here. Until recently I was obliged to live at Gardula, a hundred miles to the north-

---

[17] Grooms (Arabic, Swahili)

west – took me a long time to get the Abyssinians to agree to let me move here. There's another consulate at Maji, three hundred miles away as the crow flies in the south-west corner of the country. And another at Gore in the west. Then there's one at Harar, as you know. HBM's purpose is to collaborate with the Abyssinian government to help secure these outlying provinces that border on HBM's possessions of the Sudan, Kenya and Somaliland. As I'm sure Kitters will have told you, this province of Borana is completely dominated by Abyssinian brigands – *tigre*, they're called, or *shifta*[18] as you would know them. The truth is that the *tigre* bigwigs are as often as not the Abyssinian government officials, or at least people in cahoots with the officials. Everybody knows this, but it's simply too far from Addis Ababa for the empress (not that the old bag Zauditu gives a toss) or Ras Tafari to do anything about. Ras Tafari himself calls Borana a *madbet*,[19] which it most certainly is. Kitters probably put you in the picture, but the *tigre* play merry hell among the Boran and Rendille of the N.F.D., reiving across the border and then scuttling back to Abyssinia to mock us stuck behind the international boundary. Not that the location of the border has ever been formally delineated, but in practice we know more or less where it's assumed to be. The Abyssinians, of course, invariably know *exactly* where it is and it's not necessarily always in the same spot. We're responsible for the welfare of the N.F.D. Boran – they're British subjects, dammit – and it simply isn't on that these Abyssinian *tigre* should be free to plunder and abduct and kill them. They treat the Boran on their own side of the border just the same. Ever since Menelik conquered the Galla and annexed their country in the 1880s

---

[18] Bandit. Widely used term. (*shufto*, Somali; *shafta*, Amharic)
[19] Kitchen (Amharic). Used by Abyssinians in the sense of the French *bordel*, to describe a shambles.

52

they have been treated as the slaves of the Amhara so that whatever official line is spun in Addis the truth is that the Abyssinians don't give a monkey's what happens to the Boran or any other Galla anywhere."

' "But what can you actually do to rein in these *tigre*?"

' "Damn little, I'd have to say. I can really only use diplomacy – the few armed men I have are for my own protection. It's never been agreed that HBM can take punitive action of His own accord inside Abyssinia. Here – look at this." He rummaged around among some papers and produced a remarkable letter that read as follows:

> *Let it reach the English Government Consul, Mr Hodson. How are you? I am well.*
>
> *The post goes to Moyale and returns to Mega. Why do you not send me a letter? You despise my friendship. Now because of this I have stolen your post. Send me either 50,000 dollars or 50,000 cartridges, whichever you like. I have not opened the secret letters yet. Send me either the dollars or the cartridges that I do not do so.*
>
> *I, Alamu Woyessa, say this.*

' "Who the hell's Alamu Woyessa?"

' "A dab hand at cold-blooded murder and pillage. Leader of the biggest band of cutthroats in this area; they boast at least fifty rifles. Then there's Aba Boka's gang with thirty, Haili's with fifty or so and Ayala's with ten. That's a hundred and forty *tigre* rifles just in this neck of the woods – they can and do wreak havoc from Liban to Moyale to here. Then there's Gabra Hidan, Lij Balai down near Moyale and Tugla over towards Malka Murri on the Daua. You can imagine how much plunder it takes to support such large numbers of brigands who live entirely on what they extort from the unfortunate Boran who are absolutely prevented by the Abyssinians from arming themselves. And by us, for that matter, across the border. We fail to protect our own Boran subjects yet we forbid them guns. Pretty poor show, what?"

' "This bandit Alamu – he seems a pretty cocky sod writing letters like that to you. Waylaid your mail runners, did he?"

' "Yes – the insolent bastard. The worst of it is that I'll complain like hell to Fitaurari Hapta Georgis – he's Minister for War and the 'owner' as the Abyssinians see it of Borana – who'll despatch a couple of *dajazmachs*, with orders to bring the *tigre* to heel. Once here and out of reach of Hapta Georgis – who would be as good as his word were he on the spot – they'll fart about and eventually piss off, making damn sure they keep well out of the brigands' way. And to pass the time while they *are* here they'll like as not carry out a bit of pillage on the Boran themselves. Or even sell some of their guns to the *tigre*."

'Hutcheon and I marvelled at how the lone *faranj* Arnold, without a smoothly distilled nightcap or other conventional forms of tender solace, slept as soundly as he did while all around him roamed such monsters as Alamu Woyessa. No telegraph, three weeks' trek from Addis, four days' trek from Moyale – not many *okes* would survive five years of such a bleak life without falling off their perches.

' "They're wary of attacking me," he said, "because they know that such a move wouldn't be playing the game. It's one thing to be threatened by some posturing Abyssinian government official with a bunch of sabre-rattling soldiers who are never going to risk their lives by getting too close to any *tigre*; but quite another to incur the wrath of the British in general whom they basically hold in some awe. At any rate, that's what I tell myself," he grinned.

' "Seems to me," I said, "that you aren't ever going to suppress brigandry by diplomacy – yet you're still here after five years of proving that true. HBM must surely have another purpose?" He said nothing to that, so I went on. "I'd guess that what HBM really keeps you here for is to keep tabs on what the other *faranj* are up to politically. When Menelik curled his toes up in 1913 you Pongos got really jumpy, because that berserk maniac Lij Yasu upped and grabbed the throne. Not only was he as psychopathic as the Emperor Tewdros had been, but he was also a Moslem, which gave the Turks and the Krauts the idea that by supporting him and al-Islam generally they could incite a revolt against the other European powers, grab Christian Ethiopia, see off the Frogs and Pongos, take over the Suez Canal and rule the entire Middle East, Horn of Africa and East Africa. Am I not right, Arnold?"

' "Historically, yes. That's about the size of it."

'I went on. "Once the war against Germany began, keeping the Turks and al-Islam at bay became really urgent and it wasn't until halfway through the war that the pongos managed to orchestrate the locking up of Lij Yasu in a cage and replace him with a sane, friendly Christian. You're all still as jumpy as baboons on a moonlit night. I reckon your diplomatic mission is more to keep your ear to the ground than it is to protect HBM's Sudanese and East African borders against the *tigre*."

' "You can hear just about anything if you listen long enough," Arnold said enigmatically and refused to be further drawn on such matters. I wasn't that much interested anyway so we concentrated more on such things as the niceties of *afaan* Oromo, the language of the Oromo. When HBM posted Arnold to southern Ethiopia – the Oromo or Galla heartland – he was ordered to learn their language as quickly as he could in order to engage diplomacy or, as I figured it, garner intelligence without having to use interpreters. He not only taught himself the lingo, but wrote the first book on it. He showed us the nearly complete manuscript of his treatise on *afaan* Oromo and we spent some pleasant hours discussing various aspects of the grammar. His only other interest was in hunting big game – lions in particular – and he grilled us relentlessly on all matters hunting. Of course, what I wanted to hear was what he knew about gold in southern Abyssinia. Unfortunately, gold wasn't one of his interests and he came up with precious little in the way of information.

' "There *is* gold about," he said, "but I'm sorry – I just haven't tried to find out where exactly. Not so long ago the King of Jima is said to have given the Empress Zauditu a huge amount of gold as a token of fidelity at the time of the collapse of Lij Yasu's bid for the throne."

' "But Jima's on the west side of the Rift," I pointed out, "and it's been well known for thousands of years that there's a lot of gold all along the western highlands of Abyssinia. But here in the south, on the east side of the Rift, there's no legendary source of gold. Yet I just can't believe that there isn't any, that it's all on the other side of the valley. Makes no geological sense. There *has* to be gold here too."

' "Oh there is," said Arnold, "you're right about that. It's just that I can't tell you where. For a start, the Boran aren't going to blab about such things, because the *tigre* will stop at no gory outrage to force the Boran into revealing something like the whereabouts of a source of gold they hadn't previously known of. So if the Boran *do* know something they aren't going to be slack-mouthed about it to me."

' "I have heard, though," Arnold went on, "that there's placer gold up on the Daua headwaters somewhere north of Negele. But I don't travel the Negele route, because that's in Liban, which really is *tigre* country. Liban's considered to be somewhat outside my territorial area of operations in that it's the Abyssinian interior a long way from the Kenya border. So, to keep the Abyssinian authorities on side, I take the established route via Gardula when I go to Addis. If I were to trek from Mega to Negele the *tigre* would

assume I was either planning to attack them in their heartland or to propose some shady deal. So, for diplomatic
reasons, I never go there. But the gold is scattered about, I
believe – there's no single mine as such."

'I pumped him for more information on the Negele gold,
but he really hadn't anything other than vague stories to
relate. He did have some intriguing information about
another place, though – in many ways a much more interesting area than Negele. Arnold was an indefatigable traveller, who'd notched up a huge mileage on mule-back or on
foot during his time on the border. One of the first things
he did on taking up his post as consul was to find out for
himself what the Kenya–Abyssinia border country looked
like. Although the boundary was not demarcated it was,
geographically, a logical separation of the two countries in
that it ran more or less east–west along the foot of the great
Abyssinian highland swell.

'"Mongrel country," Arnold said, "real badlands if ever I
saw any. From Moyale to Lake Rudolf it's an endless succession of canyons and ravines scouring the foot of the
Abyssinian escarpment. The plain on the Kenya side is
either black-cotton soil or lava scree – either way it's hot
and dry as hell with typical thorny N.F.D. scrub. The many
streams above the escarpment on the Abyssinian side dry
up before they reach the N.F.D. so that the luggas are just
dry sand except for a brief period after rain – only it hardly
ever rains in the vicinity of the border! Once past Burroli
it's really bleak country that's seen a lot of volcanic activity.
The Huri Hills are just a group of old volcanoes – quite
high, about five thousand feet above sea level – but dry, dry,
dry. The border runs between the Huri Hills and the
escarpment south of Mega and, after the hills, goes north-
west up to Chew Bahir, which is nowadays a dry pan though
in times past it's been one of the many lakes on the floor of
the Rift Valley.

57

' "That stretch of country from El Adi at the Huri Hills to Chew Bahir is one of the roughest I've ever been through – actually, *the* roughest. On the northern horizon you always see the mountains of Abyssinia, looming blue-grey through the haze, to over eight thousand feet in many places, sometimes only twenty or thirty miles from the border, so abrupt is the change in terrain. But down in the border country it's all lava and sand and basalt boulders. Stinking hot, with patches of thick, ground-hugging scrub with branches like spring steel and thorns to match. The camels and mules make heavy weather of it and you are always worried sick about failing to find a well or waterhole at nightfall. No way can you travel at night – the bush is like a net in the dark. Bloody lions growling round you and frightening the camels – terrible place.

' "I got as far as El Sardu on the southern edge of Chew Bahir, where there's a small lugga running north-west into the lake. You're in the Rift Valley at that point, which has a narrow range of very high mountains on its eastern edge after the long gap without mountains to the south. In the valley itself it's flat and you can see for miles so that you get at least some sense of openness and space. But as you head back east and skirt the foot of the mountains that mark the edge of the valley you start to feel claustrophobic. These mountains are cut deep, right down to the level of the plain, by the Bullul River gorge thirty miles east of El Sardu. Then, twenty miles east of the Bullul is the equally deeply incised Rirribba gorge. This whole area of high mountains – they rise five or six thousand feet above the plain and seem from below to be almost vertical cliffs all the way up – is incredibly spectacular. But forbidding – this must be one of the most isolated, unvisited, unused corners in the whole of the Horn of Africa. I can tell you, much as I love to travel and explore new places I was glad to get out of there. I couldn't shake off a sense of foreboding, even during the day. Not from *tigre* or *shifta* – even they have little reason to go there. It's just the place. The gloomy gorges and the grasping bush that seems to actually go after you; the lions, the towering mountains, the dryness and the heat. The heat – bloody hell, it's hot there, down in the gullies surrounded by that dense, low bush that would give even a rhino the shits. All the time that hot wind blows, you can hardly hear yourself think, and there's never ever a shady spot. Scary place, let me tell you."

' "You didn't by any chance try panning for gold in any of those luggas?"

'Arnold stared at me in amazement. "Bloody hell! Gold! All you can think of when you reach one of those luggas is water. Water, water, maybe there's some water – and you trudge up and down hoping like hell to find a place that the elephants or the baboons have been scraping at for water. And of course you never do. Gold! No, chum, it never occurred to me that I might spend a few hours panning for gold. If I'd ever found any water in those devilish luggas I sure as hell wouldn't have used it for that!"

'I saw in my mind's eye those deep canyons of the Bullul and Rirribba Rivers that Arnold spoke of, cutting right down through thousands of feet of sandstone and basalt to the level of the plain. That's where some really old basement metamorphic rocks buried under the sediments and volcanic stuff could get exposed revealing perhaps some veins of quartz with gold in the cracks . . .'

Dad's voice would tail off at this point and I remember once that Hutcheon laughed and said, 'The banal Eldorados of all the old fools, ay.' Dad chuckled and said, 'You've been reading my books again, Hutcheon, I see.'

We all laughed, unaware at the time just how ironic Hutcheon's remark would prove to be.

6

Unholy Deeds in the Holy City

'Having done what we could to ease Arnold's appetite for competitive golf we got ourselves together for the journey on to Harar. Arnold advised us to use mules from Mega onwards, pointing out that our lowland camels would become even more evil-tempered in the cold, wet highlands that we would be travelling through from now on. "Avoid donkeys," he said, "their small hooves ball up in the mud. Abyssinian mules are real tough buggers and will take you anywhere as long as you use good pack saddles and don't overload 'em. I reckon about eighty pounds a beast is enough. They'll carry much more, but you risk saddle-sores and in the long run you lose time." That was only a third of what our camels had been carrying so it meant a bigger train of animals, but as Arnold was nothing if not an expert traveller we took his advice and after much haggling with the Boran we finally put together a bunch of mules and got going late in July.

'We waved goodbye to the diminutive, lonely consul standing in front of His Britannic Majesty's little grass castle in regulation pith helmet, khaki drill, boots and puttees, abjuring him to keep one up the spout for when Ato Alamu came visiting. The last we heard was him shouting, "WATCH YOUR CODS – THOSE AFAR KNAVES WOULD LOVE TO SPORT A SET OF PEARLY WHITE B . . ." The wind took the end of his sentence, but we knew of course what it was.

60

Whenever we kidded him about his meagre chances of living long enough to draw his pension in the *tigre* heartland, he would gleefully anticipate our fate when we reached Harar and the land of the Somal Bedouin. The Somal of that region – Afar and Issa – are notorious throughout the Horn of Africa for their custom of scalping their enemies, or indeed anyone they can get the drop on. In fact, enmity has nothing to do with it – even their best friends are not safe. But the hairy bit they're after is not on your head; it's lower down. The dream of every Afar and Issa brave is to dangle a brace of sun-dried testicles from their necks or arms. As such a handsome trophy will guarantee the possessor the uninhibited adoration of every girl in the tribe it pays to sleep with both eyes open in that part of the world.

'From Mega the track wound up onto the watershed of the eastern Rift mountains through the juniper forests that are home to the rarest of all the eighteen or so species of turaco in Africa – Prince Ruspoli's turaco. As it only eats juniper berries it's confined to these southern Ethiopian juniper forests and is found nowhere else in the world. Seeing for the first time these exotic birds that we had only known about from books led many years later to an idea that was to have important consequences; but that story will have to wait.

'We trekked on, taking the north-eastern route from Yabelo that threads its way through Sidamo and then down onto the Rift Valley floor past Shashamene, Lakes Shala and Ziway, past Awash and on to Dire Daua where the road to Harar leaves the valley and, turning south-east, climbs steeply back up on to the high Chercher Mountains that fringe the eastern edge of the Rift. The whole of this journey is through land peopled by various Galla tribes all now subjugated by the Amhara (or so the Amhara would like to think) of central Ethiopia. To ease the long rides we did what everyone in the Abyssinian highlands does – chew *chat*[20] or *jima* as the Oromo call it, the Arabs' so-called 'food of the pious'. The forests of these mountains east of the Rift Valley are where both *chat* and coffee evolved and the *chat* at least is the world's best – tender and juicy, as much as *chat* could ever be called tender and juicy; it's an acquired taste, that's for sure. But once you're over the initial desiccating bitterness it lives up to its reputation for buzzing you up a bit so you can stay awake, do without food and keep going far into the night.

'When at last we came to the final hilltop overlooking Harar we stopped and gazed for a while at the little whitish town crammed behind the dilapidated five hundred year-old encircling wall. That was a great moment for me . . . couldn't ever tell you just what an extraordinary sensation it was to be standing there looking down on that scruffy little dorp. Because we were looking at Punt's back door. Might not seem that grand, I grant you, but think about it a bit. Travel south from here and you will not find a single structure inland from the coast of such antiquity anywhere else in the entire eastern continent right down to the end of the Cape. *Nikkies,* nothing. Those stones piled on top of each other at Great Zimbabwe are the next nearest thing, but architecturally they are totally naïve and in any case nothing like as old. There are a few comparable places down the *sawahil,* the eastern coast, ancient Zinj, built by the same Arab civilisation that built this town. But that's it. Barbaria as it was so accurately labelled on the ancient maps – the very heart of darkness of darkest Africa.

'Now, I'm not suggesting that the present town is as old as Punt – it was built by Arabs in the seventh century in the early days of the Islamic hegemony. That's one *moerava* long

---

[20] Mild amphetamine-like drug from leaves and shoots of *Catta edulis*, chewed all over the Horn of Africa and exported to Arabia

time ago, but still a couple of thousand years after the heyday of the Land of Punt. But you can't tell me that this old town we're looking at was the first settlement at this location. When the Arabs set up the Zeila Empire centred on the port of Zeila – that's a bit east of Djibouti – they made Harar the capital of the province of Hadiyah. There were six other provinces with many old ruins as yet unstudied by archaeologists. I guarantee that when they do dig under the Harar we're looking at they'll find the relics of much older settlements, remains that could easily go back thousands of years – who knows? Remember that the *Periplus*, written five hundred years before the Zeila Empirc, already maps the port of Zeila. Now, if Zeila was already there so was Harar – or some such place up in these hills. Zeila and particularly the province of Hadiyah, was, according to the Arab historian Makrizi, principally known for its top quality eunuchs and other slaves. The best and most expensive slaves were from the interior, not the coast. You can be sure Harar was simply the last big town on an ancient route to who knows where in Barbaria, a route that you began at Zeila.

'When the Egyptian queen Hatshepsut, the great female pharaoh, sailed down the Red Sea three and a half thousand years ago and came back with shiploads of myrrh, ivory, ebony, gold, baboons, giraffes, leopard skins, slaves and whatnot I'll bet my life one of the places she shopped at was Zeila. Just had to be – it's in such a logical location from every point of view. However, Zeila and the other coastal ports themselves produced nothing; everything Hatshepsut acquired came from the hinterland. But when she spoke of Pun she was referring to ports like Zeila. And when the authors of the Old Testament books spoke of Ophir, the balance of probabilities says it was Punt. Or in Punt – opinions differ as to whether it was a specific place or a general area.'

This part of Dad's story was always the one that I found the most exciting back when I first heard him tell it. The romantic names glowed in my mind like fires in the night, vivid yet distant, too remote to know exactly what they were but all the same you felt they were familiar. Ophir, Punt, gold, Barbaria, the Old Testament, Solomon's Golden Temple, Harar, Hatshepsut, Egypt, Zeila, Kush, King Solomon's mines, the Heart of Darkness – oh what magic these words had, what romantic images they evoked, what enormous spans of time they covered, what amazing adventures they implied!

The first time he described that fine sunny morning when he and Hutcheon stood looking down on Harar I asked him. 'So you're saying this is where the gold of Ophir came from, from Harar? When I was a kid you used to say it was impossible to know, didn't you?'

'Ah . . . now you're getting complicated.' Dad said. 'The gold . . . about the gold history is aggravatingly vague. I'm saying the gold came from somewhere round here – and by round here I'm talking about the entire Horn of Africa and Abyssinian highlands. The ancient references to Punt always say it supplied gold, and Ophir was unquestionably the greatest source of gold in the ancient world. The only problem is that history omits to tell us exactly where Punt and Ophir were. King David's gold, King Solomon's gold, the gold of Ophir . . . it's a mystery where it came from.'

'So you're saying this is *not* where the gold of Ophir came from?'

'No, no . . . I'm saying I don't know – nobody knows, not even Professor Keane or any of the other brain-boxes knows, for all that they'd like us to believe they do. I'm saying I think it came from somewhere round here because if it didn't then where in the hell did it come from? You can rule out the whole of Arabia. There just isn't any gold to speak of there. And you can rule out Somalia – nothing's turned up there. And Great Zimbabwe – that gold was only found long after the days of Ophir during the Arab hegemony. It's the northern and western perimeter of the Ethiopian highland swell that has all the known gold sources of the right antiquity. Plus the Kush and Egyptian deserts between the Nile and the Red Sea. But all these were dominated by Egypt, or at least by Kush, which passed its gold onto Egypt. So, although I think Ophir and Punt were one and the same I also think that the detail of where Solomon's gold came from remains obscure. Don't forget, Ophir may simply have meant what later came to be called Africa, the mysterious country beyond Egypt and Kush.'

'So, did you think that in Harar you were going to solve the mystery of Ophir?'

'No, Alan, not solve it, but maybe get some more ideas about where to look. Ever since I first read Richard Burton's fantastic book about his visit here in 1855 I'd wanted to see the place for myself. You can't deny its romance. It stands smack on the boundary between the historic world and the authentic heart of darkness, the Barbaria of the ancients. Just imagine what's gone on here over the millennia!'

And imagine I did – still do for that matter and no doubt always will. Because even if they eventually turn out to be less than magical, as places do when too much is found out about them I shall pay no attention. Like Dad, I'd far rather hoard my romantic perceptions; protect them from the scourge of banal reality.

Dad's story continued. 'We rode on down and entered the town through one of its five gates. A noisy, crowded, smelly place of small, flat-topped rectangular buildings without windows, interspersed with thatched *tukuls* and corrugated iron lean-tos, separated by ravine-like, stony alleyways often barely wide enough for a loaded donkey. The barn-like

Jamil mosque with artless conical minarets (a legacy of some dull Turkish architect of centuries past) is at one end of the town and on the other side, across the horse market, is a Christian church so that the muezzins' chanting mixes with pealing Christian church bells. There are a multitude of crude little private mosques and many small, crowded graveyards. We took rooms in the Lion d'Or, said to be the least uncomfortable hotel in town and which had facilities for our horses and mules. It claimed by way of distinction to have originally been Arthur Rimbaud's warehouse, which some might regard as more ill-omened than good given the luck Rimbaud had with it. We ostentatiously deposited our money in the Bank of Abyssinia to discourage the many rogues we knew would be spending long hours chewing *chat* while drawing up schemes to rob us as long as there was any chance that the *ferenjes* would be stupid enough to keep their money on them.

'When we entered the town there was an air of excitement about the place with small boys scuttling around frenetically like *kukus*[21] and groups of Amhara men with rifles over their shoulders moving among the population. We soon heard that Ras Tafari himself was in town along with his entourage and other dignitaries. The Ras had until recently been the governor of Harar, but was now the de facto prince regent alongside the Empress Zauditu. It was he who was destined a decade later to become the Emperor Holy Trinity,[22] King of Kings, Conquering Lion of Judah, the last such emperor in one of the world's most ancient dynasties. The following morning we presented ourselves at the governor's residence overlooking the town and asked for an audience in order to present our credentials and obtain official sanction for our intention to trade. After a

---

[21] Chickens (Swahili)
[22] In Amharic, Haile Selassie (Ed)

couple of hours wait while various officials came and went a lackey handed us a letter, which turned out to be an invitation to attend a banquet that evening at the governor's residence as the guests of Ras Tafari. It proved a memorable evening. The Ras was a short, slight young man in his mid-twenties with classic Amhara features and a courteous, dignified manner. He was well educated with impeccable manners and made us feel very welcome. He had come to Harar with the British minister from HBM's legation in Addis, Captain Thesiger, on some diplomatic business or other. Thesiger had brought along his two sons, one of whom was Wilfred – you know, that *ou* who's always trekking around exploring. Also there that night was old Monseigneur Jarrouseau, introduced as the Bishop of Harar, which sounded rather grand I thought for such a dorp. He was very entertaining though, and remembered the mad poet Rimbaud well, about whom he had some weird stories to tell.

'As the evening wore on Ras Tafari relaxed his formal manner and partook liberally of the excellent cognac he'd laid on for us. We made it clear that we weren't here just to trade or to look for investment possibilities in a developing Ethiopia – something the Ras was clearly much preoccupied by. It was exciting to have three really interesting people to talk to who might easily have some light to throw on the legendary mines of Ophir. The Ras had been born and brought up in Harar, though both his parents were Amhara, not Harari, and was a well-informed student of his own and his country's history. His father, Ras Mekonnen, had been an outstanding general under the great warrior emperor Menelik, and although the Ethiopian royal line from Queen Makeda, as the Amhara call the Queen of Sheba, up to the young prince Tafari was not the genetically continuous lineage tradition held it to be he was nevertheless the most recent in the amazing Abyssinian dynasty that went back twenty nine centuries to the seduction by Solomon of Sheba – or, as was more likely the case, of Solomon by Makeda. There was nothing to say that Ras Tafari was not descended from Queen Makeda – he could easily have been, and I certainly found it a most romantic notion to assume that he was. Thesiger was also a keen student of Abyssinian history and it was not surprising, therefore, that we stayed up late into the night, long after all the other guests had gone and the servants fallen asleep, drinking cognac and talking about King Solomon's mines.

'Neither man was able to shed much light on the mystery of their whereabouts, though, for all that they had some intriguing things to say. Ras Tafari pointed out that asking him, the heir apparent to the Ethiopian throne, about the sources of gold in his country was a bit like asking a man for his bank account number. Gold, he'd explained, was a royal prerogative in Abyssinia, always had been and, he hoped, always would be. Traditionally, gold was one of the main – often the principal – sources of a king's personal wealth. Of course, people didn't always respect that and considerable amounts of gold had always been diverted by unscrupulous individuals from the emperor's personal coffers; but, in principle, gold was supposed to be handed over to the emperor. The sources and amounts were as a consequence always shrouded in uncertainty. It was well known, though, that the bulk of the emperors' gold had always come from the west – especially the area known as Beni Shangul. The mines in question had always been referred to as Queen Makeda's mines. There had never been any doubt about that. They were Sheba's mines, not Solomon's mines. Nobody with any knowledge of history had ever suggested that King Solomon had at any time held any lien over these mines. The only other people to have had access to them historically were the Egyptian pharaohs – but that was in the time before Makeda.

'But not all the emperor's gold came from the north and west. Ras Tafari described how, between 1880 and 1885, the Emperor Menelik subjugated the Moslem Oromo kingdoms of Southern Ethiopia between Gibe and Didessa of which the wealthiest was Jima. The main products of these places were gold and ivory (which Menelik reserved exclusively for himself), slaves, civet, leopard skins and coffee. At the time, Jima was a huge slave market trading mainly other Oromo and Shankalla, as the Abyssinians dismissively called anyone who was not an Oromo or highland Abyssinian. In 1886, Menelik seized the Gamo Gofa province of south-west Ethiopia, in large part for its gold. He licensed a prospector called Ilg who re-opened an old Kush mine at Nejo that yielded vast amounts of gold of which Menelik took half. Etiquette ruled out enquiring about the present arrangements concerning this and other large gold operations on the western frontier of Ethiopia; but there was no reason to suppose that they differed from Menelik's day.

'But, by the south, they weren't referring to the country east of the Rift Valley, the true south. They were referring to places like Jima on the west side of the valley, whose kings had always had plenty of gold. Furthermore, the kings of Jima – Galla kings it must be remembered – had always been a thorn in the side of the Ethiopian emperors in that they stubbornly resisted Amhara royal prerogatives and operated far too independently. At the time of the Empress Zauditu's successful resistance to the attempted throne grab of Lij Yasu, the King of Jima as a mark of endorsement had sent her a huge present of gold. That was, in Ras Tafari's view, a typical bit of *samenna werk*.[23] The king was with one hand acknowledging Zauditu's throne, and with the other reminding her that in Jima he ran his business as he pleased. Any gold she got from him would be a present, not

---

[23] Literally, wax-gold. Amharic verse with a hidden meaning (Ed)

a due. We Galla are no longer the slaves of you Amhara. But where the king of Jima actually got his gold from – that was a mystery. There were no mines around Jima itself. Some came from the south-west, from the Maji area where the Surma people panned gold at many small alluvial sites. But by all accounts the Surma gold didn't account for the very large quantities the kings of Jima were thought to deal in.

'As for Harar, well, according to the Ras there wasn't that much gold passing through the town. Even in his father's day, and before that, gold was not a big part of Harar's trade – officially, at least – although the Ras did say that Arthur Rimbaud regularly bought gold. In Sir Richard Burton's[24] detailed list of the trade goods of Harar in 1855 there was no mention of gold. On the other hand, Ras Tafari said, the old sheiks of the town always stated that in times long past, in the days of the Zeila Empire, large amounts of gold were traded through Harar. But history was rather ambiguous about this. One mediaeval historian, Bartema, wrote of "the marvellous abundance of gold in Zeila". Other historians make no mention of it.

'One thing that Ras Tafari did agree with us about was that whether or not gold figured much in the recent history of Harar said nothing about what might have been the case long ago. For there is one thing about Harar that speaks for its great antiquity more than any other and that is a very singular thing. He pointed out that Harar has its own unique people and language – a tiny, isolated little population confined, at least today, to the city and its near environs. This is a most extraordinary thing with a profound implication; for the Harari language is not a dialect of another tongue – it's a unique and highly evolved language as distinct as any other. Linguistically, it's a Semitic graft

---

[24] See Burton's *First Footsteps in East Africa*, 1855

onto an indigenous stock, one of four such languages along the west coast of the Red Sea that include Tigrinya, Amharic and Gurage. The other principal languages of the Horn are the completely different Cushitic Oromo and Somali tongues. If, as some have supposed, Harar and the Harari only go back to the beginnings of the Arabic Zeila Empire then the Semitic root of their language would inevitably have been Arabic. But, while Harari, like all Horn of Africa languages, has absorbed many Arabic words, it is not derived from Arabic. It must therefore predate the seventh century Arab invasion, which implies a powerful Middle Eastern Semitic influence before ever the Arabs and their distinctive language dominated the region. It's impossible not to view the Harari nation as a remnant of the string of four Hamitic peoples down the west coast of the Red Sea (the coast of Punt) who several millennia ago adopted a Middle Eastern Semitic language.

'By the time we finished the Ras's excellent cognac that convivial night in the governor's residence we were all in complete agreement with the proposition that Harar, or at any rate its predecessor, was none other than Ophir itself, the location of its gold mines now forgotten, or – regrettably but undeniably possible – the mines exhausted.'

'We had no difficulty getting to meet people in Harar – the advent of two obviously well-heeled *ferenjes* in those days drew the attention of everyone. And when we let it be known that we were interested in buying gold all sorts of little cons, big cons and more respectable men of affairs got in touch with us. We bought a fair bit of gold quite quickly, paying, as we intended, appreciably more than a local would in the hopes of dislodging old gold that might otherwise have remained hoarded. There was a lot of silver jewellery, amber and indifferent gemstones offered to us, most of which we turned down as we hadn't the means of moving stuff in any volume. But the gold was interesting, because it seemed there was raw gold about, as well as worked stuff. Raw gold implies an origin in the region. People are hardly likely to bring raw gold to Harar from anywhere except the hinterland. Worked gold might come from any direction, but raw gold would be moving eastwards on its way out of Southern Ethiopia to the gold markets.'

Dad's stories always ended here, more or less. He'd say how they brought 'quite a lot' of gold back to Luoniek and talk about how the visit to Harar had crystallised a lot of his thoughts about Ophir and King Solomon's mines; but there'd been no great revelations, no great mysteries solved. He'd fulfilled his wish to walk through 'Punt's back door' and seen for himself much that hitherto he'd only read about. It wasn't until I and my sister Leila were well into our teens that Hutcheon told us what else had happened on that safari. And he didn't have to explain why Dad had always left these bits out.

This, then, is the missing story as Hutcheon told it. His tone was far less jocular than usual, almost formal. Too many echoes, I suppose, of matters he took very seriously for all that there were some droll elements.

'We'd been three or four days in Harar when a Somali approached us saying that a certain Abd el Hai wished to discuss business. Of course we assumed that Abd el Hai was an Arab trader and for sure he looked like one, ay. Actually, though, he was a Frog with a *moerava* big hook nose. *Magtig*[25] man, it'd have looked big even on a Arab, ay. This *oke*, Abd el Hai as the people called him – and everyone seemed to know him – was to have a profound influence on our lives, not that he really meant to, at least I don't think he did. But, knowingly or not, he marked out the course of

---

[25] Expletive. Corruption of (God) Almighty. (Afrikaans)

72

the rest of our lives – and yours, too, Alan – as surely as if he'd been God himself, ay.

'As soon as we met up with this Abd el Hai we realised we were in many ways kindred spirits. His real name was Henry de Monfreid[26] and he'd baled out of France back in 1910 to live the life of a *vrai flibustier* – that's what your dad called him – in the Land of Punt. His Arabic nickname meant, he said, the Servant of Life, which signified about as much to me as any crossword puzzle clue, ay. Anyway, it seems the Servant of Life started off as a trader here in Harar, like *cet autre fou* as he put it, the crazy Frog poet Arthur Rimbaud, thirty years before him, but soon set about freebooting on the Red Sea. He said all the Frog officials in French Somaliland moaned like hell about him being completely *bougnoulisé,* dressing Somali-style and keeping the company of Somali and Dankali men – and women, ay, there was usually a young Somali bint somewhere in the background. They must've had the hell in with his gun-running and the other smuggling that he flagrantly carried on right under their noses. He didn't care, ay – made bloody fools of them all the time. The *rooineks* were similarly irritated by the ease with which he dodged them on the Red Sea, though I heard that when they did eventually catch the *skellum* they treated him more as a trophy than a villain.

'He reminded me of a klipspringer – small and wiry with frenetic, springy movements. He seemed to jump from place to place rather than simply walk as ordinary *okes* do. Didn't do a lot of laughing for all that he couldn't take authority or convention seriously. But most of all he didn't talk *kak* – or not as far as we could tell. He clearly knew the country and people extremely well and we talked for hours about all manner of things. Sooner or later, of course, your

---

[26] See Ida Treat's biography of this remarkable man, *Pearls, Arms & Hashish,* 1930

dad brought up the subject of gold, asking if he'd ever traded much of it. Seems he himself had never got into that side of things, ay, at least not in a big way, as most of his time was spent farting around the Red Sea and in that part of the world gold didn't figure. But up here in Harar, he said, there was some about. He said that although Burton had not listed gold as one of the principal trade goods of his day it was a matter of record that Arthur Rimbaud had regularly traded gold during his time in Harar in the 1880s. Not any great quantity to be sure, but then *cet fou* Rimbaud, as he put it, never made a killing out of anything while he was in Harar, except himself, ay.

'Anyway, this De Monfreid *oke* went on to say that there was a businessman of his acquaintance who he had heard dealt in gold and silver and suchlike. This man he said was often in Harar. He had got to know him back in 1911 when he, de Monfreid, was living here; however, he had not seen him since that time. But he had heard that he still operated in this part of the world. He remembered him as an unusual man, well educated and very knowledgeable in business matters. De Monfreid seemed to feel very strongly that he would be the best contact Rider could make if he was interested in gold.

'Always I will remember that day,' said Hutcheon, 'not only for the fateful arrangement to introduce us to this gold dealer, but also for another quite different sort of introduction, ay. We'd been talking all afternoon and as it got towards evening we suggested a drink. De Monfreid declined, said he was a Moslem. But we soon discovered that anything he lost out on by not drinking he more than made up for in other ways.

'*Allez*,' he said, 'we visit the Daughters of the Danakil. You know the place?'

'When we said that we didn't he allowed himself a rare smile and chuckle and said something to the effect that by

74

this time tomorrow we would be changed men. Man – he wasn't wrong.'

Richard Burton, celebrated connoisseur of all things erotic, had remarked on the 'laxity of morals' in Harar, and both Hutcheon and Dad told me later that in that respect things had evidently not changed since his day. Mention to Hutcheon the Daughters of the Danakil and a Mona Lisa smile spreads over his face that speaks of unrepeatable recollections of the very best kind.

'*Krars*, man – the Daughters of the Danakil. *Nou dars 'n ding*, ay! A little whorehouse tucked away in one of those muddy alleys you have to walk down sideways they so narrow, ay. A small scruffy-looking place – but, *jussus*, I don't believe there's a better brothel on earth. The entrance is just a little low door that a pygmy would have to stoop for. There's no sign outside – just the small red cross that in Ethiopia signifies succour inside for the needy; but it doesn't mean medical help. In point of fact, you're more likely to need medical help after heeding the red cross sign than before. Inside, on the wall, there's an old sign in Arabic that reads *Binti el Danakil.* It's dark in this room and there's always myrrh burning, but just a little, just enough to catch a whiff. Then this tall, swishy bint comes up and greets you, polite as hell, quiet-spoken and gracious, finds out who you are and what you want to drink and sit down there, sir, make yourself at home. She's obviously the boss and somehow you act quite deferential because she just has that air about her. She's not so young, but not so old either and still good-looking and attractive. Tall, with slender arms and legs – but big breasts, I mean huge, ay, really *lekker*[27] tits – hard, like a young Afar girl's. Spectacular. Nicely dressed, but you can see her body move under the clothes – after all, she's not dressed for the bioscope, ay. She has a very

---

[27] Nice (Afrikaans)

pale complexion, even for a Harari, with piercing black eyes and big, dark eyebrows. Brings your drink and sits down opposite you.

'She explains that her prices are much higher than the other salons of venery in Harar, of which, she says, there are "too many". But they, she says dismissively, are "just toilets". She's expensive, she says, because she only caters for the best clientele, the wealthy and discerning. Furthermore, her girls are experts, not common prostitutes like the other tarts in town. That's why there are not a lot of customers and why you are welcome to stay for as long as you like – days, if you feel like it. No hurry, here – in fact we encourage you to take your time. After all, it's pleasure we provide, and why take five minutes over something that could be spread over many hours, properly conducted? Why indeed.

'Her name, she says, is Nigist, which is Amharic for queen (although she is Harari, not Amhara) and she then calls in her "daughters" and introduces them one by one. They don't call her Nigist, though, referring to her instead as Bilqis – the Arabic name for the Queen of Sheba. Later on, when I got to know some of the daughters better they told me that among themselves they call her simply *Tut*.[28] Among the girls I particularly remember Dinkanesh, a busty Amhara girl (though flat-chested compared to Nigist) who dances the Amhara shoulder-shake so erotically that your eyes ache from trying to keep them in your head; Jamila, a young Afar girl who never wears anything above the waist (and rarely below it, come to that); Amira, a pure Harari who, if sexual gymnastics were an Olympic sport, would be a multiple gold medallist; and Salome, whose particular speciality I will not go into here, but if you know what the women of Tahiti are legendary for you'll not need me to

---

[28] Breast (Amharic)

explain. Each was as sexily voluptuous as the other and all possessed powerful libidos and a knowledge of creative fornication out of all proportion to their youth and lack of other education. Real professionals, man,' Hutcheon recalled, 'Just when you thought there couldn't be any other way to put the hump on the camel they'd show you how ingenious the divine design really was and come up with yet another way to turn over the kudu's hoof.'

There was another thing about Madame *Tut* that Hutcheon related, something very intriguing. 'After we'd got to know her better,' Hutcheon recalled, 'she said she had something to show us and went off to fetch an old book.

' "Look at this," she said, "it was given to my grandmother who gave it to me before she died. My mother and my grandmother were all in the same business," she added proudly. "It runs in our family."

'She handed us an old book, nicely bound and still in fair condition. It proved to be a copy of the *Thousand and One Nights* in Arabic.

'*Tut* pointed to a short inscription on the flyleaf, written in Arabic, saying, "my grandmother was also called Bilqis, like me."

'Now, I can't read Arabic,' Hutcheon said, 'but Rider can, more or less. Took him a while in the dim light, but eventually he worked it out.

' "It reads," he said, "For Bilqis, beautiful flower of the Perfumed Garden. And it's initialled RFB". Well, those initials could stand for many names, but it only took Rider a couple of minutes to realise that one of the many is of course none other than Richard Francis Burton. *Nou dars 'n ding*, ay – puts the great man's famous safari to Harar in a slightly different light, doesn't it? It's certain that he had a copy of the book with him, because he writes of reading stories from it to his companions during his journey to Harar in 1855, sixty-four years earlier. Furthermore, if you have the kind of imagination that your dad had you'll find it significant, as he did, that in his book Burton states unequivocally that the emir made him welcome in every possible way. Make of it what you will, but there's no doubt that it's an intriguing little fact and all the more so if you let your imagination wander a little further and wonder at the elegant Bilqis' flashing black eyes, prominent dark eyebrows and pale, pale complexion . . .

'When we'd recovered from that first encounter with the Daughters we made an effort to concentrate on business and set about getting to know the big men of Harar.

"There are people in all places," your dad would say, "who maintain memories of the past. People come and go, but some families stay put for generations in an isolated, introspective town like Harar. The extraordinary persistence of the Harari race and language is proof of that. There must be many people here who've never budged over the generations and who must therefore preserve information that's been handed down through the generations."

'This was one of your dad's favourite themes,' Hutcheon said, 'and I told him what I thought, ay, that in my experience people's memories dry up faster than buffalo shit on a hot day, what did you really expect to learn by asking people what they remembered?

'Well, as you know, your dad always said that it wasn't individuals' singular memories he was referring to; it was their collective memory he was after, the stories that were told over and over until they gradually became part of their perceived world.

'You'll get very few people writing stuff down, even if they know how to write, and not many people do. The history of the ancient world was written by an extraordinarily small number of people. And this minuscule band of men was in any case, for the most part, recording the collective memories of their day. History offers precious little firsthand observation. It's rare for a man who makes history to also record it. Richard Burton was one of those rarities and as such was the exception that proves the rule.

' "Anyway," your dad would say, "it's all there is to go by, so I've always reckoned to go after it."

'He was good at it, too. For all that he was a hard man in the sense of making his way in a rough, often hostile, seldom accommodating world, he had an engaging manner that encouraged people to talk. He never argued if he could possibly avoid it, could listen tirelessly to the interminable drivel that so many *ous* can dispense so much of and had a knack of asking questions in such a way as to flatter a person's opinion of his own noteworthy ability to answer them. As I say, he could listen to almost anything he was told, but part of his knack of extracting information – I suppose good police interrogators have the same ability – was that he was seldom fooled into believing what he was told. Crafty people realised that, once they got to know him, but his willingness to listen to their bullshit flattered the dissemblers, so that sometimes they embellished their bullshit, so to speak, with facts when their imagination ran a bit dry. And Rider had a keen nose for facts, which, as he put it, stood out like spots on a zebra when someone's trying to baffle you with bullshit.

'So we spent two or three days talking to some of the old Arab traders of the town who of course were delighted to have someone actually want to listen to all the amazing twaddle they could dish up incessantly once they got a good wad of *chat* lodged in their scrawny old cheeks. I have to say, though, that your dad did unearth a surprising amount of gold by talking to these old reprobates and what's more, some of it was in the form of ingots, rough little slabs weighing a pound or two – but obviously old, that's for sure. Stuff they'd been hoarding for donkeys' years, which, so they claimed, had been handed down to them by their fathers and grandfathers. It was only by offering three or four times the market value that we dislodged this gold; otherwise it'd been left where it was, hidden away in dark forgotten corners with the silverfish and spiders. Of course, I didn't realise it then but meeting these fusty old Arabs whose families had lived in Harar for as long as they knew and discovering that they did indeed possess at least some old gold tuned, so to speak, your dad's mind to a certain frequency that resonated with romantic tales of old men with hoards of gold – the kind of fairy stories that, after all, he was a sucker for at the best of times.

'Then our Frog friend Abd el Hai showed up again. I thought then and I think now that Burton summed up this type of *bougnoulisé* man perfectly with his epithet of "amateur barbarian"; for, looking back on it all as I have a million times over, I suspect that *le flibustier* was a bit out of his depth. Unless he was a great deal more villainous than we took him to be, the real barbarians he was consorting with were simply using him to puff up the trustworthy impression they wished to impart to us. Anyway, de Monfreid said he'd located the man he'd been looking for who was apparently keen to meet us. He took us to a pleasant little *buna-bet*[29] on a clear sunny morning when the town was looking and feeling good. People bustling about shouting and singing and swearing, donkeys braying, children squealing, dogs barking, the visiting Dankali and Afar girls looking their giggly, near-naked best – all in all a fine day on which to do a little business, ay.

'I must say this acquaintance of de Monfreid's made a good impression on that first meeting; a tall, sparely built man in his forties, well-spoken and well-dressed. A handsome man, but with inscrutable features in that I couldn't place him ethnically. He claimed to be Harari and for all I

---

[29] Coffee shop (Amharic)

know, he was, though as I say he could've come from just about anywhere. His skin was pale with the yellowish cast that is much coveted in a woman in this part of world and goes by the epithet *turk*, pronounced *toorrk*, for most Abyssinian languages roll the "r's" and sound "u" as "oo". *Turk* means, literally, just that and harks back to the time several centuries ago when for more than a hundred years the Turks occupied Harar and Zeila. He said with some pride that he was directly descended from these Turkish occupiers, which accounted for his skin colour (though I have to say I thought it just as possible that he was descended from Harar's Egyptian occupiers of the 1880s – not that any of it matters).

'De Monfreid introduced him as Abdulkader Mandit and as we were exchanging greetings a second man joined us whom de Monfreid introduced as Sheik Mâki. Something told me I'd heard this name Mâki before, but at the time I couldn't place it and we soon moved on to the purpose of our meeting. He was an engaging, friendly *oke*, this Abdulkader, with the ability to hold your attention. The sheik was a reserved, taciturn Arab, well mannered and cultivated, but impossible to fathom. He rarely spoke, leaving the conversation almost entirely to his companion. Your dad was immediately intrigued – anyone would've been as these two were clearly of a different cut to your average Harar rascal – and we spent hours together at that first meeting. We met up again every day for the next few days, but your dad and the *turk* spent so much time just talking that I eventually got bored and went off, leaving them to it.'

Hutcheon always claims that he never took to the man as Dad did and never found his many stories as convincing as Dad did. Sometimes, though, I think Hutcheon is using hindsight when he says this – it would be understandable if he were, in the light of what happened.

'Between them Abdulkader and Sheik Mâki did come up

with a sizeable amount of old raw gold in small, crude ingots, like that we'd already bought. Unlike the old Arabs, though, they didn't angle for a grossly inflated price, saying they were content to accept a price equivalent to what they would expect to get in Arabia. Abdulkader said that there was in reality quite a bit of gold moving through Harar, but clandestinely, because if the Abyssinians got wind of who controlled it they would seize it, an explanation that fitted well with what Ras Tafari himself had told us. What really got your dad listening, though, were Abdulkader's remarks on the gold's origin. He never claimed to know for sure where it came from – probably the single most persuasive element of his *racontage*, that he didn't pretend to know for sure – but he said that everything he'd ever heard pointed to its originating from somewhere in the south-west. That of course was what resonated with your dad's romantic obsession – somewhere in the south-west, the Ogaden, Barbaria, the Heart of Darkness as he used to say.'

Hutcheon certainly had Dad figured in this respect, as I too now realise. The Ogaden covers some fifty thousand square miles, all of it mysterious, none of it then mapped, all of it forbidding, none of it accessible. There is no doubt whatsoever that this element of the vast unknown was essential to the Quatermain obsession with finding King Solomon's mines. What Dad really wanted, the thing that really got his gooseflesh up, was an intriguing pointer, a romantic possibility, a hitherto untried tack. I realise now that if someone had told him exactly where these mines of Ophir were he'd have found some excuse for *not* going to look. He perfectly exemplified Stevenson's maxim that to travel hopefully is a better thing than to arrive. It's the very lack of specificity and finality that so grips people like Dad, that constitutes a vital trace element for the romantic spirit. Romance needs indeterminacy; bring everything to a clear-cut conclusion and you kill romance. It took me a long time to grasp all this about my father, whereas Hutcheon knew it all along.

'Your dad of course wanted to know who *did* control the gold trade, something Abdulkader proved reticent about. He kept saying that if he divulged such information to a visiting *ferenje* his life would be on the line. Your dad of course swore that he would never reveal such information to anyone, least of all to an Abyssinian. Anyway, Abdulkader kept him on the hook for a couple of days until I suppose he felt he had your dad's confidence. He then alluded to an old, wealthy Arab who lived about twenty miles out of Harar on the road to Jijiga. Shcik Ibrahim, he said, was of an old Harar trading family whose roots went right back to the golden days of the Zeila Empire. When the Christian Emperor Menelik had captured Moslem Harar back in 1887 he delivered by that victory the *coup de grâce* to the remnants of the ancient Hadiyah province of the once glorious Zeila Empire. The sheik, disgusted at this turn of events, had moved out of town to set up a little personal stronghold on top of a hill a day's ride from Harar, where he still lived, old now, and no longer interested in the effort and aggravation of politics and trading.

'This inactivity, Abdulkader said, meant that from time to time he was short of cash, which he sometimes solved by selling some silver or amber jewellery, of which he had a huge collection. But, Abdulkader said, he also kept a considerable hoard of gold against the possible day when he might have to flee the usurping Abyssinian infidels and buy rapid, safe passage down to the coast and across the Red Sea. He was sure the sheik would sell a substantial quantity of gold for the sort of price your dad was prepared to pay. He would also be one of the region's most knowledgeable people when it came to the history of trade in these parts. That assertion, of course, was the one that really got your dad's attention and though he didn't make a point of his interest in the history, or so he thought, there is no doubt looking back on it all that Abdulkader had spotted his true obsession and knew he had him as surely as a duiker in a snare. Abdulkader, I think, was more than a match for even your dad when it came to sniffing the important facts out of an afternoon's verbal excavation.

'Your dad soon proposed a visit to Sheik Ibrahim to which Abdulkader at first agreed, but then opined that there would be a problem. The sheik, he said, was a devout Moslem and not as tolerant of the infidel as the Prophet had been. On top of that, he had been appalled when the infidel European powers in concert with the Abyssinians had arbitrarily and arrogantly assigned the ancient Zeila Empire to one another. Such outrage! Regardless of whether or not we were French, Abdulkader said, the old man would place us in the category of usurping infidel, the accursed *faranj*. He, Abdulkader, on the other hand was a good Moslem and an old family friend with whom the sheik would willingly deal. In time, no doubt, Abdulkader said, he could be persuaded to accept us as having no interest in the Abyssinians or the French or infidel colonialism and agree to deal directly with us.

'So your dad decided to stake out Abdulkader for a trial run and see what he came up with. It would have to be a substantial trade, Abdulkader said – the sheik was not a small-time man and would be insulted unless serious business was being proposed. So your dad set up Abdulkader with three thousand dollars (no small sum in those days) and sent him on his way. Abdulkader had offered, as tokens of good faith, his horse and a Koran. Rider had admired his horse when he first met Abdulkader, and he saw that the animal meant a great deal to its owner. It was an unusually fine beast even in an area where there were many good horses, a head-tossing black gelding a hand or two higher than anything else in Harar and in exceptionally good condition, with finely wrought saddlery. It was well-shod, too, a rare thing in that part of the world.

'The Koran was also remarkable in that it had old, yellow ivory covers measuring some six inches by four with finely worked Arabic inscriptions. Rider reckoned the sentimental value of these tokens was considerable and readily agreed to accept them as collateral. The Koran was locked in the hotel safe and the horse stabled along with ours in the hotel stables. Abdulkader was to return on the evening of the third day, and we agreed that this appointment would not be postponed for any reason.

'Your dad was well pleased with the arrangement and we celebrated with a lengthy visit to the Daughters of the Danakil. We didn't return to the hotel until midday of the second day, barely capable as I recollect of making it up the stairs to our rooms. Your dad emerged the following day at around eleven in the morning and made his way downstairs to the hotel lounge. There were always people in the lounge and that day was no exception. I joined your dad a bit later and we had lunch together, after which I went out saying I'd be back in the evening to hear the news.

'As best I can piece it together your dad spent the afternoon in the lounge reading, for the umpteenth time, Sir Richard Burton's absorbing account of his epic visit to Harar back in 1855. As the day wore on towards evening he started to take note of the people coming and going, looking out for Abdulkader. After a while, he noticed a young girl sitting by herself in a corner of the lounge. In contrast to everyone else who came and eventually went she stayed put, hardly moving – just sitting. She often stared at your dad, he told me, but at the time he scarcely noticed her, other than to vaguely think it was unusual for a child to be in such a place alone for so long.

'Your dad stuck it out until long after the agreed time and when I returned later that afternoon he told me that

Abdulkader had not shown up. Anything could explain that, we agreed, but by then we were both very suspicious. Abdulkader had in all our other rendezvous and deals been punctilious and had seemed in every way a punctual, predictable man. Then your dad suddenly stood up and told me he was going to check on the horse.'

Hutcheon recalled how when Dad left the room the girl who'd been sitting alone all afternoon in the corner jumped to her feet and walked quickly after him to the exit from the lounge. She was clearly agitated, dithered around the exit for a bit and then returned uncertainly to her seat. But, as Hutcheon said, it would never have stuck in his mind at all were it not for subsequent events. Then, after a few minutes, Dad came back into the lounge looking extremely pissed off, strode up to their table and said to Hutcheon. 'Fucking horse is gone. The bastard's done a flit.'

'No! *Krars*, man – for *krars* sakes!'

They'd stared at each other in disbelief. 'What about that Koran?' Hutcheon said.

They strode over to the hotel office and got the duty factotum to open the safe. No Koran. Rider blew it then, a rare thing for him, and shouted at the man. 'What happened? What the hell is going on? Who did you give that Koran to?'

The man swore he didn't know what Rider was talking about; he'd only come on duty after lunch that day. Rider then insisted the other duty manager be found immediately to explain what was going on. It took some time and much swearing but eventually the other receptionist appeared, a fat, surly woman who smelled of stale tobacco smoke unsuccessfully masked by the pungent *Binti el Sudan* perfume that, as Hutcheon put it, 'is to be found in any whore's handbag from Mombasa to Djibouti.'

On being questioned she said quite openly that, yes, she'd given the Koran to a man who came that morning

saying it was due to be returned to Abdulkader. 'He told
me to give this letter to the *ferenjes*,' the woman said,
rummaging around and producing an envelope addressed
to Mr Kortman. Rider tore it open to find nothing inside –
just an empty envelope.

'Bloody hell, Hutcheon, I've been swindled, man.'

'Why the hell didn't you give me this letter this morning?'
Rider roared at the woman, who was clearly little concerned
and in any case didn't understand English. She had that
glassy indifference to the anger of others, especially *ferenjes*,
that so many people find almost intolerably infuriating
when things go wrong.

Dad, Hutcheon recalled, was in a fury he'd rarely, if ever,
seen before, the fury of someone who's been duped for all
to see, made all the more unbearable by the rapidly growing
realisation that nothing was going to get better.

He repeated in Oromo, 'I said – why didn't you give me
this letter this morning?'

'You were asleep.'

'She actually yawned as she spoke,' Hutcheon said,
'looked at Rider and yawned. I thought he was going to
knock her down.'

' "I was not asleep when I came downstairs. I've been here
ever since. You must've seen me sitting over there."

' "I was busy."

' "It was your responsibility to give me that letter. What's
the matter with you?"

' "Too many things to do first." Then, after a pause, she
added. "I didn't know who you were."

' "Fucking hell," said your dad, turning away, defeated.

' "Call the owner," I said to the two hotel employees.
"Now. Go and get him. *Tolo bel* – move it."

'They didn't budge. The woman yawned again and the
man began to pick his nose. "He cannot be disturbed at this
hour," the man said, "he is taking *chat*."

At this, Hutcheon said, he casually drew his revolver (in those days anyone of any substance went armed everywhere), swung out the chamber, dropped and then rechambered the cartridges, slowly, one by one, and snapped it shut.

'Stopped the bint yawning, man. Cheeky cow. They soon went to fetch the owner.

'After some time the Armenian owner of the Lion d'Or appeared, still with a large wad of *chat* in his cheek, his eyes glazed and a dreamy expression on his face. Your dad explained what was going on and he invited us to discuss it more privately in his office. It soon became clear that he was not surprised by our story. Rider asked him if he knew Abdulkader.

' "Yes," said the hotel owner, "I know that man, the *turk*. But I never heard of the name Abdulkader. I do not know anyone by that name round here. He is called Hussein, I think. Yes – Hussein. He lives in Djibouti and sometimes comes here to Harar for business. He is a . . . he is an exporter. A black market exporter."

' "What does he export?"

' "*Bagul*.[30] He deals in *bagul*, among other things."

'The hotel owner had a funny look on his face as he said this, the look of someone who expects you to query what he just said, ay. But your dad wasn't really paying attention – he was impatient I suppose to get to the heart of the matter. Before I could say anything, your dad interrupted and related to the hotel owner the gist of the arrangement to get in touch with Sheik Ibrahim.

' "Sheik Ibrahim?" said the owner, "I do not know of a Sheik Ibrahim."

'He then added, "You know, this man Hussein, his head is loose. When he speaks sometimes it is as if another

---

[30] Mule (Arabic)

person is speaking. He is like two people. Everybody knows it. Did you not see it for yourself?" '

'That pretty well silenced us. What else was there to say? We complained about his staff, their failure to deliver the letter, their allowing the horse and Koran to be spirited away. ' "You know," said the Armenian, "you gave this man Hussein a lot of money. He will have used a little of it to make certain necessary arrangements. Such things cannot be prevented. My staff will not confess to any wrongdoing and neither you nor I can prove otherwise. I'm sure you will agree that the matter is unfortunate, but – and he shrugged – well, not unexpected. After all, you are *ferenjes*."

'That started to wind your dad up again.

' "What's that got to do with it?"

'This Armenian *oke* said, "You must realise, surely, that with *ferenjes* –" he paused, looking at us uncertainly, "with *ferenjes* it is normal to do business in a more . . ." Again he paused, before continuing, "a more simple way. The *ferenje* doesn't understand us, it is not necessary to observe all the normal protocols."

' "Ah. So that is why you charge us three times as much for our rooms as you charge that man over there?" said Rider, pointing to a prosperous-looking Arab from Djibouti who had checked in some days previously.

' "Of course. There is the price for *ferenjes* and . . ." He paused for a moment, scratched his head and then said, "I charge you the full price. He (indicating the Arab) is entitled to a discount. That is why he pays less than you." He smiled, pleased with his explanation. Again he paused, then added, "and you are definitely *ferenjes*. What can I say – I am a businessman . . ."

'We really were silent now, bereft of anything more to say. The Armenian called for drinks, invited us to take *chat* with him and then said something that got us sitting up and talking again.

' "You have the girl, though?" he said.

' "Pardon?" said Rider.

' "The girl."

' "What girl – who are you talking about?" said Rider.

' "You didn't know?" asked the hotel owner. "You didn't know that that girl has been left here for you?"

' "I don't know what you're talking about," said Rider. "What girl?"

'The Armenian went to the door of his office and spoke in Harari to someone. A few minutes later the girl who'd been sitting in the lounge all day came in, trembling and breathing rapidly.

' "This is Amina. She is Hussein's daughter. He left her for you as recompense for your – your – your inconvenience. I thought you knew." '

And that is how my father came by my mother.

7

The Course of True Love

As I said, Dad would never talk to me about the events in Harar that April day in 1919 that led to his acquisition of the girl Amina as his personal property. His reticence was not so much due to the events themselves, bizarre though they were, but to what transpired later. That part of the story, however, will have to wait. In the meantime, I can only continue the tale as told to me and my sister by Hutcheon in answer to the natural curiosity of any child as to their parents' lives before they are old enough to interpret such things for themselves. As it happens, Hutcheon's version of what happened may well be more accurate than Dad's would have been, had he been willing to recount it, given that Hutcheon was not so deeply embroiled. I will never know.

Hutcheon says, hardly surprisingly, that he remembers it all as clearly as if he were still there in that dingy Harar hotel lounge watching what he thought of later as something akin to a play. Bizarre events sometimes have that make-believe quality that arises directly out of their unfamiliarity to us. If we ourselves have not experienced what is taking place to some extent we are bound to see the participants as acting out roles that are not supposed to represent the real world as it is, but rather as we might suppose it to be if we could escape banal reality. Just as a painter will try to render an impression or expression or abstraction of some person or emotion or place. We react primarily with our own emotions; it takes time and some effort to grasp the emotions of others, of the players in a drama, which do not necessarily coincide with our own. As Hutcheon said, he saw and reacted to things in accordance with his own views and emotions. Each of the others must have seen things somewhat differently, according to their particular views, their moral judgements, their wishes and intentions.

You have to realise that to the owner of the Lion d'Or and to people generally in that part of the world at that time there was nothing particularly noteworthy about trafficking in people. Out and out slaving of men was a dying – though far from dead – trade; but women and children were still highly transactionable goods. The ageing emperor Menelik, nagged incessantly by the meddling British, had reluctantly agreed to outlaw the slaving that had, since the beginning of time, been one of the mainstays – if not the principal element – of the economy of much of Abyssinia. To begin with, of course, the ban simply made the slavers more discreet; it wasn't enforced enough to actually deter them. But the patrolling of the Red Sea by the busybody British put paid to large-scale shipping of slaves across to Arabia, leaving the remnants of the business in the hands of small, mobile operators no longer dealing in expensive eunuchs (the high mortality following castration was what bumped the price) but in the much easier to handle female side of things. Women as consumer goods is after all not such a foreign notion in almost any society. In most African tribal systems, for example, daughters are customarily traded by their fathers as wives in a manner not so far removed from slavery – so that for Hussein and all those party to the affair, compensating the *ferenje* by means of his daughter would not have seemed an exceptionally outlandish way to conclude a nefarious deal. The hotel owner had obviously thought nothing of it.

But – I should get on with Hutcheon's story.

'Your dad, for all that he knew Africa and its people's ways, was shocked, ay. At first, he had said to the hotel owner, "I don't want this girl. What on earth do you think I would do with her?"

'The hotel owner had smiled, then, and said, "Have you not tried a young girl? It's a nice change, many people – "

' "What do you take me for?" Rider had interrupted, getting angry again. "I am not the kind of man to, to – to take pleasure with a child."

'The hotel owner had looked away and shrugged, and started to say that he himself was not averse to a young girl, implying, as just about everyone does in the surety of their own prejudice, that if he found it acceptable then what was Rider's problem?

'But your dad was in a *moerava* bait by now. "I will do no such thing," he said. "It's out of the question, completely out of the question."

' "Well," said this Armenian *oke*, "I don't want her. If you do not take her I will dispose of her to someone else. I cannot afford for her to remain here."

'At this point I said to your dad, "Rider, I think you have to go along with this, man. The only alternative is to walk away and know that she will be sold into prostitution. You are about as far up shit creek as it's possible to get. Come on, man, it'll do you good having a woman about the place. Knock some bloody manners into your head, *kêrel.*"

' "She's *not* a woman, man, she's just a child. I don't need children, man. Nor manners, come to that."

'I must admit that I was beginning to find the whole thing funny – after all, you couldn't have concocted such a *lekker* practical joke on someone however hard you tried. You just had to see the humour of it. There was your dad getting all high and mighty about the morals of it all when, really, he hadn't the luxury, ay. He was stuffed, man, well and truly stuffed. It just seemed so funny that in such a fix he should get up on his high horse and lecture us all about morals. Only your dad could do that. I really admired him for it, but, *krars*, man, he just had to accept that he had been well and truly swindled in front of us all and there was nothing he could do but accept his new possession and get on with it. What else could he do, man? I told him that Abdullahi and Hawa could foster the girl and bring her up, told him not to make such a big deal out of it, ay.'

Moreover, it was, in Hutcheon's view, a self-inflicted injury. Typical Quatermain folly – so carried away with implausible day-dreams that he couldn't see Ali Baba and the Forty Thieves gypping him in broad daylight.

Amina for her part, it transpired, had already made up her mind. She was going with Dad, and that was that. 'It was really impressive to see the determination in her,' Hutcheon said. 'Of course later, when I knew her well, I wasn't so surprised as she turned out to be a very strong character, very single-minded, ay. She never took her eyes off your dad and though very frightened and no doubt confused she must have seen the susceptibility in him, the Quatermain trait he had that made it impossible for him to be cruel to an innocent or to turn his back on a genuine supplicant. Pulling thorns out of lions' feet was always his Achilles heel. I'm sure that she figured Rider out on the run so to speak, as she watched and listened. And when you're desperate, as she was, you're super observant. You know what I mean, ay.

'So she latched on to him. Literally grasped his arm and wouldn't let go. Each time he dislodged her grip she quickly grabbed him or his clothing with her other hand – it was just like being caught up in a *wag 'n bietjie*.[31] He would've had to push her hard – rather even hit her – to get away

---

[31] Wait-a-bit thorn (Afrikaans)

and of course Rider could never bring himself to be so rough with a child. He was so embarrassed, ay – I just had to laugh! But he didn't laugh. Deadly serious for him, ay, the whole business.'

Later, though, Hutcheon said, he realised that Amina must have rationalised things a good deal more clearly than any of us could have understood, lacking, as we did, any real knowledge of the world as perceived by someone like her. We would naturally see her as callously abandoned by her father – of her mother she never spoke, except presumably to Dad, and he never repeated anything of what passed between them – and wonder at how terrible she must feel about it. But we are almost certainly wrong. It's more likely – much more likely, given the girl's extraordinary self-possession – that she saw it more as the process by which she was to be entered into marriage, or concubinage or whatever it was she thought was happening to her.

Hutcheon surprised me a little when he spoke of all this – he usually came over as much too matter of fact, too unsentimental to explore such emotional pathways. But as my sister and I both knew he was for all his reticence towards overt sentimentality actually very affectionate and considerate to those close to him. He'd adored our mother and by all accounts they'd been close friends. So it was perhaps not so surprising that he should have understood her so well.

We all of us knew that she would have been brought up in the absolute certainty that her ideal destiny was marriage, and that the arrangements for it would be made by her father. Such marriage contracts are commonly made when the girls are still only eight or nine years old and their opinion is not, of course, relevant to any aspect of it. Knowing this, Amina must have rationalised whatever her father told her when he left her (or sent her) at the hotel as the process by which she was being entered into marriage. Hence her single-minded determination to attach herself to Dad. It could not, Hutcheon opined, have been otherwise.

In the end, Dad accepted Hutcheon's view and agreed to give up on the affair, cut his losses and head back for Kenya. Hutcheon remembers how he got Dad to have a couple of drinks to calm him down a bit and how Dad shook his head despairingly when it really sank into his comprehension that the barefoot, skinny, rag-tag little girl had absolutely no possessions other than the dirty dress she was standing in – absolutely *nothing* more than that tatty garment.

'As your dad sourly observed, her father's horse had been well shod (not to mention well-fed and smartly orna-mented), while his daughter went barefoot. I found that really funny, ay – but, *jussus* – he didn't!'

Neither would she accept on any account being put in a separate room of her own. That, Hutcheon recalls, was clearly in her mind nothing more than a ruse to give her the slip. So Dad had to get another bed installed in his room and, as Hutcheon told him, 'Start getting used to married life.'

'I couldn't resist teasing him. He was so bloody serious, man – nothing would get a laugh out of him. Of course, the longer his face got the more I yokked, ay! Then there was the hilarious business of him outfitting her the day after the events in the hotel. Naturally, your dad bought her plenty of clothes and suchlike, which she inevitably took as hard evidence of her new status as *his* woman, ay. She so loved getting those clothes – nothing remotely like it could ever have happened to her before – and your dad knew absolutely what it made her think! And there was nothing whatever he could do to disabuse her, ay – nothing! Man, I laughed so hard! It wasn't until we were past Shashamene on the way home that he finally gave in to the funny side. After that, we laughed a lot about it – even Amina smiled when she listened to us kidding each other, for even before she spoke English she understood well enough what we were joking about. She was very smart – yeah, very smart – and with enough of the raw African in her to enjoy a *ferenje*'s discomfiture as well!

'Then one day we stopped for a midday break under the shade of some acacias and got some tea and something to eat on the go. We were sitting there chatting about this and that and your dad made a casual remark about slaves and suddenly something clicked. It was a trivial remark in itself – can't remember the context – but always I will remember what it triggered in my mind: that Arab friend of de Monfreid's, Sheik Mâki. I suddenly remembered where I'd heard his name before: at the governor's residence in Harar that night we sat up drinking cognac with Thesiger and Ras Tafari. Thesiger had been waffling on about the slave trade and how it continued to flourish in spite of the efforts of Ras Tafari and the European powers to stop it. They'd been telling us how Harar had long been one of the great slaving emporia of the region and how the trade still flourished, with the King of Jima continuing to despatch slaves that nowadays bypassed Harar to go straight to the Danakil coast, where such notorious outlaws as Sheik Mâki[32] would slip them across the Red Sea in between the British patrols. *Sheik Mâki*, for *krar's* sakes! And the hotel owner's reference to *bagul* – mules! I don't know why it took my brain so long to click it, but *bagul* is one of the many euphemisms for slaves. He'd said that Hussein dealt in slaves – we just didn't absorb the significance at the time. And we'd been taking coffee and talking business with this ruffian Mâki just days before, introduced, along with that other toe-rag Hussein, courtesy of our amateur barbarian de Monfreid! Well, *nou*

---

[32] For an account of de Monfreid's dealings with the slaver Mâki see Ida Treat's *Pearls, Arms and Hashish*, 1930

dars 'n ding, ay! Because you see what it had me thinking, ay? That your mother might not have been Hussein's daughter after all, but rather one of Sheik Mâki's slaves. Deals within deals – Mâki doing some deal with Hussein who was busy two-timing us while *le fameuse flibustier* was maybe taking a commission or two, ay? I don't know, of course – we'll never know – though I couldn't help recalling that all three *skellums* had managed to fade the scene at more or less the same time. For years afterwards we heard all sorts of hairy tales about de Monfreid, how he smuggled hashish and ran guns up and down the Red Sea, the Frogs and Pongos racing around after him blowing their whistles and waving their arms, tut-tut. Some of these stories had him shifting a few *bagul* as well. As to the facts, well, I can't say. But I've always wondered just exactly what deals were struck and by whom in the affair of your mother, ay.

'But all that's neither here nor there any more and in any case I'm getting ahead of the story,' said Hutcheon. 'We rounded up our crew and organised horses, mules and food for the Rift Valley leg of the return journey. The *watu* expressed due admiration for your dad's choice of wife, though they were of course only being polite as they must in reality have been astonished at his purchase when a *tajiri*[33] like him could have afforded a much more expensive and fashionable woman. They were happy, though, to have a woman cook for them and Amina for her part gained considerable confidence from being allowed to assume a formal role in her new ménage. The food itself wasn't any different – just cooked by a woman, ay.'

To begin with, as Hutcheon told it, they retraced their steps, descending the steep escarpment from Harar down to Dire Dawa on the edge of the Rift Valley floor, through Awash and on past Lakes Ziway and Shala. Before reaching

---

[33] Rich man (Swahili)

Lake Abaya, instead of continuing south-west down the valley the way they'd come, they branched south-east at Shashamene and climbed the steep escarpment of the Rift into the high mountains to Chenchya. From there they headed along the ridge that runs for fifty miles or so at about seven thousand feet above sea level before it finally starts to descend to Negele. The trail from Negele actually runs on south-east almost in a straight line for four hundred miles right to Mogadisho on the Somaliland coast. There's plenty of water all along the highland part of this trail and when it finally descends to the hot, dry lowlands of Somaliland travel by caravans of camels was always sustained by the water and browse of the Juba River valley. The long high spur that Negele lies in the middle of is the watershed between the Juba's two main tributaries: the Dawa on the south and the Ganale Dorya on the north.

Dad had told me how excited he was to be on this trail from Negele to Mogadisho and Kismayu, because, he said, it was undoubtedly an ancient trading route between the southern highlands of Abyssinia and the Somaliland coastal ports of Mogadisho and Kismayu. Though the eastern Somaliland coast is south of what the earliest maps depict as the Land of Punt it must, in Dad's view, have been an integral part of Punt, because there was a good, direct, year-round caravan route between Harar and Mogadisho. This trail runs almost due north from Mogadisho on the coast to Jijiga, in the highlands just east of Harar. For its entire distance of five hundred miles this route runs along the Shebeli River and its eastern tributary, the Fafen, that provided the water and browse essential for camel-based caravans. Dad always regarded it as significant that Mogadisho was connected by well-watered trails to both the southern edge of the eastern highlands of Abyssinia at Negele and the northern edge at the capital city of Punt – Harar. It meant that if Suleiman's fabled gold originated from the eastern Ogaden, as Dad believed it did, it could easily reach the main export points of the Land of Punt – Harar and Djibouti – either by the shortest route along the Rift Valley, or, if that was unsuitable for some reason, via Mogadisho.

There was a very good reason why, in Dad's view, a valuable trade good such as gold might be difficult if not impossible to transport from the eastern Ogaden to Harar and on to Djibouti by the relatively short (though still four hundred long camel miles) direct route along the Rift Valley – the route he and Hutcheon had followed – and that was extortion, plain old common or garden extortion. The Rift Valley route meant that people from the Ogaden – Borana – would have to pass through densely populated country belonging to other Galla tribes. This part of Ethiopia has always been – and still is – notorious for the endless succession of tollgates that force caravans to pay arbitrary, often absurd, tolls on their trade goods.

The alternative was to move the stuff to Mogadisho through the Ogaden and Somaliland. While such an enterprise was always going to be fraught with danger and uncertainty, it would nevertheless have been easier to manage than to run the four hundred-mile long Oromo tollgate gauntlet. The division between the Ogaden and the Abyssinian highlands is a natural one both ethnically and geographically. The division between the Ogaden and Somaliland has neither geographic nor ethnic boundaries being purely a political artefact. The Somalis have never recognised Ethiopia's sovereignty over the Ogaden, and never will. For all that the Borana are ethnically distinct from the Somalis they live, in the minds of the Somalis, in Somaliland. If you were from the Ogaden it would always have been easier to trade with Somalis than Abyssinians – of that there was no doubt.

'Mind you,' said Hutcheon, 'choosing to go home via

Negele was really typical Quatermain idiocy, ay. Negele was in Liban, the *tigre* heartland that Arnold had so vividly described to us. While we could be attacked anywhere in the Ogaden, heading straight for Ato Alamu's lair was asking for trouble. Not that I particularly cared – if the *tigre* wanted a fight they were welcome, ay. They had the numbers; but they couldn't shoot for peanuts and knew very well that we could, which would make them as skitsy and disorganised as a bunch of *bobejaans* pretending to attack a leopard, ay. We'd have to be very unlucky not to get the best of them. All the same, ay, stray bullets are as deadly as any if they happen to be going your way. But nothing was going to deter your dad from checking out the gold situation in Negele, so there was no point in arguing, though he agreed not to *tanga-tanga*[34] there.'

'As soon as we arrived I set about trading in our horses for camels and listening to the gossip about the whereabouts of the *tigre* while your dad found out what he could about gold. He soon got friendly with an old man who'd been born there and knew the area well. He confirmed what Arnold had said: that there was indeed gold to be found some fifty miles or so back along the trail we'd just come down, on the headwaters of the Dawa around Kebre Mengist. But no way would anyone dream of panning for it these days, because the *tigre* would immediately steal it. So, although there was plenty of gold there no one ever admitted to even knowing where to look, though of course some of the older people knew well enough where it was. As for showing your dad, well, that would simply be the kiss of death, ay.

'So the upshot was that we decided to split for home before the *tigre* could make a plan. Several people had warned us that Ato Alamu was in the Arero area and likely

---

[34] Dawdle (Swahili)

101

to ambush us, Arero being on the main route south-west to Mega and Moyale. To finesse the *tigre* we therefore hired a guide to take us due south across the Dawa and straight on to Moyale, a plan that worked well and saw us to the Kenya border without hassles. We left Negele at night as a further safeguard and shortly before we departed the old man your dad had been talking to appeared and asked to accompany us. He very reasonably said that once the *tigre* got to hear that he'd been talking to us so much they would twist his tail unmercifully on the assumption that he had got money from us or had some useful information. Better he leave the district for a while until they forgot about him. Before he parted with us in Moyale, your dad had ascertained that although there was a lot of gold in the mountains above the Dawa there were no stories about ancient mines there. The old man was certain about this and swore that he would've known if there was any evidence of old gold mines. He said that as a young man he had panned gold there and never came across any sign of really old mine workings. One thing he did come up with, though, was a bit of gold. Once safely out of Negele he produced a crude gold amulet that looked as if it had been made by hammering two separate nuggets together. It was obviously old – he said he'd buried it thirty years back – and your dad was really pleased to get it. As to its origin, the old man was vague. He'd always understood, he said, that it was local; but he couldn't say for sure if it came from the mines he'd worked as a youth. It had clearly been worn a lot before the old man got it and your dad gave it to Amina who wore it for a while. An interesting hunk of gold this turned out to be, as you know, ay.'

From Moyale they took a detour via Buna to see Wajir after which they turned south-west to pass Habaswein, Mudo Gashi and Garba Tula. From there they followed the Uaso Nyiro up to Rumuruti arriving at Luoniek nearly four months after leaving Harar. By that time, Hutcheon recalled, the events of Harar were overshadowed by the change in Rider's relationship with Amina. 'I was really amazed at what was taking place, man,' said Hutcheon. 'I was beginning to see a side to your dad I hadn't anticipated. He'd been so genuinely pissed off at being saddled with this waif that it never occurred to me – or him, I reckon – that he might actually see her as something other than a total nuisance, ay. Quite the contrary, though. Within a week or two of quitting Harar I realised he was growing quite fond of her. He invariably spoke really softly to her and was actually quite deferential, ay. In our sort of life we give orders. It's expected of us, you do it without thinking, ay. It's just the way things are. I noticed, though, that he never ordered Amina about; her he asked, never commanded. Quite something, this little slip of a bint thrust upon him, and right away she's got him taped, ay! Not in a conniving way – nothing like that. She always subordinated herself to him, never questioned anything he said. Come to think of it, ay, I don't think I ever saw her pout, never saw a hint of sulkiness. Nothing at all of your typical bint's mannerisms. You know how when they balk at something they scowl like snared leopards, drop their hands on their hips, arch their shoulders back and shove their tits forward – and then look past you over your shoulder? You know that mannerism, ay – all African bints do it. Not Amina; never saw her pull those little feminine tricks. She was a lady, actually, a born natural lady, ay.

'Anyway, as we trekked back to the plaas I saw that she and Rider were more and more taken up with each other. They always rode together; if the going was easy they'd be side by side, chattering. Your dad, well, as you know, he can talk like a weaver bird, ay – on and on. They were like a couple of guinea fowl, always saying something quiet to each other as they went, just so there was no risk of losing sight of each other. As if! You know how it is on a long day,

103

just riding to cover the miles, ay? After the first couple of
hours even the *watu* go quiet. You fall into a *dwaal*, all of
you, horses – everyone. You go for hours like that, ay, can't
even remember the country you just passed through. But
not Rider and Amina. All the time, mostly in low voices,
they'd be saying something to one another. Or he'd whistle,
she'd sing a bit, one of those melodic highland songs they
were so good at in Harar. *Magtig*,[35] man – I was starjarbued.[36] Your old man – he was falling in love with his little
bagul, ay!

'At first of course they had to converse in Oromo, but
she was dead keen to learn English. So a lot of their chit-
chat was him teaching her the lingo. I guess with an all-day
class like that, dawn to dusk for several months, it's hardly
surprising that by the time we got back to Rumuruti she was
speaking English. And reading and writing too, ay. And
arithmetic. She was smart, ay, really smart, and had the
power of total concentration, amazing concentration.
Maybe she'd had a bit of schooling before, I don't know.
But usually these bints don't get any education, ay. I don't
know, but learning just came naturally to her. Very smart,
she was, very smart.

'After we got back to Rumuruti we settled back into the
daily routines of cattle trading and so forth – only now
there was a difference, with Amina well and truly part of
the household. There was no longer any mention of her
going to live with Abdullahi and his wife Hawa as a foster
child; she stayed with your dad. But it was a long time
before they became lovers. Two or three months after
getting back to the plaas, probably – I don't remember
exactly. Well, for *krar's* sakes, I wasn't actually present when
Rider finally bit the apple that had been hanging above

---

[35] Expletive: Corruption of (God) Almighty (Afrikaans)
[36] Corruption of *sitaajabu*, to be amazed (Swahili)

him for so long it must've been about to go rotten – *jussus*
man – you know what I mean! But I can remember that
quite suddenly I noticed a change in them. Rider was less
touchy about her – he'd always got all uppity when I teased
him about her, ay. Like one time he complained that his
back was aching and I asked him was it because he was
getting too much or too little. Hell, he got cross, ay! Got in
a *moerava* bait!

'Of course he was only touchy because he wasn't getting
any, still all snarled up in his mustn't-touch-a-child morals
or whatever the hell his problem was; but he must've been
thinking about it, ay. Even a eunuch would've been thinking
about it in the presence of such a nubile bint. He was
bogged in a moral quagmire of his own making; the problem of sex with a minor as he saw it. But of course he was
the only one of all of us with the problem. For sure, it
wasn't Amina's problem. Her age in years, twelve or thirteen
or whatever she was, bore no relation to her real physical
or mental age. In the context of Rider, that is. It would not
have been the same in connection with anyone else, ay. In
relation to anyone else she'd have been the immature girl
that Rider kept telling himself she was. That was his problem; his romantic conscience, ay. He felt he should continue treating her as untouchable, to observe the
convention between a man and a young girl; whereas by
now those distinctions no longer applied to them. They'd
both actually committed themselves to each other. Amina,
though, much more completely than Rider.

'I suspect in the end she just gave up wondering what his
problem was and seduced him – he'd have been a pushover
by then, ay! I don't know, of course – but it wouldn't
surprise me. However it happened, I suddenly noticed it
didn't bother him any more, me pulling his leg about her.
And she got even more relaxed, too, didn't fret when he
was late getting in, didn't – well, I mean, she just got

broody, ay. Don't know how to explain it, man, but it suddenly dawned on me one day that Rider'd finally given up all his moral reservations and was at last playing snakes and apples with her. Had to happen, of course – only someone like Rider would've taken so long to get around to it.

'You have to remember that Amina was really beautiful, ay. Very sensual – for sure she must've known all along the physical effect she had on Rider. He made her dress modestly, but she might just as well've gone naked, the way she handled herself. You know how clothes actually cover some women up, whereas others, the really sexy ones, move their bodies inside their clothes so you don't notice the garments, only the body underneath. Well – she was one of those. Couldn't help it. Wasn't putting it on – didn't have to. Even before she was fully grown up, her figure was really well developed – no mistaking that she came from the Land of Poont, ay! The volcano breasts and symmetrical curves that never fold however they move their bodies – no question that she was a girl from the Land of the Perfect Poont! Long black hair that glistened in the sun like wet obsidian and that wonderful, pale *turk* complexion – your sister has it just like her mother – I don't know how he resisted her for so long. But once they started spooring the kudu their fate was well and truly sealed, ay. I've never seen two people so completely immersed in each other. In point of fact, tell the truth, I thought that sort of stuff between a man and a woman only happened in books, ay. I didn't know it could actually be for real. Quite something, ay, quite something.

'Then she got pregnant with you – must've been about three years after we got back from Harar, ay. You were born in, when – 1922, wasn't it? Yeah. Then Leila in 1923. They were so content, so wrapped up in themselves and you kids. It was a fantastic time, and for me also. As you know, I never had gold fever – that was always your dad's disease, the

Quatermain family handicap; never mine. I mean, we had a great time chasing Rider's day-dreams around the country, but – shit, man, it's like galloping after dust-devils. You can see the bastards, you can catch up with them – you can even feel the buggers, ay! But no ways you can pin the sods down! So when Amina and your dad started a family I thought, thank *krars* for that, ay. Now we can kick all this King Solomon *kak* down the long-drop, where it belongs, ay, and get on with some serious business. As you know, I'm happy making money buying and selling cattle, and taking out a few safaris now and then. Chasing after some bint or other. I was sure that Rider'd got over it all, too, as he hadn't mentioned doing another gold safari for ages.

'By the time we got back from Harar we'd bought four or five hundred ounces of gold, most of which Rider shipped off to Amsterdam to recover what he'd spent. So we were flush and he seemed happy enough to get stuck into some serious cattle trading, which meant he could be on the plaas a lot of the time, with Amina and you kids. It was around this time that I went across the Rift Valley to Kitale to see my cousin, Malcolm – D'Arcy – Graham, who'd also baled out of Grahamstown and headed up to Kenya some years before. He and a couple of other toerags had a transport business, mostly hauling supplies for the King's African Rifles' outposts up in Lodwar and Lokichoggio on the Sudan border. They were using T-Model Ford lorries and Rider and I wanted to learn how to work these things. Up to then we'd only ever used camels and horses and donkeys – we hadn't caught up with motor vehicles. There were no roads in our part of the world, which was one reason why we'd never got around to it; but things were changing fast even in the N.F.D. and we reckoned it was time to catch up. So I did a safari with D'Arcy and learnt how these lorries worked – or didn't work. I used to think camels were hell with humps on, ay – and they are – but I soon learnt that motor cars are just as evil in their own way. The difference was that one lorry could carry two tons – and that's a hell of a lot less trouble than five or six bloody-minded camels, ay.

'So we bought a couple of T-Models and concentrated on cattle trading. We'd buy cattle cheaply off the Samburu and Borana in the dry season when they were running out of grazing and water, get them back to the plaas for a while to get some weight back on them, then move them on for slaughter. Made a little money, kept out of trouble – mostly – had a fantastic time.

'It could've stayed like that forever, ay. But it didn't.'

8

Even the Tightest Knot Comes Undone

'Then as you know, the whole thing unravelled.' Neither I
nor my sister are likely to forget those words of Hutcheon's
that still, grey day when Leila was I think about thirteen and
I a couple of years older. There was thick low cloud, so
thick it was still dark at ten in the morning, with no wind,
and cold. Hardly a sound, even from the birds. Hutcheon
hadn't meant to choose a sombre day when he asked the
two of us to come and listen to something he had to say. I'd
guess it was rather the day that chose him, that reminded
him that he had something sombre to say, something he'd
been gearing himself up to broach for a long time. Dad was
away for a few days so that Hutcheon probably felt the time
had come. He was fidgety and uncomfortable and spoke for
a while about destiny, how if you believe in destiny you
might, if you have a really good imagination and no sense
of reality, you might just come up with a justification for
why things happened the way they did. But, Hutcheon said,
neither he nor Rider believed in *twak* like destiny. Nor were
either of them religious or superstitious. It was easy, he
opined, to see how religion evolved, to help people deal
with the fear of death. The fear of death and the incalcul-
ably cruel way that Nature has of pulling the carpet out
from under you just when you think you've got it so admi-
rably laid down. Only religion, or superstition, can explain
the fact that whatever emotional capital you accumulate,

however hard you try in your life to do the right thing, it counts for absolutely nothing in Nature's book. Live like an angel or a shit – it's all the same to Nature and either way you have equal chances of drawing the short straw. The problem as Hutcheon saw it was that however clearly you understand that Nature has no favourites, that no amount of good behaviour will score you a single Brownie point if you happen to be there when lightning strikes, you simply cannot shrug your shoulders the way Nature does if lightning *does* strike. Religion helps you cope; the laws of probability leave you completely exposed to the devastating kicks Nature delivers so callously. You're on your own with reality.

Well, we weren't sure what all that was leading up to, but he didn't leave us guessing.

What follows is something Hutcheon wrote down soon after the events in question took place. I've never talked about it to him – for a start he doesn't want to and neither do I. Or Leila. My father – well no one ever thought to raise the subject with him. But Hutcheon always felt he should record these events, though he wasn't sure exactly why. I suspect it was for me and my sister's sake. I think he felt we ought to know what transpired, but didn't relish the thought of talking about it. It's the sort of reason why Hutcheon would've gone to the trouble, because he doesn't like writing for all that he's actually quite good at it. His English is full of what teachers would call mistakes but that doesn't stop him from painting a pretty good picture of things if he has a mind to. I've corrected his English, but it's as he wrote it as far as the facts are concerned.

It's an old adage that when things do come undone there's often not a single, simple cause. It's the combined effect of several things, inconsequential in themselves, that just happen to occur one after the other which leads to the ultimate

110

catastrophe. It was like that that night in April 1923 when your little sister was still only one year old. We were all out together on a recce for a big safari that Rider and I had booked for a Yank who wanted a greater kudu as well as the conventional Big Five as the clients love us to call them. For the kudu, the rhino, the leopard, the lion – even the buffalo and the elephant if we were lucky – we planned to go right up north in Borana, across the Ngaso plain near the Abyssinian border where it's wetter and there's more game. There were several Boran we knew well up there who were always on the lookout for big trophies as we paid good money for information that resulted in a happy client. We camped near a big Boran kraal that drew its water from a well beside one of the many luggas that originate in the Abyssinian highlands to the north. Now, if you are a lion and required by Nature to engage in vigorous callisthenics not to say fisticuffs every time you want to eat, you soon learn that cattle and camels are much easier to catch and kill than wild game. And long pig easier still. If you are a Samburu or Boran or Somali or any other inhabitant of the N.F.D. you will opine that every lion – and there are many – that ever lived there is a born man-eater. Nobody but the ignorant or the stupid plays silly buggers with N.F.D. lions, because they eat people; always have, always will. It's not an aberration if an N.F.D. lion kills and eats a man – it's par for the course with them; it's in their genes.

Amina loved going on safari and having the kids didn't put her off at all. Hawa was usually along to help, and there was always a large camp crew so that things were always well organised. He and Amina and you kids were in a large tent. Tents are pretty safe – a lion can easily tear through a tent, but they rarely actually do so. People that get taken by lions in the N.F.D. are the herdsmen who have to sleep in the open with their livestock. People don't as a rule get taken from inside a tent or dwelling.

The first thing that went wrong that night was the weather. A thunderstorm started to brew up in the vicinity and it blew like hell – the gusty, dusty wind that always blows out from under an active storm cell. Though it didn't rain, at least not on us, the wind loosened the tent pegs that are hard to hammer firmly into the sandy ground of the N.F.D. Then a ridge pole corner peg was uprooted and the outer fly and its rope started flailing against the tent. Once one peg goes, it often unzips the rest and Rider decided to fix it before the whole tent collapsed. So he got up, buckled on his gun belt with his revolver, took a torch and went outside to secure the guy ropes. It was really blowing a gale; the sky was completely clouded over so that it was pitch dark. He shone briefly around the tent and started to make his way round to the back. The next thing that went wrong was that the bulb in his torch failed. He went back into the tent and got Amina's torch. You kids started crying, Amina was in total darkness trying to calm you down, Rider was crashing about outside trying to sort the ropes out. The wind was blowing from directly behind the tent and it was those ropes that he had to secure first to prevent the whole thing collapsing.

Lions weren't on his mind. We'd been in that camp three days and not heard lions at all, or seen any tracks. The people in the area, always quick to grumble about lions if they were about, hadn't mentioned the subject. Then the next thing that went wrong was that the whipping guy rope knocked Amina's torch out of his hand. It fell to the ground and went out. As it did, the wind dropped for a moment, as it does on those gusty nights when you think it's going to rain, but it doesn't. Rider swore loudly as the torch went out and he's sure now that in that brief lull before the wind picked up again Amina heard him curse the torch for failing. She knew that it was next to impossible for Rider to do anything in the dark – it was cloudy and absolutely inky black that night. She had been trying to fix the first torch and had in fact put in a new bulb and got it working again. It's almost certain she stepped out of the tent to bring Rider the torch she'd fixed. It was like her to anticipate things and just do whatever was required without saying anything.

Well, there was a whole bunch of lions in camp though no one knew it They'd no doubt come from downwind and if lions choose to remain silent, as of course they do when hunting, there's no man alive would be able to guess they were already right on him. Unless you happen to shine a light in their eyes there is simply no way of knowing. So when Amina stepped out of the tent, immediately upwind of the lions, she was stepping, quite literally, into the jaws of death. She probably only shone the torch at her feet so as not to trip over the guy ropes, meaning to move quickly round to the rear to join Rider. She had her revolver in one hand, just as Rider had told her she always must, no exceptions, whenever she went anywhere at night. The wind by now was blowing again and Rider says he never heard anything for sure, though he thinks that in retrospect he heard the grunt of a lion. But in the wind you can hear just about anything, if you try hard enough, there's so much ambiguous noise. He finished the rope he'd been working on when the light had gone out, knotting it in the dark, and then made his way round to the front of the tent to see if he could fix one of the torches. Inside the tent he called Amina – and well, of course, she wasn't there. In the dark and the noise it took Rider an appreciable time to realise she really wasn't there, maybe a minute or so. Then he says he went all cold and stood for a second or two, paralysed. For that second his mind just didn't want to get in gear and think the unthinkable – bloody lions. But he knew, he says, he knew then as sure as hell what had happened. 'I just knew,' he recalled, 'I tried so hard to deny it – but, somehow I knew she was gone and why.'

The sheer overwhelming frustration of the next period of time, he says, he can feel to this day. Frustration at not being able to do anything of any use. He groped in the darkness for the rifle from beside his bed and charged out the tent. But for what? It was so dark it was like racing around with your eyes tight shut. He fired both barrels well up from the ground just for the noise – but of course in the wind it was nothing much. It didn't wake me up. He screamed for me – for anyone – to bring a light. He got to my tent and got my torch and woke me up. At last, a light. He yelled at me to hold the light so he could shoot – hoping, hoping, as any one would, that he might somehow still be in time to reverse what was happening.

'Lions, Hutcheon,' he bellowed. 'Fucking lions in camp. I can't . . . I can't – shit, I can't find Amina.'

I was on my feet and with him before he finished speaking. The alarm in his voice was like cold air blowing – I started immediately to feel a chill like a fever starting. I remember that so clearly – the sensation of cold, though it was a hot night. I hadn't the strength to ask about Amina, because I felt something of what your dad must've been feeling, the cold, cold horror of the words 'I can't find Amina.' There was no point in dwelling on it, asking for amplification.

We ran to his tent, not far, and, with Rider standing up close, directly behind me, I shone the torch slowly around, holding it at head height so that if it lit up a lion's eyes he would see it too. He knew I'd just stand still so he could get a shot in quickly. Nothing, just nothing. At that point, we were joined by some of the *watu* who came in a tight, nervous group with more torches and rifles. Rider told me quickly what he knew and I told the *watu* to start looking for tracks immediately downwind of the tent, while Rider went to start the T-Model up and use the lights to scan the surrounds again.

What does a man do who is faced with the absolute certainty that he has just lost the only person in the world who really matters to him (although there is still a lack of detail to confirm that). What can a person actually do in the minutes immediately following such a realisation? There seem to be two alternatives: to untie the knot that bound you to that person and fall apart; or to tighten the knot, try to keep yourself firmly bound up until you can gradually loosen the bond in your own time. A man like Rider is almost certainly going to choose the latter course, to slip his moorings as far as he is able by paying out the rope slowly and deliberately, so as to prevent the ties from flying apart out of control. In the still impenetrable black night he thought and moved at the edge of frenzy, allowing himself only those words and actions that instructed the rest of us as to what he wanted from us. The wind was dying now, the storm that had been gathering decaying before it could mature. I had the sensation that the storm was reflecting the events on the ground: it had had its chance, and missed it. It was all over now. Men were assigned to look after the children. Others to prepare a rapid meal. The two men who were gifted trackers – Abdullahi and Ndaragus – were to pick up the spoor, then go and prepare for a possibly long day or more following up the tracks until the matter of the lions was resolved. There was a short discussion about using the truck. Its headlights gave far more light than hand torches and wild animals can often be more readily approached from a vehicle because they do not always associate it with man. On foot, you are always at a disadvantage because wild animals have far superior senses than any human. But the bush around camp was too thick, the car would be too unmanoeuvrable; we had to work on foot.

Ndaragus approached me in the dark and spoke in a nervous whisper to say he had found blood. Once again, I had that sensation of cold running down my body, as if little dribbles of icy water were working their way down the small of my back, right down onto my legs. This was it, the confirmation of what we all expected to hear, but dreaded. I went with him and, wordlessly, in the dim light of a fading torch, he indicated the unmistakable footprint of a lion maybe twenty yards from the tent, and, on a pebble next to it, two little spots of blood. I felt the blood – congealed but still soft, consistent with the time that had passed since the lions were presumed to have been there at the entrance to the tent. Then Ndaragus took my arm and walked me, wordlessly, another three or four paces. The torchlight reflected off something bright: Amina's revolver. Ndaragus spoke softly in Oromo. 'She died here. Her fingers loosened here and the gun fell to the ground.' Words I shall hear for the rest of my life, so poignant, so charged with finality. This is where she died, Ndaragus had said, where her fingers relaxed and let fall the gun. The saddest words I ever heard anyone speak, the loneliest moment I ever felt. I told myself then, and keep telling myself now, that she must by then have been unconscious, that from the moment the lion sprang on her and bit deep into her she must have been out of it, or else she would've fired her gun. But she never had the strength to, or rather I hope never had the awareness that she was still holding the gun.

We stood together for some seconds, the knowledge of what we were looking at seeping deeper into our minds. Then I picked up the gun and, turning to peer at Ndaragus in the darkness to confirm, so to speak, what we two must do though in reality we could not clearly see each other's faces, I went to find Rider. I gave him the gun saying we had found it about twenty-five yards from the tent. In the torchlight reflecting off the gun in Rider's hand we could just see each other's faces. He was tight-lipped, eyes nearly closed, still as a dead tree and slightly hunched. He looked up from the gun and asked tonelessly. 'Did you find the tracks?'

'Yes.'

'Blood?'

'Yes.'

'What does Ndaragus say?'

'He says – ' Here I paused. I was about to tell my friend, the man who stands for so much in my life that is precious to me, that his beloved Amina had without doubt been killed and carried off by a lion. 'He says a lion has killed her.'

We looked at each other for a while, quite a long time. Then he let his arms fall loose, he sagged, man, he sagged like a bag of wet mealie-meal, all limp and lumpy and useless. I thought his body would just fold down over his legs.

'We'll go as soon as the *watu* are ready,' he said, and wandered slowly back towards his empty tent.

I looked at my watch. It was 3.55 a.m. Half an hour later the clouds started breaking up, letting some starlight through. Soon their faint light was smothered by the pre-dawn luminosity of the approaching sun. Time to start moving. We were all dressed now, had eaten something (though Rider as you might guess could not eat) and Abdullahi and Ndaragus were conversing rapidly, huddled over a torch as they deciphered the spoor. Rider stood apart, waiting for them to say they could see well enough to start tracking. I joined them and as the light increased listened to their discussion. They moved up and down the spoor in the camp area, which was easily recapitulated. The

117

lions had traversed the fifty yards or so of open ground from the edge of the bush to the tent in a straight line, bellies to the ground. Two of them. They had returned almost retracing their steps. The lion carrying Amina had held her high so that her limbs only scuffed the ground occasionally. At the edge of the campsite they had joined two more lions and all had moved off quickly.

Ndaragus eventually came up to me and said in Oromo, '*Lenca. Lenca dhaltu.*' Lionesses. 'Four of them,' he added. 'They went very fast.' As the light picked up, we moved off, slowly at first, until there was enough light to move at a steady walk. Tracking was easy in the dry sandy ground and I started to brace myself for the next inevitable part of our day. At this pace, we would soon come to where the lions had stopped to feed. I started to say to myself, over and over, there must not be anything left, nothing left, please, nothing left. I absolutely dreaded what we might find, some remnant of Amina overlooked by the lions. At the same time, I kept saying, 'Four lions, big lionesses – there won't be much left.' Then, about a mile from camp, the spoor of the lionesses was joined by that of two other lions. '*Lenca dhira,*' said Ndaragus, tersely, male lions. Lions often shadow other lions hoping to freeload on their kills – just what these two were doing.

Not long after we reached the spot that I had been so dreading to get to – where they'd stopped to feed. We saw a spotted hyena about seventy-five yards ahead of us that loped off as we approached, and we all knew what that was likely to mean. I was shaking, man, shaking like a chameleon, ay – terrified at the thought of what we might find. The only good thing that happened that day was that they had consumed Amina completely. I cannot tell you how much I dreaded finding some part of her still intact that I would have to confront – and worse still perhaps have to confront Rider with. The two male lions had either joined the lionesses to feed, or, more likely, been obliged to wait until the four had finished. Between six lions and a hyena something little bigger than a gerenuk doesn't go far and all that was left was a bloody mess on the sandy ground. Grisly enough that's for sure but far easier to handle than some recognisable part of her body.

In point of fact, there was something more tangible left – her *kanga*[37] When we reached this spot and the two trackers in front paused and then conversed before fanning out and looking around them Rider knew what they'd come upon and without saying anything made a wide detour and waited for us fifty yards ahead. They found the garment a few yards away from where the lions had fed, torn and bloodied, and when one of the men brought it to me I quickly balled it up and stuffed it in my pocket. My intention was to wait and see how Rider fared in the days ahead before telling him I had it. None of us looked any closer than we had to, or lingered any longer than was necessary to sum things up. We moved on quickly, the lionesses' spoor now without the two males who'd followed them to where they'd fed.

We were five people: Rider and I, Abdullahi and Ndaragus, and one other man to carry food and water, Abdullahi's only son, Osman. We had to expect to be out all day and possibly through to the next, as the lions typically would go many miles before stopping during the heat of the day. I spoke quietly with Abdullahi and Ndaragus. The time now was 6.10, making it about three hours since Amina had been taken. Even if the tracking was easy we could not expect to close the gap between us and the lions, now anything up to ten miles away and no doubt walking steadily as we stood there conversing. Our plan would be to assume that they would keep going until it got really hot when they

---

[37] Sarong (Swahili)

119

would find a shady spot and lie up to sleep over the hottest part of the day. Lions don't like the heat and on a day like this was going to be, stinking hot and muggy, they'd move as little as possible between eleven and four. They might easily stop before eleven, specially since they'd eaten. Provided that we could spoor them about as fast as they were moving we could expect to catch up with them where they were resting at about 2 p.m. – two hours or so before they would move again. So we had about two hours in hand – time enough if the tracking was easy, but not that much time if we ran into problems that delayed us.

We did run into problems. The lions headed south-west until they hit a dry lugga that ran roughly east west. They then followed the lugga eastwards, perhaps because there was water somewhere along it. About two miles along the dry river bed the spoor suddenly split with three lionesses going up one side of the river bed, and the fourth to the other side. The trackers told us to wait while they figured out what was going on. We waited twenty minutes or so before they returned. It seems the lions had realised there was a herd of buffalo just ahead and had set about hunting them. The buffalo had presumably got wind of or heard the lions and stampeded along the river bed further ahead. It shouldn't have affected tracking much except that other buffalo had subsequently overrun the lions' spoor, presumably trying to catch up with the rest of the herd. Tracking now became very slow as we successively lost and re-found the spoor several times. It had obviously been a confused stampede of buffalo charging around, splitting up and reforming in the dark as the lions, handicapped themselves by the really dark night, tried to catch one. In the end, they failed to make a kill and abandoned the pursuit at a muddy pool where they'd stopped to drink. From there the spoor became easier again, but by now it was late morning and I calculated that we'd pretty well lost the two hours we'd had in hand. It was going to be a close run thing, to catch up with them before four o'clock.

We made good ground over the next four hours and would've made better if we had not lost the spoor two more times where other buffalo had overrun the lions' tracks. At one o'clock I called a brief rest. Spooring is hard work, even for the best trackers. Not so much physically, the pace is rarely that fast, but mentally. Although to see a tracker work it seems as if nothing much is going on, that's only because it's all in the mind. It's rare that a European white man can acquire the knack of tracking; I've never come across any white man that really has it, though we can all follow a clear spoor. There's something going on in the brain of a gifted tracker that is totally foreign to the white man's make-up, something he lacks altogether. Rider says it's all to do with eidetic vision, that African people tend to form a relational picture of what they see where the white man synthesises and abstracts. It's the experience of all white men who work with trackers that the tracker sees all sorts of signs that are all but invisible to a white man even when pointed out to him. Tiny disturbances to the ground that appear indistinguishable from all sorts of other disturbances nearby. But what the tracker is doing is mentally reconstructing the animal he is following and what it is doing. He then sees the effect of the animal's passage on the ground and looks for confirmation of those effects. He has an expectation of what he should see and can therefore narrow down the area he scrutinises. Much of the time what he sees may be imaginary – it should be there and sometimes it really is, sometimes it probably just looks as if it is. But every now and then an unequivocal sign shows up and permits him to readjust or strengthen his running mental picture of what the animal is doing. Most of this of course becomes intuitive with practise, allowing him to apply his conscious mind to the difficult bits or to where the running image changes as the animal changes pace or direction. Maintaining the concentration required is exhausting.

Both trackers said the spoor hadn't changed, which is to say that when the lions had passed this spot maybe four or five hours ago they were still moving steadily. Most of the time, they said, three of them went more or less in file, while the fourth was always off to one side. After a ten-minute spell, we moved on again. By two-thirty, I was getting nervous. In half an hour or so the lions would be stirring and thinking about moving on again. The only thing in our favour was the heat. With no wind, the air just above the ground had been absorbing heat over the midday period at a tremendous rate, making it breathlessly hot. Too hot for tsetse flies, at least, but not for the little meliponid sweat bees that relentlessly scoured out the edges of your eyes and nose and mouth. The trackers, for all that today was one on which they would muster everything they had for the task in hand, had been slowing up for some hours now, spelling each other at shorter and shorter intervals as it became ever harder to concentrate. Time was running out.

Then, at about 3 p.m., Abdullahi and Ndaragus paused and beckoned to me. The lions' spoor, they said, indicated that they had slowed their pace, which meant that by now they had probably stopped to rest. A few yards further on, Abdullahi, who was a few yards to the side, stopped and pointed wordlessly to the ground under a low, scrubby tree. I saw where the ground was smoothed a bit – a lion had lain down here, sure sign it was tiring. That meant that they might now be very close. I'd had the impression we'd been going very slightly uphill for the last mile or so and kept looking back to see if we were indeed higher. But the bush was always too high to see over and I couldn't be sure. We closed up behind the trackers, moving as quietly as possible. The wind, or rather the lack of it, was good. A short time later Abdullahi and Ndaragus paused and indicated that

Rider and I should now take the spoor and lead. That meant they thought the lions were very close. Then, after just a few yards, one of the trackers tapped me on the shoulder. I turned and saw him pointing ahead. We could just see the crown of a baobab tree, maybe fifty yards ahead, to which he was drawing my attention. Baobabs are in leaf at that time of year and we all thought the same thing; its shade was a very likely spot in which to find the lions. We covered the distance to the tree very slowly to be sure not to make any noise. We got to within twenty-five yards without being able to see the trunk of the tree at all through the thick bushes. But any moment now we could expect to get a view of the base of the tree. Still on the lions' spoor, we edged round a thick bush and gradually the tree trunk came into view. There were no bushes growing under the tree – just long yellow grass almost the same colour as the lions. We took a few slow steps and suddenly Ndaragus reached past me with the stick he was carrying to tap Rider, in front of me, on the arm. We froze and Ndaragus flicked his stick off to the left a bit. I saw it before Rider, just a tawny patch in the dappled shade of the baobab tree, hardly distinguishable from the dry grass around it. I slowly stepped up alongside Rider, moved a bit to his side and raised my rifle, my .473 – you know the one. I waited a bit so he could see what I was aiming at, and fired. The shot was a good fluke – I couldn't see much of the sleeping lion – and though it thrashed about a bit, it never got up. The other three, also asleep, were a bit beyond, and at the sound of the shot scrambled to their feet. One was a lot slower than the others and Rider took that one easily. I got off my second barrel to hit the third lion as it began running directly away from us – an easy shot, though it went down still alive. The fourth took off away from us, but somewhat diagonally – not so easy a shot – and though Rider's second barrel was a hit, it only stumbled, and then kept going.

Abdullahi got one shot off from his .500, but I think he missed. By the time we'd reloaded, it was out of sight. Rider and Abdullahi ran after it and I went for the second lion I'd shot, as it was far from dead. When it saw me it got a second wind and charged straight at me, very quick and low on the ground. I took my time to be sure and waited until it was about fifteen yards away, looking very big along the barrels. A lion coming for you is as nasty as it looks, but an easy shot when close and moving directly at you provided you stay cool, which, mark you, is sometimes easier said than done. Then I heard a shot from the direction Rider had gone in and shortly after the two men returned, Abdullahi saying Rider's first shot had in fact been spot on the heart and the lion had only run a short distance. He'd only fired again to be doubly sure.

Abdullahi, Ndaragus and Osman had a close look at each dead lioness, but Rider couldn't even look towards them. I joined the three of them and we pieced together, as hunters always will, the last seconds of the hunt. Abdullahi and Ndaragus had correctly deduced from the spoor that the pride comprised an old lioness and three younger ones – in all our minds unquestionably her daughters, though of course one can never really know such things for sure. The one that had got up more slowly than the others was the old lioness, not so old that she was incapacitated, but ageing and slower than her offspring.

'Kalas',[38] said Abdullahi harshly, spitting with eloquent finality onto the ground beside the old lioness. For the men there was an immeasurably strong and satisfying sense of retribution in having killed all four assassins – for that is how they perceived these lions: as killers, murderers. For them the old adage that 'without shedding of blood is no remission' was a self-evident truism that had absolutely to

---

[38] Finished, done with (Arabic)

be observed. In this respect they were worlds apart from Rider, though they did not know that.

Then Rider addressed us all again, saying that he wanted the lions piled together up against the base of the tree on the south-west side of the trunk. It didn't take long to get the three nearest ones in place, but it took us a bit longer to drag the three hundred-pound carcass of the fourth back to the tree. At last, Rider seemed satisfied and for quite some time he stood and gazed at the tawny bodies heaped around the wide tree trunk. As we waited I heard him muttering quietly, to himself, not to us. 'Seeking whom they may devour' was all I heard before he finally turned and indicated that we could now go. We picked up our gear and prepared to leave the spot. The shadows were long now and guinea-fowl were calling not far away. The cool of the evening felt infinitely cooler than it really was now that the sun no longer touched us. We were played out, having gone all day with only short breaks, as we walked slowly away half a mile or so to choose a spot for the night off our incoming tracks. It was quite possible that the two male lions would follow our tracks to keep in touch with the lionesses and any other kills that they may make. They themselves if they came upon us asleep would be highly likely to consider us as prey. We chose an open patch of ground and the men set a fire to get a *sufuria* of *posho* cooking. Abdullahi and Ndaragus then asked if they might return to the carcasses. Rider ignored them, but I nodded and they set off, returning as darkness fell about an hour and a half later.

Nothing was said, but of course you can guess what they'd been up to. (Hutcheon was referring here to the fact that in a lion's shoulder there is a small, vestigial bone that floats in the muscle, unconnected to any part of the skeleton. The anomaly of this floating bone, not found in any other large animal, confers upon it in the superstitious mind of man all kinds of supernatural qualities. It is powerful *muti*, the mother of all snake oils, invaluable in the casting of mortal spells on those you hate, or of generating incandescent lust in those you desire. And the floating bones of a man-eater are supercharged compared with those of a common or garden, zebra-eating lion.) I laughed to myself – but not out loud – to see that even the dour Moslem Abdullahi, bitingly scornful of his animist fellow men, as cool a customer as there is, could not resist such virulent *muti*; without doubt, he had a couple in his pocket.

We ate some *ugali*, drank heavily sugared black tea and, scooping out the sand to make an indentation for the hips, quickly fell asleep. The men would try to spell each other, so that someone was on watch for lions, but I knew they would not succeed for more than a few hours. We were all completely wiped out and the only strategy that could keep us watching out for lions was for four of us to sleep as early as possible, while the other two tried to keep themselves awake for as long as they could. After a few hours we would be so uncomfortable that sleep would become fitful and as the night wore on at least one of us would be half awake most of the time. Fatigue made this seem like a perfectly good strategy.

The night passed uneventfully and I was half-awake for the last three or four hours before dawn. There was just enough water to brew a *sufuria* of tea and we were ready to go before the sun was even up. Then Rider spoke for the first time since I'd heard him muttering over the lion carcasses. 'I want you all to come with me back to the lions,' he said. He said nothing more, so we all got up and made our way back to the baobab tree. Rider walked straight past the tree and carried on for about sixty or seventy yards or so, then stopped. The ground was much more open on this side of the tree with patches of long grass that rustled quietly in the slight breeze that was blowing towards us. I saw now that when I had thought the ground was rising

126

yesterday I'd been right, because when I turned to look back at the baobab the ground beyond was appreciably lower. Then when I joined Rider I saw that he'd come to the quite abrupt edge of a small escarpment that fell away steeply to the south-east. We were, I suppose, about two hundred feet above the plain below, not much, but in that flat country even a weathered escarpment of two hundred feet is striking terrain. The rim of the low scarp turned gradually round to the east on the one side and disappeared into nothing looking the other way, south-west. On the eastern edge, maybe a thousand yards away, were two quite large baobabs standing side by side. Beyond them, on the horizon, was the outline of a conical hill, an old volcano. To the south, just visible on the horizon, was a line of low hills. Rider had a piece of paper in his hip pocket, and a pencil (I never knew why – probably no reason at all), and he sat and sketched a map showing all these features with the estimated distances. He then asked me to estimate the bearings to the baobabs and the hills, using the just-risen sun as the compass reference. We discussed our bearing estimates and he noted our best guesses on his map. Then he told us all to listen carefully.

'I want you all to remember this place,' he said, speaking in Oromo. 'Can you do that?' We all allowed that we could remember it.

'Well enough to find your way back here?'

'*Hai*,' exclaimed Ndaragus, '*Hai*.' He looked along the escarpment and spoke to Abdullahi. They discussed for a bit the ins and outs of finding their way back to such a remote spot. Beyond the two baobabs, invisible from where we were, a dry lugga obviously descended the escarpment, evident as a line of slightly larger shrubs and small thorn trees as it meandered across the plain below us.

'Is that the same lugga where the buffalo were?' Rider asked. Abdullahi and Ndaragus agreed that it probably was.

'Then you could find your way back here by going down the lugga until it reached the scarp, then walking along the rim of the scarp to here?' They agreed that such a strategy was feasible.

'Good,' said Rider, and led us back to the dead lions. He made no comment about the very obvious incisions on the carcasses made the evening before to extract the floating bones. He abjured us all one more time 'to remember this place as long as you live, *bila shaka*,'[39] after which he said no more. There was an insistency in his tone of voice that all of us noticed. It made us look closely, but silently, at each other, each trying to figure out what Rider had left unsaid. I think we all thought that because Rider was undoubtedly under an enormous strain he could be expected to behave a little oddly. It was clear he didn't want to talk so no one felt like addressing any sort of question to him. Just not the time or place. On top of which we were all exhausted. So we all dutifully looked around again to indicate as best we could that we would indeed endeavour to 'remember this place as long as we lived.' In point of fact, it would be hard to imagine any of us forgetting.

As we got ready to go, Abdullahi suddenly spoke rapidly to Ndaragus and the two of them asked us to wait a moment. They walked back quickly to the grassy ground beyond the tree and cast around until they found a loose stone each. These they tossed[40] onto the lion carcasses, mumbling something under their breaths, and then rejoined us. It spurred me to do likewise though Rider at first just waited, expressionless. Then he too went and found a stone as the rest of us had, and dropped it onto the lions.

Then, just when we all thought we'd finished with this

---

[39] Without fail (Swahili)
[40] Among the Galla and others it is respectful to toss a stone onto a grave as you pass by

sad place and would be moving on he abruptly said that he wanted to be left alone for a while and told us to walk off out of sight and wait for him. I suddenly felt very suspicious and looked closely at him. He caught my gaze and held it unflinchingly. 'Give us your guns, man,' I said, 'think I'll hold on to them until you rejoin us.'

He stared at me for a moment, then he just unbuckled his gun belt and handed it and his rifle to me, saying, 'I'll be half an hour or so.' He paused a bit, then added, 'There'll be no funny business. I just want some time alone with her.'

Her? Gave me a bit of a creepy feeling, that, I can tell you. *Ja*, for sure she was there under the baobab tree – but inside the carcasses of a bunch of stinking lions. Then I kicked myself for turning the thing back onto myself. This wasn't for me to feel bad about. It wasn't my business – it was Rider's. He hadn't chosen this. He just had to put up with it, find some way to pay his last respects to the woman he loved so very dearly. Our duty was to help if we could – not to feel squeamish. But help? How could we? Where she was was where Nature had discarded her, with all the indifference that Nature has towards human sentiment. Well, we sloped off uneasily as he'd requested and though I'd been suspicious I was pretty sure he wasn't going to top himself, though I've no doubt he'd been over all that in his mind. All the same, I have to admit I was relieved when after about forty minutes he showed up and indicated that we could all get going now.

I do remember one thing that struck me as a bit odd, but which I didn't attach any particular significance to, and that was his knife. He had it buckled round his waist when he rejoined us. Nothing odd about that you might say – except that he hadn't had it there when I disarmed him. Crafty bastard, I thought, you fooled me there. No point in taking your guns and leaving you with your knife. Where was it all this time? Did you hide it, and if so why? But I was just very relieved that my oversight hadn't resulted in just what I was trying to prevent, and thought no more about it.

That was it. We moved off and Rider lapsed again into the sombre silence of the day before. He only spoke once on the way back, and that was to say, quietly, so that I had to ask him to repeat it. 'Lion shit. All that's left of her is lion shit. Just bloody lion shit.' After a pause, he added, cryptically, 'Zoroaster would approve, though.'

Now that was a terrible thing to have to hear a man say, that the woman he had loved so deeply, whom he had absolutely adored and idolised, had been reduced in a matter of hours to nothing more than a pile of lion shit. There's nothing comforting, at least I couldn't come up with anything, you can say in reply to such an indisputable statement of fact, however much you may want to soften its harshness. In fact, there's very little of any use at all that you can say to a man at such a time, even if you felt anything of what he felt. We all did feel something of what he felt, because all of us adored Amina and all of us knew just how much he loved her. But none of us was hurt quite as he was – how could we be? The *watu* have a very sympathetic Swahili expression at such times. '*Pole, bwana, pole,*' they'd say to Rider, which means literally 'slowly', or 'carefully', but which conveys the wish that you will be able to cope with the pain reasonably peacefully and without unnecessary suffering. The sympathy of your friends and compatriots is indeed comforting when you have suffered as Rider just had. Even so, the enormity of such pain is vastly greater than the relief that sympathy can provide and for the most part you are on your own in such matters.

Rider, however, did not pass that remark in order to elicit a sympathetic response from me. He just wanted to spit it out, get it said and, as far as saying something can ever substitute for the thing itself, obviate any false softening of the awful, bitter fact. At the time I hadn't any idea what the remark about Zoroaster meant and, not wanting to trouble Rider, didn't ask. I looked it up though and learnt that the Zoroastrians didn't bury their dead. Rather they left the corpses out in the open to be disposed of by dogs and vultures, which they revered for exorcising the spirit of decomposition.

Hutcheon's story ended here. I've been over it in my mind many times, as I know Leila has too. We've both of us cried more than once and many years later were to cry again, bitterly, when the day came that revealed to us just what Hutcheon's story of the missing knife meant.

BOOK TWO

9

The Ancient Eldorado of all the Old Fools

'If you really were my friend you'd ask me to walk out in the bush with you and when I wasn't looking put a bullet through the back of my head.' We'd got back to camp the day before at about midday, absolutely creased, and without saying anything to each other had washed and eaten and then slept. The following morning shortly before dawn, when it was still quite dark, Rider and I got up and wandered over to the embers of last night's cooking fire. Two bush francolin were rasping out their clattering, oddly musical calls from the thicket to one side of the camp. A robin chat was singing near the kitchen fire, going through his repertoire of local bird calls in the grey half-light. Usually, Rider would sit and listen to these sounds of dawn that he loved so much; listen for as long as he could before he had to turn his mind to the day's work. But not today; he obviously wasn't hearing them at all. In point of fact, from his initial apathy I'd thought that it was going to be a sombre, brooding day, with Rider depressed and withdrawn and me wandering around like a lost fart wondering what on earth I could do to help him and coming up with *nikkies*. Depression is not something either sufferer or sympathiser can alleviate; it simply has to run its course. It was a huge relief to hear Rider not only break his dark silence, but with a sarcastic remark as well.

' "Why should I dirty my gun when you could do it

135

yourself?" I replied, happy to begin talking again without being all long-faced and solemn. Kidding aside, though, there was a deadly serious element to it, because what Rider was really telling me was that suicide had been – still was – very much on his mind. So as to minimise the time he spent by himself I'd ordered him to sleep in my tent, no questions, do as you're bloody well told. One of the first things I'd done that morning we followed up the lions was to leave instructions for Rider's tent to be packed away while we were out. I was (rightly) sure he'd never want to see it again, but I was also worried that once the matter of the lions had been dealt with and he was no longer concentrating on pressing practical things he might start feeling sorry for himself and get really down. Rider's tendency to depression was always there and he sure as hell had reason to despise the world and himself right now. The less time he spent on his tod the better.

' "What the hell am I going to do now, Hutcheon?" he asked, but more of himself than of me.

' "Be a good father to Alan and Leila, and don't ever let yourself forget it," I said. "That she would expect of you without question and you can't tell me or yourself otherwise. And when you aren't looking after Amina's kickers, you've got plenty of *kazi*.[41] Lot of *watu* have changed their lives to work for you, lot of really loyal *watu*, really good people. You're not on your own, you know, you owe a lot to all of us. You're not nearly ready for the bullet. So you can forget that *kak*, ay.

' "And when you are ready for the bullet, make no mistake, we'll let you know," I added, trying to keep some flippancy in what was really grim business. The burden of loneliness is borne by all of us at one time or another in our lives, but for some it gets too heavy and they founder.

---

[41] Work (Swahili)

Rider must've felt so lonely then, so utterly lonely. And cheated and humiliated and guilty and all those ugly thoughts that accompany an event that really lies a bit beyond our comprehension in the sense that it defies all reason or logic. I was not that confident of Rider's mental strength not to worry what he might do if left on his own for any length of time.

' "Listen to the francolin," I said, "and the guinea-fowl – hay – don't pretend you didn't hear the zebra down towards the lugga a while back. All these things and a hundred other sounds and sights are still there. The bushveld keeps going just the same – you may as well stay part of it. Right now, you can hardly see or hear any of it, even less feel any of it; but it'll come back. You know that as well as I do. You also know that when it does come back the loneliness will diminish. The *watu* and I, we all know what you're feeling. We all know that some loneliness will shadow you forever; like a kudu with wild dog on its spoor, you know you'll never really shake it off. But that's just too bad, it's not our burden and you haven't the freedom to bale out now and dump all the loneliness and pain and suffering on us. We're in it together, Rider."

'He was silent for a while, and then said. "You know what her name means in Arabic?"

' "Amina? No, can't say I do."

' "Trusting. Trustworthy. That's exactly what she was – trusting and trustworthy. She trusted me implicitly. And what did I do? I let her down – totally."

' "Rider – for the rest of your days you will be haunted by that demon of having let her down. It's one of the cruel penalties you will pay for being the decent man you are. But you are wrong, all the same. She herself would never have thought that, never. In that respect, you have to turn your back on your feelings and concentrate on reason. This romantic conscience of yours that you've tried to explain to me – it's a bloody tyrant, man. You have to fight it off, ay. Nature has dealt with the two of you very harshly, very cruelly – as we are bound to see it. But you would be the first to remind us that Nature has no compassion, no fury, no guilt, no bad, no good. Nature only acts; it doesn't judge, it has no motive. What happened was an act of Nature and you can only accept it and keep going. Your judgements in such affairs will not help you or Amina or your children. You are the one who's always saying we can't judge Nature, because Nature is truly innocent."

'He said nothing for a long time, and we just sat there, silent. We sat for ages like that. I wished I could've thought of more to say – you want to try to say things as if, somehow, it might help, though I suppose that really it makes little if any difference. It wasn't as if I could say something Rider didn't know or hadn't thought of himself. Then, at last, to my enormous relief, he got up and said, "Better *hama*[42] then."

'Well, we upped sticks that morning and headed back to the plaas. There followed a bad spell that lasted quite a while – six months or more – with Rider deeply depressed and apathetic. Wouldn't eat, wouldn't talk, couldn't sleep, couldn't work. Only you kids kept him going – if you hadn't been there he'd have inspanned himself for the Last Great Trek pretty damn quickly. He wanted to, of that there's no doubt. But to orphan you at that age – he couldn't do it, although I know he teetered on the brink many times. I used to slip in a sly one now and then (at least I thought I was being sly – your dad probably thought I was about as subtle as a white-tailed mongoose, ay!) and comment on how trusting kickers are – clever stuff like that! You were five and Leila three – a great age and there was no way he couldn't respond to your liveliness. You were very active

---

[42] Move your abode (Swahili)

kids, always up to something, always demanding his attention over this and that. Gradually he fought off the
depression and when he did he went over the top the other
way. The years with Amina had got him semi-domesticated,
but he went feral again pretty damn quickly, let me tell you!
Made safari after safari, buying cattle and ivory and leopard
skins – didn't give a damn whether he made money out of
it all or not. Though all in all we did make money, specially
from safari hunting, which was good business. Whenever he
could he took you kids with him, as you know, and you had
the time of your lives. And when he'd had a bellyful of
safari we'd head off down to Nairobi for a break. We were
friendly with all the rogues and knaves in the colony – the
English remission men, the chancers and dreamers, the
safari hunters and other drones, the guilty on the lam from
who knows what devilry. Those were the so-called Happy
Valley days of Kenya and, *krars*, we had some good times,
ay. We'd get to town and call in on Blix[43] or Joss Erroll or
some other *mokora*[44] – whoever was around – and get stuck
in; drinking and gambling and shagging the wives and
mistresses who were always keen for a bit of Rumuruti Root
as one of them put it, and maybe stoking the fires with a bit
of cocaine from time to time. Of course, we could bolt after
a week or so, make tracks before the husbands could pluck
up the courage to load up their *bandooks*[45] and take revenge.
Blokes like Joss Erroll who lived there weren't always so
lucky – as you know, he eventually got the husband's bullet[46]
to no one's surprise; but he wasn't any more deserving than
several others of us.

---

[43] Baron Bror von Blixen-Finecke, Swedish hunter and playboy who helped establish
the scandahooligan label
[44] Rascal (Swahili)
[45] Corruption of *bunduki* (Arabic, Swahili for gun)
[46] Hutcheon Graham is referring to the celebrated murder in 1941 of Lord Erroll by,
it was assumed, Sir Delves Broughton, whose wife, later Lady Delamere, was Erroll's
lover.

'As for old Suleiman's gold, well, that got put away for a long time. After all, Amina only came into his life as a direct consequence of looking for King Solomon's mines so it was only to be expected that Rider would avoid that subject in the aftermath of her death. In point of fact, several years went by before he picked up on Suleiman's gold again, so long a time that I wondered if he'd ever get back onto it. I brought the subject up from time to time, more as a therapeutic thing than anything else. I thought it would be good for his mind to get back into it, remembering how the legend had so absorbed him in years gone by. Sometimes he'd start to get interested again and then the interest would fade and he'd drop it. He still had all his bits of gold and all the books and papers he'd accumulated on the subject. I was a little surprised that he kept them because one of the things that Rider did after Amina's death was expunge all physical reminders of her. Their tent of the fatal night he burnt with everything in it – clothes, bedding, everything. I heard a din over in the workshop one day and went to look. It was Rider pulverising her revolver. The beautiful little .32, Webley's pocket hammerless model that he'd had silver-plated with her name inlaid in Ethiopian gold. All her jewellery and other possessions – he got rid of it all. None of us ever said anything; I think we all understood that he needed to do it and also that it was a completely private matter for all that much of it had to be done in our sight. He didn't even keep a picture.

'I'm not a romantic sort of bloke, but I found what Rider did very romantic because he put her memory onto a much higher plane than is possible by using material things to remind him or recreate her image. He installed her totally and completely into his mind. She never left him in that respect, or he her. Years later, I saw him one day sitting under a tree and I went and joined him. He was quite still for a very long time and then I saw that he was whispering

– very quietly, so that you had to look closely to see that that was in point of fact what he was doing. Eventually I asked him, "What're you thinking, Rider?" Nothing. He didn't budge, didn't seem to have heard me at all. I wondered if something was wrong and peered into his face. He couldn't seem to see me, his lips just moving, his eyes open but unseeing. It worried me for a moment. "Hey, Rider – what's up, man?" I demanded. Finally, he seemed to come to, and sat up straight and looked at me. "What?"

'"What're you doing, man; you're in a complete *dwaal*, ay?"

'"Amina,' he said, 'I was just talking to Amina."

'I said nothing more then and we sat there for a long time. Finally, he said, "You know, I think of her every day. Sometimes I worry myself because she's right there with me, talks to me, touches me. There's never been a day that I don't think of her at some point. I don't feel so lonely then – just for a while. It's what keeps me going. I dread the day when I discover that I haven't thought of her in twenty-four hours. If that day ever comes then I'll know our time is up. Truth is, though, I don't think it *will* ever come – she's always there. And because we never had any bad times I never feel bad when I think of her."

'After that, I knew exactly why he'd destroyed all the material things associated with her. Except that he didn't quite destroy everything. He thought he had, but two things got overlooked. One was her *kanga*, the one she was wearing when the lions took her. I'd picked it up, all bloodied and dirty, and balled it up into my pocket. At the time I didn't give it to Rider because I thought it would be too difficult for him to hold something so much a part of her. I washed it and put it away meaning to give it to him when time had passed. But the more time *did* pass the harder it got to raise such a ghost, the more so when I saw him rid himself of all such objects. So, I decided that I would give it to Leila when she was of an age to understand it and not just be squeamish – lot of old brown bloodstaining on it, you know, that not everyone might cope with. I still haven't found the right moment to give it to Leila; though something in me tells me I should one day. She's so like her mother it seems like it's a little thing I could do to bring the two women together. The moment will come, I'm sure.

'The second thing – well, there's a story attached to that.'

10

Flashman's Gold

The other thing that survived Dad's obliteration of the material objects that he associated with my mother was to play a crucial part in his quest to solve the puzzle of where King Solomon's mines were. By itself it meant little – it was only when its link to another piece of information was made that its real significance became apparent. This other piece of information, and the object attached to it, has an interesting story, one that has been passed down through the Quatermain and Graham families for two generations.

Some sixty or so years ago, in January 1859 to be precise, my great-grandfather Allan Quatermain met up with a colourful character named Harry Flashman in Cape Town in the old Cape Colony of South Africa. Colonel Flashman, VC, no less, was – or so he said, and, as Allan soon found out Flashman's own account of things did not always exactly match the truth – on his way back from India to England where he was to be knighted for his heroic exploits in the recent Mutiny. People were already referring to him as Sir Harry and he created something of a stir in Cape Town society when he disembarked from the tea ship that had brought him over from Calcutta. He was so personable and engaging, especially when togged up in full Seventeenth Lancers' fig that most people took him at face value: and there's no denying that he cut a fine dash. A good-looking – according to many women devastatingly so – man, who must've stood six feet two in his socks, he could charm the knickers off a nun and had, apparently, distinguished himself exceptionally in several famous and not a few notorious military adventures all over he world. He had just been awarded the Victoria Cross for outstanding bravery at Lucknow in the Indian Mutiny, according to the stories the papers were full of at the time. He seemed to personally know the queen and hobnobbed with – at any rate dropped the names of – all sorts of celebrated politicians, soldiers and others. He could – and frequently did – tell the most gaspingly lewd stories in several languages and was much in demand as a guest by society ladies.

Allan had come down to Cape Town from his farm outside Grahamstown to meet a recently widowed cousin and her daughter who had sailed out from England to start a new life in Cape Colony. He'd travelled in style on the personal yacht of his neighbour, John Charity Spring and his young daughter, who'd settled at Grahamstown some years before. Spring was an enigmatic character about whom there were all sorts of dark rumours of a past life of piracy and slaving off the West African coast. He had apparently started life as an Oxford don and peppered his conversation with affected Latin quotations that understandably fell on uncomprehending ears in his new home at Grahamstown, populated as it was mainly by soldiers (it was an army town), farmers, hunters and traders. The university had been obliged as the result of some scandal or other to terminate Spring's services and he had abandoned academia for a career as a freebooter, out of which he had evidently made a million, mainly, it was said, from West African black bullion. There were especially dark rumours about his notorious young daughter, Miranda. She was a captivating chichi girl about whose allegedly Arab mother nothing was known. Though only seventeen, she was, according to some of the army officers in the garrison, extraordinarily well-versed in the art of exotic fornication and possessed what's more, they said, an insatiable appetite. Her father was jealously protective of her, and had already murdered a visiting French officer who, unaware of the nature of John Spring, had thought he was on to an amazingly good thing and been too careless of where and when he bit into the sumptuous Miranda apple. He'd been found savagely beaten to death with a *sjambok* and no one wondered by whom. Because of this, few men were prepared to risk galloping the undeniably tempting Miranda even though she made it plain that all were welcome. The question that everyone asked was how, given her youth and the fact that so few men were prepared to risk being brutally murdered by the father, had the young Miranda acquired such carnal expertise? The universally agreed answer was of course that she had been taught by none other than John Charity Spring himself.

It wasn't that Allan was a friend of Spring's – few if any men were – but he'd helped him when the latter originally bought land at Grahamstown and they got on well. The chance to avoid the long ride down to Cape Town by sailing instead on Spring's ship from Port Elizabeth was too good to pass up and as Allan was too smart by far to spoor the kudu with Miranda he kept on the right side of Spring.

Spring had a house in Cape Town, but Allan put up at the Masonic where he met the newly arrived Colonel Flashman. They were of an age and as Allan knew Cape Town well his new-found acquaintance asked him to organise a trek round the many shebeens and brothels of what had been known in years past as 'the tavern of the seas'. Flashman, citing the weeks of starvation at sea, made a pig of himself among the whores and, during the lulls in his recuperative rut, they played a lot of poker. Allan was apparently a good poker player, keeping his cool even when drunk, whereas Flashman once pissed fell to bluffing and braggadocio. Inevitably, like others before him, he ended up owing Allan a fair bit of money. Well, the end result, a few weeks later, was that Flashman shot through without paying; not that he'd planned to. Allan wasn't that concerned about the gambling debt – he'd fallen in with a good many rascals like Flashman in his time and was owed money by many of them – but quite by chance he found a way to cancel it that left his own conscience clear enough and which, ironically, Flashman himself probably never was aware of.

What led to Flashman's precipitous departure was an invitation to the two of them including Miranda to a reception held by the governor of Cape Colony, Sir George Grey. Flashman was in his element at such gatherings; drinking, telling long, tall stories and swaggering about making suggestive remarks to the ladies. The inevitable happened when Flashman met Miranda and Allan says he thought the *oke's* britches were going to split. He considered warning him about this particular honey pot, but then saw that Spring and Flashman were acquainted and so kept his nose out of it. All sorts of stories were put about concerning what happened next, but it seems that John Spring, using Miranda as infallible bait, lured Flashman onto a ship of his in Table Bay and shanghaied him. At all events, Spring, Miranda, the ship and Flashman all disappeared at the same time, bound apparently for America.

It transpired that during the month or so that he spent in Cape Town Flashman left behind much more than a gambling debt. Allan's cousin arrived the day after he did and also stayed at the Masonic. This relative, Harriet Fleischmann, was a Quatermain who'd married a German businessman and had a teenage daughter by him. The husband had died a year or so back and she and her daughter had found things very difficult, as he had not left them a great deal of money. Allan had proposed that they come out to

South Africa and settle in Grahamstown where he would help them to get on their feet again. Allan had business to do in Cape Town and after the first few days of carousing with Colonel Flashman he'd spent most of his time attending to his affairs, leaving his cousin and her daughter much to their own devices. Flashman, with nothing to do but wait for a ship to take him on to England, did what he always did with time on his hands and that was put himself out to stud. First, he relieved Mrs Fleischmann of the drought she'd endured since her husband died, and then moved on to curing her daughter's virginity. Towards the end of the year, the daughter gave birth to a little boy. In an effort to legitimise the child and suppress scandal the Quatermain family concocted an elaborate tale to the effect that the girl and Flashman had secretly married and, helped by the similarity in names, Allan's good connections with Grahamstown officialdom and no doubt a suitable consideration they managed to register the child's birth in the name of Buckley Flashman.

All this is not just by the by for nearly three decades later Sir Harry Flashman's bastard son Buckley was to marry a Graham of Grahamstown. As I've already mentioned, their only child was Hutcheon – my father's lifelong friend and virtually a second father to my sister and me. What is intriguing, though, about the connection between the swashbuckling Colonel Flashman, the Quatermains and the Grahams is something that happened shortly before the events that took place in Cape Town.

Flashman had sailed for England from India on the only ship he could find at short notice, a Downeaster tea ship bound for New York, the skipper of which agreed to drop him off at the Cape where Flashman would have to find another vessel to take him on to England. He had indicated to Allan that he'd been obliged to make this rather hurried and unsatisfactory arrangement as the result of an angry husband – an explanation that Allan remarked seemed entirely in keeping with Flashman's character. Before reaching the Cape they had anchored for a few days off Mogadisho, the principal town of the east coast of what is now Italian Somaliland. Sober, Flashman would probably have kept his mouth shut; but drunk his mouth was as easily unfastened as his fly buttons and he'd blabbed to Allan about this clandestine visit to the Land of Punt. 'Don't worry about my capacity to meet my gambling debts,' he had drunkenly boasted to Allan late one evening after losing heavily yet again, 'I'm dripping with blunt. Or as good as. I've a deal of gold that I picked up a few weeks back in Mogadisho. Always meet my debts, what?'

'How's that?' Allan had asked, initially only mildly curious as he'd already begun to write Flashman's debt off as hopeless. Besides, he rather liked the man seeing in him perhaps the same streak of rascality that undeniably typified the Quatermains. He'd enjoyed his rambunctious company and shared many a good laugh; the gambling debt wasn't important.

'The captain of that rat-ridden old tea ship – Ridley was his name – cut me in on a little perquisite he'd arranged on his outbound voyage to India. He'd fallen in with an Arab trader who operated in the Horn of Africa – hah!' Flashman had banged his hand on the table at this point and beckoned to an exceptionally buxom whore he'd been addressing bawdy remarks to all the time they'd been playing and bellowed, 'The Land of Poont is in the Horn of Africa, my dear – what do you say to that? Or is the Horn of Africa in the Land of Poonts? Could go either way, don't you think? I'd allow your poonts have gotten a few horns of Africa blowing in their time, wouldn't you say?' and fell about laughing and coughing at his own wittiness. The woman, who was behind the bar, gazed unsmilingly at Flashman, boredom oozing from every pore. Still looking at him impassively she leant lazily over the bar, plumping her enormous breasts heavily on the bar top so that they billowed most of the way out of her bodice. 'Don't know what you're talking about, I'm sure,' she said.

'The devil you don't, Madam Poonts, the devil you don't,' replied Flashman, making an effort to return to the matter at hand.

'Now, where was I?' Flashman asked, turning back to Allan.

'Mogadisho, I think.'

'Mogadisho? Where in hell – ah, yes, Mogadisho. By Jove, they breed fine whores there, don't you know? I've strolled the Perfumed Garden in some pretty far-flung parts of the world, but – '

Here Allan interrupted him. 'You were talking about gold – '

'Ah yes, so I was, so I was. That bang-tail's monstrous poonts make my mind wander, I have to say.' Flashman belched loudly and called for a fresh bottle of brandy. They'd been on Klipdrift Green Label all evening, a fine brandy to be sure, but they're all liable to unsettle one if taken to excess. And Flashman exemplified excess. 'You see,' he said to Allan, 'this blasted brandy of yours is heady stuff and making me see double if I'm not damned careful. Two of those udders lying side by side like a couple of one-eyed elephant seals are distracting enough. When they slowly multiply into four, all heaving about in unison, it's damned unnerving, don't you know.'

Flashman shifted his chair round the table the better to concentrate on his story, took a sip of Klipdrift's best, belched again and lit a cigar.

'Yes – this Arab *banyani* said he could assemble a fair hoard of gold in Mogadisho if Ridley paid somewhat over the local price. The going rate in Mogadisho was such that the skipper reckoned he could turn a good profit in New

York, the ship's owners would never get wind of what he was up to – at least never get the evidence to do anything about it – and he'd end up supplementing his wages very nicely. So a deal was made and Ridley arranged to stop there on his way back to New York. He cut me in as he no doubt reckoned I'd be sure to sniff his little racket out and with my connections might make things uncomfortable for him back home.'

As Allan said, once he saw what sort of man Flashman was, he'd no doubt that the truth was that Flashman had blackmailed Ridley into cutting him in, by threatening to expose his racket to the ship's owners.

'We were a few days anchored off the town – there's no sheltered harbour at Mogadisho – waiting for the gold to be assembled and the business settled. With nothing else to do I put a representative sample of the local pussy vendors through their paces, and was mightily pleased with the standard of service, I have to say. They could play tunes on the horns of Africa that would get you dancing a jolly hornpipe or two, let me tell you, Allan old boy! Phoa! Anyway, I discovered that they weren't just for rent – you could buy 'em freehold so to speak and for a very reasonable price at that. So I proposed to this flat-hatted blackguard Ridley that we supplement the gold trading with a couple of dozen frisky young tarts that we could flog off to the madam midnights of New York at a good profit. Keeping them in good working order would also ease the long passage home.

'But he would have nothing of it – amazing how a ruffian who'd slit a throat for a bent rupee can be so high and mighty about someone else's brand of knavery. "Damn your eyes, Flashman," says he, "what do you take me for? I'm no slaver and I want no truck with those who are. Have ye no conscience man?"

' "Oh, I've a conscience," says I, "and a very healthy one, too. Never known it to bother me."

'Anyway, we bought a tidy quantity of gold, mostly raw unworked stuff that was very cheap. Also, some worked jewellery that the son of Ishmael insisted on a higher price for. We pointed out that the craftsmanship was indifferent, not to say piss-poor, and we would have to re-melt it all anyway before we could sell it on. But Ali Baba wouldn't hear of it and altogether we paid somewhat more than we'd hoped. All the same, we'll do nicely out of it.'

Flashman proposed to settle his debt to Allan with an appropriate amount of the Mogadisho gold and came up with a small, crude ingot that Allan wanted to take to a jewellers of his acquaintance to have valued. The proprietor was away at the time and so the gold was left at his establishment pending his return. It was then that the invitation to Government House had been extended that was to presage Flashman's unscheduled and precipitous departure for America. He left without his dunnage and Allan took it upon himself to put it into safekeeping, expecting in due course to hear from his new friend regarding its disposal. But no word came from Flashman and so Allan asked Sir George Grey if he knew how he might contact Flashman's home in England. Sir George obtained an address for him, but he never received an answer to his several letters of enquiry. Years later, he met an officer of the Seventeenth Lancers who knew Flashman well, who'd guffawed like a hornbill when Allan said he'd never got any response to his enquiries. 'Flashy's establishment receives innumerable letters concerning gambling debts, outstanding loans, allegations of bigamy, paternity and I don't know what other skulduggery. They get so many I'll wager they don't even open letters from unknown sources any more. You're wasting your time.'

So Allan gave up trying to return Flashman's possessions and handed out the Lancers uniforms and other clothing to his Hottentot farm hands. There was a collection of small clay figures depicting the more athletically challenging positions of the *Karma Sutra* that he sold to an art dealer in Port Elizabeth. There was nothing else of any value save of course the Mogadisho gold, which turned out to be something less than the grand hoard Flashman had bragged about. All the same, it fetched the amount of the debt several times over. He kept one small, rough ingot as a memento. This little block of gold was part of the estate that his son Harry inherited, which in turn passed to my father when Harry died. And a very influential little slab of gold it turned out to be.

11

Sweat of the Sun and Tears of the Moon

As kids, Leila and I loved to get Dad to show us his gold collection. He always kept a bit of every gold purchase he made, whether of alluvial dust, worked gold, ore or ingots. It made a change from reading us *Jock of the Bushveld* or the *Just So* stories, though he enjoyed all these too – just as much as we did, I suspect. He loved to go over his reference collection and tell us, again and again, the facts of life as they pertain to gold.

He'd explain to us that for all practical purposes – at least at ordinary temperatures – gold won't react chemically with anything and so is rarely found as a compound with other elements: it stays just gold. This means that it doesn't corrode or tarnish or break down and this remarkable durability is undoubtedly one of its attractions to man, why it's called a noble element. The others are its unique colour and the way it can be beaten wispily thin or drawn out filamentously long – more so than any other substance.

Although gold scarcely reacts chemically, it readily blends with silver to form the alloy electrum. The two metals associate in Nature and also in men's minds; it's always been gold and silver and though silver is the lesser of the two it's nevertheless held in high esteem. The Incas perceived gold as the stronger, and silver the softer. They had a wonderfully lyrical conception of the two metals, calling gold the sweat of the sun, and silver the tears of the moon.

153

The natural association of the sweat with the tears, Dad would explain, is very strong. Even though natural gold always looks like gold, it's hardly ever pure; it's nearly always electrum. And that's actually a very useful fact, Dad would say, as you'll see.

Because there's no chemical reaction in an alloy the components of electrum can be physically separated out as the pure elements. But the process is not easy and the way to do it wasn't figured out until about two thousand six hundred years ago – centuries after King Solomon's day. The kings of Crete, notably King Croesus, were anxious to make their gold coins pure to dispel the uncertain value of currency made from electrum. To do this, they invented the world's first parting furnaces by packing a clay crucible with a mixture of salt and silicate. Electrum was placed in the crucible and kept at dull red heat for several days. Tricky, because the temperature had to be kept just below the melting point of electrum. Under these conditions the silver separated from the electrum, leaving pure gold. Another tricky bit was to know when all the silver had left the electrum. This was done by periodically cooling a bit and scraping it on a touchstone. The colour of the trace was then compared with that of pure gold. Prior to this people just had to put up with electrum.

The point of the story, Dad would explain, is that in King Solomon's day they didn't have the metallurgical know-how to separate pure gold from their electrum and had to live with the degradation caused by the silver. The more silver in the electrum the greyer and less admired the colour. Naturally occurring electrum is usually from five to fifty per cent silver; only very rarely is it nearly pure gold. The ancients were very conscious of purity and the intriguing fact is that the biblical reference to the gold of Ophir – King Solomon's gold – mentions its unusual purity. That makes it very distinctive, gives it a fingerprint.

Fingerprints, Dad explained, are unique. Thus, the gold:silver ratio of a given piece of elctrum distinguishes it from all others. Theoretically, the silver content of gold bought in a market far from any mine could indicate where it came from. Dad spent a good deal of time mapping the distribution in the Horn of Africa of the gold:silver ratios of as many different bits of gold as he could lay his hands on. As this map developed, he hoped it might help to pin down the likely locality of the fabled gold of Ophir. He wanted to see if particular markets dealt with distinct electrum types, and if the gold on sale could be traced back to its sources.

He explained how in making this map he was helped by the fact that electrum usually contains impurities that sharpen the gold:silver fingerprint. Iron, tin and copper are often found in electrum in minute, but distinctive, amounts. Taken together, these elements can accurately distinguish one source of gold from another.

Unfortunately, Dad would tell us, Mother Nature sometimes paints an extra stripe or two on the zebra's bum, just to remind us who's in charge in paradise.

Fingerprinting electrum suffers from the zebra stripe anomaly. Up until the Industrial Revolution (I won't say that of course we knew what *that* was) the gold grubbed by mankind was placer gold; weathered out of exposed ore and placed by gravity and running water in sediments sometimes far removed from the source. It happens that electrum tumbled along river beds progressively loses its silver so that the original gold:silver ratio changes – by a lot if the bits have travelled far, or been severely bumped. The silver goes more easily than tin, iron or copper, which are therefore better indicators of origin than the silver content; but they also get lost.

On the other hand, he'd say, there's another thing that sometimes happens to placer gold that actually helps. It mostly starts as gold dust, but much of it ends up as bigger flakes or nuggets. Because it's heavy, gold dust sinks to the bottom of the river gravels and accumulates as it travels downhill. As the small flecks bump into one another they gradually get hammered together to form bigger flakes and lumps called nuggets. The ancients were often exasperated by a particular consequence of this process of nugget formation; namely, the incorporation of what they called adamans. These adamans – things that adamantly refuse to budge – are little pellets of platinum. Platinum is even heavier than gold and also sinks to the bottom of the river sediments. Sometimes, tiny, hard platinum nuggets get embedded in the gold nuggets. These adamans greatly irritated the early jewellers, because they are much harder than gold and almost impossible to separate from it. But, said Dad, they help identify gold sources because they only occur in certain places.

It was impossible not to get caught up in his fascination for all things gold even if we didn't always grasp the whole story. It was exciting to finger the various bits, to heft their weight, to look at their colour and see how one piece differed from another, to listen as Dad explained about electrum and platinum and placer gold and ore bodies and all the ways that people had figured out for riddling it out of river beds. He had a gorgeous shiny black basalt touchstone that we loved to scrape bits of gold on to see which gave the purest yellow. Then, as we grew older, we began to comprehend the really interesting part: the way in which the map could be interpreted to suggest where the legendary King Solomon's mines might be. Dad would show us the twelve passages in the Bible that referred to Ophir and the immense amount of gold it yielded to King Solomon and his father King David. He would show us, too, the many other references to gold in the context of Solomon and the Queen of Sheba and of Solomon's stupendous golden temple.

Although a patchy sampling for such a huge area, his map was intriguing. The gold from the western side of the Rift, from the south-west edge of the Abyssinian swell, the land of the Surma, around to Tigrê on the northern border with Eritrea, was different to that from east of the Rift. Western gold had more silver in it than eastern gold and often had platinum adamans that didn't occur east of the valley. The differences of course didn't of themselves reveal the mines' location; but for someone with a gold-feverish imagination like Dad they suggested possibilities.

What would be really interesting to know, Dad used to say, was the impurity pattern of gold that made its way to Solomon's kingdom from the fabled Ophir nearly three thousand years ago. If such a piece could be assayed, would the impurity pattern be allied with the modern western or eastern Ethiopian type, or neither or both? How choosy was old Suleiman? Did he want the gold inlays of his temple, and the many gold objects and pieces of furniture, to be made exclusively from the purest available electrum; or did he use any gold, even the dullest, most silvery electrum? Ah – what fascinating conjecture, what captivating trains of thought all this elicited in our minds. But Solomon's gold is untraceable now. Six hundred years after his death his marvellous gold-plated temple, one of the most extraordinary buildings ever made – ever likely to be made – was demolished by King Nebuchadnezzar and the gold looted. The raiders in turn were raided and the raiders raided as men are bound by their natures to do until the original gold of Ophir was mingled with other gold and spread all over the civilised world. Not lost – very little gold ever gets lost – just untraceable.

As the original temple was knocked down and rebuilt and knocked down again it is more than likely that some small fragments of its gold found their way into crevices in the foundations from where they could in theory be recovered and analysed. But even that isn't possible because although parts of the foundations are still visible today they lie beneath yet another temple – the famous Moslem Dome of the Rock whose guardians most certainly would not permit any such excavations underneath their mosque.

'Doesn't matter,' Dad would say, 'there's a gap in the story that I'm certain holds the key to the location of King Solomon's mines. Back in 1919 when Hutcheon and I went to Harar, we did so for several reasons. We might just as well have journeyed up the western side of the Great Rift Valley and gone on round the western edge of the highland swell where, historically, there are many rich sources of gold. One reason for staying on the east side of the Rift was simply that from the N.F.D. a journey up the east side was shorter and easier than to head off across the valley and up the west side of the Ethiopian swell – by all accounts a wild and difficult part of the world about which we knew very little. Another was that I couldn't find any reference to known gold sources on the east side – and that seemed strange. Didn't make sense to me that gold should only occur on the west side of the Rift. I felt that there must be gold on both sides – just a matter of locating it. Maybe if we went there we'd pick up some local knowledge.

'But another reason – I guess the most compelling at the time – was my desire to visit Harar, Punt's back door, maybe even the gateway to Ophir. Then there was the odd case of the mad French poet, Arthur Rimbaud, who lived in Harar on and off for the last eleven years of his life between 1880 and 1891. He'd baled out of France after writing his famous prose poem *Une Saison en Enfer* and, working as a trader, proceeded to live out his personal season in hell in Harar. It certainly knocked the rhymes out of him for he never wrote a line of poetry in Africa, though his many devotees have searched diligently for some overlooked but brilliant manuscript of the – as so many seem to see him – tragic

158

young poet. But that's not what makes his name stick in my mind. You see, it's a matter of record that Rimbaud regularly bought gold while he was in Harar – that's what I remember about him. But, where did the gold he bought come from? He doesn't say, damn it.

'Incidentally, I often wondered if Allan Quatermain, my grandfather, hadn't ended up in Harar on that last journey of his to look for King Solomon's mines. Rider Haggard wrote that they all became *bougnoulisé*, 'amateur barbarians', somewhere far north of Mount Kenya, using as his source of information Allan's diaries that a Frenchman had posted to him from Aden. Well, Rimbaud's employer lived in Aden. Hard not to put two and two together and come up with Harar as the place where they all ended their days . . .

'Anyway,' Dad went on, 'it turned out to be a good choice, one that saved us a lot of unnecessary travel into western Ethiopia. First off, we met the golfing consul Arnold Hodson. Arnold wasn't interested in gold, but he got me several bits of gold from mines along the western edge of the swell. These have been mined for placer gold for as long as anyone knows. It was the Kush civilisation who originally controlled them, trading the gold with the Ancient Egyptians. There are many historical allusions to a connection between Egypt and gold from Ethiopia and for the first few thousand years of the old Egyptian civilisation all the gold from this part of Africa ended up in the hands of pharaohs. It wasn't until Abyssinia was invaded by Semitic people around two millennia ago that the gold from the Ethiopian swell began to be commandeered by the Abyssinians rather than the Kush. This period coincided with the final collapse of the Kush and from then until today the gold from the western edge of the swell has been controlled by the emperors of Abyssinia.

'Now, this gold from western Ethiopia has quite a high silver content and – and this is crucial – platinum adamans.

159

None of the gold we got in Harar had adamans. And although some of our Harar gold was high in silver, most of what we bought there was much purer than anything I've seen from the west.

'The question is: where *did* the gold we bought in Harar come from? To my mind, it must have come from somewhere east of the Rift Valley. The old sheiks asserted that it does. Harar is the portal to an ancient trade route that runs from Red Sea ports such as Berbera, Zeila and Djibouti up onto the mountains at Harar and then along the mountains fringing the east side of the valley to where they give out along the present day Ethiopia–Kenya border. This route linked to another that ran south-east along the long spur from Negele that descended the mountains and ran along the Juba River to Mogadisho and Kismayu. This is the trade route along which came the slaves and ivory and gold that history states came from the Land of Punt and Ophir.

'Or was it? There *is* some gold about fifty miles north-west of Negele panned out of various streams that drain into the Daua, the main tributary of the Juba. I'm sure some of the Harar gold comes from here. But they're not King Solomon's mines. They're too small and there's no evidence of ancient workings. Nor are there any parent ore bodies at the surface because the gold is placed there by laterisation – a complex underground process.

'I said earlier that there's a gap in the story. Actually more than one gap, but the first one is the mystery of Flashman's gold. When I sent that old ingot of my grandfather's for assay, the one that Colonel Flashman got in Mogadisho in 1859, the result didn't match anything from Harar. It was very pure – only about three per cent silver, which makes it twenty-three carat gold – and what made the fingerprint really different was that it contained traces of tin – something that none of the other gold from anywhere in Ethiopia has. So where did it come from? Obviously, the first thing I thought was maybe it came from Negele. Well – that's one of the gaps. On our way back from Harar I got some gold from Negele, from an old man who'd lived there all his life. But I lost it. When I destroyed all your mother's possessions I think it got thrown out with everything else. I don't know, but I can't find it. Maybe someone stole it. So I asked Arnold if he could get me some and he sent me several small nuggets that were riddled out of the ground at that place north of Negele. Think he called it Shakiso or Lega Dembi – some name like that. Anyway, the assay was similar to several pieces we'd got in Harar, but – and here's the rub – quite different to Flashman's gold.

'So you see, there's *another* source of gold somewhere on the east side of the Rift Valley, and what's more it's very pure, like the gold from Ophir was. Like Flashman's gold. Cut a long story short – I reckon Flashman's gold came from King Solomon's mines. Out of the question that there could be a mine yielding the sort of pure gold that Flashman came by – and that mine have no connection with the pure gold of Ophir.'

When I first began to visualise what Dad was saying there was something that I didn't grasp. 'Why, Dad,' I asked, 'are you so sure the gold came from round Ethiopia? Why not somewhere else – Somaliland, Kenya, say?'

'Ah,' he said, 'that's easy. You have to know something about gold generally, something that rules out everywhere else. All basement rock contains some gold, but far too little to extract. Something has to concentrate it before there's enough for we humans to get at. Now, the classic circumstance in which gold collects is when ancient igneous rocks are pushed and pulled and twisted and crushed by some immensely powerful event, such as the collision of crustal plates, or the folding of mountains, to form metamorphic rocks. If there are also massive volumes of hot water containing various reactive chemicals accompanying these events

161

then dissolved gold can percolate through cracks in the metamorphic rocks – along with minerals such as quartz – and eventually crystallize out of solution. These are the gold-bearing veins of a classic ore body. In this way, the background incidence of gold (a minuscule fraction of an ounce per ton of the earth's parent rock) can be concentrated thousands of times over to form veins containing several ounces of gold per ton – very occasionally even more.

'There is,' said Dad, 'only one place in the Horn where such high energy events took place: Ethiopia. The geologists call it the Ethiopian swell and it's a truly remarkable thing. A patch of the earth's crust some five hundred miles in diameter was pushed up vertically nine thousand feet – and then topped in places by another three thousand feet of molten magma that oozed out of huge fissures and holes in the raised crust. It's the highest lifting of the earth's crust in the world, except for the folded mountain chains along colliding continental plates – such as the Andes and the Himalayas. Nothing like it has happened anywhere else. Clearly, the edges of this huge blister would have been distorted and cracked as they bent upwards. If dissolved gold were transported by hydrothermal action during and after this swelling it would be into the broken rocks at the edge of the swell – which is where many pockets of gold have indeed been found.

'That's why King Solomon's mines could only of been in the Horn of Africa.'

Once Dad had explained about the Ethiopian swell I could see why he was so certain about the general location of King Solomon's mines. Equally I began to see why the exact location wasn't obvious, given that the edge of the swell covers such a huge area. In terms of earth history, it's a recent phenomenon that took place in the Eocene, forty million years ago. Shortly after, the huge three-way crack of the Rift Valley separated a smaller eastern part of the swell from a larger western sector. The lack of gold mines east of the Rift Valley is not because the geology is radically different. The Rift itself had nothing to do with it, Dad reasoned, because it occurred after the swell; the geology was already settled. What *was* different east of the Rift Valley, radically different, was the people. The eastern highlanders were – and always had been – exclusively Oromo-speaking people; Galla as they were known to the outside world. As you went further east the Galla gave way to Somali, whose language, like Oromo, is Cushitic, or Hamitic if you will. The ancient Abyssinians, the Queen of Sheba's people, who became the Axumites, were of an altogether different stock and spoke a Semitic language. There *are* some Galla living west of the Rift Valley; but there are no highlanders east of the valley, nor have there ever been.

This difference, was, Dad reckoned, the key to understanding why there were *apparently* no big gold mines east of the valley. The Galla and Somali it seems had a common ancestor, the legendary giants, the Madanle. If these people mined gold they would have taken it to the Red Sea through their own country east of the Rift, not across it into hostile territory. Suppose, Dad would muse, suppose there were some gold mines being worked on the east side of the Rift Valley, low down at the foot of the escarpment where the swell begins, and something catastrophic happened to wipe out the miners. If those miners had no dealings with people higher up on the swell, but only with their relatives to their east, then nobody in Abyssinia would necessarily know about the mines, or be aware except by rumour of any disaster. It could go unnoticed west of the Rift.

It only required one devastating epidemic disease, like the rinderpest pandemic started by the Italians in 1888, followed by successive years of drought to exterminate all human beings from vast areas of the Horn of Africa's bleak

SULEIMAN'S GOLD

hinterland, the Ogaden, for as much as a generation. Such
a generational discontinuity of occupation is all it takes for
a body of folklore to lose a myth or a legend among people
who do not write. As long as folklore is passed on solely by
word of mouth, the displacement of a complete generation
can easily blur the memory of a remote locality.

This then is how I understood Dad's tentative theory to
account for the mystery of King Solomon's mines. The
mines were located somewhere around the Ethiopian swell,
east of the Great Rift Valley, low down at the foot of the
swell in relatively dry country where the inhabitants were
necessarily nomadic. Sometime after the death of King
Solomon in 922 BC, almost three millennia ago, an
unusually long-lasting calamity such as a long series of
drought years had exterminated the nomadic people who
lived in the vicinity of these mines for at least a generation.
This broke the continuity of collective memory about them,
their location was forgotten and the legend faded. And such
things certainly happen. The entire Madanle nation disappeared leaving only the vaguest of folklore behind them,
little more than their name and giant stature. And one
other thing that of course Dad found intriguing: their wells.
In the desert all around the eastern foot of the swell are
many deep, extraordinarily well-engineered wells that the
Boran say were made by the Madanle. If they could dig such
sophisticated wells, Dad would say, they could dig mines.

A remote location habitable only by nomads on the eastern side of the Great Rift Valley meant somewhere between
the Chalbi Desert in the N.F.D. of Kenya and the north-
eastern tip of the Ogaden where it pushes into Somaliland.
As Hutcheon would sarcastically observe, 'That's only fifty
thousand square miles of stinking hot desert, crawling with
shifta and scorpions – should be a piece of piss to find, ay,
Rider, piece of piss, man.

164

'I just need a few more clues,' Rider would reply (according to Hutcheon), 'and then I'll know where to look.'

'Why waste time sleuthing it out, man? Why not just wander about looking for a *kopje* with a sign saying Chief Suleiman's Mining Company Pty Ltd?'

'You can laugh, Hutcheon, but the irony is that you can bet your *kransie's* hairy back that there *will* be a sign. Not the painted board you *yok* about, maybe; but a clear sign all the same. Many signs in point of fact, the telltale signs of human activity, bits of worked rock, unnatural markings on stones, even the mine workings themselves if they haven't collapsed or been covered up.'

'*Ja* so, but even if the locals *had* been wiped out, for a long time even, sooner or later someone would have moved back into the area, I reckon. Moreover, these *okes* would for sure have noticed the signs you think are there. They would know that people had been there before them, ay.'

'So?'

'So the "forgotten" locality would have been rediscovered.'

'For sure,' said Dad. 'No question this place has been "found" again, maybe several times over. But what would some Gabbra or Borana make of it? *Nikkies*, nothing. They would see that people had been there long, long ago. Madanle, they'd say, our forefathers, the giants. They might even realise what the Madanle had been up to there, but so what? They'd talk about it among their own clan, but there'd be no reason for them to make anything of it, to want to spread the information. Even if you talked to such people they wouldn't bring the subject up of their own accord.'

Hutcheon allowed that this was undoubtedly what you would expect, that such things would not of themselves strike people such as the Gabbra as having any particular

165

significance. And their inclination would never be to spread such information around. On the contrary, such people are naturally tight-lipped and for visitors it can be extremely difficult to extract local information. You just do not blab about your country to strangers until you are quite certain as to their motives.

The fact that other people had no doubt 'rediscovered' the location of King Solomon's mines probably wasn't going to make Dad's rediscovery any easier. He was still going to have to find his own way there. Proving his theory wasn't going to be, as the Nigerians say, a one-day job.

12

A Snake Story

In *Jock of the Bushveld* Sir Percy Fitzpatrick warned against telling snake stories if you wanted to avoid a reputation as a bullshitter. During his years transport riding in the Bushveld he discovered that even the most sober and reliable of men are apt to liken their gorged pythons to borassus palms; to overstate the whirling of the dust-devils generated by the black mambas that overtake their fleeing horses; and to equate the venom expectorated by the spitting cobras on their stoeps with piddling elephants. Sir Percy was an astute observer of the Bushveld and its inhabitants, and I would not normally spurn his advice; but not all snake stories simply strain the athleticism of bakkops, spuugslangs and mambas. Some concern the treachery of vipers, which is altogether another matter.

For some years after my mother's death, as I learnt from Hutcheon, Dad avoided the subject of Suleiman's gold or indeed anything at all to do with gold. In 1930, there was something of a gold rush in western Kenya following the discovery of placer gold in a river running off the Uasin Guishu plateau. All the rogues and knaves in the colony at the time – and there were a fair few – raced off to such grand eldorados as Kakamega and Lolgorien where they burrowed and scraped and drank and cheated and fought and generally behaved like dogs quarrelling over a bitch too small to mount. There *was* some gold, little bits here and there, but it soon fizzled out. Hutcheon's cousin, D'Arcy Graham, tried his luck at Lolgorien and told Hutcheon that he knew why aardvarks only dig for termites: it's more rewarding. All the same, Hutcheon was intrigued. The two preceding years of 1928 and 1929 had been drought years exacerbated by plagues of desert locusts that poured out of Somaliland like ravening *shifta*, laying waste to huge swathes of veld throughout East Africa. Such cattle as survived were emaciated wrecks and even if they were put up for sale were impossible to fatten on non-existent pasture. The Great Depression had caused most of the would-be Nimrods of Europe and America to cancel their trophy hunting safaris, leaving Dad and Hutcheon somewhat the worse for wear. But when Hutcheon asked Dad if he was interested in maybe having a go Dad said he never wanted to hear the word gold again.

Then one day a clapped-out Rugby one and a half ton truck sputtered noisily into camp. The exhaust silencer had ruptured, the mudguards shook like wet dogs over every bump and it was down on one wheel from a de-tempered spring. Out of this heap of smoky scrap clambered a fattish bloke in his twenties who looked as if he needed as much attention as his *gharry*. Dusty, sweaty and freshly sunscorched, he looked as if he'd just fitted himself out in a dude's Mowgli-green safari suit from one of the cheaper Nairobi emporiums, which as it transpired was exactly what he had done. He asked someone where Dad was and, finding him, walked up with a pink hand outstretched.

'Ranulph Hudson-Doone,' he announced himself in lordly fashion.

Dad, who'd been writing at a table under the shade of the grove of trees where we used to eat, looked up and stared for a moment before getting up to shake hands. 'Howd'you do. Rider Quatermain. What brings you here?'

'I say, old chap, I have a letter of introduction from my

uncle Sir Ensor Doone,' he said, 'an old friend of yours, I gather?'

Dad jibbed perceptibly, startled by this caricature of a Pongo. He said afterwards that he thought it must be someone he knew, but momentarily didn't recognise, taking the piss. But in a moment he realised the apparition was definitely a stranger.

'Yes, I know Sir Ensor well,' said Dad, taking the proffered envelope.

The man they referred to as Sir Ensor was in fact Charles Doone, son of one Lord Doone, but known universally as Sir Ensor after the fallen aristocrat in Blackmore's *Lorna Doone*, whom he was considered to resemble in character as well as looks. The nickname was so pervasive that few people actually knew it to be such and if a stranger had enquired after Charles Doone, it's doubtful that anyone would have known who was being referred to. Its possessor considered it flattering rather than derisory and had long adopted it himself and, in keeping with the spirit of things, had named his Wanjohi Valley farm, Glen Doone. Sir Ensor was one of Kenya's many so-called remittance men; bourgeois or aristocratic sons and brothers and cousins whose characters like Dorian Grey portraits were deemed to be predestined to a progressive and irreversible degeneracy that would inevitably expose their families to intolerable embarrassment. Their knavery ranged from plain uselessness to outright criminality; but whatever their specific shortcomings, the families had rid themselves of their problem children by transporting them to the colonies and making sure they stayed there by remitting enough money to pay their debts and court fines, support their illegitimate children and generally hush them up. It was a splendid custom that populated the highlands of Kenya with many colourful and often likeable if deplorable cads and bounders of whom Sir Ensor was archetypal. He lived with the scullery maid he had impregnated on the billiard table in his father's stately home while still at school. With the maid he had sired three daughters and with the maid's sister, who had rashly spent a holiday at Glen Doone, a fourth. These four girls were renowned for the promiscuity that everyone agreed showed them to be chips off the old block, a characteristic that led to them being collectively known as the Woodchip Kids.

Sir Ensor arranged his deplorable life around his two abiding interests of wanton entertainment and feckless gambling. He was an obsessive poker player and a member of a group of like-minded veranda farmers, professional hunters and plain ordinary wasters, not all remittance men, but all of similar character, whose dissolute lives created the notorious Happy Valley legend of the twenties and thirties. The infamous valley was the Wanjohi Valley of the Kinangop, where Glen Doone was located. Rider and Hutcheon often called in at Glen Doone on their periodic journeys to Nairobi. Quite often they never made it to Nairobi at all, depending on who else happened to be there at the time and how involved they got in the parties and gambling sessions. Sir Ensor was a natural buffoon who loved to play the goat and was forever devising practical jokes to play on his friends and guests. There was a memorable occasion when Dad and Hutcheon happened to call in at Glen Doone just as a number of guests arrived to attend a particularly lavish party that Sir Ensor had organised. Quite by chance they walked into the house behind a group of people that included Lord Delamere, Lord Erroll, Baron von Blixen and one or two other nobles. Sir Ensor stood at the entrance to his living room as if it was a stately ballroom, loudly announcing lord this and baron that as each person entered, finishing up with 'Sir Rider Quatermain and Sir Hutcheon Graham.' He'd paused as Dad and Hutcheon strolled into the room and then loudly added, 'Methinks twill not be long ere miladies' vaginas start fluttering like cormorants' throats and milords' trigger fingers begin twitching like shed geckos' tails.'

Dad opened the envelope that Sir Ensor's nephew had given him and drew out a letter that read as follows.

My Dear Sir Rider,

   I hope you won't mind my taking the liberty of introducing my nephew, young Ranulph to you. He recently took an MA in Social Anthropology from Oxford and has come out to Kenya to work on his dissertation for a doctorate that will shed new and astounding light on the ancient mystery of the hitherto baffling disappearance of the great Meroë nation nearly two millennia ago – something that we will all be on tenterhooks to learn, I have no doubt. His professor tells me that he is something of a dab hand at anthropology who shews, as well, a nimble and imaginative aptitude for a variety of other pursuits.

   Knowing you to be an exceptional student of human nature yourself, and recalling that you are fluent in the Galla tongue among several others and recognising that there is unlikely to be anyone who knows the N.F.D. as well as you do, I am of the certain opinion that Ranulph should make your acquaintance as the essential first step towards familiarising himself with his prospective study area and the particular challenges he may expect to encounter there.

   I am taking a liberty, I know, making such an imposition on your time without prior notice, but I am confident that we are good enough friends to occasionally take such liberties. I recall that on your last visit up-country to refresh yourself in our cool highland air you mentioned that the trials and tribulations of the last few years had conspired to deprive you of both the four-legged and two-legged creatures from which you normally glean a hard-won living. I take it, therefore, that you are reading this letter whilst relaxing under a shady kameeldoorn tree as I believe they are called, gin and tonic at your elbow, butler within easy calling distance and nothing much to distract you until the time comes to rise and dress for

171

dinner. Forgive me if I have perchance misjudged things. Should that prove to be the case you will put me straight, I have no doubt, when next you come to lay waste to the players not to mention their consorts at our humble card table.

Both I and my elder brother, Hector, Ranulph's pater, will be eternally grateful for any assistance you may be pleased to give to this promising young fellow as he sets out on the dawn of his career to unravel some of the more arcane anthropological mysteries of the great Galla nation. I have lent him one of my carriages and an old ex-army .303 that, whilst its rifling may now be largely inferred rather than demonstrated, and its action not as tight as it was in the days of its virginity, may yet serve to protect him from the attentions of those lords of the jungle that may not necessarily accord him the respect due to the scion of one of England's noble families.

I remain respectfully yours,
Sir Ensor Doone
April 1st, 1932

The subject of the letter was standing watching Dad as he read it so that for the time being Dad kept a straight face and simply folded the letter and replaced it in its envelope.

'Sit down, Ranulph,' he said, 'and I'll call for my business partner, Hutcheon Graham. You should meet him, too.'

When Hutcheon came, Dad got up and walked a few paces to intercept him. He thrust the letter into Hutcheon's hand and whispered, 'Read this. That bastard Doone thinks he's *so* bloody funny. He's going to pay for this, the *kants.*'[47]
Hutcheon read the letter and a grin spread over his face. But he managed to control himself and came and met the newcomer.

The introduction done, Hutcheon eyed Ranulph's newly

---

[47] Literally, hermaphrodite dog. Highly derogatory epithet (Somali).

made dude safari suit with unabashed amusement. 'Where did you get that *lekker* suit, man?'

'I say, it's smashing, isn't it? It was a place in Government Road,' said Ranulph, 'the Nairobi Emporium. Do you know it?'

'*Ja*, I know it,' said Hutcheon. 'This your first trip to Africa, ay?'

'Yes – I flew out two weeks ago on the Imperial Airways flying boat and then took the train from Kisumu. My uncle met me in Nairobi and helped me get organised to start my field work for my dissertation. Are those Oromo people that I saw on the way here?'

'No, no – they'd have been Samburu, probably. Quite unrelated to the Galla. The Samburu are Nilo-Hamites – quite different. Different language and society. You won't see any Galla this far west. But you must know all that?'

'A bit, yes. I've read everything I can find on the Oromo and the people around them. There's not that much, really, I suppose because they mostly live in such remote places. I have Arnold Hodson's book on the Oromo language – do you know it?'

'Yes,' said Dad, 'I know Arnold himself quite well. It's a handy book to start you off with. We had to teach ourselves to speak *afaan* Oromo as Arnold hadn't even got to Ethiopia when Hutcheon and I first started moving around this part of the world. It's a pretty easy language, though.'

Dad's soft heart of course resulted in Ranulph being invited to stay for a bit while he planned his first trip among the Galla of the N.F.D. The fact that Sir Ensor had taken the opportunity to have a laugh at Dad and Hutcheon's expense could be attended to later, and of course, they thought it quite funny themselves. But then Dad started to get interested in what Ranulph had come to do, in spite of his own reservations and Hutcheon's overtly expressed ones.

'Tell him to v*oetsek*, Rider,' said Hutcheon. 'A *pampoen* like that belongs in Pongoland, balancing teacups. We haven't got time for noble savage *fundis*.[48] He'll be trouble, man, mark my words. He's another bloody lion with thorns in his feet – leave 'em where they are, man.'

'You're just jealous of his safari suits,' Dad would retort, though he too must have seen the soggier aspects of Ranulph's character just as Hutcheon did. But, whereas Hutcheon always took people and things as he found them, and reacted accordingly, Dad was forever expecting something better in people and what they did. It was the difference between them and no doubt an integral element of their enduring friendship – the admiration of the one for the quality of the other missing in himself.

Although Dad had systematically dismissed all mention of things gold for the last few years, Ranulph's anthropological mission unexpectedly reawakened it. This came about, undoubtedly, by virtue of the seemingly unrelated nature of the anthropology of the Oromo and Suleiman's gold. Any direct reference to gold Dad had come to reject outright, almost as a reflex. Deep in his subconscious, though, the old fascination was still there, dormant but intact like a lungfish in the dry season, waiting for the right signal to reincarnate. Dad was always far too much of a lyrical dreamer for something as unequivocally romantic as the legend of King Solomon's mines to be permanently repressed. It was bound to worm its way back into his conscious mind sooner or later.

The link, the stimulus that brought the subject of Suleiman's gold out of aestivation in Dad's mind, was the Galla. Up on the Kenya–Abyssinia border the people are all Galla – the Borana and Gabbra of the greater Oromo nation. The area of Solomon's Triangle is in fact the Gabbra heartland.

---

[48] Expert (Swahili)

174

As you go further into Abyssinia you enter the territory of the Boran, considered by many Oromo to preserve the nation's traditions in their most original form, who rub shoulders with the many other Galla people living on the east side of the Rift Valley. So it came as no surprise, really, that the more Dad talked to Ranulph about his project the more he started to think that it might just shed some light on the mystery of Suleiman's gold. Perhaps if this anthropologist dug deep enough into the collective memory of the Galla he might unearth some hint of an ancient mine. It was just possible. Quite apart from all that, Dad was also genuinely interested in people and had always had a particular liking for the Galla. They had nothing of the drive to violence and plunder that seemed so deeply ingrained in the Somali psyche. They were true nomads absolutely bound to their livestock and lived with a demonstrable and impressive satisfaction in their harsh, dry land. They had no sense of the other side being greener – not that green was a colour they saw much of in their near-desert land – and always expressed an innocent devotion to their traditional lands. This was in such contrast to the other people of the region, the Somalis, who seemed so dissatisfied with their lot, always itching to move into new lands and in so doing fall upon the inhabitants like starving hyenas. And such beautiful people, too, the Oromo. To see the Hamer people of south-western Ethiopia is to witness a physical beauty that has no like. Their copper-red complexion seems actually alight, it's so lustrous, and their classical figures are as perfect to the western eye as anything ever sculpted in ancient Greece or Rome. Such beauty is all the more striking when encountered in such a harsh, unremittingly dry and difficult land as the Rift Valley floor between Lake Rudolf and the Ethiopian highlands.

It was Ranulph's research topic that sealed the matter. When Dad had asked what he was proposing to study for his doctorate he'd replied. 'My thesis is "*Does Oromo oral history provide evidence for a Meroitic ancestry of the modern nation? A comparative analysis.*"'

'*Meroitic* ancestry? I'll be damned – are you suggesting the Oromo came from the old Kingdom of Kush, from Meroë?'

'Yes – it's my professor's pet theory. He's convinced that the Meroë empire didn't just vanish without a trace in 400 AD after it was allegedly overrun by the Axumites, as received opinion has it. He believes they retreated southwards down the western edge of the Abyssinian swell and that the modern Oromo nation developed from the survivors of that catastrophe.'

'Phew,' said Dad, 'that's quite a theory. The mysterious Madanle were none other than the Kush. Not impossible, I grant you – but what about the writing? The Kush had a highly developed cursive script and alphabet, every bit as sophisticated as that of ancient Egypt. On top of that, it seems most Kush could read and write – not just a few priests. But the Galla are completely illiterate as a nation. Why would they survive, but not their written language?'

'Oh, I think that's easily explained,' said Ranulph. 'If a civilisation is completely overrun by a conquering horde it's the very young and the very old that get killed outright. The survivors will be those young adults that are nimble enough to escape. It's the older folk who are the most skilled in such things as writing – and they don't survive. The survivors have no use for writing if they've been displaced from where the ability to write is utilitarian and understood by others. So they'd soon lose the knowledge because it's no longer valuable.'

Of course, this suggestion that the Oromo were the survivors of a once great civilisation that rivalled the Ancient Egyptians was just the sort of romantic notion that Dad adored. On top of which, there was the fact that the Kush dealt in gold.

Kush – later Nubia – began at the Ancient Egyptian frontier at Aswan on the First Cataract of the Nile. The country south to the Second Cataract was Wawat, the scene of endless conflict between Egypt and Kush because of the two long eastern wadis – Allaqi and Gabgaba – along which lay a string of gold mines. None were really big, but over the millennia they yielded a significant proportion of the gold amassed by the pharaohs, for the Kush traded all their gold with Egypt. The ancient Egyptians mined gold from more than a hundred places in the eastern desert of Egypt between the Nile and the Red Sea, but supply never met the pharoahs' demand. As long as the Kush retained control of the eastern desert south of Egypt as far as the Ethiopian swell – where the Abyssinians held sway – they were assured of a steady revenue from the gold that the pharaohs could never get enough of. As well as the famous wadis of Allaqi and Gabgaba there were dozens of other places in the eastern desert where the Kush mined gold. Like the Egyptian mines at El Sid and elsewhere to the north, these were never big sources. In the beginning, at the start of the great Egyptian civilisation, they may have found large deposits of placer gold; history doesn't say. But if they did, it was soon picked up, after which they laboriously chipped away at the many exposed seams, ground the ore and riddled and melted the gold out of the dust.

What is specially intriguing, though, is what the Kush did about the gold of the Ethiopian swell. On the northern rim of the swell – Eritrea – there are several large gold mines. Down the long western edge there are several other quite large sources. These are much richer sources than the modest though numerous mines of the eastern desert. They were well known to the ancients, and historians variously allude to their exploitation by the Egyptians, the Kush and the Abyssinians. The rather ambiguous record probably reflects a constantly shifting pattern of control depending on the relative power of the three nations at any given moment. We shall never know how this ebbed and flowed over the immense span of time involved: some five thousand years. It seems, though, that for the first three millennia of this period the gold of the Ethiopian swell was controlled by Egypt through the intermediary of the Kush and their predecessors. It wasn't until the invasion of Abyssinia by Semitic people two thousand years ago, and the subsequent evolution of the Axumite people, that Egyptian domination of this gold was seriously challenged. It wasn't long after this that history, in this case unequivocally, records the remarkably abrupt disappearance altogether of the Meroitic Kush. Almost overnight they simply vanished. That the remnants of this once great people found their way south to found the modern Oromo nation is indeed a plausible and undeniably romantic notion.

Thus it was that in spite of Ranulph's unprepossessing appearance and manner, at least to men like Hutcheon and Dad who were instinctively uneasy with his affected Pongo speech, his dude dress and his blundering about the countryside, Dad went out of his way to help him. He hired a Boran man to help Ranulph find his way, act as turney-boy[49] for his *gharry* and help him to learn Oromo. As soon as Ranulph was more or less fitted out and operational, Dad drove with him across the Chalbi Desert up to North Horr and on into Gabbra territory. There he introduced him to a Gabbra family that Dad knew well and generally did all sorts of things to smooth his way and get him started a lot sooner than had he been on his own. Ranulph seemed

---

[49] Driver's offsider. Before electric starters, car and truck engines were hand-started by turning with a starting handle.

grateful for all Dad's help and guidance and sought his views and opinions on all that concerned the people of the N.F.D., especially their history and customs. So, while it could not be said that a friendship was established, a pleasant acquaintanceship was set up that Dad put no little effort into. Once settled in, Ranulph got into his work and began spending a month or two months at a time with the Gabbra before coming down to Rumuruti for supplies. When he did, he would always come up to Luoniek to meet up with Dad and discuss his experiences up north.

I suppose it was about six months after Ranulph appeared on the scene that Hutcheon was talking one day to some Samburu up near Barsaloi where he sometimes bought cattle. Notwithstanding the droughts and locusts there were a few cattle available and Hutcheon was busy trying to settle a price. The men enquired about Ranulph, asking Hutcheon if he knew about this *mzungu* who was writing down all sorts of twaddle about the Gabbra who were known liars and why did he waste his time with savages? Why did he want to know about the customs of such people as the Gabbra? Surely, if he wanted to know such things he would ask the Samburu? Hutcheon tried to explain what Ranulph was doing; but of course, it meant little to his interlocutors in whose world such things as anthropology and sociology were not relevant and therefore incomprehensible subjects. But as the conversation progressed Hutcheon began to wonder a little at what was going on. The Samburu seemed more than usually interested in Hutcheon's business, asking him all sorts of questions about where he took their cattle after buying them, how much he sold them on for, what he did with his money, and so on. Eventually it all came out. One of the younger Samburu asked Hutcheon if he knew what Ranulph had been telling them, the Samburu, about cattle trading. He told Hutcheon that Ranulph had been advising many Samburu that they should not sell their cattle to Hutcheon and Dad because they were cheating them. At first Hutcheon pooh-poohed the story, seeing it as just a normal ploy in the endless haggling process. Most of the people from whom they bought cattle enjoyed far more the wheeling and dealing than the actual money they got, and they were always coming up with sometimes quite creative tactics for gaining some advantage over him in negotiations. So Hutcheon dismissed the story as humbug, an attempt at common or garden *fitina*[50] But the Samburu man was adamant and others claimed to corroborate his intelligence.

At all events, Hutcheon relayed the information to Dad in due course, who, like Hutcheon, thought it must just be *fitina*. All the same, the next time Ranulph passed by our place Dad found an opportunity to raise the matter.

'I was up in the Barsaloi area a while back, trading cattle with the Samburu. Met a young fellah by name of Sokot who said he knew you.'

'Sokot,' mused Ranulph, 'doesn't ring a bell. From Barsaloi, you say?'

'He was sure he knew you, said you'd been talking to him about cattle traders,' said Dad.

'Cattle traders? No way – sounds like a story to me.'

'We thought at the time that he was probably talking shit,' said Dad, 'because on this occasion the Samburu spent bloody days haggling over the *goi-goi 'gombi*[51] they were trying to palm off on us. Most cattle – even the best – are pretty poor these days, but half of what they were trying to dump were so *goi-goi* they would never fatten, whatever you did to them. So what this bloke Sokot was saying sounded like just another attempt to get at us and improve the price.'

'Why,' asked Ranulph, 'what was he saying?'

---

[50] Intrigue, discord (Arabic, Swahili)
[51] Sickly cattle (Swahili)

A SNAKE STORY

'You won't want to hear,' said Dad, watching Ranulph closely as he spoke.

'I say – tell me, I want to know.'

'They said you'd advised them not to trade cattle with me and Hutcheon, because we were cheats.'

Ranulph sat up in his seat with a start. 'I say – what tosh! I've never said any such thing to anybody.'

'Must say, I was inclined to put it down to shit-stirring all along,' said Dad.

'I can't think why else they'd come up with such bloody tripe,' said Ranulph. 'There's certainly no truth in it. Very mischievous of the Samburu to spread such slander about.'

Dad told Hutcheon what had transpired and that Ranulph seemed genuinely astonished at the Samburu's allegation. 'But you can't help wondering, ay,' said Hutcheon, 'why the Samburu would want to make *chiqachiq*[52] between us and Ranulph. It'd make sense if he was a competitor, try and play the two of us off against each other.' Dad shrugged his shoulders. 'Just a naïve way of trying to make us feel bad about the price we're offering. Not that any of them are naïve when it comes to trading.'

The months passed and they saw less and less of Ranulph as he got to know the people and country and learnt how to organise things for himself. Then one day while Hutcheon was working on their business accounts with Patel, their accountant, the latter let slip a strange remark. 'So you are getting new competition in the cattle business, isn't it?'

'Not that I know of,' said Hutcheon.

'Oh yes, definitely. That young fellow from Pongo-side, the one they call "I Say" – he is selling the cattle, you know.'

Hutcheon gaped. 'Serious?'

'Oh yes, serious, man. That Somali fellow, Hassan Omar, he is telling me.'

---

[52] Intrigue, discord (Oromo)

181

'You must be confusing him with someone else – although for that matter I hadn't heard of anyone new in the business, let alone Ranulph.'

'Not confusing, man – that fellow "I say" – he is selling the cattle. I'm definitely certain, man.'

Well, it transpired that Patel was right to be 'definitely certain'. Hutcheon started asking around and eventually discovered that Ranulph had sold two lots of cattle over the past two months, cattle he'd bought from the Samburu. All of a sudden, the allegation of bad-mouthing that the Samburu had made some seven or eight months ago began to add up to a true story. When Dad heard the news, he at first just couldn't believe it. 'You sure, Hutcheon? This can't be true, man.'

'S'true's God, ay. I've checked it out and there's no doubt about it. He sold at least two mobs of *gombi* in the last couple of months. That half-Somali bloke, Hassan Omar, he took them. You know the bloke that buys for that group of ranchers? I tackled him myself and he was quite open about it. Said he assumed I must know, was surprised when I said I didn't.'

'But you know how the little sod accuses us of exploiting the *watu* when we buy cattle. The last time he was in camp he really got up me on that subject.'

'I know.'

'So how come he's into cattle trading? Doesn't add up, man.'

'Beats me. But I can tell you it's a fact, ay. No word of a lie.'

The realisation that Ranulph was double-crossing him really hurt Dad. Hutcheon was more philosophical, saying he wasn't surprised; he'd taken him for a shifty little bastard all along. But Hutcheon had never got to know Ranulph or been at all friendly with him, whereas Dad had.

'If you want to really screw someone, first become his

friend, ay. You'd be the first to spout that at me,' said Hutcheon. 'I'm not pretending I really saw this coming, but unlike you it doesn't surprise me. By taking the thorn out of his foot of ineptitude and ignorance you felt you were being friendly; he, like the proverbial lion, forgot the thorn and began to feel his appetite coming back . . .'

Dad was silent for a while. 'I've got to get to the bottom of this. I suppose I know you're right, but all the same, I find it hard to believe someone you've gone so far out of your way to help and befriend can be so two-faced.'

'He's a fucking snake, Rider. Crawled out from under a stone, ay. Hatched with his moral belly already on the ground – can't get lower. He's bad news, man. Just have to hope he plays one dirty trick too many and provokes someone to *twanga*[53] him one dark night . . .' Hutcheon flicked his hand to snap his fingers in emphasis and wandered off, leaving Dad to himself.

He brooded over the matter for days and, as he was so prone to do, got quite depressed. Eventually he decided to take off to find Snake, as he had begun to call Ranulph, and confront him over the matter. Snake, however, had apparently gone back to England for a while and it was a couple of months before Dad finally caught up with him. During that time, Dad had been down to Nairobi on business and ran into Sir Ensor one evening in the bar of Torr's Hotel. Dad lost no time in bringing his friend up to date on the unfolding story of Snake. Sir Ensor had long ago tried to make amends for directing Snake to Dad in the first place, explaining how he'd thought it would be a great practical joke to foist his asinine nephew onto Dad for a bit. He'd supposed that the joke would end there with young Ranulph moving on; or as he'd supposed would more likely be the case, giving up and returning to England. He was as

---

[53] Hit repeatedly; literally, thresh grain with stick (Swahili)

angry as Dad when he heard about the cattle trading treachery and told Dad how he, too, had suffered a bit of snakebite. The old Rugby car and the rifle he'd loaned to Ranulph for his first trip up north had always been just that: loans. On his arrival in Nairobi Ranulph had told Sir Ensor that his grant money had not yet been transferred to Kenya, but that as soon as it arrived he would sort out his own transport, and return Sir Ensor's loaned items to him. 'Promised me faithfully, the little swine, and I took him at his word. Should've known my own flesh and blood better. D'you know what the prick said when I finally lost patience and asked when he was going to return my car and gun?'

'What'd he say?'

'"I say, old boy, that car was in pretty rough shape, you know."

'"That's what I told you when I lent it to you. Get you up to Rumuruti all right, but it's well past its heyday and you'll have to sort yourself out with your own *gharry* right away."

'"I've had to invest a lot of money in that old heap,' the blighter says, 'I reckon by now I've more than paid for it."

'Well,' as you can imagine, 'I was staggered. "Paid for it? You haven't paid me for it."

'"Oh but I have, when you think about it. The money I spent you would've otherwise have had to spend. Financially, you've done quite well out of it, really, because it's cost me more than its market value. By rights, you should be paying me to keep it."

'I lost my temper then and sent the little fart packing. I saw from his demeanour that he was one of those people who lack a conscience – they just don't have one and despise it in others as a weakness. Unable to feel remorse, too – just don't have whatever it is in the soul that generates remorse. I may myself be a species of rascal – there's many who think so – but I don't lie or cheat or let the side down. Play the game, even if the game's a bit dubious in the eyes of polite society. But sods like that – they start off lying to themselves and once they've swallowed their own bullshit they really can't see the lie any more. There's something missing in their make-up, something that makes it impossible for them to sense another person's feelings. They know *about* the feelings – just can't sense them. Everything is expressed in practical terms; they never judge things as good or bad, right or wrong. Simply as plus or minus, available or unavailable, useful or useless. It's one of the defining characteristics of what we label criminal. If he was a dog he's the sort that would have to be put down.'

'He is a dog,' said Dad. 'He's a bloody *kants.* If the Boran were better Moslems they'd stone him.'

Not long after this Dad caught up with Snake one day near Laisamis on the Marsabit road. Dad lost no time in demanding to know the truth behind the rumours that Ranulph was trading cattle. Somewhat to his astonishment, Ranulph admitted that the story was true – in point of fact, he acted quite annoyed, as if Dad was prying.

'Not that it's really any business of yours, Rider, but yes, I do trade cattle from time to time. Why do you ask?'

Dad was astonished at his snooty manner. This callow Pongo twit, who just a year ago had to be taught not to piss into wind, was now looking down his swinish snout at Dad and his impertinent questions, his little, close-set eyes swivelling from side to side.

'Why do I ask? Because not long ago you had the fucking nerve to accuse me of exploiting the *watu* by buying their cattle. What's your game, ay?'

'I say, old boy, keep your hair on. There's a world of difference between what you and I do.'

'Too fucking right there is – more of a difference than you will ever grasp, that much is sure.'

'Don't know what you mean by that, old boy, but you seem to have got yourself worked up about something. What's the matter?'

Dad told us afterwards that the desire to put a bullet through Snake's ear absolutely consumed him for a while, so much so that he had to turn away and make a real effort to control himself. 'Thanked my lucky stars I didn't have a gun handy – I swear I would've given him the bullet, the arrogant little shit.'

'Look, Ranulph,' said Dad, 'don't overdo it. Just explain why it's okay for you to buy cattle, but not me.'

'I say – think I see what's eating you, old boy.' said Ranulph. 'You must know that I'm not buying cattle on my account?'

'No I don't know. On whose account, then?'

'If you'd made a few enquiries before blurting out at me like this you'd know that I buy and sell cattle on behalf of the true owners – the Samburu and Boran. Unlike you, I do it for them, not for myself.'

His supercilious manner was aggravating Dad almost unbearably, but he managed to contain himself.

'How very high-minded,' said Dad, 'but what's the difference? I pay them, you pay them. As far as they're concerned it comes to the same thing.'

'Not the same thing at all, old boy. You do it to profit yourself by their industry – it's what imperialism is all about, the strong exploiting the weak. You're nothing but a colonial overlord. A hundred years ago you'd have been trading slaves.'

'Go on.'

'I don't buy the people's cattle. I sell them on their behalf. They get the full worth of their cattle.'

'The last mob of cattle you sold on their behalf – how much did you pay them?'

'I say, that's confidential information, old boy. I'd have to get the people's permission to divulge private information like that. Not for me to talk about such things, wouldn't you agree?'

'No I wouldn't. Everybody knows what I pay. I can easily enough find out what you paid. If you won't tell me I must assume that either you paid them a poor price or got yourself a high profit margin.'

'I say, old boy, you don't understand, do you? I take nothing for myself, nothing at all. All the money I sell the cattle for goes to the owners of the cattle.'

'So you're telling me you do this out of the goodness of your heart?'

'If you want to put it that way – yes.'

'You take no money for yourself, no fee, no commission, nothing?'

'That's right – nothing.'

Dad recalled how he looked at Ranulph as he said this, and thought to himself that he must be lying.

'His eyes give him away,' said Hutcheon. 'I tell you, man, they swivel faster when he's lying.'

'I remembered what you said about that,' said Dad, 'and I watched closely. But I couldn't see any difference. Maybe you can – I believe it – but I just can't see the difference. They swivel all the time.'

Dad went on to tell Ranulph that he had helped him when he first arrived because he'd told Dad he was here as a social anthropologist and Dad had taken him at his word. If Dad had known that he was planning to spoil his business he would never have assisted him. He told Ranulph that what he was doing was unethical and little short of deceitful. Ranulph retorted that things change, business was business and for Dad, an imperialist exploiter, to invoke ethics was absurd. They parted on bad terms, at least as far as Dad was concerned. Snake, he said, acted as if nothing untoward had happened and that Dad was being unreasonable and angry because his lucrative racket was exposed.

Dad was angry and not a little hurt by Snake's treachery, but he probably wouldn't have pursued the matter had it ended there. Hutcheon told him to forget it, Snake wouldn't be around for that long and when all was said and done the *watu* themselves by all accounts didn't like him. Dad usually took Hutcheon's advice about people and after a while he seemed to let the matter of Snake die a natural death. But it didn't die.

13

Scotching the Snake

One day a while after Dad's confrontation with Ranulph concerning the latter's entry into the cattle trade Hutcheon was reckoning up his and Dad's account with Hassan Omar, the buyer with whom they did business from time to time. Hutcheon took the opportunity to ferret out some information. He asked Hassan how much he'd paid Ranulph for the cattle he'd bought from him, whether he'd got them for less than he normally paid Hutcheon. Hassan had said that he'd paid the same price. He'd tried, he said, to pay less, but Ranulph it seems knew what he usually paid Dad and Hutcheon and insisted on getting the same. Hassan knew N.F.D. cattle well and said they'd been typical Samburu stock, most likely, he thought, originating from the Maralal or Wamba area. Hutcheon decided to make a cattle buying safari in that area himself during which he could perhaps find out who Ranulph had bought his cattle from.

It didn't take Hutcheon long to run down the source of Ranulph's livestock purchase and when he did he lost no time in finding out what the Samburu sellers had been paid by Ranulph. And, just as he was certain would be the case, it was considerably less than what Hassan said he'd paid Ranulph. In fact, they complained bitterly to Hutcheon that they'd been paid a lot less than promised and what was Hutcheon going to do about it? This Ranulph was *mzungu* like Hutcheon, they said, and with a certain undeniable logic that meant in their eyes that Hutcheon by association of race was partly responsible for the raw deal. Hutcheon always said that Ranulph's assertion that he paid the original owners what he got from Hassan, that he was doing the trade solely for the Samburu's benefit, was bound to be a lie. 'From the moment he tapped up in camp that day in his dude outfit and Pongo-posh talk I knew he was a phoney, ay. Stood out like a vervet's scrotum, ay.'

The confirmation of Hutcheon's suspicions didn't come as any surprise to Dad though he probably nursed a secret wish that it wasn't so, that somewhere in Snake's character there was at least a hint of a redeeming feature. For Hutcheon it was cut and dried; the man was a shit, a two-timing *kants* that even a snake eagle wouldn't soil his beak on. But Dad as ever wanted his emotional investment so to speak to generate some worthwhile return, something that justified his effort and goodwill; something that matched his commitment to what was right and proper. But Snake was yet another disillusionment in Dad's life, another gra-tuitous kick from behind, another example of the folly of pulling thorns out of lions' feet. And, as Hutcheon remarked, snakes shed their skins from time to time to freshen up. Shiny and gleaming in the sunlight, all the ticks and tatty bits shaken off, they get all frisky and keen, anxious to make a new start. 'But,' said Hutcheon, 'it's still the same poisonous snake, ay, same appetites, same morals. The gleaming eye of the cobra,' here he laughed sardon-ically, 'is still as cold and heartless as it ever was.'

'Bloody hell, Hutcheon, you've been reading my books again. Go on like that and you'll be reciting poetry next.'

'Sooner or later he'll shed his skin, ay, and when he does we better watch our steps.'

Hutcheon was seldom wrong about people and as it turned out, he wasn't wrong about Snake.

During the lean years when cattle and safari clients were

really thin on the ground, Dad and Hutcheon had supplemented their income from time to time by selling a few wild animals to zoos and private collectors. They didn't try to get into the large animal business apart from a few of the easier beasts like cheetahs, servals, and caracals but concentrated mainly on a few species of birds – the eagles and falcons and finches that always found a ready market. They did it in a small way and only when their usual business dried up. But one bird in particular they did unusually well out of. In the southern highlands of Ethiopia, there grows an endemic species of juniper tree and associated with it is a rare bird that feeds on the juniper fruit. This bird, Prince Ruspoli's turaco, is as limited in its distribution as the juniper it depends on and living as it does in one of the remotest and least visited parts of Africa is a rare and exotic bird in the world of collectors. There are only about twenty species of turacos and plantain eaters in the whole of Africa. Although most are quite large, gaudy birds they're seldom seen because they live high up in dark forest trees. Prince Ruspoli's turaco is ranked by many enthusiasts as the most exotic of all turacos by virtue of its rarity.

Dad had remembered seeing Prince Ruspoli's turaco back in 1919 on his safari to Harar and in 1928 he came across them again while with a client hunting up near the Kenya–Ethiopia border. This client knew something of the bird fanciers' world and told Dad that a pair of young Ruspoli's would fetch a small fortune from the big collectors in Europe and America. They were camped north-east of the Huri Hills near Gara Dimptu where Dad knew an old Gabbra man, Dassen, who had been in his day a mighty hunter of elephant and rhino. He loved hunting and knew the country inside out so that Dad or Hutcheon always retained him as a guide when they took clients to that part of the N.F.D. Dad asked Dassen if he thought he could organise the capture of a few Ruspoli's turacos. Dassen said they were plentiful on the highlands round Mega thirty or forty miles to the north-east. He knew many of the Boran whose country that was and was sure he could work something out with them. This was well into Ethiopia, a fact that made the enterprise all the more enticing to Dad and Dassen, both natural poachers under the skin. So it was that Dad and Dassen put together a scheme whereby Dassen would arrange with the Boran he knew across the border in Ethiopia to locate some turacos' nests, keep them under surveillance and take the fledglings just before they were old enough to fly. Dad would then come north to pick up the birds. The arrangement worked well and the half dozen or so pairs of birds they managed to spirit overseas fetched more money than they made from all their other activities combined over the same period.

It was midway through 1934 when Dad once again set off for the border country to meet up with old Dassen and see if he could get hold of another pair or two of turacos. When he reached Dara Dimtu and located Dassen's kraal, he found the old man furious and quite distant. It took a while to get the story for Dassen seemed reluctant to tell Dad, acting as if he'd been insulted. What had happened to upset the old man so much was, for Dad, the final straw in the episode of Snake. A couple of months before, Snake had been carrying out his anthropological research in the area. Dassen knew Snake as Dad had advised Ranulph to contact him at the beginning of his research and he'd been a very useful and helpful contact. He was a respected Gabbra elder and freely gave Ranulph much invaluable information and eased his way among the Gabbra in all sorts of ways. But Snake had got wind of Dad's turaco scheme and the next thing Dassen knew was that Ranulph was acting in Dad's name. He said it had been agreed that he would take the next pair of birds on his behalf as Dad was unable to come himself. But when Dassen got the birds and told Ranulph they were ready to collect Ranulph refused to pay him, saying he would get his money from Dad in due course. He, Dassen, was very offended by all this. Dad had not bothered to inform him of these new arrangements and in the past they had always done business in a straightforward way. Dassen expected to be paid when he handed over the birds and Dad had always respected this understanding. Furthermore, this young man Ranulph had become very rude and disrespectful and he, Dassen, did not wish to do any further business with Dad if this was going to be the way of things. Ranulph it seems had taken to demanding the services of young Gabbra women when camped in the area and he, Dassen, and other elders were being treated as if they were pimps.

Dad of course was horrified and enraged. It took him some time and patience to convince Dassen of what had actually transpired, so offended had the old man become. Finally, he made his peace with Dassen, but it was clear that unless he saw to it that Ranulph kept well away from this part of the world he would make an enemy of Dassen and his people. Dad's mind was in turmoil all the way back to Luoniek. He toyed with the idea of physically manhandling Snake onto the flying boat in Kisumu, but he knew now that there was no skulduggery the reptile wouldn't stoop to in resisting such a move or continuing to make life a misery for him and Hutcheon. Simply ignoring him hadn't worked and wasn't going to work. He simply couldn't accede to the realisation that if people like Snake wanted to behave as he did there wasn't anything to prevent them. However wrong or bad such behaviour was, or frowned upon or deplored, it worked. If you didn't feel bad doing such things, if you weren't squeamish about them, then doing them was all too easy, and got easier the more used to doing them you became. If the perpetrator was indifferent to anger or censure he soon learned to ignore these reactions in victims. Quite often, the reactions themselves became pleasurable – human beings generally like to see victims squirm. There were only two potential remedies: the law and violence. The law was of no help to Dad because the law does not concern itself with treachery (except against the State) or gentlemen's understandings or ethics or any such nebulous things, whatever store may be set by them. And Dad had a deep-seated aversion to the law – it wasn't something he ever wished to employ.

Violence – well that was a bit like one of those big yellow and black hornets: a good bite, yes, but a sting at the other end too. Overt violence would only invoke the law against himself. And crude violence wasn't very long-lasting. Giving Snake a hiding would be immensely pleasurable – indeed, he'd day-dreamed about the administration of it several times – but the effect would soon wear off as it always does in the case of untrainable dogs, and only provoke Snake into worse outrages. The sense of powerlessness and the frustration it engendered was extraordinarily depressing and by the time Dad got back to Luoniek, he was very low.

We all spent considerable time going over the affair and trying to come up with a solution. We agreed on one thing: that something would have to be done. But what! Easy enough to agree that he had to be persuaded that messing us about wasn't worth it. But exactly what sort of persuasion? He wouldn't believe a verbal threat, however sinister. Roughing him up would be fun – maybe, though the thought was probably much better than the fact – but ineffectual. No, it had to be something more intellectual, something that would cause him to slither away of his own volition. No point in any sort of appeal to conscience, or to ethics or to anything that didn't threaten his own sense of well-being.

Having come to that conclusion, however, did focus Dad's mind and helped lift him out of the depressed state he'd got into. And I suppose it was not surprising that it was Dad, the emotional and creative one amongst us, who suddenly came up with what we all agreed was a truly brilliant way to scotch a snake. We were sitting round the fire one evening, drinking beer and shaving flakes of biltong (even Leila did this) when Dad yelled and jerked upright, just about falling out of his chair. We all thought exactly the same thing – that he'd been stung by a scorpion. Leila even jumped up squealing, 'Where did it get you?' But Dad paid her no attention, instead bellowing, 'I've got it, I've got it. I know how to teach Snake a lesson he'll never want repeated.'

'Listen everybody,' he said, 'I've got the perfect answer.'

He paused and Hutcheon impatiently demanded, 'C'mon, *jong*, spit it out. What's the answer?'

'Baobab owls,' said Dad, looking at us, grinning.

We all stared at him uncomprehendingly. 'What he hell is a baobab owl?' said Hutcheon. 'I never heard of a baobab owl, ay. You're talking *twak*, Rider, have another beer, man, and talk sense.'

We all knew our birds well enough to say with confidence that none of the leading twitchers had labelled any species of owl a baobab owl. So what was Dad on about?

'No,' said Dad, 'you *okes* never heard of the rare and wonderful baobab owl – nobody in the world has – but I recently discovered it. As from today, it's one of Kenya's rarest birds, harder to find than a finfoot. Hitherto it's been known only from Somaliland, but has recently been confirmed in the N.F.D. where it typically nests in baobab trees – hence its common name.'

'So what?' said Hutcheon.

'You'll see,' said Dad. 'You remember I said that during the night I spent next to that big baobab tree I noticed a pair of eagle owls going to and from it. In the morning, I couldn't see them in the tree – in any tree – and wondered where the hell their nest was. Ndaragus said it was probably inside the tree, that the tree was almost certainly hollow, old baobabs are always hollow. As you know, I'd stopped for the night there because a centre bolt had broken just before dark and the axle had begun to slew round. It was going to take a while to repair; everybody was wiped out and so we gave up and decided to fix it in the morning. So, the following day while the *watu* graunched the spring apart, I got Ndaragus to help me climb the tree and look inside. There was a commiphora growing right next to it that made it quite easy to get to where the tree's trunk ended and the branches radiated out. Sure enough, just as Ndaragus had surmised, the tree was hollow with a surprisingly small hole at the top, where the branches started. I peered in and shone my torch around. At first I saw nothing, no owls – just the inside surface of the tree, gleaming in the torchlight as if it was wet. Then I saw the owls. They were way down, at least ten feet below the entrance. It looked as if they were on a fold in the trunk that stuck out a few inches. Somehow they'd got a nest stuck in this little fold, just enough to hold a bunch of sticks and feathers. They had two eggs in the nest. A nesting pair of baobab owls – quite something in the twitchers' world, ay?'

'So you shot 'em and cooked 'em up for breakfast, ay. Is that the point of all this banana oil?' asked Hutcheon. Dad ignored him.

'I shone the torch around inside that tree and, hell, man, I got gooseflesh, ay. You know how smooth and slippery the trunk of a baobab is?' We all nodded. There's no way you can climb a big baobab seven or eight feet in diameter by shinning up the trunk. There are no branches until the trunk ends, it's mostly shiny smooth and the few knobs and lumps that occur are so slippery even a baboon can't do it.

'Well,' continued Dad, 'the inside is smoother and greasier still, because it's protected from the weather and animals. This particular tree was tall for a baobab – eighteen

196

feet or so – and very symmetrical. As I peered around, I thought how it looked like the inside of a huge bottle; how if you fell in you'd never get out again without help. The only foothold was the little fold where the nest was and it was way below the hole at the top. If you were alone . . .'

'We all stared at Dad for a bit as the implication of what he was saying gradually sunk in. Finally, Hutcheon exclaimed, '*God, jong,* Rider – so you're saying . . .' His eyes flashed and the most wicked smile spread across his face. 'Push the *kants* in and leave him to howl at the moon . . . *krars,* man, Rider – you really are a bloody *mokora,* ay.'

'No, no – we don't push the *kants* in. We trap him. Get him to sneak in of his own volition like a *nugu*[54] that thinks he's stealing your mealies when you aren't looking.'

'How the hell are you going to trap him? No *oke* is going to drop in there all by himself.'

'*As a dog returneth to his own vomit, so a fool returneth to his folly.* You know that old saying?' said Dad. We all shook our heads.

'He's a fool, he's a hermaphrodite dog as you reminded us, Hutcheon, and for sure he's about to engage in the folly of his life. We got all the ingredients. Now let's cook.'

'First, the bait. We need to get the story of the baobab owl fermenting in his thieving little brain. Piece of piss. I have to go to Nairobi anyway tomorrow or the day after. Whilst there I'll get one of those little printing businesses to knock up a fake reprint from *The Ostrich* – you know – that little twitchers' journal? I'll write an article by a certain Rider Quatermain describing the discovery of the rare Somaliland baobab owl nesting in a baobab in the N.F.D., giving the location of the tree, and so on. That'll be really easy. All we need to do is post it to ourselves in an envelope marked urgent, so it has a cancelled stamp. Don't stick the

---

[54] Monkey (Swahili)

flap down – just tuck it in so it can be easily opened and closed again. Then drop it in Snake's post box as if the post office put it there by mistake – as they often enough do in Rumuruti. No way he'll turn up the chance to look and see what it says. Without a shadow of doubt the scaly little *kants* will think he's on to a winner; a pair of baobab owls with eggs – must be worth a fortune, ay!'

We all agreed that Snake would jump at so fine a chance to stab us in the back.

'Next, we go to the tree and set the trap.'

'I don't know how you're going to do that, ay,' said Hutcheon. 'Sounds too complicated to me.'

'True – I haven't figured it all out yet, but there's got to be a way. We make a rope ladder up through the commiphora to the opening in the baobab trunk. That's easy. And it's easy to make a ladder leading into the hollow so as to take an egg or a fledgling bird from the nest. But how to seal the opening once he's inside . . . must say, I can't see a way to do that. Any ideas anyone? Must be possible, somehow.'

We all sat around and discussed it for a bit, tossing various unworkable suggestions around. Then it struck me.

'Forget sealing the entrance, Dad, there's another way to do it. Pull the ladder up once he's gone down it.'

They looked at me quizzically. 'You mean have someone hidden there who pulls it up after he's in? You'd have to hide there for days, surely . . .'

'No – some sort of automatic device that gets sprung as a result of his going in.'

'But what device, Alan?' asked Dad. 'I don't see where you're going; I've never come across anything like that.'

I admitted that I'd not thought it through, but as I mulled over the idea I began to see a way.

'When he's climbing down the ladder into the tree his weight has to pull some sort of trigger mechanism. I know

– do it like this. The ladder has to be tied to the tree at the top, obviously, but then pull it up a couple of inches, get some slack. Hold it up with a string that is attached via a trigger to a weight. When he gets on the ladder, it pulls down a bit, takes up the slack, and in so doing dislodges the trigger. As soon as he jumps off the ladder the weight, no longer held up by the trigger, falls, and pulls another string – attached to the bottom of the ladder – which pulls up the ladder.'

'You'll have to draw that for me,' said Dad, 'but it sounds bloody brilliant. I can see you aren't wasting *all* your time at school.'

I went off and made a drawing of what I had in mind and brought it back to show Dad. He was thrilled and we spent half an hour or so fiddling with the design until we reckoned we had it taped.

Dad was all fired up now and dead set on putting the snake trap into operation. He wrote the fake article for *The Ostrich* and left for Nairobi, saying he'd be back in about a week. While he was away, I was to drive out to the tree and set up the trap mechanism. I was to go alone as we didn't want anyone to know what we were up to in case, somehow, word leaked out to Snake.

He was, if anything, even more fired up when he got back to Luoniek. 'Had a bit of luck,' he said, 'A good omen, I reckon. When I checked the post in Rumuruti today there was an unsealed letter from Hyman (Hyman was Dad's lawyer in Nairobi) with an invitation to his daughter's wedding. The envelope had his business logo on it – perfect, ay? I just substituted the article for the invite and stuck it in Snake's post box. No way on earth he won't pry into a letter to me from a lawyer, ay!

'How d'you go setting up the trap, Alan?'

'Fine. It's ready to go. I had a good idea for the weight. I was worried that if we hung a rock or a log up in the tree and Snake saw it he would wonder how it got there and possibly spot the mechanism. So I got an old beehive made from rolled up bark and rammed a rock in the middle. Snake'll think it's just a beehive and pay no attention, I reckon.'

Dad wanted to see what I'd done so early next morning we drove out to the place and had a last look. Dad thought I'd done a great job setting it up and concealing the string from the ladder to the trigger, plus the other string from the bottom of the ladder to the weighted beehive. I'd positioned a lot of mostly superfluous rope that held the top of the ladder in place so that it hid the strings. The owls were there, blinking as we shone a torch inside the hollow tree for a last look round.

'Well, that's it,' said Dad. 'Now we wait for the snake to slither in. I'll check with the postmaster to find out when Snake next comes to check his mail. Then, when we know he's swallowed the bait, we'll come and check the trap once a week or so. That gives him anything up to seven days without food or water stewing inside the tree, by which time he won't be as full of shit – literally and metaphorically speaking – as he is now. Think he'd be about ready to have his fangs pulled, ay?'

It was a sobering thought as we drove back to Luoniek, Snake inside that tree wondering what was going to happen next. I asked Dad what in point of fact *was* going to happen after we had our reptile securely bottled up. 'Can't just leave him there forever, can we, Dad?'

'No, Alan, I guess not, much as I'd like to. Haven't figured out what we do. Depends on Snake, really. I guess we'll talk to him through the hole, find out just how much he values his life. But he has to be the one who gives in, obviously. Until I'm certain he's got the message and knows he has to fuck off forever – really forever – he stays there.'

It was a long drive back and we didn't get in until 3 a.m.

We headed straight for bed and sleepily agreed that a long lie-in tomorrow morning was next on the list of things to do.

Well, someone else it transpired was planning an early start for us and sometime just before dawn all hell broke loose.

14

The Unreliability of Men's Memories

I awoke slowly and reluctantly, vaguely aware that something was up. Then a rifle shot cracked, and another and yet more. All drowsiness gone I rolled out of bed, groping frantically underneath it for my rifle and then ran out to find Dad. He was yelling for me to join him and I ran towards his voice in the dark. 'Stay with me,' yelled Dad, 'for *krar's* sake don't separate.' Then two more shots went off and now I saw the flashes, close to each other, in the direction of where Abdullahi and the others slept. Then there came a lot of yelling and shouting and yet more shots. If we headed over there in the dark, we'd risk being shot by our own. Dad spoke rapidly. 'Go and switch the car lights on, Alan. I'll cover you. But duck and get back – don't for *krar's* sake stay near the car.' I raced over to the car, only yards away, reached through the window, turned on the lights and ran, crouching, back towards Dad. I saw his purpose – he'd realised the car was pointing towards the commotion over at Abdullahi's side of the camp and suddenly the area was partially illuminated. We both saw a man aiming a rifle, caught in the lights, who obviously wasn't one of us. Dad fired quickly and I too a moment later. The man dropped instantly and I remember his legs kicking a bit, but immediately my attention was drawn back to the camp. Shadowy figures were running everywhere it seemed, far too indistinct to risk shooting at. 'C'mon,' said Dad, 'round the back of the car.' We ran round and as we passed behind the direct line of the lights, a man ran fast through the light beam away from the camp towards the fringing trees. He carried a gun and I remember his *shuka* streaming behind him as he legged it. Dad's rifle followed his motion and when he fired the man fell headlong onto the ground, then he half got up, half fell again, crawling and running, and as he was getting up again we both fired and he dropped.

Suddenly it was silent, absolutely dead quiet. The whole scene seemed frozen, a still life of trees and bushes and tents and the fallen man dimly lit at the edge of the car lights' beam. There was no wind and the silence was weirdly complete, after the turmoil and din of a few moments back. Then Dad shouted in Oromo, 'Abdullahi, are you all right? What's happening?'

'We are all right,' he shouted back. 'I think they are gone.'

'Don't move yet,' shouted Dad. 'We wait and see if they are still there.'

We waited with the dawn light gradually turning the black to mauve then grey. A robin chat began to sing, indifferent to us and our rude treatment of the sunrise. Then Abdullahi started yelling to Dad that Osman was hurt.

'C'mon, run for it,' Dad said, 'and keep down.'

We ran, crouching, over to the other camp, towards Abdullahi's voice. The commotion was starting up again, it seemed to me, but no shots this time. Someone was shining a torch at a figure on the ground. Dad told me to keep a watch all round in case the attackers were still around, while he knelt and examined the figure on the ground.

'He's taken a bullet through the chest,' said Dad, 'right side, must be through his lung. At least the bullet's gone right through.'

Then Abdullahi found another wound in Osman's right

leg. 'We better move fast,' muttered Dad, 'he's badly hurt. If he doesn't get into hospital quickly, he'll die.' Osman was very limp and motionless, his eyes closed, obviously shocked and in a bad way. His breathing was quick and shallow, and with an ugly hoarse sound to it. We stopped the bleeding and got a comfortable litter made up to move him while a mattress was put in the back of the car.

While tending to Osman, Dad asked me what the blood was on my arm. I looked where he pointed and found a long graze on my left forearm, which until then I'd been unaware of. It was a narrow, superficial wound about three inches long. I thought I must've bumped into something during the commotion, but I couldn't recall doing so. Then Dad said he reckoned it was caused by a bullet and I suppose in retrospect that it was. While very proud, of course, to lay claim to an honourable wound I was secretly disappointed not to have had the much more satisfying experience of knowing what it was at the time and being able to capitalise on the excitement and danger of seeing a man shoot at me. But as long as Dad said it was a bullet wound I was happy: even when he added that it was just as likely caused by a friendly as a hostile bullet. No need to bring that up when telling other people about it.

What *was* disappointing when recalling the *shifta* raid was how quickly the whole thing was over. We'd talked about such things so many times in the past, reminding each other that raids were always possible and trying to anticipate what might happen should the day come when we were attacked. These discussions lasted much longer and covered many more eventualities than the affair itself when it did finally happen. Everything was over and done with so quickly that I had no time to feel any great emotion – certainly no sense of fear or dread or danger or any of the emotions normally associated with a real battle. The only lasting emotional memory was the anxiety over Osman.

Dad and I were gone within twenty minutes in Dad's Ford V8 hunting car with Osman on a couple of mattresses in the back and a man to nurse him. I spelled Dad with the driving and, going non-stop, we reached Nairobi about nine o'clock that night and got Osman into the emergency ward. As I was due back at school in a few days time Dad stayed down to see to that as well as see how things went with Osman. For quite a while it was touch and go for him, but he was young and healthy and tough, and he pulled through.

If one thing goes wrong it's not uncommon for another problem to arise at the same time – or so at least it seems to me. Leila had not been with us this school holidays, because she'd chosen instead to spend them with her best friend, Benta, the daughter of a professional hunter, Lars Olsen. Lars was one of Dad's and Hutcheon's drinking muckers when they descended on Nairobi, one of the original Kenya scandahooligans as the Danes and other Scandinavians were called. Whether their behaviour as a group was any more deplorable than that of the Pongo and other hunters isn't certain; but it is certain that they worshipped Bacchus and diligently observed the pagan rites of their ancestors. Lars' wife, Karen-Lise, was known as the Long Blonde Animal, feared by wives and fantasised about by husbands. A tall, slim, leggy woman who rippled when she moved like a sandsnake in the afternoon leaves, she would glide around a party room with the eyes of every man in it following her every undulation like mongooses. It was rumoured that she and Dad had been or were lovers. I tend to doubt it, because Hutcheon told me that Dad never loved any woman but my mother, though that didn't mean he was celibate. There were many whom Karen-Lise had taken as lovers according to folklore. She was the kind of seductive woman around whom rumours accrete like safari ants; but such rumours are of the same provenance as day-dreams and not necessarily spun from reality. She liked her reputation and did her bit to help keep the stories lively. Certainly she and Dad were close friends – but so was Lars, which made me sure that friends was all.

Their house was the scene of much carousing and playing of the goat and it transpired that Leila's choosing to spend the school holiday with Benta wasn't only because the two were close friends. It seems they both had other friends, boyfriends, and not just boyfriends but scandahooligan boyfriends; the worst kind. The night before we arrived in Nairobi with the wounded Osman, Benta's mother found the two girls in Benta's bedroom with their boyfriends whom they'd contrived to sneak into the house. When Dad went round to see Leila in the morning Karen-Lise told him what had happened. Privately, I suspect it only made Dad and Karen-Lise giggle, but publicly they made a scene of it, as they had to I suppose, as parents. In reality, it must have worried Dad who always fretted over the fact that Leila had no mother and that as a father he wasn't exactly a good model. Away for protracted periods, affectionate, but not very confiding, he expected both us kids to become adults at an early age, to assume a lot of responsibility ahead of our years and never to stuff-up or complain. Somehow, we were to be well behaved when both he and Hutcheon frequently were anything but. I know that he talked a lot to Leila about things in general following the boyfriend inci-dent, trying to figure out whether his nubile, twelve-year-old daughter was hiding some real and serious insecurity about her family that was going to present as teenage promiscuity. She wasn't, as it turned out, and she told me afterwards that she felt much guiltier about Dad's sense of guilt than she did about the boyfriend matter itself. They'd done it for the hell of it, the thrill, and when I vicariously tried to worm out of her the lurid (as I hoped so much they'd be) details of what they'd actually done with the enviable boys I ended up with a hard smack across the ear and no details. All this meant that when I got back to school I had hero status to an almost unimaginable degree. I lived the high life on it for a long time, as any thirteen-year-old Kenya hick would have, describing the fight with the *shifta*, my wound, Osman's wounds and the dead bodies – especially the dead bodies – in, I have to confess I suppose – a gradually exfoliating level of detail. When you are incessantly interrogated over the same thing by people with an insatiable appetite for sanguinary detail, it seems almost a duty to supply that detail, which, if missing from reality can be conjured up from virtual reality. And when the dawn battle with the *shifta* story was for the moment worked out there was always the story of my incredibly randy sister and her equally sex-starved mucker, caught, as the story almost immediately had it, actually poking – stark naked, mark you – in the middle of the night, all of them together in the same bed. There was little I could do to adjust the story or influence its evolution; but it added vastly to my already elevated status that I was the brother of this unbelievably lascivious dame. After a few weeks it got to the point where sweaty, hard-breathing hicks would ask me what it was like to 'poke a dame' on the muzzy assumption by association that what my sister allegedly did I did too, or at least knew all about. When your authority is absolute, it seems churlish not to live up to it. So, I painted as lurid a picture as I reckoned I could get away with. Heady days indeed.

It greatly helped my racontage that Dad kept me informed by letter of the aftermath of the *shifta* raid. The police of course were summoned and came to investigate and cart off the corpses. The assistant superintendent of police in charge was officious and somewhat condemnatory about the number of dead. It turned out that after Dad and I left with Osman the *watu* spent some time examining the tracks of the incoming and departing *shifta*. While doing so they came across a fourth body of one who'd been wounded and got some distance away before expiring. Of the seven men in the raiding party, only three had survived. There was also a blood spoor that showed at least one of these three to be wounded, though probably not seriously to judge by the speed with which he fled. The ASP made disparaging remarks to the effect that we were a bloodthirsty crowd of people and seemed unwilling to accept that, given the chance, the attacking *shifta* would undoubtedly have slaughtered the lot of us. As Hutcheon remarked, they hadn't come for early morning tea.

Dad and Hutcheon enjoyed a prickly relationship with the authorities that went back to the intervention by Rider Haggard many years before when they first settled at Luoniek. An instruction from Whitehall over the heads of the local authorities to more or less ignore Dad and Hutcheon and not put obstacles in their way was always going to be deeply resented – and it was. It meant that there was always some mongoose-faced functionary (pith helmet practically resting on his shoulders, as Hutcheon would say) on the look out for a breach of the law that could be used to give them a hard time. Although no charges had ever been brought, it was openly said that lack of evidence was the only reason for that. It was impossible to conduct the considerable ivory, rhino horn and leopard skin trading that they engaged in without people knowing about it. But catching them at it had eluded the game wardens and policemen of the N.F.D. who were often mocked by Dad's sympathisers for their failure to outwit those toerags Quatermain and Graham. So, a friendly visit from the police was never on the cards. The ASP gave it as his opinion that this excessive carnage would never have occurred if we weren't there in the first place attracting these *shifta* with the stories, certainly in wide currency, of the large amounts of money and firearms we kept at Luoniek. Hutcheon gave it as his opinion that the whole district would be much more peaceful and law abiding if people like he, Hutcheon, were in charge of security and game rather than the fart-arsed Kenya police and narcoleptic Game Department. The ASP bridled at that and said he would have to determine whether or not to charge Dad with manslaughter, given that it was his, the ASP's, opinion that the alleged *shifta* had probably been shot before firing any shots at us. Hutcheon fetched a piece of paper and a pen and said he would write all that down and get the ASP to sign it, remarking that he'd attended kangaroo courts before and knew the form.

The ASP was getting angrier by the minute and ordered his men to start searching our camp for as he put it 'evidence'. Hutcheon demanded to see his search warrant, at which point the furious policeman gave up and with a cursory look around loaded the bodies of the slain *shifta* and departed, saying Dad and I would be summoned to give statements. Hutcheon asked if he really had to go so soon, saying he'd been hoping he would stay for tea and a chat.

Apart from the necessary formalities, the affair was soon forgotten by the authorities. The administration of the N.F.D. had been a headache for the British ever since they first laid claim to the land back in 1885 and one more raid by Somali *shifta* was just par for the course. The Ethiopian *tigre* never tired of raiding the Gabbra and Borana all along the northern border and the Somalis never forgot His Britannic Majesty's effort to push the north-east border of the British East Africa Protectorate right up to the Juba River, which gave them a wonderful and permanent excuse to send endless raiding parties into Kenya. Although the ASP would never admit it, our defeat of the *shifta* raid was actually a relief to the administration and would send a useful message to other *shifta* regarding their chances of success with such raids on civilians.

A great school term that was, the only one I remember enjoying from start to finish. Term ended and Dad drove down to pick Leila and me up for the holidays. After a short stay in Nairobi we set off up to Rumuruti and Luoniek. I remember that it had been, as always, a long day's rough, dusty drive. It was late afternoon and we'd descended the higher part of the Laikipia Plateau, passed through Rumuruti and were on the last leg home, driving slowly on the very bumpy track past Mugi Springs towards Luoniek. Suddenly Dad braked hard to avoid a monster puff-adder that was slowly inching its way across the track. It was a really big fellow, four feet or more and fat. There'd been a veritable plague of striped rats and voles that year and the puff-adder nation had done exceptionally well on them. We watched the huge snake complete its careful crossing of the road and disappear into the grass, but Dad didn't move – just sat there staring ahead through the windscreen. Puzzled, I said, 'Anything the matter, Dad?'

He didn't reply, so I asked again. 'Dad – what's up?'

He turned and looked at me and Leila. '*Krar's* sakes,' he muttered, an 'Oh-my-God' look on his face.

'Dad*yyy* . . .' Leila immediately said, 'what've you forgotten *now*? You men are *always* forgetting things.'

'Snake,' he said. Just the one word 'snake'. I still didn't twig, and looked at him quizzically. 'Yeah – we saw it. What's the form, Dad?'

'Can we *go*?' said Leila. 'This is *so* boring. I'm tired – can't we just get home and then talk about snakes?'

Slowly Dad engaged first gear and let in the clutch. I'd got it now, after Leila's prescient remark had sunk in. As she had so ironically observed, us men were always forgetting things.

210

15

Solomon's Triangle

Well, what would you have done? It's all very well to cluck your tongue and shake your head, to deplore the unreliability of men's memories or even that of men in general and all the regrettable behaviour for which they are notorious. You may well take the ever popular 'I told you so' stance, or assert that you would never have even contemplated such a silly, irresponsible thing in the first place. Maybe. Ifs and buts and maybes – how irresistible and useless they are. I went over all this and much more for a long time afterwards and still do, occasionally. But, there's no unstuffing the well and truly stuffed. What if we *had* caught Snake? No, it simply didn't bear thinking about too much. 'If we never, never go, we'll never, never know,' said Dad. 'For all anyone knows he never even knew about the trap we set. It's been a while, now, and no one's mentioned him. There's nothing to say he's gone missing. Let's just assume he's buggered off and leave it at that.'

So, what Dad and I ended up doing (Hutcheon was never part of this particular Quatermain folly) was nothing. He told me never to answer anyone's questions about Snake – should anyone pose any – and that if anything came of it he, Dad, was fully and solely responsible. Very few questions were ever asked, as it happens. Various people from time to time asked about that Pongo *pumbavu*[55] the *watu* called 'I

---

55 Fool (Swahili)

Say', but only casually. Sir Ensor observed that he didn't miss him and added that his brother, Snake's father, had confided to him when his son left for Africa that he'd hoped he'd end up in a three-legged pot. 'That'd give 'em the runs, what?' was Sir Ensor's comment at the time.

In point of fact, we never did hear what became of Snake, which does, I admit, mean that we two are the only people in the world who could, should anyone want us to, possibly – just possibly – explain his whereabouts. But it's not certain. Everyone who ever got to know him wished they hadn't. He could've gone anywhere, got into all kinds of trouble. Considering all the people he'd cheated or double-crossed or otherwise stabbed in the back it could very well have been that he'd upped sticks and done the traditional bunk before the angrier ones caught up with him.

On the other hand, he may well have taken the bait – who knows? On the long, dusty Marsabit road there is a small grove of baobabs about a quarter of a mile away out in the *porini* that you might one day notice as you hammer by with your back seizing up and your head throbbing. Baobabs live a long, long time, two thousand years say some, but certainly for many centuries. The big old ones become hollow and often there is an opening at the top of the trunk where the branches start, which provides eagle owls and bats and geckos with a cool, quiet, secure place to hole up in, though the inside surface of the tree is very smooth and slippery with not too many footholds even for small animals. The floor of the cavity preserves layer upon layer of debris from the owl casts and other detritus that finds its way in. The curious natural historian can, by sifting through this sediment, reconstruct something of the sequence of occupation of the hollow tree as the cool, dry, dark environment favours the preservation of organic material for much longer than would be the case outside the tree . . . Take a look if you're that curious – who knows what you might find?

Whatever jolt the plan to punish Snake gave Dad it seemed to be the final shove that got him out of his long depression and rejection of all things gold. There must've been some connection, because from that time on he seemed to perk up enormously and shake off the recurring bouts of depression that had become so much a part of his life in recent years. He began to talk a lot about Ophir and King Solomon's mines again and I must say I was completely caught up in the romance and magic of it all.

Then, not long after the affair of Snake, something happened to make Dad doubly certain he was right about the area that Suleiman's gold came from. Way back in 1919 when he and Hutcheon were getting ready to quit Harar Dad had bought Amina two leather saddlebags for the journey home. They'd been well made from good soft leather, with Arabic inscriptions tooled into them. He'd got them as her personal saddlebags for her new possessions, her clothes and such things as her mirror and combs and whatnot. He also bought her various bits of jewellery on the way back, mostly silver and amber stuff from the markets they stopped at to buy food.

Apparently, she absolutely loved jewellery and took great care of anything Dad gave her. As I've mentioned already, on their journey back to Kenya from Harar they took the route over the mountains via Negele where they'd met up with an old man who sold them a small gold amulet that he said he'd acquired from his father many years before. Hutcheon had told me that it was very roughly made by hammering separate bits of gold together – you could see the different pieces – but nicely proportioned and a perfect fit round Amina's forearm. She wore it a lot until two of the obviously disparate pieces of gold it was made from began to separate. She'd stopped wearing it then, presumably in case it broke right apart. Hutcheon recounted what happened years later.

'I never knew it at the time, but she hid it in one of the saddlebags. These had, as well as the open pockets with flaps, another pocket that was sewn on all its edges to the back of the main pockets on the inside. The idea was that anything you wanted to hide you would put in these blind pockets by unpicking the leather thread and re-sewing them again after placing the object inside. She'd done this with the gold amulet.'

'Well, as you know, after Amina's death your dad destroyed all the physical reminders of her – all her clothes, the tent from the night she was killed, jewellery – the lot. But he missed the saddlebags. After she got pregnant and stopped riding, the saddlebags were put away and at the time of her death hadn't been used for ages. It wasn't until some time after Rider destroyed the relics of her that I came across the saddlebags under some saddlery I was clearing out. The rats had been at them and while I was assessing the damage, the amulet fell to the ground. The rats had gnawed open the pocket where it must've come from and I realised what must have happened – for I recognised it easily as Rider's gift to Amina. The old join between the two pieces of gold had been loosened even more, presumably from heavy things being piled on top of the saddlebags in the store, and as I fiddled with it the pieces almost completely separated.

'Anyway, I passed the thing on to Rider, ay. Time had passed and he was better able to consider the object as just a chunk of gold rather than primarily a reminder of Amina. And his fascination with all things gold made him look closely at what he had. He separated the two pieces completely and pointed out that one piece, the smaller, was yellower than the other.

' "It's purer gold," he said, "much purer than all the other gold we've come by, I reckon."

'I couldn't really see that much difference, but I've never tried that hard to learn subtle differences in the look of gold. I'm willing to believe your dad really can spot such small differences in appearance.

'Well, in due course he sent it off for assay and when the results came back some months later he started carrying on like a bloody *bobejaan* – yelling and racing about, calling for me to come and look.'

' "*Ky' dar*, Hutcheon, *ky' dar*, man," he bellowed, thrusting the assay report at me. I looked at it, but of course I didn't grasp the significance, ay.

' "What, man?"

' "There. *Ky dar, jong* – the ratio, man."

'I still didn't get it – only your dad memorises every blasted bit of assay information he gets.

' "It's bloody well the same as Flashman's stuff. Look – "

'So I read the assay, which gave the silver content of the electrum as 2.8 per cent. I knew this meant that it was for a naturally occurring source unusually pure: twenty-three carat gold. There were no other impurities except for traces of tin.

' "You see?' said your dad, "it's virtually the same assay as Flashman's gold. These two bits are the only ones with that fingerprint that we've ever come by. They come from the same place, man."

'Now of course I started to pay attention. If the assays meant what Rider said they did then the gold from Mogadisho came from the same place as the gold amulet from Negele. You couldn't hang about with Rider as long as I had without getting at least a *bietjie* excited about Chief Suleiman's gold, ay. But of course, I wasn't going to let on.

' "C'mon, Rider, for *krar's* sakes, man, get a grip. These bits of gold have been floating about the Horn of Africa since Eve was flashing the kudu's hoof at Adam, man. Thousands of years, ay. They could've been to Suleiman's kraal and back three times by now. It's probably just coincidence, ay."

' "Coincidence hell. You never *listen*, man. Old Solomon curled his toes up nearly three thousand years ago, *ja*, but that wouldn't have stopped people digging *his* gold. Those Old Testament stories were scratched out thousands of years ago, too, then nothing more like them. The point is – I've told you before, man – history doesn't record when the gold of Ophir dried up. It might've been a long time ago; but it's just as possible it wasn't very long ago. Nobody was keeping a record, man, there's no continuous history of events since the time of Solomon. Even such stuff as was written by the few *okes* that knew how to write has mostly been trashed by silverfish over the centuries – you can be sure of that.

' "Take the history of Harar, for example. There's no such thing – it doesn't exist. The town's been there since man first began living in settlements – you can bet your hairy arse on that. But a written history – no way! The archaeologists'll have a ball there one day, if they ever get round to it.'

' "They won't get much digging done if the Daughters of the Danakil are still operating,' Hutcheon interrupted. 'At least not that kind of digging.'

' "Yeah, well – probably not. *Krars*, the first westerner to visit Harar was Sir Richard Burton, only seventy years ago, man. Think of what that means, ay. Gold from King Solomon's mines could've been traded through Harar until just a few generations ago and we would have no inkling of it. The gold that old Allan got off Colonel Flashman could – at the time – have been quite recently mined. There's nothing to say that it wasn't – nothing at all.'

'Of course, much as I liked to argue the toss with Rider

what he said was completely logical. You could choose to believe that the location of old Suleiman's mines was forgotten way back, some time after his death some three millennia ago; or, you could rather believe they operated until only a hundred years ago or so. There was absolutely nothing that ruled out the latter alternative. The recorded legend of Ophir spans six centuries – and the surviving records are like the fragments left by white ants after trashing a tree: very, very tiny bits. Naturally, Rider preferred to assume that their location was not lost until a few generations back or so.

' "You can't deny, Hutcheon, that a chunk of gold from Mogadisho and a chunk of similar gold from Negele suggests a common origin not so very long ago somewhere in the area."

' "Yeah, man, that really narrows it down, ay? Somewhere in the Horn of Africa – should be a cinch to find the exact spot, a pit in the ground about the size of an elephant's arsehole."

' "*Voetsek*, Hutcheon – you know what I mean; the Ogaden, not the Horn of Africa. You can rule out most of the Horn."

' "And the Ogaden's only about fifty thousand square miles, you say, about the size of Pongoland. That's still one *moerava* lot of elephants' poop-holes, ay?"

' "Negele, Hutcheon, Negele. That's the key to it, man. There's no gold mined anywhere near Mogadisho, or anywhere else in Somalia for that matter. Flashman's gold was brought there. From where? Somewhere in the direction of Negele. Stands to reason, man. Otherwise there's no explaining how two pieces of gold from the same vein came to be in Negele and Mogadisho, that is to say, two places along the same ancient trade route."

'For sure it was a logical explanation, no denying that. It was an easy trade route from Negele down the Daua River valley to its junction with the other main tributaries of the Juba, then either on down to Kismayu with water all the way, and then up the lower Shebele to Mogadisho; or the shorter but somewhat harder route across the dry country via Baidoa and Bur Acaba.

'Then I remembered something that didn't seem to fit – the bits of gold Arnold had got your dad from the mines north of Negele. The assay of that gold didn't match the amulet at all, ay – completely different. I pointed that out to your dad.

' "I know, Hutcheon. Those mines north of Negele were never King Solomon's mines – too recent, for a start. The point is that Negele lies on the route that Solomon's gold took on its way out. It's an old market town, bit of a trading centre, the first highland town you get to when you leave the lowlands of the Ogaden and start ascending the mountains of southern Abyssinia. That's exactly what it is nowadays – no reason to think it was any different a couple of generations ago. Now, none of the gold from the other side of the Rift Valley – the western side – matches the amulet or Flashman's gold. That means that Negele must be near King Solomon's mines, which must be on the east side of the valley. And if they fit the pattern of gold deposits generally in this part of the world they must be somewhere near the edge of the Ethiopian highland swell. That narrows things down considerably.

' "Those two bits of gold must've come from somewhere quite close and furthermore I reckon it must be south-west of Negele, because if it was from the north-east then the chances are it would have found its way to Harar rather than Negele. I admit that's not a very strong argument, but I have a hunch the south-west is likelier than the north-east. All the other mines round the edge of the highland swell have been exposed by the rivers cutting through the edge of the basalt mantle and into the raised basement. Somewhere along one of those luggas draining the south-west quadrant of the Abyssinian highlands east of the Rift Valley there's a quartz outcrop . . ."'

Hutcheon had gone on to describe how Dad's voice trailed away then and he fell silent. When all's said and done he had to accept that the Negele clue wasn't exactly a roadmap to eldorado. Rather it was a flimsy signpost pointing vaguely at the blue beyond that consisted of miles upon miles of mostly waterless semi desert, rife with bandits, scorpions, vipers, lions, camel flies, sand and black lava scree. And, as the Mad Mullah of Somaliland had once put it, 'There are also many ant heaps. The sun is very hot'. If logic and reason were the only criteria then the location of King Solomon's mines would have to be dismissed as apocryphal – about as apocryphal as it had ever been since old Allan Quatermain's fruitless safari of 1885. But there's the rub, of course. Dad, cool customer that in so many ways he was, wasn't driven by reason or logic for all that he could – and did – employ those faculties better than most men. No, he was driven by passion. In that sense, he had a touch of the artist. He could and did use technique very skilfully, whether to hunt or to think or, I have no doubt, to make love to a woman. But what mattered to him, what drove him, what enabled him to overcome set-backs, was passion. His passion for my mother was, by all accounts, spectacular and all-consuming. And lifelong – that's what really impressed me as it obviously had Hutcheon from whom I learnt all this. After she died, he never abandoned her or his passion for her. Hutcheon told me that Dad had said to him once, many, many years after her death, that he still thought about her every day, that he never fell asleep without imagining that she was there beside him, that sometime almost every day he'd fantasise about something they were doing together; he'd place her into the circumstances of whatever he was doing at the time. 'He was a

219

totally monogamous man,' Hutcheon said. 'Oh, yeah, he went with enough other women, sure, but only to shag them; he never fell in love again. I don't believe he could've. His passion for Amina was all-consuming, it completely ruled out another person. Completely, ay. He'd always had this obsessive passion for gold, of course, got it from his grandfather, Allan. But after your mother's death it was, psychologically, enhanced by the transference of some of his passion for her – at least, that's how I see it. And passion, of course, is in itself unreasonable. There doesn't have to be anything logical about a passion, or anything that makes much sense. If I asked Rider what he was going to do with these mines once he'd found them he'd always dismiss the subject by saying he'd think about that after he'd found them. All that mattered, he'd say, is to find them. Plenty of time to think about what next. He was the exemplar, as I've said before, of Stevenson's view that it's better to travel hopefully than to arrive.'

The assay of the gold from Negele marked a turning point in the whole matter of locating Chief Suleiman's gold mines, because for Dad it greatly narrowed the field of search. Up to now, he'd had to consider the whole Ogaden, which led us to make some very long and rather aimless safaris over the years. Now he was certain that the balance of probabilities pointed very strongly to a stretch of Borana country that he started referring to as Solomon's Triangle. Hutcheon preferred to call it Cloud Kukuanaland, and said so.

'Cloud Kukuanaland where the famous Wafakawe wander round aimlessly trying to figure out which way points to hell, ay, Rider. That's where we're headed, ay?'

'*Voetsek*, Hutcheon – the day will come when you'll have to wipe the silly grin off your *kransie's* hairy face, I'm telling you.'

'Then why don't you call it Kukuanaland – that's where

your grandfather said Chief Suleiman had his mines? Better than this airy-fairy Solomon's Triangle *twak*. Stick to the original name, man – why change it?'

'You have a point,' Dad admitted, 'for once in your philistine life. Kukuanaland . . .' He laughed and said it again. 'Kukuanaland. Yeah, old Allan would approve, I guess.'

' "So that's it, then. We call it Cloud Kukuanaland?" I said. But Rider just spat in the dust, as a Boran would in response to some piece of humbug someone was trying to hand him, and walked off.

'The truth was, though, that I was picking up on Rider's passion a bit, whatever I may have said about Cloud Kukuanaland. After all these years of searching and dreaming there was now a very compelling reason to think – or to hope or to believe – that we might just have narrowed the field down to what was, in relation to the Horn of Africa as a whole, a very small patch of ground. Not more than four thousand square miles . . . A doddle really.'

'I was actually beginning to get quite excited about exploring this bit of Cloud Kukuanaland and even caught myself referring to it as Solomon's Triangle when I wasn't paying attention to what I was saying, ay. We sat down and went over the map of northern Kenya many times to review the logic of it all in the light of the Negele gold assay.

' "Forget the country beyond Moyale towards Mandera,' your dad said, 'because if there was gold there it'd most likely be taken east directly on to the Dire Dawa and down to Kismayu or Mogadisho. Unlikely to be taken north-west to Negele as that'd be a long way round. No well established routes that way, either. But anywhere west of Moyale to, say, North Horr – gold from there would naturally be taken north towards Negele. Stands to reason.'

' "Reason? You must mean Quatermain reason," I'd say, "and why not? No *oke's* ever going to prove you wrong, ay?"

221

' "So, draw a shallow triangle from Moyale west to Chew Bahir, Lake Chalbe or whatever you want to call it, with Mega in Ethiopia at the apex. That's the country at the foot of the Ethiopian swell. A few volcanoes scattered around, but basically any lugga flowing west off the Mega watershed doesn't have far to go to cut through to basement rocks."

' "That's quite a few luggas, Rider. Should keep us busy until we're about a hundred and twenty years old, ay."

'As you know, this so-called Solomon's Triangle is mongrel country – *jussus*. In only about twenty miles, it drops from seven thousand feet down to about two thousand feet. Really bust-up terrain with boulders and scree slopes and steep canyons. Dense vegetation high up but it rapidly disappears down the hillsides. Hardly any soil in all the rocks and you get the impression no rain ever falls on the low country. In a bad year it doesn't; in a good year you'd have to stay awake twenty-four hours a day to be sure not to miss it.

'Well, we made a couple of safaris up into Kukuanaland in the name of Quatermain reason. Much too far from which to drove cattle back to Laikipia so we had to find something else to offset the cost. There were still elephant and rhino along the escarpment, but they've been so heavily caned by Abyssinian *tigre* for so long that numbers were nowhere large. So ivory and rhino horn weren't going to help much. We managed to talk a couple of clients into hunting there, alluding to good leopard, kudu, Grevy's zebra, dibatag, eland – stuff like that. The trophies aren't specially good in point of fact, and from any client's perspective the safaris there are all *tabu*[56] safaris. It's hot and dusty, even at midnight; you are perpetually thirsty, always itching, constantly at risk from bloody lions at night so that you can't afford to sleep out in the open to stay cool.

---

[56] Trouble (Swahili)

Instead, you have to sweat it out in a stinking hot tent under a mossy net.

'Then we had a series of really dry years from 1929 right through to 1934, with locusts as well. Rider was unwilling to spend a lot of money on speculative safaris at such a time – it was hard enough just making ends meet with few cattle to buy and no grazing for them anyway. So all in all we made relatively little exploration in the early thirties. In 1936, I think it was, we were sitting round the fire one evening drinking beer and talking when Rider fell silent for a long time, deep in thought. Eventually he sat back in his chair, stretched his arms above his head and said, "'*N Boer maak altyd 'n plan.*" It'd been a while since he'd used that expression, so I was interested to see what new piece of idiocy he was concocting. The result was certainly unexpected.

' "Have to get a geologist," he said.

' "Why not?" I said, though of course I hadn't the foggiest idea why we had to get a geologist.

' "Seriously, Hutcheon, we need a geologist."

' "Have done for ages, don't know what's been holding us up."

' "C'mon, Hutcheon, man, you must know what I'm getting at?" Rider said.

' "Well, it must be something to do with gold, yeah – but, no, I don't know what you're on about, man."

' "We've had a pretty good look at the country in Solomon's Triangle, and a hell of a lot of country elsewhere, and we're getting nowhere. I know the basics when it comes to geology and the types of rock associated with gold. If I stubbed my toe on the right piece of rock, I'd recognise it for what it was. But what if it's not that obvious? We could be looking at the right country and not know it, because we don't know enough about the fine detail. Geologists sometimes have to use minute bits of evidence to lead them to the real thing.

' "You know how the real *fundis* at this game find buried diamond pipes, for instance? They sift through the sand in old fossilised river beds looking for tiny bits of garnet, because garnet is associated with diamonds and occurs in much larger quantities than diamond itself. So you can find alluvial garnet a lot easier than you can find alluvial diamonds – there's so much more of it, relatively speaking. Then you follow the garnet traces upstream until they stop. Then you know you're standing above the place they came from, which may look like nothing, because of millions of years of erosion and sedimentation and so forth.

' "But for all that the idea is simple the devil's in the detail. What you're looking for may only be there in microscopic amounts. You have to be a real *fundi* to pull that sort of stunt off."

'I was beginning to see what your dad was getting at. We'd – I'd – been looking all along for an old mine. Rider was now thinking maybe we should be prospecting for the source of the gold as if it hadn't already been discovered. Gold forms in cracks in quartz rock so that you get a vein of gold running through the rock. Where these rocks reach the surface they gradually crumble away due to weathering. The crumbs of weathered rock including any gold in them slowly work their way downhill, pulled by gravity and pushed by rainwater. Over millions and millions of years this process, imperceptible to us during our short lifetimes, can move the bits of gold many miles from their source, spreading a long trail of clues to what might prove to be a rich, but in itself hard to find, lode.

' "All this time," Rider continued, "I've been looking for outcrops of metamorphic rock – any sort of basement rock sticking out of all this basalt and volcanic *taka-taka*. And let's face it, man, I've found sweet fuck all. *Nikkies. Yelem.* Zilch."

' "We have to start racking our brains, Hutcheon, get crafty, man. Blundering around hoping to fall down an old mineshaft isn't making the best use of what's rotting away inside our heads. Oom Schalk Lourens would have some caustic comments to make, ay?"

'By now, of course, I'd figured out what he was on about.

' "So we get ourselves a geologist, Hutcheon – a proper *fundi* who can point us in the right direction. No other way to go."

' "It'll cost you a fortune, Rider."

' "I've thought of that," said Rider, "and there's a way to keep the cost down. We advertise for a young graduate and dress up the task to make it sound like a great adventure as well as valuable field experience. That way we can get someone we don't have a pay a huge salary to – maybe even no salary at all, just their expenses."

' "I think I hear the sound of Quatermain dreaming," I said. "Like white ants inside a safari box that's been left lying under a tree for too long: ominous little cracking noises."

' "Lose your dreams and you lose your mind, *kêrel*."

'The truth was, though, that I reckoned your dad was on to a good thing. I loved to take the piss, sure, but underneath I really admired his ideas and more than anything I envied him his passion. Always wished I could've got as carried away as he did with whatever crazy scheme he conjured up. He sure as hell made life interesting for those around him. We talked a lot about getting a geologist and eventually cobbled together an advertisement that we placed in the "Wanted" column of a couple of newspapers in Pongoland and the States. It read:

Graduate geologist specialising in gold prospecting. Six months in Kenya's fabulous Northern Frontier District. Nominal salary, but all found. Gain invaluable experience while enjoying holiday of lifetime in tropical paradise. Apply Quatermain Safaris, P.O. Box 3, Rumuruti, Kenya.

'We didn't get many enquiries. In those days geology graduates had no trouble moving straight from university into well-paid jobs, and the only responses we did get were from very dodgy sounding people. We'd pretty well given up on the idea when, after placing the ad yet again, we got a much more promising enquiry. This letter came from someone in New Mexico, D.L. Verlasques, expressing great interest and asking for more detail. It stated that the respondent was a graduate geologist from the University of New Mexico, competent in all aspects of gold prospecting geology, and listed the equipment and materials that we'd have to provide. It was well written and sounded sensible and businesslike. Your dad replied and there was an exchange of several letters, all of which took quite a while before a deal was eventually struck and arrangements made for this Verlasques to sail to Mombasa and spend half a year with us investigating the geology of Cloud Kukuanaland.

'Well – you know what a sporting prospector D.L. Verlasques turned out to be, and how much we all learnt about geology. Or maybe I should say how little we learnt about geology; depends how you look at it, ay? But you'd know more about that than I do, Alan.'

BOOK THREE

16

The Geologist

I was just turning sixteen when life for me suddenly changed radically and I became a fully operational Quatermain so to speak, and in more ways than one, I'd have to add. The year was 1937 and up to then I'd been more of an onlooker than a participant in my family's business, apart from twangering the odd snake or two. Hitherto, most of the time my sister and I had been away at boarding school and though we spent every holiday with Dad and Hutcheon and the people they employed we were kids and as such were playing rather than working. We looked on rather than conducted the activities that constituted Dad's daily business. While at school, we were virtually out of touch with Dad as there were no telephones and the post was a long drawn-out way of communicating at best. Nor could I claim letter writing as my forte. So life was for the most part a separate affair during our school years.

The sudden change came about as the consequence of what might seem to some a rather deplorable incident. The headmaster of Prince-o, the school I was incarcerated in, which he would've insisted on calling the Prince of Wales School, certainly described the events as deplorable, as indeed he described the entire tribe of Quatermains. It all began with a rare visit by Dad and Hutcheon on one of the so-called Sunday leave-outs. Two or three times a term we were allowed out of school on a Sunday, provided there was a parent or relative to take you. For many of us, like me, there was no parent near enough and no other relatives at all; so leave-outs for us were usually just another boring day at school. But Dad and Hutcheon happened to be in Nairobi on the weekend in question and arranged to pick up both my sister and me for a leave-out. Coed schools were of course out of the question in a late-Victorian colony and Leila attended the Heifer Boma, or just the Boma as it was universally known (that would've been pedantically referred to by the Education Department as the Kenya Girls High School). On that fantastic Sunday evening Dad and Hutcheon returned us to our respective schools, dropping me off first at Prince-o. It'd been a good day out for all of us in the course of which Dad and Hutcheon had predictably quaffed a fair few Tuskers.[57] Meaning to impress my school fellows, Dad drove his scruffy Ford V8 hunting car up the school driveway like a *matatu*,[58] coming to a stylish halt at the end of the gravel drive with a flamboyantly executed handbrake turn (not that the handbrake actually worked) that brought the vehicle to rest in a dense cloud of dust in the flower border flanking the main entrance. It was a heavy car and the skidding wheels uprooted a fine swathe of lawn on the way to the flowerbed and threw up large chunks of ironstone murram, one of which cracked the large, glass-paned main entrance door.

As far as impressing my compatriots went it was a brilliantly executed manoeuvre. As far as the headmaster was concerned, it was an outrage.

It was unfortunate that the head was on hand to witness my stylish entrance, and his failure to impress either Dad or Hutcheon with his pompous authority only worsened things. Hutcheon just sat where he was and smirked while

---

[57] A proprietary brand of beer (Ed)
[58] Rural taxis notorious for reckless driving (Swahili)

Dad got out and, leaning across the bonnet, airily wrote out a cheque for the damage, apologising in a patently insincere manner for his crass behaviour. Just about the entire school assembled to gape admiringly at the car, the damage and the fuming headmaster. That done they then ogled Leila, seated nonchalantly between Hutcheon and Dad on the front seat, her hands clasped behind her head (the better, I accused her later, to show off her burgeoning tits). Dames (girls were invariably called dames) were a rare occurrence within the school perimeter and a really smooth dame like Leila virtually unknown. Then, inevitably, someone remembered who Leila was.

'It's that nympho, Leila Quatermain. *Krars,* man, look at those tits, ay.'

It might never have worked out the way it did if only Dad had dropped Leila off first instead of me. But he hadn't, and she was there in all her nymphomanic glory to add the last proverbial straw. About an hour after Dad had gone some bum-sucking little rabble sidled up to inform me that Apie (better known simply as The Ape) van der Merwe, a *kaburu* from '64'[59] whom I hated, was telling everyone that he was going to fuck my sister. This intelligence was delivered in the hearing of a couple of my muckers, leaving me with no choice but to announce that I was going to 'thump that bloody *kaburu*'. I didn't feel like it at all – The Ape was a tough shit and the thumping could go either way – but chivalry is a merciless taskmaster. A scrap on top of the earlier incident fired the testosterone and adrenalin-saturated mob up to previously unknown levels of manic excitation and very soon the two of us were supported by several of our respective followers. Then the toughest guys in the school, the Tanganyika Greeks, decided to exploit the mêlée to settle

---

[59] The town of Eldoret, built on Farm 64; also 64 miles from the nearest railhead at Londiani. Scene of a small Boer trek in 1908, following the Second Boer War.

a few private scores of their own and the result was a monumental brawl. An impressive amount of blood was spilled and a creditable amount of school property damaged. Several of us required treatment in the sick-bay after the staff had broken up the fight and the enraged headmaster was by now spitting like a cobra cornered in a hot shithouse. Another rabble took it upon himself to inform the head that the fight had been started by none other than Alan Quatermain and, still bleeding, I was summoned to the head's study. When asked what the blazes I thought I was up to I said, quite innocently, that Apie van der Merwe had announced that he was going to 'fuck my sister'. I had naïvely assumed that this would elicit due sympathy; but of course it did no such thing. 'Don't talk such filthy language to me,' he bellowed, 'you foul-mouthed little hick,' and set about caning me with one of the polo-stick handles he kept for the purpose. He then demanded to know where Dad was staying and drove straight down to Torrs Hotel to insist that I be withdrawn from the school forthwith.

So it was that my schooldays came to a sudden and for me wondrous end somewhat before time. I went back to Rumuruti to begin life as a fully-fledged Quatermain, vaguely proud of myself at having to assume the responsibilities of adulthood – not that I had the faintest idea what they really were – at so young an age. I was, as the headmaster had disparagingly observed, a typical Kenya hick, well able to hunt dangerous game, drive an overloaded, mechanically unsafe vehicle on rough, slippery tracks, supervise a large crew of unruly staff and play the goat. I knew all the words to such grand ballads as 'Goodnight Irene' and 'Vat Jou Goed en Trek Ferreira', the admittedly rudimentary rules of *jukskei*,[60] and was aware that the fork was held in the left hand. But in most matters of polite

---

[60] In Kenya, a crude, rough version of the game, involving the batting of a short stick

society I was little more than a savage. In defending Leila's honour I was dealing with a subject about which I knew absolutely nothing. I could say the words easily enough – at school we read contraband 'dirty' books rapturously – but my virginity was as pure as the proverbial Mary's.

'Not to worry,' said Dad, 'it was a bloody useless school, anyway.' In truth, he *was* a bit worried about the premature end to my formal education and told me quite sternly that I was going to 'have to learn one *moerava* lot by teaching myself from books'. He himself was a compulsive reader and had a huge collection of books on an enormous range of subjects. Luckily I had his appetite for reading and was already well into his library. His knowledge was inspiring and he was a good and patient explainer so that over the next few years I did in point of fact learn a great deal, the bulk of which I would not have learnt at school.

At the same time, I had to deal with the fact that my principal role models – Dad and Hutcheon – were *mokoras*; perpetually playing the goat, habitually defying authority, rarely getting haircuts and never having regular paid jobs. I could easily have been badly influenced, or, perhaps I should say, influenced worse than I was. The circumstances of my leaving school were, you might think, about the worst example any parent could set their child. Luckily, I suppose, I was able to work that out for myself. I'd read enough and had a lively enough imagination to see that the events of that day, however funny I thought they were – and I thought they were hilarious, as I knew Dad and Hutcheon did too – were not to be taken as a guide to the future. I knew that the headmaster's reaction was the one to be expected, probably even the 'right' one and that if I chose to behave like that I would have to accept the consequences; just as Dad had to accept the consequences in the form of my precipitous expulsion from school.

But I was as happy as a baboon in a pawpaw tree to be

finished with school and ready, I thought, for anything that Dad might give me to do. My first task wasn't long in coming.

'I want you to take the new V8, go to Mombasa and pick up our geologist,' he announced one afternoon after getting back from Rumuruti where he'd been all day. 'There's a cable just arrived to say that the ship's docking on Thursday – that's in three days' time. Hutcheon and I can't go; we've got a lot of cattle coming in all this week. You'll have to do it. Take Osman with you in case you have trouble on the road.'

'Who's the geologist and why is he coming?' I asked.

Though I knew a good deal about Dad's search for King Solomon's mines from the innumerable discussions over the years that I'd listened to, I wasn't up to date on the geologist.

'We're just not making any progress in Solomon's Triangle – '

'He means Cloud Kukuanaland, Alan,' interrupted Hutcheon. 'Put it another way, the banal eldorado of all the old fools – won't swear to it, but I think that Frog poet Baudelaire said that. Anyways, you know the place, ay?'

Dad ignored him. 'We need to look in much more detail at the geology of the area. I just don't have the know-how to interpret it. It all looks volcanic to me, but there's got to be more to it. So I've got someone to come and teach you to be a geologist.'

'Me?' I said, startled. 'How come?'

'Perfect timing,' said Dad, 'your leaving school at this point in time. Perfect timing. In six months you'll be a fully fledged geologist and lead us straight to the banal eldorado of all the old fools . . .' He laughed, and sat back in his chair. 'Simple as that.'

'What's going on, Hutcheon?' I said, appealing to Hutcheon as I always did when Dad was being apocryphal.

'Your old man's got this hare-brained scheme to hire a

geologist to teach you how to analyse rocks and work out where the gold-bearing ones are. There aren't really any gold-bearing ones – we all know that – but it'll be a lot of fun pretending there are.'
I turned back to Dad. 'What sort of analysis?'
'Haven't the foggiest,' said Dad. 'That's why I've got a geologist coming. He's bringing a bunch of stuff – microscopes, books, chemicals; all kinds of *nini hiis.*[61] Be your job to learn the tricks of the trade. Should be a cinch for you, fresh from school, your brain working at peak capacity, hungry for knowledge . . .'
And that was all I got from them. Dad gave me money for the journey and told me to list everything I should take in the way of fuel, tools and spares. When I'd done that, he went over it with me and generated an even longer list of what I'd forgotten or wrongly estimated. Rumuruti to Mombasa – around five hundred and fifty miles of dirt road, much of it so corrugated that the truck would skip and dance and pirouette like a vervet monkey on fermenting mangoes. The corrugations would be gingered up by spring-snapping potholes, spine-jarring washaways and sump-cracking rocks. Every passing lorry would blanket you in dust as impenetrable as fog that would inexorably cement up your eyes and nose and eventually mouth. If it rained, the dust would turn to doughy mud slipperier than corrugations and far more than axle-deep in the ditches into which you were bound to slither sooner or later. The mere thought of it induced a teenage ecstasy made all the more intense by the accompanying realisation that this was now the daily grind, never again to be spoiled by having to go to school.
This safari was going to mean that I'd be driving all day for two solid days if all went well – longer if I had too many punctures or broke down or the Kibwezi drifts were up. But

---

[61] Thingamajigs (Swahili)

I looked forward to it with more excitement than I think I could ever remember – Osman and I all on our own in Dad's nearly new, albeit already well-scratched, Ford V8 hunting car; a Model 48 no less (of course I knew everything there was to know about the *gharry* as I did about all of Dad's mesmerisingly beautiful guns and vehicles). Magic, pure magic! The sixteen-year-old Kenya hick didn't exist who wouldn't have thought the same.

Within a couple of hours Osman and I were ready to go. As I got in Dad slammed the cutaway door for me with one of his favourite remarks. 'Boot, saddle, to horse and away, *kêrel.* And NO TOERAGGIN' ABOUT, AY? Turn my *gharry* upside down and I'll send you straight to boarding school in Pongoland – I swear, s'true 's God. Stuff it up and there will be no excuses, just no excuses – not even the kind that you could think up. I mean it, ay.' His admonition didn't fall on deaf ears. At that point in my life I was absolutely determined not to balls things up. Dad's approval was everything to me and as far as I could manage it I wasn't going to shatter his confidence. Besides, the threat of school in Pongoland was a boy's equivalent of a girl's fate worse than death; simply not to be contemplated.

I was glad to have Osman come along. He was Abdullahi's only son, a lot older than me and, like his father, a pretty cool customer (which was of course why Dad had picked him). Ever since the affair of the *shifta* and his wound we had shared a close camaraderie and as Dad well knew could be relied on to look after one another. We had a good journey with no serious problems and I was on the docks when the ship bearing our geologist berthed. I waited for hours in the huge, sweltering customs shed for the passengers to come through. I had no idea who I was looking for. Dad had told me that he'd asked for a photograph or a description but never got a reply to his questions. I didn't think to hold up a placard with the person's name on it and simply hung about hoping for inspiration. As it happened, the geologist was one of the last to clear customs and eventually, with nearly all the passengers dispersed, I was left with only half a dozen or so potential candidates. Four of them sounded like Italians from their speech and the other two were both women. Something was wrong, so I approached a customs officer and asked if a passenger named Verlasques had been through. The officer looked up and pointed to the person nearest me. 'That's Mrs Verlasques,' he said. I gaped at the woman, a young, sun-tanned blonde with eye-tugging tits and long, swishy legs, sparingly clad in light summer clothes.

'I'm Dolores Verlasques,' said this scarily sexy creature, 'I'm waiting for Mr Rider Quatermain. Do you know him?' As she spoke, she stepped right up to me. I'd never been so close to a young, strange, exotic woman who was directing all her attention to me; it was terrifying. My face must have looked like a punctured tyre, all slack and shapeless. I just had no idea how to cope with physical intimidation of this kind. Her civet-like scent wafted up, further deranging me.

'No,' I gasped, 'I mean, yes. But it's not me.'

Now she smiled and stepped even closer. 'No matter,' she said, 'you're probably better-looking than he is.'

I looked frantically around for something familiar to cling to. Nothing. No one. Osman was waiting in the car. One of the customs officers was looking at me, frowning. Alone in a strange place with a real woman, unarmed. *Krar's* sakes, what to do?

I looked back at my tormentor, openly grinning at me, and blurted out, 'Dad told me to look out for Mr Verlasques, the geologist.'

'I'm sure he did,' she said, laughing. 'Poor Mr Verlasques the geologist is no more, because I just divorced him. Would've been silly of me to go into all those details before arriving – I'm pretty sure I never would've been invited had

I done so. Too late to send me back, I reckon, so here I am. I'm guessing that you're his son. What's your name?'

Jussus. Not only a fearsome dame, but a divorcee to boot. I knew what divorcees were like from all those dirty books: relentless nymphomaniacs.

'Alan Quatermain,' I said, defensively.

'Well gee, how do you do, Mr Quatermain? Dolores Verlasques, at your service, sir.'

I shifted my weight from one leg to the other, and back again and looked around frantically for something to lock on to. Nothing presented itself.

'How's about we saddle up and mosey on outa here,' said Dolores. 'It's hotter'n a Gila monster's armpit in this shed, don't you think?'

With something practical to do I pulled myself together at last and organised porters for her baggage, loaded up the car and drove to the Manor Hotel where I'd already made reservations. We spent the rest of the day driving around Mombasa while she did her shopping. I'd already made the necessary arrangements for the return journey and after a pleasant evening during which I managed to get a grip of my terror and behave a little less like a hick we agreed to make a five a.m. start the next morning.

Everything was new to her and she wanted to know about it all. She'd said nothing about me driving the day before, but when we set off in the morning she'd obviously presumed that there would be a driver, someone older.

'Don't you have a driver?' she asked.

'No – only me. Osman doesn't know how.'

'Guess the laws are different round here – back in the States you have to be eighteen to get a licence.'

'It's the same age here,' I said, and bit my tongue. Damn, I thought, this bloody dame is turning me into an idiot. Keep your dumb mouth shut, I mentally admonished myself; but of course, I'd already said too much.

She looked at me. 'But you're not eighteen.'

Dad had instructed me that if the police were to raise the subject of drivers' licences I should do what I'd been doing for years at school when interrogated by the staff: dissemble. 'That's one of the things schools are for,' he'd said, 'to teach you how to look after yourself when the authorities try to bugger you around.'

'You have to be eighteen to get a driver's licence,' I said.

She laughed. 'And how long have you had your driver's licence, Mr Quatermain – sir?'

'Dad wouldn't let me drive his new V8 if he thought I was going to stuff it up.'

She laughed again. 'I'm guessing sixteen.'

'Most people in Africa don't know their exact age,' I said. 'Even if they're literate – and the majority aren't – they don't refer to calendars much. So you have to guess their ages.'

She chuckled and gave up the topic.

We drove on with Dolores obviously revelling in what was for her a completely new and exciting landscape. Answering all her questions began to relax me and after a while I started to feel more comfortable than I had since our unsettling meeting in the customs shed. It was a fine day and the first part of the road out of Mombasa had been newly graded, giving the car an easy smooth surface to ride on. From Voi on though the road hadn't been graded for a long time and was as rough and uneven as most Kenya roads usually are. It wasn't long before my new-found equanimity evaporated and I returned to yesterday's state of helpless nerves. It wasn't the road itself – I enjoyed the driving challenge it provided. It was Dolores, unconsciously – or maybe not, come to think of it – who set me shivering with dimly understood unease once again. I noticed, and once noticed couldn't help seeing all the time, how her breasts wriggled and squirmed like catfish under her blouse

every time we went over a bump. And there were many
bumps. By midday, I was exhausted. I hoped she would put
down my profuse perspiration to the heat; but as she wasn't
sweating at all, she probably knew the climate had nothing
to do with it. As we approached the Kiboko River shortly
after noon I was more than ready for a break and so I
decided to stop and have some lunch, which we'd brought
with us. As we made ourselves comfortable under some
shady trees, I heard a troop of baboons approaching. Before
they showed themselves one of them screamed from close
by and I suppose if you've not heard it before it sounds
quite alarming.

'What was *that?*' Dolores asked, scrambling to her feet.

'Rockapes.'

'Rockapes? What're rockapes, for Pete's sake?'

'*Die burgers van die berge. Bobejaans,* baboons, babs – the
bandalog. They want to see what we're doing.'

She sat down and we watched as the first of the troop
wandered into view. Soon there were dozens of them – it
was a big troop. The closer they got to us the more they
clowned about.

'You sure they're safe?' Dolores asked, 'they look like
gorillas behaving badly to me.'

'They're safe. They're scared of people. They can see
we're eating something and they'd love to steal it – but
they'll keep their distance.'

She was fascinated and we watched them for quite a
while. I know what's coming next, I thought resignedly to
myself and sure enough she began taking an interest in
their mating behaviour once she saw what we couldn't help
seeing, for there were at least three females on heat. I'd
hoped all that would be lost on her; but of course, it wasn't
long before one of them was mounted right in front of us.

'Oh my *God*,' she exclaimed, 'is that *it?* I mean . . . most men don't last long – but . . . he was quicker than Speedy Gonzales.'

She turned to me as she spoke, waiting for an answer, her big eyes wide and a look of anticipation on her face. *Krar's* sakes, I thought, what'm I going to do? At least we were talking about animals, which helped to dispel – slightly – the wretched nervousness I'd started to feel again. The only way out was to stick to natural history.

'Yeah, that's it. Just as well for him, though, because if he'd been spotted by the big cheese of this bunch of *cynocephali* he'd 've had the living shit beaten out of him for such insolence.'

'Which is the head honcho?'

'Reckon it's him over there. See that really big sod? His attention's being taken by that female next to him that's also on heat. With more than one on heat, he can't watch everyone all the time. So these inferior males try to sneak in for a quickie when they think he's not looking.'

But Dolores was no longer listening.

'Am I really *seeing* this?' said Dolores. I looked where she was pointing. 'That female is actually backing her ass up at that male. Surely he doesn't need so much prompting?'

'It's because he's scared of the boss,' I said, desperately trying to keep my cool. 'She couldn't give a monkey's – but he's windy as hell.'

As we watched the female backed again at the male and this time he capitulated. And as I'd surmised on this occasion he was spotted and the big male I'd guessed to be the boss raced over and chased him. There was a brief and ferocious encounter between the two males with tremendous screaming and carrying on among the others.

'I see what you mean,' said Dolores. 'But at least she got herself laid.'

I managed to keep my mouth shut about that and

suggested we get going again. I thought no more about the interlude with the baboons and was glad that for the rest of the journey up to Nairobi Dolores seemed more interested in the geology of the country we drove through than the sex lives of the animals. We got into Nairobi well after dark and checked into the Norfolk Hotel where I'd already made reservations. Dinner passed uneventfully and I thanked my lucky stars that Dolores was tired and went off to her room without starting any more terrifying conversations. She agreed to make another early start the following morning as we would be all day again on the road to Rumuruti.

I was exhausted from the intimidation I'd suffered from keeping the company of this physically alarming dame and her candid conversation all day long and at first fell into a deep sleep. But instead of waking refreshed, I spent the hours before morning in a twitching state of half sleep driven by anxious, lurid dreams. I'd be walking around the base of a *kopjie* when suddenly I'd be surrounded by baboons. Everywhere I turned there'd be baboons fornicating, baboons screaming, baboons fighting – but above all baboons fornicating. I'd wake and fall asleep again and find myself in the flat plains of the N.F.D. Everywhere there were the circular waterholes that last for a short while after the rains and then dry up completely. At the last stage, when they are simply round, shallow pools of liquid mud, the catfish heave and billow in a concentrated, rippling mass, each trying to get under the others as the ring of marabout storks round each pool lunges repeatedly into the endlessly ballooning throng. I was up well before dawn, feeling tired and uneasy and was almost grateful to greet Dolores at the breakfast table and get ready to leave.

The drive up-country went smoothly enough and we made good time. I was enormously relieved to discover early on in the journey that she'd got on a heavy-duty bra for the trip that kept the behaviour of the catfish down to a dull roar by comparison with yesterday's unnerving performance. I hope they ache like hell, I thought uncharitably, but it certainly helped me get a grip of myself. Concerning women there was a limit to how much I could cope with all in one go. As it happened nothing occurred that day to unnerve me and Dolores spent a good deal of the time dozing. She didn't get into any awkward subjects but concentrated on finding out about the country and the people we passed through. In fact, by the time we made it back to the plaas I was beginning to get quite carried away by the experience of spending all day in the company of just the sort of blonde nympho I used to read about in the dog-eared, gruesomely stained paperbacks at school. She seemed to treat me as an adult and was always smiling and tossing her hair back, and making fun of the sort of people we were and the life we led. She couldn't believe the half of it and if I'd known at the time the sort of life she'd led in America I'd have better appreciated how surreal she thought we all were.

It was after dark by the time we reached the plaas. Dad and Hutcheon were sitting by the fire drinking beer and shaving sticks of biltong with their knives. Dolores and I walked over in the darkness and they got up to meet us.

'Hello, Dad – this is Dolores Verlasques, the geologist,' I said.

'How'd you do?' said Dad, suspiciously. 'Rider Quatermain. This is Hutcheon Graham.' He peered at her in the darkness, trying to figure it out. There was a distinct pause before he added, 'But you're a woman?'

'I'll be doggoned,' said Dolores, laughing, 'looks like I've blown my cover already. You must be rather disappointed?'

'But you are the geologist I hired?' asked Dad.

'Sure am.'

'So that's why . . .' Dad's voice trailed off and he laughed. 'Disappointed? No, not at all, not at all. Just as long as you can spoor gold . . .'

Of course, Dolores soon had the full attention of both of them, once they'd been able to appraise her in the firelight and discover that not only was she a dame but a good-looking, sexy one as well. All of a sudden I dropped out of the equation altogether and after a while just sloped off to bed, my nose quite out of joint. I needn't have worried, though. Dolores Verlasques hadn't forgotten me.

17

The Tsetse Fly

Dolores's arrival added a lot of zip to things in general and Dad soon organised a safari up into Solomon's Triangle to familiarise The Geologist, as we all called Dolores, with the lie of the land. Long before she came, he'd made me swear never to mention the real purpose behind our interest in gold, the legend of King Solomon's mines, but always to make out that we were simply prospecting for gold. So, Dad had to explain part of the story, that the edge of the great Ethiopian swell was studded with small gold mines, many of which had been worked since the time of the Ancient Egyptians. North of the swell, all along the western coast of the Red Sea right up to its most northern point, there were similar ancient gold workings in the desert. The curious thing, Dad said, was that all but one of these gold mines – and altogether there were hundreds – were west of the Rift Valley. The valley cut off nearly a third of the swell in which only one gold source had ever been found – yet the geology was the same. Or was it, Dad asked? Perhaps he'd been wrong in assuming that the geology of the swell was the same on either side of the Rift Valley.

Dolores, it transpired, had done her homework before setting off to enjoy her holiday in a tropical paradise. She'd read the work of the foremost Italian geologists such as Stefanini and Dainelli and was able to confirm that Dad was quite right in assuming that the geology of the swell was essentially the same on both sides of the Rift Valley. She, too, saw no reason why there should not be more gold sources on the east side – our side. She explained a bit more about the reason why the known gold mines are where they are.

Before the swell happened, she explained, the surface geology of the Horn of Africa and of Kush and Egypt was a very uniform, flat peneplain of extremely old marine sediments dating back more than half a billion years. These sediments, often hundreds of feet thick, lie on the original basement rocks of the earth's first continental crusts. The basement rocks rarely protrude through the sediments – except for one place where the sediments have largely eroded away. This is the long strip of desert between the Nile and the Red Sea, from Ethiopia to northern Egypt, where the basement rocks, particularly along the wadis, are at the surface. These exposures contain the hundreds of small gold mines that supplied the Egyptian pharaohs with nearly all the gold they acquired over the four millennia of their civilisation.

The whole region must, in the very distant past, have been the scene of considerable tectonic turmoil, because the original granites of the basement are highly metamorphosed. Just what happened to break up the original rocks is not known, but the swell, the separation of the Arabian peninsular from Africa and the breaking off of the Horn of Africa from the rest of the continent are almost certainly the most recent manifestation of huge tectonic processes that have been going on in the region probably since the earth began. Rock that is metamorphosed by such tectonics is the kind of rock where, if other conditions are also met, gold accumulates.

Such gold, originally near the surface, was subsequently buried under millions of years of marine sedimentation. Then a patch of crust swelled up in the Ethiopian region, lifting the buried basement rocks and the sediments capping them high above the surrounding country. This exposed the basement rocks in a band around the shoulder of the swell, which is why all the little gold mines are where they are: on the edge of the swell somewhat above the level of the surrounding plains. The swell was of a height that precipitated rain that eroded the edges of the swell exposing even more of the raised basement rocks and their veins of gold.

Dolores readily agreed that there was only one thing to do and that was to go and look. Both Dad and Hutcheon had safaris booked, so Dad assigned me to guide Dolores over the next few weeks. Our mission was to systematically collect samples of sand from every lugga running south off the hills of Solomon's Triangle. This meant a lot of *tabu* safari through really rugged country, as we had to travel against the grain so to speak, moving westwards up each valley side and down into the next dry watercourse. The valley sides were usually steep, always eroded and often nothing more than boulder fields. In the valley bottoms we'd collect two samples: one from the surface and another from as deep as we could dig.

Dolores arrived at the height of the 1938 dry season in late March. By the time the first good rains could be expected, in May, we were well into our task up in the foothills of Solomon's Triangle. Late that month there were several thunderstorms in the area after which water flowed down some of the luggas for a day or two. We were camped at the western end of the triangle on a large lugga just where it fanned out onto the plain below the Abyssinian escarpment. It had been building up for rain and one night there was a big storm on the high ground behind us. The rain was widespread, for we could see lightning everywhere we looked along the northern horizon. Sure enough, the following morning water started running down the lugga, building up to quite a flood for several hours. With the rains setting in on the high ground we would soon have to give up sampling until the next dry season, as we risked getting the car bogged on the frequent black cotton patches along the foot of the escarpment.

We decided to take a couple of days off while we waited for the lugga to dry up again so we could finish sampling it. The runoff from the rain above the escarpment had created a string of quite large waterholes along the lugga's course over the plain. These would rapidly dry up, but before they did I knew they would attract large numbers of birds and other animals that I figured Dolores would enjoy seeing. So it was that we set off on foot from camp to spend the day wandering around these waterholes. There was quite a bit of game in the area as evidenced by the vigorous tsetse fly population wherever the bush was thick.

The rain had stirred everything up and the tsetse were especially *moto* that morning, which was one of the reasons I thought to head out onto the flood plain where the vegetation was much sparser and the tsetse flies therefore fewer. *Moto* means hot in Swahili and is an apt metaphor for these, the most painful of all the many biting flies of Africa. Though a large fly, they are not the largest; but they are the rudest, roughest and most impatient. Their only subtlety is the one they share with all blood-sucking flies: the extraordinary ability to alight on tiptoe so that if your attention is elsewhere you will, almost without fail, feel nothing as the brutes touch down. But you will feel what comes next. As most of their lives are spent drilling instant boreholes into the thick skin of large wild animals from which they must suck up as much blood as possible before a large tail strikes them senseless, it's hardly surprising that upon landing they stab one deep with a mighty dagger that feels as if it's been pre-heated to red heat. They don't need to; human skins are like cellophane compared to the hides they normally pierce. But tsetse cannot seem to adjust their stabbing action; humans get the same fiery clout an elephant does. A lot of these bites, one after the other, can be *moto sana.*

It was a hot, sultry day after the rain and when, at about noon, we came to a particularly large, deep waterhole, we decided to stop there and eat the lunch we'd brought with us. There was a candelabra tree quite close to the water's edge that gave a little patch of good shade while we ate. A flock of red-billed ducks was sculling about, looking very cool and contented and as we watched they were joined by some tree ducks. We'd been there about half an hour or so, watching the ducks splashing about, when Dolores announced that she couldn't stand it any longer.

'I can't sit here sweating and panting while those ducks are having such a cool time in all that water,' she said. 'Don't you jungle junkies ever get in and cool off?'

'Not as a rule, no. Well, yeah, sometimes,' I said. 'But out in the bush most pools are about as inviting as Death Row.'

'What do you mean?'

'Flatdogs.'

'Flatdogs?'

'Crocodiles.'

'Crocodiles are flatdogs? Why flatdogs, Jungle Boy?'

'It's from the Afrikaans word *plathond*, which means, literally, flat dog. If you think about it, the legs of most animals stick down from their bodies – their legs hold them up like chairs. But the legs of a croc stick out sideways – like a dog that's been flattened.'

Dolores laughed. 'Well, Mowgli,' she said, 'that's one *Just So* story old Rudyard missed.'

'I'm not kidding, though. Jump in a big pool almost anywhere out in the *porini* and you can expect the kind of welcome a steer gets in an abattoir. Crocs while away the time day-dreaming of animals jumping into pools.

When they have insomnia they count wildebeest crossing rivers.'

'How charming,' she said. 'You certainly know how to make a gal feel comfortable on safari.'

'But you have a point,' I said. 'This pool is brand new. Only yesterday it was all dry sand here. There are definitely no flatdogs in this part of the world. No crocs, no hippos, no sharks, no sting-rays – not even a few piranhas to keep you on your toes.'

'Seriously?' she said. 'No bities?'

'No chance – this'd be as good as it gets.'

'Swear on your maternal grandmother's knickers?'

'On my maternal grandmother's knickers, I declare this waterhole free of all nasties.'

'Men are such liars. You have no idea who your maternal grandmother was or if she even knew what knickers were, let alone wore any. From what you've told me you come from a long line of barbarian slaves and concubines . . .'

She was quiet for a bit and gazed out over the waterhole. There were a few tsetse about, even down here on the plain; but it was very hot and they didn't bother us much. Suddenly, she sat up and looked at me. She had a strange, quizzical look on her face that I didn't understand. There'd been a couple of times recently when we'd been sitting alone together and she'd taken on this expression. It made me a bit apprehensive, as if I were being sized up in some mysterious way. She said nothing for a bit, just sat there with this disturbing expression. Then, after a while, she spoke.

'Turn around,' she said, 'and put your hands on the tree trunk. Do not move until I yell. DO NOT MOVE. You're under oath, remember.'

I did what she said and heard her get up and walk off. Then I heard splashing in the water. A minute later, she shouted. 'OK. You can turn around, Jungle Boy.'

She was swimming about forty yards out from the water's

edge, just where the lugga's channel ran and the deep water began.

'Now you,' she yelled. 'Off with your loincloth, Jungle Boy. I promise not to look until you say.' With that, she turned round and shouted, 'You have one minute to make it to deep water.'

My new-found aplomb was shattered. Bloody hell – this dame was something else. But I couldn't just stand there like an idiot. There was no way out – or rather the only way out was in. So I stripped off my shirt, then my *chaplis*[62] and last of all (of course) my shorts. Stark naked, only yards away from a near-naked woman. Fear is a shameful thing to feel in any circumstances, but shame doesn't disperse it. I started nervously for the pool and passed by her clothes where she'd left them at the water's edge. The two upper-most garments were a bra and knickers . . . right there – laughing at me! Near-naked, *hell* – she was *kaalgat*![63]

I got to deep water – keeping my distance – and sank in gratefully, just my eyes and ears showing, like a hippo. Or so it felt, I was so relieved to be underwater.

'Can I look now?' she said.

She turned to look at me and laughed.

'My – you look so different without any clothes on.'

'But you can't tell,' I said. 'For all you know I might be fully dressed.'

'Oh yes I can,' says she. 'I can tell by the look on your face.'

We paddled about for a bit in the deep water and then she moved towards a sandbank that was just sticking out of the water on the inside of a meander of the lugga. The water was quite deep right up to the edge of the sand.

---

[62] Sandals (Hindi), specifically a Punjabi style worn as an act of faith by all Kenya hicks
[63] Literally bare-arse, nude (Afrikaans slang)

'Come over here,' she said, 'it's a lovely sandy bottom.'

I saw that she had that strange quizzical look on her face again that for the life of me I couldn't figure out. I swam towards her, hesitating to get too close. I watched nervously as she moved into shallower and shallower water. Her back was just breaking the surface now. Then she raised her head and shoulders and pointed in front of her.

'Hey, Alan, come here. What on earth is that?'

I moved up behind her, a bit to one side, squinting along her pointing arm. Then she started whispering, 'Look, look. What is it?'

'Don't know what you're looking at,' I said, leaning forward to squint along her outstretched arm.

'There,' she said, 'just on the other side of that bush sticking up above the water. That yellow thing. You really are blind, Jungle Boy.'

Then suddenly she exclaimed, 'Oh, my God – it's *moving*!' and drew back onto her knees, her bum bumping into me as she crawled backwards right up against me. She was half out of the water now and pushing me up onto my knees as well.

She'd asked me a few days back what my star sign was. I hadn't a clue and so she'd told me that as my birthday was the first of April that my sign was Aries. Hers, she'd said, was Virgo. Well, Dolores must've been a good astrologist as well as geologist because on that sunny day on the flooded lugga up in Solomon's Triangle the planets had just positioned themselves so that Venus was in exact alignment with Mars, right smack on the cusp. Such perfect synchromeshing of the celestial orbits should be matched, if quantum theory is to be realised, by a corresponding event here on earth. That outcome was serendipitously mediated by the simple act of a lowly tsetse fly alighting surreptitiously on my exposed buttock, glistening invitingly in the midday sunlight. The plunging of its dagger deep into my bum, like the small detonation of dynamite that sets off the huge nuclear chain reaction of an atomic bomb, caused a mighty thrust of my loins as I straightened up with a yell. The noise Dolores made was exactly like the opening half-bellow-half-squeal of a hippo that prefaces the series of diminishing grunts that follow. I can never listen again to a hippo without that happy memory springing to mind.

Nature took over from then on and, as Dolores said a little while later, we generated quite an impressive little tsunami that frightened the ducks and lapped right over our clothes at the water's edge.

As I lay awash in the shallows, in that glorious state of shock and awe that all former virgins find themselves in at such times, she chided me for my brutish sexual manners. 'You could've done one of us an injury charging in like that – specially when you're packing a heavy calibre elephant gun. We've got all day, you know, Jungle Boy.'

'It wasn't me,' I blurted out.

'Oh my *God* – I was raped by an *ngoloko*! Is that what you're trying to tell me?'

'No, no – I mean – you see, just when . . .' Once more, embarrassment started to take over.

'Just when what, Jungle Boy? Just when you were about to take advantage of a damsel in distress?'

'No, no. You see . . . you see – you see, just when you, you bumped into me a tsetse bit me on the bum, and – '

'You're *kidding* me, Mowgli?'

'No. I swear, s'trus'God – it was a tsetse made me, um, well, um . . .'

She looked at me and then started laughing. Laughed and laughed.

'Well I'll be doggoned,' she said. 'Swear on your other grandma's knickers, Jungle Boy, or I'll kill you.'

'I swear – it was a tsetse.'

'Stand up and show me your bum. There'd better be a

253

tsetse bite there or I promise you you'll suffer dreadfully. I think you're bullshitting me. Which side?'

'The left side – high up.'

'C'mon – turn round and stand up.'

I did as she said and she fingered the red welt where I'd indicated.

'That bite is days old – who're you trying to kid, Mowgli?' She laughed and finally said, 'OK, I believe you,' and started laughing again as I subsided gratefully back into the water. I turned to face her and saw that she was still kneeling in the loin-deep water. I looked at her breasts, the catfish tormentors that had given me such headaches for so long, water still dripping off the ends of her nipples. She laughed even more.

'There you are, Big Eyes, all yours now. Show and tell is over – it's touch and feel from now on.'

She looked down and said. 'Oh *my* – he's coming up for air! Does that mean you're ready for seconds, Jungle Boy?'

18

The Bobejaan

I have no doubt that that safari into Solomon's Triangle will remain as clearly stuck in my memory as photographs in an album. Being relieved of the burden of my virginity was of itself a memorable enough thing, as it should be for all those fortunate enough to slip the handicap in such friendly circumstances. But to then have a crash course in the age-old game of snakes and apples under the tutelage of a beautiful, sexy blonde who would only give lessons in the open air on sunny afternoons when most other men and animals were taking a siesta was to enjoy good fortune far above the lot of most men. She refused to sleep with me in a 'hot, dark, sweaty, cramped little tent on a creaky camp bed with everyone else in the darned camp listening'. It had to be out in the bush where we had the place to ourselves and could make as much of a commotion as we liked. By the time we returned to the plaas I was, according to The Geologist, 'beginning to get the hang of how a lady likes to experience the Horn of Africa'.

'Patience, Jungle Boy,' she'd say, 'savour the moment. Calm down – it's not a race against time.' But men it seems are more likely to be sprinters than marathon runners, though she coached me diligently in the sport of long distance running.

We often laughed about the incident of the tsetse fly, but it was not until the last day of the sand sampling that she divulged a snippet of information that completed the full story of my seduction by my adored Dolores. I suppose I felt a little twinge of pique, but only a twinge. In reality, I thought it was as funny as she did and we laughed a lot about it.

We were driving back to camp the evening before we were due to up sticks and head back when we came across a small troop of baboons. They're not that common in this dry country and she asked me to stop so we could watch them for a bit. They soon disappeared, though, as it was late and they were heading home. Then Dolores said, 'Remember those baboons we watched on the Kiboko River on the way to Nairobi?'

'Sure.'

'I guess you probably don't realise how big a part they played that afternoon when we made the tsunami on that waterhole?'

I looked blankly at her. 'The babs?'

She laughed and then said, 'I remembered how that female monkey got herself laid, and I figured maybe the same tactic would work for me. You were so painfully shy I figured, well, if I treat you like a baboon maybe you'll get the idea. You know – imitate the wild animals. You're used to seeing them screw so I thought maybe that's how to get past your inhibitions. So I organised it to back up into you, as if you were a baboon.'

A bloody rockape. She had me down as a bare-arsed, eyebrow-flicking, lip-smacking *bobejaan*.

'You're *kidding*?'

'Why, not at all, Jungle Boy. That's really what I figured. Just act kinda like a . . . a baboon, I reckoned, and you should get the message.'

'Hell's teeth, Dolores – and all the time I thought you loved me as a human.' I started giggling and soon we were laughing like hyenas.

'Even without the help of the tsetse fly I think it would've worked,' she said.

'Thank god your arse doesn't look like a baboon's on heat,' I said, drawing on the sort of romantic resources that your average Kenya hick is most at home with. 'If it had that day a whole swarm of tsetse flies wouldn't of made any difference. I'd 've been out of there like a jerrymungolin.'[64]

Then suddenly I remembered something else. 'So what was it that you saw that afternoon that you were trying to point out to me?'

She looked at me with her mouth open and her eyebrows arched, and started laughing again.

'Sometimes I think you really are a bit of a baboon, Jungle Boy.'

In due course, we headed back to the plaas and spent a pleasant month working on the samples. Dolores taught me how to make microscope slides of bits of rock and taught me how to identify the common minerals of the area. Finally, in June, her time was up and she got ready to return to America. I was devastated at the thought of her leaving for of course I had progressed from helpless apprehension in her presence to hopeless infatuation. For her part, Dolores was very tender and kind to me and for all that I miss her still I am grateful for what she taught me about life and love – and laughter. Of course, I was convinced that I was in love with her, and I must have made it difficult for her sometimes to stay patient with me. But she had the gift of honesty in the areas where honesty is so valuable and that more than anything kept me from behaving like a complete baboon.

---

[64] Large, extraordinarily fast-moving, spider-like animal (Family: Solifugidae). Also called jerrymanders or wind-scorpions

The last night we spent together I pleaded with her not to go, and, as one does, declared my everlasting love for her.

'You don't have to go, Dolores. Stay here with me.'

'Don't be silly, Jungle Boy,' she'd say, 'what on earth would I be doing in six months' time if I stayed? You have to be realistic – there's life as well as love.'

'But I love you. You can't just ride off into the sunset.'

'No, Jungle Boy, you don't love me. You don't know me well enough to love me. So far, I've only shown you my nice side. How do you know I'm not a bitch in angel's feathers? You don't know – believe me, you don't know.'

'But if I don't love you why do I feel the way I do?'

'Ah – the answer to that is very simple. You've discovered you like apples, as we all do. The kudu's hoof as you so quaintly describe it has got you in its spell. You are – forgive me if I sound a bit blunt – you are, quite simply, cunt-struck rather than love-sick.'

She reached forward and felt my forehead with her hand, looking very serious.

'As I thought, you've got a temperature. It's pussy fever. A bad case – and why wouldn't you? After all, I infected you on purpose and kept on re-infecting you. But look on the bright side. Play your cards right and you could have the condition for years. There's a lot of it about; it's hard to cure.'

She was smiling now. 'C'mon, Jungle Boy, don't be so glum. We had the time of our lives. Of course you love me and I love you – to tell the truth I fancied you from the moment I saw you, notwithstanding the callow youth that you were – are? Don't spoil it by thinking it could go on forever.'

'Besides,' she said, 'I have business to do back home. I told you I was divorced, but I didn't tell you the whole story. You see, I grew up poor, very poor, and I decided at an early age that I would marry for money. That's exactly what I did. I married Verlasques in order to divorce him and collect a big settlement. Not nice, I know, but he was never a nice man, nor ever intended to be. His lawyers are even shittier than he is and I've got my work cut out to get my money. You saw that I got a lot of cables recently. Well, they aren't giving me any good news and I must get back. I thought I had it all buttoned up, which was why I decided to come here and get a fresh look at life – in a tropical paradise what's more, as I recall.

'So you see, Jungle Boy, I'm not as sweet as you would like to think. For sure, I never felt for Verlasques even a tiny bit of what I feel for you. I do love you and there's no way I'll ever forget the wonderful time we had. You'll probably never know how happy you've made me over these last few months. But we have to part, Jungle Boy. Something of both of us will die a little as a result; but there's really no other way, believe me. Love is awfully pricey stuff.

'Even our ages makes it all impossible. I've a pretty good idea how old you really are and it doesn't bear thinking about. Why, back home people go to gaol for messing around with . . . And I told y'all I was in my early twenties. Such fun, really tickles my vanity! The truth is I'm thirty-four. I'm pretty sure Hutcheon had me figured, but he was kind enough to keep his mouth shut. So you see, when I'm fifty-five you'll only be the age I am now and still laying waste to every bit of fresh poon you can get the knickers off of. I'll be a vicious, jealous bitch and want to murder you. That's no recipe for a long-lasting love affair.'

19

Shifta

The first thing that Dad did after The Geologist left was review what we'd found out as a result of her visit. Although we hadn't found evidence of some huge deposit of placer gold or anything like that, we had found something interesting – extremely interesting in point of fact. The lugga sands were, as they were bound to be, derived from the sandstone, basalt, trachyte and other volcanic material that makes up most of the Abyssinian highlands. Dolores had told us that quite large amounts of gold are mined from porphyry – veins of copper, molybdenum and gold that form in cracks in basalt. Obviously, there could be porphyry in the region, but even if there was it is primarily a source of copper with gold really only a by-product. No, the thing that really caught her attention was something infinitely more intriguing: particles of greenstone. These came from two luggas – one of the first we'd sampled at the eastern corner of the triangle and the last lugga we'd sampled over on the western side of the triangle; the one that would remain forever in my memory for reasons unconnected with the geology of gold.

Greenstones are interesting – as Dolores had explained to us – because they are highly metamorphosed basalts that formed under exceptionally high pressure and quite hot temperatures. They are some of the world's most ancient rocks dating back nearly four billion years and something of a geological puzzle because they sometimes include chunks of lava of a kind only known from deep ocean plates. That suggests that they could only have made their way to the surface of present-day continents as the result of massive tectonic upheavals in the distant past. The immense forces needed to metamorphose greenstones out of basalt typically occur where continental plates collide or split apart, or where some vast igneous intrusion occurred under the earth's crust.

But the most interesting thing of all about greenstones is that they often have rich veins of gold in the faults that cracked them after they originally formed.

Most of the world's gold, aside from the huge but atypical Witwatersrand deposit, is concentrated either along continental collision belts, both the ancient quiescent ones as well as the recent, active volcanic arcs of the Pacific, or in islands of ancient metamorphic rocks on the continental plates. Ethiopia is not near a collision belt, but it is the site of an exceptionally powerful disturbance that caused the huge swelling culminating in the Y-shaped split centred on the Danakil that created the three arms of the Great Rift Valley. The surface geology of most of Africa north of the equator is comparatively recent – half a billion years old or so – but the greenstone of the Abyssinian highlands is a remnant of the much older underlying rock that was lifted by the magma pushing the crust upwards.

We spent a lot of time with Dolores going over the significance of the tiny bits of greenstone in our samples. The fact that they didn't include any visible gold was neither here nor there, she'd said. They could have been located right next to a rich gold vein for all that anyone knew – or not. A few bits in river sand many miles from the source didn't prove anything either way. What it did tell us, she said, was that there was exposed greenstone somewhere up in the southern highlands and if we were interested in gold then we should definitely look a lot harder in the two luggas in question. It could be hard to find the parent rock if the exposure was very small, she'd said. So rather than blunder off up the luggas and risk crossing the border into Ethiopia, she advised us to sample the riverbeds more thoroughly to see if there really was a lot of greenstone and whether there was any alluvial gold with it. That would help focus our effort on the most rewarding sites.

Of course, it didn't take much of this sort of talk to stoke Dad's enthusiasm up and as soon as she'd left he got down to organising the next step.

'You remember, Alan, how we were talking to The Geologist about the depth of the samples?'

'Not sure what you mean, Dad – '

'Those samples you collected were from two levels in each lugga: one from the surface and then one from well below the surface – correct?'

'Yeah.'

'At the time, though, you told me that in a couple of the luggas the sand was really deep and you thought you probably weren't anywhere near the bottom of the riverbed.'

'That's right – there were two luggas with really deep sand. We hadn't the labour and the time to get to the bottom. It's a bastard of a job, ay. When we did those luggas, it was dry and the sand just runs into the hole you dig. To get deep you have to dig a *moer-on* big pit, ay.'

'Moreover, you had other more important business to attend to, ay?' broke in Hutcheon with a smirk. 'I reckon you spent more time filling in holes than emptying them out.'

Dad laughed and Hutcheon added. 'A bit of *mzuri sana,* ay, Alan – must say I quite envied you. It's not every father looks after his son so well, ay?'

'Bloody hell, Hutcheon,' Dad said, 'you make it sound

like I was pimping for my son. Trust a *kransie* like you to get the conversation where it is.'

'But seriously, Alan, you say there were two luggas with really deep sand?'

'Yeah. I remember there was one at the eastern end – one of the first we did. Then the last one we did, right over to the west.'

'Did you mark them on the map?'

'For sure – it'll all be in the original field notes.'

We left it there that night and it was another few days before Dad got back to it. He unpacked the boxes we'd stored all the information in and found my original field notes. We pored over the maps and saw which luggas I'd noted as having particularly deep sand. As I'd recalled there was one at each end of the base of Solomon's Triangle and we soon realised they were the ones that had yielded the grains of greenstone. That in itself was an intriguing link though it could just as easily have been coincidence. I had a pretty good idea what Dad was thinking and he confirmed my suspicions when he said, 'We have to go deeper, down to the bottom of these luggas.'

'Thought you were coming up with that,' I said.

'Point is, if people had found gold in the area they might well have altered the terrain so that sand from the gold-bearing outcrops no longer got washed down the luggas.'

'Bit of a remote possibility, don't you think, Dad?'

'Maybe. But there's also another. There's a lot of volcanic activity up and down the Rift Valley, as you know. Lots of small earthquakes; some of the volcanoes are active – some still erupt. From a geological perspective, the Rift Valley is still active. As you know, it continues to widen an inch a year – that's a lot of movement.'

'Yeah . . . what's your point?'

'My point is that there could've been volcanic activity that blocked off runoff into one of the luggas. Could happen any time.'

What I knew about such things confirmed what Dad had said about the considerable volcanic activity up and down the length of the Rift Valley. Geologically it was an exceptionally active part of the world – no question whatever about that. And what Dad said about the possibility of local changes to the pattern of runoff was indisputable; such things could happen at any time in a thousand places along the valley.

'Worth a try, Alan, don't you think? Forget all the other luggas – we can treat them as eliminated. But the two deep ones – if we never, never, go, we'll never, never know.'

'So, you want me to head off back there and do the aardvark thing again?'

'You're the geologist round here,' he said.

That's how, once again, I came to be camped in Solomon's Triangle late in August 1939 with a gang of labourers digging a deep pit in a large lugga that ran south off the Abyssinian highlands into the sandy wastes of the N.F.D. Dad and I had driven up there and reconnoitred the deep-sand lugga at the eastern edge of the triangle. He was all excited and reviewed over and over again the facts we'd assembled so far. Of course, the more he talked about it and recapitulated the sequence of events thus far the more he believed his own reasoning. I had no reason to dispute it with him – after all, I was every bit his son when it came to romantic day-dreams about lost mines and other such dust-devils of the mind. And his knowledge of the bush and all he'd taught me about it made him, in my mind, something of a Delphic oracle. I often thought back to everything he'd told me about the bush as I grew up and how it had all turned out to be just as he'd said so that when he opined that the secret of King Solomon's mines lay hidden somewhere in Solomon's Triangle I quite simply believed him. I had absolutely no reason not to. Hutcheon would pull his leg about it, call it the Paradise of Fools, accuse him of being a pathological day-dreamer and worse; but even Hutcheon loved it all really. Hutcheon was my idealised cool customer; practical, sensible, hard-nosed and scornful of the world's wasters, wankers and skellums. If he of all people was also caught up in the pursuit of Sulciman's gold then it was inevitable that I would be too.

So when Dad and I had chosen a place to begin digging and he returned to his other business at Rumuruti he left me enthusiastic and happy. The only downside to it all was that I couldn't help remembering how this all began with The Geologist. Dolores, my beloved Dolores, who showed me how wonderful it is to be in love and who created memories that are as clear now as the actual events that formed them and which, I suppose, will remain as clear for the rest of my life.

We camped in the shade of a few none-too-leafy thorn trees around which we made a *boma* of thorny shrubs, with an entrance that could be closed at night. The *boma* wouldn't keep lions out if they were determined to get in; but it obliged them to make an effort to do so, and that meant making at least enough noise that one of us would be likely to wake up in time to do something about it. Camp was simple. We made our beds on the ground, with mosquito nets – more against lions and scorpions than insects, of which there were few. Three of us slept snuggled up against rifles, myself and two trusted men who could be relied on not to accidentally shoot one of us if there was a commotion in the dark. A rifle is no substitute for a woman in bed – but neither is a woman for a rifle. Under certain circumstances, a *bandook* makes better company.

Our food consisted of a sack of *posho*, a bag of beans, a tin of Kimbo lard and plenty of tea and sugar, plus salt, pepper, chilli and tobacco (I didn't smoke, but all the *watu* did). For meat, we hunted a gerenuk or dibatag or whatever else we could find. For water, we had two forty-four-gallon drums. With luck, we might find water in our pit, but there was not much chance of that. We got stuck into digging and right away things started to go awry. First, we struck rocks and had to relocate our pit several times to get above a deep-sand part of the old watercourse. Then we broke a couple of our digging tools and finally real disaster struck. Because we'd had to relocate our pit several times we'd strayed out of sight of camp and hadn't got round to relocating it. Actually, there was no shade near where we finally started digging in earnest and the truth is I took a chance on leaving it out of sight.

There were several reasons for wanting to keep the camp in sight. One was the vultures and crows that would pillage our meat as soon as we were out of the way. Another was *shifta*. It's a toss-up which is worse in the N.F.D. – lions or *shifta*. It must be said, though, that lions don't have guns. After the Great War guns became freely available in the Horn of Africa and for bandits the Iron Age gave way to the Lead Age; the spear that had served mankind so well for so many millennia deferred to the bullet.

The lions, though, were stuck with their traditional armament, which definitely shifted the balance of hazard towards *shifta*, who, as populations everywhere exploded, were becoming ever more numerous and bold. The last thing Dad had said to me when he left us to our task was to the point. 'Remember, Alan, these *shifta* bastards don't take prisoners. They can't afford to feed and guard captives. For them prisoners are simply not an option. We've had enough trouble from them already. Watch your back day and night.'

Then it happened. We downed tools on the third day

after Dad had gone and returned to camp for the midday break. We didn't notice anything wrong until we were almost there when one of the men stopped and said one word, '*Moto!*'

The fire had already burned itself out and we'd never seen any smoke from where we'd been working. A dust-devil must've whipped over the camp and picked up embers from the morning fire that should've been thoroughly extinguished, but obviously hadn't been. There was a slight breeze blowing and a fire had got going on the downwind side of the camp – the side where our food had been stashed under a pile of thorns to keep the crows and the vultures off. The thorns were dry enough to make good fuel. The fire had gone out of its own accord, but not before destroying nearly all the *posho*, the remains of which were still smouldering. Everything else was okay.

There was nothing for it but for me to head off back in the truck and get more food. We salvaged about thirty pounds of *posho*, which, with the beans and game meat, would suffice for a few days until I got back. None of the men could drive so it had to be me. I nominated one man to accompany me – as a rule one never travelled alone in this part of the world – and decided to leave my rifle with the four remaining men to strengthen their firepower in my absence. I had my revolver, which was enough.

We started back that afternoon and had only gone about ten miles when we had two punctures in quick succession. That meant repairing both the spare and one of the road wheels and it was getting dark by the time we'd finished swearing and barking our knuckles on tyre levers and recalcitrant tyre beads that always seemed to be a size too small on a hot, sandy roadside with no shade. The foot-pump gave out half way through inflating the second tyre and had to be stripped and fixed and reassembled. Finally, we fitted the wheel back on the truck, secured the spare and decided to sleep and make an early start at three in the morning. It had been a long, stinking hot, tiring day and as we cranked the jack down and put it away a puff or two of air wafted by. The shadows of the bush were long now and I listened to a flock of vulturine guinea-fowl calling, as they got ready to roost for the night. The puffs of air grew into a slight breeze that with a little imagination seemed almost cool – at least in comparison with the hot dust-devils that had blown over us all day long. I had that feeling that one sometimes gets at the end of a *tabu* day that it was all over now and things would pick up from here on. I suppose those sorts of silly, wishful thoughts are akin to the onset of delirium; certainly one learns to beware of them. At the time, though, I felt relaxed and relatively comfortable as I settled down to sleep in the cab. Ali, my turney-boy for the trip, cut some thorns and boma-ed himself up underneath the truck – always a favoured place to sleep on safari, being at once cool and secure against lions. It was a hot, still night and I had both windows half open to get some air. We were soon asleep.

I woke reluctantly, dreaming of being tied on the end of a rope tethered to a baboon that threatened to savage me. A typical ambiguous situation dream. I strained against the rope, but couldn't loosen it. The baboon lunged at me, yet seemed unable to reach me, though we were on the same rope. It must've been about midnight and I was thick with heavy, uncomfortable sleep, not quite fully awake yet. Something was in my face and I reached up to brush it away. My hand found something metallic – a hard, steel rod. I was still dreaming, trying to push away the object that was partly an animal partly inanimate, but not succeeding. The baboon was laughing now, but the laugh was mocking. The metal object was pulled away then pushed back into my face. I struck at it and the baboon laughed again. Then I was awake, trying in those last few moments of sleep to figure out what was going on. Something stank, really reeked. It was like hot, bad breath. I was awake now and instinctively covered my face with my hand to ward of the truly awful stench. The moon was nearly full that night and I could dimly see a face, from which the hoarse laughter was coming. Then I started to stiffen, to knot up as the mocking laughter, the awful smell and the hard metal object gelled into reality. The baboon of my dream was now a man prodding my face with a gun. 'Get up, dogshit,' the man said in Oromo and once again I was smothered in the odour of bad breath. That's what it smelled like, that's what it was: bad breath, really rotten, stinking breath. He opened the car door and stuck the muzzle of his rifle once more into my face. Instinctively I tried to grab it and immediately he hit my hand with the barrel, hard up against the back of the cab. 'Out,' he said, and stood back a few feet. I groped for my revolver; but of course, he'd long since become its new owner.

I remember now with knife-sharp clarity what went through my mind at that moment, as the remnants of sleep were mopped up by the realisation of what was happening. *Remember, Alan, these bastards don't take prisoners.*

Suddenly there was a commotion, excited voices in Somali, then a shot. I didn't know it yet, but Ali had woken and managed to creep out from under the car and bolt like a flushed grysbok.

My captor was joined by two other men who obviously weren't interested in Ali. The nearly full moon illuminated their figures quite clearly.

'What do you want?' I demanded, as aggressively as I could. Both Dad and Hutcheon had often told me as I grew up that if you want the upper hand in any confrontation where reason isn't going to work, always take the bullying stance, even when the odds seem stacked against you.

'Never underestimate the power of bullying,' Hutcheon used to say. 'Bullies usually get their way.'

Nevertheless, it doesn't always work and a bunch of Somali *shifta* are among the least likely people to be impressed by one of their victims trying to bully them. They simply ignored my demand and talked rapidly among themselves in Somali, which I can hear a little, but don't speak properly. I saw that one of them seemed to be in charge and again I demanded what he wanted, first in Swahili, then in Oromo. Ignoring me, he and one other searched the vehicle, going over everything carefully. The third man just watched me, his rifle at the ready.

'You move, I kill you,' he said, and laughed. 'I *want* to kill you,' he added, gratuitously. He spoke in Oromo to ensure that I got the message.

'Ah,' the first man said, 'is this your medicine?'

'Yes.'

'Where is the rest?'

'That's all of it.'

'How do I know you haven't got more?'

'Because if I had you would have found it. You've already taken my money and my clothes and my gun. There's nothing else to find.'

Simple robbery didn't seem to be their purpose. I didn't have much to steal and if they were going to kill me why hadn't they already done so? Ali's escape hadn't fazed them. I kept recalling Dad's stern admonition, so often made as I grew up – *shifta don't take prisoners.* I recalled how we'd discussed the implications of that.

'Fight to the death if you do get caught,' Dad had said. 'If you're going to die anyway you might as well go for broke, try to take some bastard with you. Because they won't kill you cleanly. They'll play with you, frighten you, hurt you, make you scream and writhe and cringe – pump themselves up on cruelty.'

Well, it sounded logical enough around a campfire – if you're for the kibosh anyway you might as well fight back

270

and force them to miss out on the torture and kill you straightaway. But there's few people with the balls to actually carry out such an excellent plan. As long as you're still alive the desire to stay that way is apt to override any other consideration, especially high-minded ones. Your mind will deluge you with wishful thoughts about how you might just survive, the odds notwithstanding, effectively dousing any idea of launching yourself onto the barrel of a gun wielded by some murderous fiend hoping that you will do just that.

At such times, one's mind is going to do one of three things: go into shock, panic or concentrate. Fortunately, mine chose the latter (I'd like to think *I* chose the latter, but that would probably be boasting) and I tried to figure out what they wanted. The problem was that trying to decide what a bunch of *shifta* wanted seemed altogether too easy. In the normal course of events it could only be what any bandits had in mind: robbery or murder, usually both. But robbery somehow didn't seem to be their purpose. I noticed that while they naturally took my money, the man who seemed to be their leader didn't give it a glance – just stuck it in a pocket.

Revenge. That was my next thought. Were these *shifta* connected with the gang that had fared so badly in that early morning attack on us five years ago? If they were, then vengeance was definitely on the cards. As soon as I turned that thought loose in my mind I started to feel *really* scared – shit-scared is the word. I came very close to shitting myself there and then and it took everything I had to keep concentrating on what was going on around me and not give way to fear. Something about the leader caught my attention, made me concentrate. It was his close interest in my medicine box, which he unpacked carefully and equally carefully repacked, looking closely at each item as he did so. Both the others seemed interested as well and were watching him as I was. Again, he demanded if I had other medicines. I said no and then demanded to know what he wanted medicine for. He flared up at that and told me to shut up. He then spoke again with the other two and seemed to make his mind up.

'We go now,' he said.

'Where?' I demanded. He just ignored me. 'Bring water,' he said, and then added, 'blanket.' That set my mind going again. I couldn't help thinking that if he wanted me to bring a blanket he wasn't about to murder me. At least not in the immediate future. Meanwhile the three of them filled their water bags and watched as I filled mine and Ali's water bottles. They then drank as much as they could from the drum in the truck, made me do the same and finally up-ended it. A good *shifta* would hate to think that someone else in that desert might benefit from a drum of water. They put everything they didn't want to steal back in the truck, made me get back in the car and with one man beside me in front and the other two on the back told me to drive the car off the track into the bush. We went about seven hundred yards or so and then the leader stopped me and we all got out and walked back to the track. Two of them then spent a while brushing out the car tracks where they went off in thc bush so that anyone driving along the track would not see where the vehicle had left it.

There followed a noisy argument between the leader and the man guarding me over my revolver. The man with dead dog's breath who'd woken me already had it buckled around his waist, but was obliged after what were no doubt bloodthirsty threats to hand it over to the leader. The third man, who I noticed seldom spoke, just stood and watched me as the other two quarrelled like baboons over a mealie cob. The hierarchy was now clear, for what is was worth.

I was dressed in the shorts and shirt I'd been wearing that day and had on a pair of *chaplis*. I told the leader that if he wanted me to walk with them I had to have my hat back, and somewhat to my surprise he made the silent one, who was already wearing it, return it to me. Which he did by dropping it on the ground and spitting on it. I couldn't help it, but it's something I suppose one learns at school, to always throw one more stick on the fire one's started even though it's bound to score you another clout. Defiance, I suppose, a way of refusing to kowtow to authority more than you absolutely have to. Whatever, but I then spat in the man's direction and ordered him to pick up the hat. He straightened up, cursed and raised his rifle.

'Pick it up,' I said again.

The leader quickly stepped in front of the man and knocked the barrel of his gun aside. They disputed furiously in Somali for a while and eventually the man turned away, muttering. The leader had my measure, though, and made no further reference to the hat so that I was obliged to retrieve it myself.

We set off into the night, heading west, the sensations of fear, anger and despair vying for control of my mind.

20

My Life as a Brigand

We marched all that night by the light of the moon and on through the day, all the time heading west. The leader and the silent one walked in front, then me, then my guard. I considered bolting when we passed through thickets that would give me cover. If I jinked like a gazelle in front of a cheetah there was every chance I'd dodge their bullets. They were probably hopelessly bad shots at anything other than point-blank range – but that wasn't certain. Some *shifta* get to be quite handy with a rifle. Theirs were clapped-out Mannlicher-Carcano carbines filched from the Italian army, but if I did get in the way of a bullet the nature of the weapon would be an entirely academic matter: they all hurt. And if I didn't get shot they would inevitably track me down sooner or later. Sooner, actually. If for some reason they didn't spoor me I'd be bushwhacked by a lion before I died of thirst. I gave up thinking of bolting.

I thought of jumping the man in front, grabbing his rifle and shooting it out. However, I knew they knew I might do that and at close range I'd be sure to get the bullet from one of the other two. These people weren't afraid of me or of anything I might do. Nor would they care about wounding or even killing their compatriot while shooting at me. The man behind me, even though he obeyed the leader, made no secret of his ambition to murder me. 'I've never killed a white man,' he soon told me, 'so you will be the first.'

He showed me his rifle stock in which he'd clumsily gouged fourteen small holes. 'See?' he said, 'count.' I ignored him. 'Fourteen,' he said. 'Fourteen men – *kalas*.' He spat, and added that he'd killed 'so many women' as well, but that he didn't bother to record them with a mark. 'They are only women.'

'You lie,' I said, 'anyone can see that those marks were made by white ants.'

He bristled, but before he could reply the leader shouted to him, presumably to tell him not to talk to me, and he shut up. To make himself feel better, he grasped his nostrils with the thumb and forefinger of his free hand and blew his nose in the African style. However neatly this is done it can never rank as a delicate or discreet operation: but somehow, he rendered it disgusting. Just the fact of his inherently repugnant personality, I suppose, but when he pinched off the resulting gob of snot and flicked it deliberately to the ground in my direction I actually retched. He saw it and distorted his ugly mug into what presumably passed in his book for a grin. '*Káfir*,'[65] he said, and shouldered his rifle, 'move, *káfir*.'

The epithet reminded me of the fact that Somalis, even such irredeemably profane individuals as these *shifta*, will insist that they are Moslems and profess the utmost contempt for all who are not. It didn't seem to matter that they probably neither understood nor practised the precepts of Islam nor did they even fool themselves into supposing that they had the remotest chance of attaining paradise. What it did, above all, was give them an excuse to despise others, to somehow gain the sense that at least in some respects they were superior to those whom they could label non-believers. Reminding me of who I was would undoubtedly be very gratifying.

*

---

[65] Infidel (Somali, Arabic)

About midday we stopped for an hour or so, then got going again. By now, I knew their names from listening to them talk. Abdi, the leader, Sufi, the silent one, and Bashir of the long-drop breath, my prospective executioner. It was stinking hot and we hadn't eaten since we started walking. We had only the uncooked food they'd rifled from my car: some *posho*, tea and sugar that wouldn't go far between four people. 'Four people?' I caught myself thinking. 'Don't assume the fourth will be included when eventually they do get around to eating. It's not hospitality I'm enjoying in the company of these murderous bastards.'

It was now obvious that for the time being at least I was a prisoner, notwithstanding Dad's admonition. But for how long, and why? That was the question. Something was afoot other than common or garden brigandry. I began to think it must be ransom. They were marching me to some awful hideout after which they would contact Dad with their invoice. The more I thought about it the more convinced I became that ransom was their plan. Nothing else explained this protracted march and the all-important fact that I was still alive. We'd mulled over such an eventuality often enough in the evenings round campfires, as it always seemed a possibility. On the other hand, *shifta* were fundamentally hit-and-run artists, disinclined to stick around in any one locality for any length of time. As with any predator the element of surprise is crucial and that's lost once you make yourself known. Moreover, ransom takes planning and organisation – qualities not normally associated with bandits drawn basically from the bottom of the heap. So, one way or another, we'd never really pursued the subject of ransom and what to do about it. Not a lot you can do about it before the event.

After it got light, Abdi had pushed the pace and at first I worried about my ability to keep up. If I can't keep up, I reasoned, they'll just give me the bullet. Trudging along, you find yourself musing obsessively over things that are as often as not irrelevant or downright unwelcome. Something to do with monotony and repetitive actions. And walking hard in the hot sun, hungry, tired and frankly scared, isn't good for the mind. 'The bullet,' I kept thinking. 'Much as these sods love guns and shooting, their life spent on the bones of their arses engenders a compulsive parsimony that is bound to take over when the time comes to slaughter me. As I'm already captive why waste a bullet? Far cheaper just to grab my head from behind, like a goat's, stretch my neck and cut my throat. *Bismillahi ar-rah...*' I couldn't stop myself, and time and again the image of being summarily gorged – though not necessarily blessed – came back to me, however hard I tried to push such thoughts away. Again and again and again. But as the morning wore on and I became more than ever convinced of the ransom motive I relaxed a bit. No point in killing the hostage – at least not until you've been paid. On the other hand, how was Dad to know whether they actually had me alive. Ransoms have been paid for defunct hostages often enough. None of it really bore thinking about.

What I should be concentrating on, I told myself, was anticipating the moment when they really were finished with me so that I could at least try some last-ditch move before they made theirs. In the meantime, I worked out roughly our track to have an idea of where we were. We weren't following a path. Our westerly heading meant that we were cutting across the general slope of the terrain, which was to the south. Nobody would make a path that cut all the time across each valley and ravine of the foothills of the high ground below Mega. Clearly, these ruffians had a definite place they wanted to get to by the shortest possible route. It made sense. Once you've shown your hand and taken possession of your hostage the clock starts ticking. They obviously didn't want Dad getting any premature information about my abduction. Two things helped slow their pace a bit, enough that I could more or less keep up. *Shifta* are members of what the Somali call *kurra-jog*, the people of the sun, as opposed to the shade dwellers who skulk around villages and towns. The *kurra-jog* live on their feet in the hot sun and can walk like camels, much faster and far longer than someone like me, who, though young and fit enough didn't spend anything like the time footing it that they did. So, I was very grateful that the day was cloudy with a fresh easterly wind that was a slight but perceptible help when walking with it. The other thing that kept them back a bit was that my guard, Bashir, had the shits. The real galloping squitters. As if he wasn't a repulsive enough oaf anyway, his festering bowels made him truly disgusting. As I said, he walked behind me and made sure he was never more than a few paces distant. The easterly wind was from behind us. It scarcely needs recording that every time he farted – and it was often – I was enveloped in a feculent miasma that would have quelled a rioting crowd better than tear gas. After the first few hits I took to skittering off sidcways as soon as I heard him let rip in the hopes of dodging the stink. Of course, this had him shouting and carrying on that he would shoot me if I so much as budged off line one more time. I demanded of Abdi that Sufi replace Bashir as the man behind me and told him why. He just scowled, of course, and warned me not to push my luck as Bashir would kill me if he thought I was trying to escape.

But the farting wasn't the end of it. Every couple of hours or so Bashir would call Abdi, who would stop briefly while Dead Dog's Breath hoicked his filthy *kikoi* up, squatted and fired off another round from his roiling innards. He insisted I keep the same distance as when walking so that not only was I obliged to breathe the polluted air but listen as well to the revolting squittering that would have embarrassed a buffalo on new green grass.

Towards evening Abdi halted and he and Sufi made a fire and prepared to cook my stolen *posho*. When it was ready, he told me to take some *ugali*[66] and we all ate. That at least was something. They made tea and then he told me to sleep for a while. From what they said, I gathered that Bashir was to sleep as well while Abdi and Sufi stood guard. I was dog tired and fell asleep quickly, vaguely wondering if I would ever wake up. But, I thought, they would hardly go to all this trouble just to finish me off while I slept. In point of fact, a bullet while I slept was highly unlikely, the more I thought about it. These sods would never be so kind. I could be sure that if they were going to slaughter me it would be preceded by a bit of lively torture, something for which *shifta* are notorious. They wouldn't waste such an opportunity. On that note I was able to go to sleep easily, confident that I would definitely be woken before they made any other move.

Sometime around midnight, to judge by the moon, I was woken by a couple of gratuitously hard kicks from Bashir and told to get moving again. We marched on, the going easier in the cool of the night. Our water, though, was finished and now my mind kept turning round thoughts of drinking and how hard it was going to be if they drove me on through the coming day. That, mercifully, didn't happen.

About an hour after sunrise we started crossing camel and goat tracks, indicating that water – and people – were somewhere in the vicinity. During the night we'd crossed a big trail that I figured must have been the track from Mega to North Horr. If it was, it meant we'd walked some fifty

---

[66] Boiled *posho*, cooked to a moist cake (Swahili)

miles or so since my capture. We'd also swung north-west after crossing this track, and were skirting some low, rough hills. We then turned north and started up a slight valley that wound through the rocky hills rising gently all the time. We'd gone about an hour like this and I noticed that we'd left the signs of livestock behind us. We'd come to where another slight valley joined the one we'd been ascending. Then, Abdi halted and the three of them conversed for a while, glancing now and then up the second valley. Finally, Abdi turned to me and told me that I was to be blindfolded. As it seemed obvious to me that we were approaching their hideout I wasn't surprised by the blindfold and decided not to kick up about it. There was of course nothing I could do about any of it as things were, so accordingly I said nothing as they told me to take off my shirt, which they tied round my head to cover my eyes.

Sufi had cut a long stick and I was told to hold one end while he walked in front holding the other end. It was an effective system and we made quite good time for another hour at least. Then Abdi halted us again and told me that we would be climbing over stones and boulders from now on, and to watch out. You're so kind, I thought, as the lamb said to himself while being fattened up. I couldn't resist asking him how I was to watch out blindfolded; but sarcasm was wasted on this one as he simply started off again without a word. It was slow, bruising going, and I stumbled often. Several times I had to reach down with my hands to stop myself falling over. The rocks I grabbed at were invariably extremely rough and sharp. I soon realised from the texture of the stones combined with the distinctive crunching underfoot that we were traversing lava, and fresh lava at that. Eventually the feel of the ground changed again and I assumed we'd left the lava section and were back on sandy, pebbly ground. We were moving slowly and changing direction all the time so I assumed we were walking around boulders. I began to hear the monotonous whistle of *dassies*, telling me that we were almost certainly near the precipitous Abyssinian escarpment. I was enormously relieved when at last Abdi stopped and told Sufi to remove the blindfold.

We were standing on sandy, stony ground, surrounded by huge black basalt boulders, some rising thirty or forty feet above the ground. The last quarter of an hour had been spent scrambling down over large rocks all the time and I now saw that we had descended into a rocky ravine with steep stony hillsides on either side. I figured it must be a dry watercourse, although I saw no signs of any water or watermarks. We now walked through a narrow defile that turned round the edge of a huge rock and opened out onto a sandy space perhaps forty-five yards in diameter. On the far side – the northern edge – the rock formed a huge overhang that shaded the ground beneath, probably all day long as the sun moved westwards. Another defile led off from this overhang.

A man was squatting under the overhang. He rose and greeted his comrades as we walked across the sand towards him. I saw what appeared to be a second man lying in a blanket in the deep shade towards the rear of the overhang. There was a fireplace, a heap of *kuni*[67] a few pots, some dried meat and various bits and pieces scattered round. I was aware of several bundles of leopard skins and a small pile of ivory up against the rock-face. Flies everywhere: big, greasy green-arsed bottle flies; even bigger stealthy, grey shit flies; a rabble of small black general-purpose flies. On the rock-faces, no doubt revelling in the bounty of flies and other camp-following insects were several huge *bloukop koggelmanders*,[68] bobbing their heads in derisive greeting. So

---

[67] Firewood (Swahili)
[68] The ubiquitous blue and orange agama lizards of Africa

this is the grand hideout, I thought to myself. What a shithole! Abdi told me to come forward and gestured towards the blanketed figure. As I did, the other three fell back and stood and watched. The first thing I noticed as I approached the overhang was the stench of rotting meat. Everything about my life stank. First, Bashir's revolting breath that would've brought tears to a hyena's eyes, then his disgusting diarrhoea of the day before, and now the sickly-sweet reek of rotting meat. My whole situation reeked, as did my prospects. I was suddenly possessed by a crushing depression that stopped me in my tracks. What the hell was I doing here, why do I bother to pay attention, why not just sit down like a gut-shot antelope and let it all wash over me as it will? Apathy and disillusion suffused me like a quick-acting anaesthetic. The combination of fatigue and fear and revulsion made me dizzy and for a long moment I lost all sense of where I was and just hung there, hardly keeping my feet.

The sharp pain of the muzzle of Abdi's gun jabbing into my kidneys cudgelled me back to the here and now, as I suppose he knew it would. Just as quickly as I'd been paralysed with depression I snapped back into reality. I turned and grabbed at the muzzle of his gun, swearing at him. He simply stepped back smartly and raised the rifle with a sharp order to do as he said. I stared into his bloodshot, baleful eyes for a bit; but of course he knew all along who was going to back down. I turned round and stepped up to the figure wrapped in the blanket, the smell intensifying as I got closer. Abdi spoke to the recumbent man who stirred slightly. He was lying on his side, completely covered by the blanket, but when he heard Abdi's voice he slowly pulled the blanket off his face with little, jerky movements and turned his head to look up at me. I realised now that the stink was coming from him. His blanket was stiff with dried blood and crawling with flies as was his face as soon as he exposed it. His movements were slow and shaky – the movements of a very sick man. Abdi brusquely told me to kneel so that I could hear the man speak.

'He is not strong,' said Abdi, 'listen carefully.'

The sick man did not waste his breath on niceties.

'You will give me medicine,' he mumbled, '*farangi* medicine.' He paused and his eyes closed. His face was sunken and the skin grey and dry, like the stretched skin on a donkey's carcass in the sun. The pungent smell coming off him was hard to bear. Imagine having your face pushed into a hot, especially rank gorgonzola cheese covered in bluebottles and you will have some idea of how I felt just then. Before I could mentally adjust to what was going on I saw his sunken eyes open and he looked at me once more. If ever I saw a man's eyes become two holes for the devil to glare through I was seeing it now. Blackmore could've been referring to this awful djinn when he wrote that, I vaguely thought to myself.

'If I die you die,' the devil said, and withdrew like a trapdoor spider. Or so it seemed to me. Thinking back over this moment I suppose I was not far off delirium from the heady cocktail of exhaustion, thirst, hunger, fear and disgust.

My mind was slowly incorporating this new information and churning out a revised assessment of reality. Forget ransom. That now seemed positively romantic in comparison to what I was beginning to grasp. A man was dying – judging by the smell a good deal of him was already well and truly dead – and I was to make him well again. If I failed – *kalas*; I too would soon smell like he did. That was why these villainous bastards had abducted me at gunpoint: to save one of their fellows' scrawny, undeserved lives. That was the reason for their interest in my medicine box. That was the reason why I was still alive. That was all very, very bad news.

I was jarred back into the here and now by the placing of my medicine box on the ground in front of me next to the sick man, and Abdi's voice urging me to get on with it. Once again I was almost overcome by the urge to make a showdown of it, lunge for one of their guns and force them to shoot it out with me. But, as before, the futility of it was just too obvious. I'd be dead probably before I could even have a go at one of them, let alone kill any of them. I couldn't do it – just didn't have the balls for it. For a bit, I just stared at Abdi, and spluttered and swore. He stepped up to me and raised his rifle, aiming at my face.

'Do it,' he snarled. 'Move.'

'Do what?' I shouted back.

'You know what to do,' he shouted, really angry, and kicked the medicine box. 'You know what to do, *káfir*.'

Sure I do, I thought . . . just lay on the old hands, take up thy rifle and walk, *shifta* . . .

'You have to tell me what happened to this man,' I said. 'And take your gun away. I will do nothing until you move your gun.'

He lowered the rifle slowly.

'Now tell me what happened. I cannot give medicine if I don't know what has happened to this man.'

'He was injured by a *shabeel*, a leopard,' said Abdi. 'Look.' With that, he moved up to the sick man and roughly pulled the blanket off him. I swear the stench was so powerful the flies had difficulty flapping through it to get at the source.

I looked at the mess on the ground in front of me and mentally cursed the unknown leopard for its incompetence. Why, I thought, must I clear up after this useless animal's bungled handiwork. Tooth-and-claw work, as it had clearly been. The man's lower right leg had been well chewed and his side and belly bore at least three long, very deep scratches – administered no doubt by the bicycling hind legs of a large and furious cat. His right forearm had also been bitten. At least that's what I reckoned had happened as best I could tell. The tissue around the wounds was massively swollen, with a purplish colour. It was suppurating heavily and I could see fly maggots surfacing like pods of tiny dolphins, rejoicing in what was presumably dipteran paradise. I didn't need (didn't want) to touch him to see that he was running a high fever. Unquestionably, he was severely dehydrated. It is part of the immutable credo of traditional African medicine to treat fever by denying the sufferer any liquid and to treat just about everything by administering purges to ensure that any lingering moisture the body may hold is expelled. *Shifta* first aid would undoubtedly hold fast to these tried and trusted principles.

'When did this man last drink?' I demanded.

'He has not eaten or drunk for . . . many days,' said Abdi, counting and recounting under his breath.

'When did this happen?'

Abdi thought for a while.

'Ten days . . . twelve days.'

I thought to myself that the combination of blood poisoning and dehydration would already have curled up the toes of a normal man. Only the fact that he was a Somali *shifta*, tough as a ratel and with the same attitude to adversity, had kept him alive thus far. But even a ratel *can* be killed if you rough him up enough – they don't all die of old age. This particular *shifta* was standing at the gates of hell – with me beside him. 'If I die you die.' Of the certainty of that assertion I had no doubt whatever.

I was concentrating hard now and weighing up what I was going to do. Dad had always been insistent on taking a medicine box wherever we went that would enable us to cope with an accident that involved serious injury, particularly bleeding. Infectious diseases, he said, had to be treated in hospital. There's usually time enough to get help for diseases and in any case you can't carry drugs for all the possibilities. But you can do something about injuries, however caused, because the problems all boil down to the same thing: bleeding and infection. So he made me always carry ex-army packs of electrolytes to make up saline, and a needle, tube and bottle to establish a drip. Plenty of swabs and bandages and a big tin of veterinary wound dressing for keeping the flies off. Sutures and a few other knick-knacks. A big tin of sulphur drugs. Had I got to this ruffian immediately after his encounter with the leopard I could have pre-empted any real problem. But twelve days after the event I had to contend with all the things pre-emptive treatment aimed to defeat: raging infection and the blood poisoning it led to; fever, loss of blood and dehydration. And if gangrene hadn't started yet it was about to. My chances of succeeding weren't good.

The first thing I needed was water to make up a saline solution for a drip. I rummaged around for the sachets of salts that had printed on them the amount of water they were to be dissolved in – sterile, distilled water, of course. Lots of that in your average *shifta* hideout, I said to myself. Looking up at Abdi I said, 'Where do you draw water? I need clean water.'

He gestured with his rifle towards the other defile I'd seen when we arrived. I got up and demanded to be shown. He pushed me with the muzzle of his rifle into the defile and we walked a few yards round the edge of the huge overhang to where it opened onto another, narrow stretch of sandy ground. The other side was a cliff of rock running the whole length of the sand, sixty or seventy yards or so. As with the place we'd just come from the rock was tilted so that it overhung the sand. At the base of this cliff I saw a series of narrow pools. Walking over to them I saw that the water was slowly flowing from right to left. Each pool ended where the water obviously went under the sand, to reappear as another pool a little further on. Each was a little lower than the one upstream of it. I saw that some of the pools extended under the overhang where it had been scoured out over time. I couldn't see how far back under the rock these pools went, as the rock was only just above the surface; but it meant that they were a good deal larger than the narrow stretch of water that was visible. The narrowness of the deep ravine combined with the overhang prevented large birds like vultures from getting to the water as it did any large animals, so that the water hadn't been polluted. All in all, these *shifta* had found themselves a very well appointed lair in a land where the few springs that do flow during the dry season are invariably churned into filthy, shitty bogs by watering animals.

I knelt beside one of the pools and scooped the clear water up to drink. As soon as I put my hands in, several small fish darted up, turning away a few inches from my fingers and circling frantically around. The deeply undercut rock-face sheltered them from the kingfishers and herons that, by the end of the dry season, normally put paid to just about everything that moves in exposed streams and pools. I started to fill my water bottles and tried holding my hands still in the water as it ran into the containers. Sure enough, within seconds the bolder ones were nibbling my skin. The fish were barbus, a familiar denizen of virtually any stream anywhere in tropical Africa. They do not have sharp teeth, but feed by rasping and sucking with their sandpapery mouths the surface of anything that might yield food – a not unpleasant sensation if you dangle your feet in a pool after a hard day's walking.

Abdi interrupted me with a curt, 'What are you doing?' I stood and told him to fill a *sufuria* with clean water and boil it. He shouted to the others and Sufi came to collect the water. We returned to the camp where they got the water on a fire. As soon as the water boiled I set the pot aside to cool. I then ostentatiously laid out a syringe and needles. It was one of those magnificent veterinary syringes for inoculating cattle, a massive stainless steel frame with a huge glass barrel containing a plunger designed to pump massive doses of vaccine into animals weighing five hundred pounds or more. This monstrosity was not in the medicine box by accident. Hutcheon and Dad had taught me that the efficacy of the *ferenge's* medicine is heavily dependent on the needle, the *sindano*, as it's known across East Africa. There is nothing that stirs the superstitious imagination more strongly than the direct insertion into the body of a powerful *muti* – indeed this perception is common to all mankind, educated or not. We are all of us inclined to think a medicine more effective if injected rather than merely swallowed. As Dad had explained to me, given the *sindano's* inherent potency, it's important to make the most of the process. The curative quality of what you inject is as often as not less efficacious than the act of injecting. Make a ceremony of it, he said, use the most imposing props you can and – very important – make sure it hurts. A skilfully administered, painless injection cannot possibly be perceived as curative as one that stings like a centipede. This perception springs from the same mental source as that of sacrifice. Prior suffering is guaranteed to sweeten the ultimate gain: it's a natural antithetical function of the brain.

In another *sufuria* I sterilised the syringe, needles and a small bottle. When the boiled water was cool enough I decanted some into the drip bottle, filtering it through a swab. I filtered some more into the small bottle to use as an injection medium. By now, I had everyone's rapt attention. They weren't even scratching or spitting – just squatting and watching every move I made like cobras watching a rat in the grass. I demanded that a stick be cut with a fork at the end, about six feet long, which was duly procured and stuck into the sandy ground beside the patient. When the drip was ready, I prepared to insert the needle into the back of the man's hand. My audience crowded round for a closer look: things were getting interesting now.

'Now's my chance,' I couldn't help thinking, 'to a man their attention is no longer on me, but on what I'm doing. They're all within a couple of yards. Grab one of their guns and go for it.'

But of course I chickened out. Their rifles held but six rounds – and what if the one I grabbed only had two or three rounds in the magazine? I was outnumbered, and while I might well get one or two of them the others would draw back like genet cats from a striking snake and then strike back before I knew it. I, of course, had been brought up to always carry a gun unloaded, to avoid accidents. To a *shifta*, such pussyfooting around would be incomprehensible. They always carried their rifles with one up the breech, cocked and the safety catch off. Ready to shoot at a moment's notice in accordance with Lesson One of basic *shifta* rifle drill.

So instead, I inserted the needle, taped it in place, connected the drip and hung the bottle from the fork at the end of the stick. That they were impressed was easy to tell. To a man, they stood and stretched, spat, scratched their crotches, picked their noses and discussed the ins and outs of the procedure – as if they had any idea, I thought. But I had one more stunt to pull and started to assemble the syringe. Once again, they readjusted their *kikois* and *shukas*, edged up closer, squatted down or peered over my shoulder, watching intently. I drew up ten cubic centimetres of the isotonic solution I'd made up in the small bottle. Then I had an idea and squirted it back into the bottle. In the medicine box I had some quinine and I remembered Hutcheon saying that quinine injections were pretty *kali*.[69] If I dissolved plenty of quinine in the injection it wouldn't do the patient any appreciable harm. Wouldn't do him any good; but it would hurt much more than plain water. It didn't take me long to decide and I was soon ready. I chose the thickest needle I had and shoved the syringe into his buttock as gracelessly as I could, pressing the plunger down as hard as I dared. Ten cubic centimetres of injectable quinine into the muscle – what there was of it. Even against his considerable background pain it made its mark and he twitched and grunted. The audience twitched and grunted in solidarity.

After thirty-three hours of purgatory, I at last experienced a fleeting moment of satisfaction. It was only a moment, but so sweet; a tiny, delicious soupçon of vengeance.

The moment passed very quickly as I stood up and contemplated the scene. I'm not particularly squeamish, but the next thing I had to do was clean up the appalling, putrefying wounds. I do not recall ever being faced with anything I wanted to do less.

---

[69] Fierce (Swahili)

21

I Do my Florence Nightingale Impression

Before setting about cleaning the sick man's suppurating wounds, I demanded food and told Abdi I would myself go for a wash. More than a wash, I wanted to lie down for a while and recuperate. The depression I'm somewhat prone to was settling thickly on my mind, no doubt catalysed by hunger and fatigue. To be so keyed up from apprehension not to say plain gut-wringing fear for so long is extraordinarily debilitating. I planned to swallow plenty of the aspirin I had in the medicine box and wallow in one of the pools for an hour or so to settle myself down and get back into gear.

They had already been cooking *ugali* and by the time I'd finished with the patient the food was ready. I insisted that they force the sick man to eat, which led to an altercation with Abdi. 'He doesn't want to eat,' he said.

'How do you know?' I said. 'You haven't asked him.'

Always quick to anger, Abdi leapt to his feet and shouted at me in Somali. I shouted back that I didn't speak like a *shufto*; I only spoke like an educated man – in Oromo. Of course, that set him off and he grabbed a piece of wood off the *kuni* pile and hit me with it. I completely lost it then and swung at him, luckily only landing my fist in uncoordinated rage on his upturned forearm. It would hardly have helped my cause to have knocked him down at this point in time. There's a good chance that his next move would have

291

been to shoot me there and then had not the fifth man started yelling in Somali and gesticulating. He was pointing at the recumbent bandit and we all turned to look. He'd seen what was happening and though too weak to make much noise had managed to attract the fifth man's attention. It probably saved my life, because for whatever reason he had their obedience. He beckoned to Abdi who went and knelt beside him. They whispered in Somali for a long time before Abdi got up and sullenly called me over. I came and knelt beside the injured man, still breathless with rage.

'What is the matter?' he demanded. I tried to take the initiative and said that it was impossible for me to treat him if the other men did not do as I said.

'You do not understand,' he whispered. 'Only I give orders. After me, Abdi.'

'I know that,' I said, 'but when it comes to medicine I give the orders. For medicine only. If these men do not obey the orders I give for your treatment I cannot make you well.'

It was an effort for the man, sick as he was, to handle the conversation, but he obviously wasn't going to give up yet. He lay for while before speaking again.

Finally, he said, 'What is it you want done?'

'You must eat and drink,' I said. 'Also, there is *dawa*[70] you must swallow.'

'I cannot eat,' he said. 'It makes me sick.'

'If you refuse to eat you will die. If you vomit, you must eat again until you do not vomit. You have no choice.'

He spoke again in Somali to Abdi who got up and told me to come with him. It seemed the ill man had told him to leave the argument alone and do what I said as Abdi then told me to prepare the food and medicine I had in mind.

---

[70] Medicine (Swahili)

It took a while, but I finally got some *uji*,[71] and a handful of sulphonamide pills into him. I could see it made him retch so I said, forcefully, 'You must not vomit. You must use all your strength not to vomit.' He was a hard-arsed bastard, no question of that. I could see him will himself not to puke – and he succeeded. I told him that if he could master his stomach in that fashion he would survive – with one further proviso: water by mouth. I told him that he would have to drink some water every half hour all through the day whether he wanted to or not. This was a hard one. Abstinence from water when you need it most is a strangely powerful compulsion among Africans and he was nothing if not traditional in this respect. But he did what I said. After all, he was anxious to stay alive and he knew I was his only chance. I told him I was a doctor; my father was a doctor – even my grandfather. Actually, I thought to myself, ironically, my grandfather *was* a doctor even if he did die swiftly of the disease he was supposed to be curing others of. Hardly something to boast about. I told him that if he was being treated by a Somali it would be correct not to drink. But if you are being treated by a *farangi* it's different, I told him. Especially a white *káfir*, I added gratuitously. Then, water has a different effect. Healthy, the humbug would simply have annoyed him. Sick, he wanted to believe it, so he did, more or less.

At last, I was finished and determined to go and rest in one of the pools. I set off across the sand. Immediately Abdi bellowed at me, demanding to know what I was doing. I was past caring by now and, without turning round, yelled back. 'Shoot. My back is toward you. That is how you would normally kill a blind man or a *káfir*.'

Well, give him his due, the bastard did shoot. But to cow, not to kill. He tried to call my bluff by firing a shot just to

---

[71] Maize flour porridge (Swahili)

293

the side of me that hit the rock in front of my face, splitting off several sharp shards, one of which cut me quite deeply on the cheek. As I said, I was past caring. Bravery under fire had nothing to do with it. The insouciance of depression, nothing more, was what saved the day for me. I just sauntered on without breaking my stride or looking to right or left and disappeared into the defile. It must have taken the wind out of even his sails and I've no doubt that his boss had plenty to say to him about it, because he let it be for the time being.

One of the others ran after me and walked behind as I went over to one of the pools, undressed and got in the water. By now, the sun was above the surrounding rocks and the day was hotting up fast. It was a delicious sensation, made all the more marvellous by real exhaustion, to slide into the warm water and wallow there for a while. My guard wandered over to squat in the shade of a rock, pick his nose and mull over whatever it is that a bandit's mind dwells on when not actually murdering and pillaging. Already the barbus were going over my feet assiduously, nibbling at the cracks in the soles, shaving off whatever tiny bits of skin they could. The many scratches on my legs from brushing past the thorny bushes on the way here were particularly attractive and they soon had all the scabby bits polished down to fresh tissue. A couple of deeper cuts commanded serious attention and eventually began to hurt a little as they worried at the tissue. The new cut on my cheek was especially delicious – even barbus prefer their steak rare. Several macrobrachium prawns had crept over from under the overhang and began competing with the fish. For half an hour or so I managed to forget where I was and the predicament I was in. I got quite drowsy and would have fallen asleep if it wasn't for the occasional twinge from an abrasion the fish were working over harder than necessary.

It's strange how some things come to you in a roundabout way, like the legendary voice out of a burning bush. When this happens, the message or idea, whatever it is, seems wholly logical, indisputable, as if it had already been thoroughly gone into. It happened to me that morning shortly after I had reluctantly got up out of the pool. I couldn't handle the fish any longer and some of the small wounds on my legs bled a little as I left the water. I was standing looking down at the injured man, trying to ready myself for the task of cleaning his revolting wounds. Where to start, I wondered? Just moments ago, a few yards away, I had been so comfortable, so relaxed. And now, this disgusting task. I suddenly felt hot and dirty again and actually shuddered at the contemplation of it all. That was when it dawned on me. The fish. The barbus. They would do it perfectly. It was their trade. It was obvious. They'd just done it for me; they could do it for him. Why hadn't I already thought of it?

It was the maggots that got my unconscious mind working on it. I'd read somewhere how surgeons had realised in some conflict of the days before antibiotics that gory battlefield wounds were actually much improved by encouraging fly maggots to feed on shattered and necrosing tissue. I'd already seen them doing just that to this man before me. The hordes of barbus, helped by the water and far bigger and more powerful than fly maggots, would have his wounds knife clean in no time.

I adopted the idea without question and immediately set about putting it into practice. The *shifta*, predictably, were *starjarbued*. Unsettling enough that I made their glorious leader drink water – now the *káfir* wanted to actually *immerse* him in the stuff. None of the three men who'd abducted me had shown the slightest inclination to wash after their long foot safari. They only went to the pools to draw water. Even when they did that, they took care not to get their hands unnecessarily wet. Ugh! Water! Among the *kurra-jog*, water is the most precious thing they know. You don't waste it by washing in it. And I hadn't mentioned the fish yet. Well, I thought, why bring up the matter of the fish. Better fudge that one for the time being – deal with it when the time comes. Going to be hard enough just getting him into the water.

I told Abdi the matter was not for him to decide and knelt down to speak to the patient. He listened while I told him that I had to take him to the water to clean his wounds. I told him that his wounds were poisoning him and that if he refused to be taken and washed he would surely die. He agreed readily enough and also agreed to order Abdi to let me do it. Abdi was as angry and sulky about it as I expected and to minimise further trouble I made an effort not to insult or humiliate him or indeed any of the others until I had my scheme implemented.

I found out from Abdi that the sick man's name was Safwaan. Before moving him, I reconnoitred the pools to see which had the most fish. The one I'd lain in seemed to show the most swirls and gleams of whirling barbus so I scraped out a trench beside it in which to lie the patient. While doing so I pondered the problem of how to ensure that the fish had free access to the man's body, given that his henchmen would be bound to want to drive them away. The more I thought about it the more I realised that getting them to accept that allowing their leader to be eaten alive by fish would take more persuasion than I had at my disposal. The role of the fish had to be downplayed. Somehow, I had to be able to cover him so they couldn't see what was going on in the water. Then I had it – the sun. Tell them he must not lie in the direct sunlight. They'd go for that for sure. Sick people would ordinarily be stuck away in the darkest, gloomiest, most unhygienic spot available. Shielding him from the sun would make total sense to the *kurra-jog*. So I ordered an armful of short sticks to be cut.

These I planned to place over him once he was immersed, the ends resting on the raised sides of the trench so that I could then cover him with a *kikoi* or blanket. The tent would serve a double purpose, because its shade would act like a black heron's wings[72] and positively attract the fish. No one, of course, would volunteer his blanket or *kikoi* for the task. So I first of all had to wash Safwaan's own blanket, reflecting as I did so that it was almost certainly the first time the object had been so treated since he'd stolen it. While I was engaged in that chore I made them put together a litter on which to carry him. It didn't have to be very strong. In his prime, after a good season's piracy, the short, spare Safwaan probably weighed no more than ten stone. In his present state I doubt he weighed eight. Finally, I was ready and we slowly got him onto the litter and carried him to the pool, with one man holding up the drip. He made no sound nor showed any sign of pain or discomfort. I laid him in the trench I'd prepared with his head resting on the sand at one end, the long gouges from the leopard's hind feet uppermost. The depth was about right, with all the wounds submerged. I laid the sticks across the trench and placed the blanket on top, shading the length of his body. Then I ordered the whole slouching gang away, saying I needed to work in peace, cleaning his wounds bit by bit. They shuffled off grudgingly to spit and scratch and swat flies in the shade of the rocks on the other side of the sand, watching closely, no doubt, to see what I was about. I simply lifted a small part of the blanket and fiddled about underneath, moving slowly from his head downward. The black heron technique worked perfectly and within minutes every fish in the pool must have been under the blanket, jostling

---

[72] Black herons stand in shallow water and arch their wings to make a parasol that nearby fish, paradoxically, swim under to hide from predators. Nature plays some dirty tricks on the innocent.

for a chance to chew at his wounds. Thank God, I thought, that fish aren't squeamish.

I debated in my mind whether or not to tell Safwaan what I was up to. He lay quite still, eyes closed, saying nothing so in the end I decided to also say nothing unless he asked. If he didn't know maybe he wouldn't even wonder what was going on. The warm water must have been pleasant and restful, and I knew from my own experience how soothing the activity of the fish can be. True, they would soon open up fresh tissue and eventually their rasping would hurt. But until then he wouldn't probably feel very much. If I kept up an appearance of activity he might, as I hoped the others would, assume it was me causing the sensations associated with his wounds.

In the end, it all worked as well as I could have hoped. The fish quickly cleaned the smaller wounds and within half an hour or so had removed most of the dead tissue and debris. Then, as I expected, they started to get through to fresh tissue and Safwaan began to twitch and eventually complain. Fresh blood appeared in the water, which caused the fish to redouble their efforts. I decided to bring the treatment to an end before I caused more damage than good. Some of the barbus were quite big and strong and getting bolder by the second. I took off the cover and called the gang over to carry him back. Florence, I thought to myself, would've been proud of me.

Though his wounds still gave off a rotten smell it was a mere whiff compared with the head-spinning stench of before. I don't think Safwaan himself or any of his pack of thieves noticed any change, or if they noticed, cared. But for me the relief was vast and it encouraged me to continue treating him with more diligence than I would have otherwise. As soon as we got back into the shade I smeared the wounds with the black, glutinous veterinary wound dressing, mainly to keep the flies and ants off, but also to create a favourable healing environment at the tissue surface. This tarry ointment worked well with cattle – it should suffice for your average *shifta*, I felt. Not that I proposed to mention this to any of the present company, who were, in point of fact, clearly impressed by the treatment as I suppose they would've been by virtually anything I did, provided it didn't resemble anything they were familiar with. There just wasn't anything else I could do. My medicine box contained only a few bandages and dressings – not nearly enough to bandage and rebandage his extensive injuries. I had a few sutures – but stitching any of his wounds closed at this stage with infection rampant would almost certainly worsen things. The less I fiddled with the injuries from now on, the better.

By now, the hideout was getting hot, really hot. The ravine lay well below the surrounding terrain so that any breeze there might have been wasn't going to have much effect on us. The huge boulders around us absorbed the uninterrupted sun's heat and were beginning to radiate it out again. The four bandits were starting to make themselves as comfortable as they could in the shadiest places along the overhang. I had an idea.

'Abdi,' I called. 'Abdi. Come.' He was clearly furious at the double irritation of being cursorily summoned by the *kafir* and having to leave his shady spot. Having progressed Safwaan's treatment this far I now felt more relaxed about coming up with ways to screw the other *shifta* around without starting something I couldn't handle. 'I'm not going to do all the work of making Safwaan better,' I told him. 'You are his people, you have to help.'

Abdi, ever quick to boil, was seething; but he managed to hold his tongue, waiting to see what I was up to.

'Are you going to leave him to suffer on the hard ground?' I demanded, pointing to the recumbent figure. 'Have you no respect for your leader? What do you think he will say when he is recovered? That his comrades left him to endure the stony ground, devoured by ants and scorpions?' I was beginning to enjoy myself, the more so as I saw how angry Abdi had become. He was literally trembling with suppressed rage, but with Safwaan in earshot he dared not respond as he would've liked to.

I saw that I was right about the awe in which they held him. I could only guess at Safwaan's hold over them, but I suppose it was all tied up in some fiendishly tortuous Somali *godoh*[73] or more likely *diya*.[74] Feuding is endemic in Somaliland. Nothing commands more attention or expends more energy than reckoning up the *godoh* between two clans, or two families or two individuals. It never ends, because by definition there can be no balance – a situation brought about by the simple fact that, over the generations, no one can indisputably demonstrate who posted the first *godoh*. Having reckoned up the score at any given moment the outstanding grievances must be settled, in as violent and telling a way as possible. That then, in the eyes of the other party, creates a fresh *godoh* – and so on *ad infinitum*. Blood grievances where someone is killed are of course the most cherished of all and in the ideal Somali world should only be avenged by a matching murder. As the ancient injunction has it: without shedding of blood there is no remission. However, as in all human affairs, money or property of one sort or another can lead to a reconsideration of a revenge killing. Thus Somalis make room in their society for *diya* – material compensation for a slaying. All human beings adore intrigue, murder and vengeance, and can bend righteousness into extraordinarily contorted shapes in the execution of these great pursuits. But none can make quite such a monkey's muddle of it all, and pursue it with such

---

[73] Grievance feuded over (Somali)
[74] Compensation in blood for major grievance (Somali, Swahili)

mindless wrath and righteousness as a Somali. If there is one thing that might turn a *shifta*'s thoughts from simple robbery with violence it is a matter concerning *godoh* or *diya*. Somewhere along the unthinkable line that Safwaan and his gang must have pursued in their reprehensible lives Abdi and the other scoundrels must have created a *diya* in which they owed their lives to Safwaan. Nothing else could explain their allegiance to him at a time when any one of them could have cut his throat one-handed. Even if the details had been available to me it's unlikely that I could have understood the intricacies that would almost certainly have shrouded the matter. Neither was I curious to know: it could only have been blood-curdling.

'You must make a bed for him, as befits a big man who lies sick among his own people.'

'How can there be a bed?' demanded Abdi. 'Do you think there are shops near here?'

I almost warmed to the man as he revealed a hitherto unsuspected flair for sarcasm.

'If there were shops near here,' I said, 'you would long ago have looted them and murdered the owners. You are nothing but *shufto*, murderers of orphans, rapers of old women and . . .'

I had been going to add donkeys, but managed at the last moment to restrain myself. Don't get too carried away, I told myself, this brute is beside himself with frustrated rage. Today is not a good day to die. Instead, I quickly told him to take the lazy fools lolling in the shade of the rock, like tired baboons I wanted to add but didn't, and cut poles and sticks with which to make a bed.

'Perhaps you have never seen a bed,' I said, 'but do not worry, I will show you what it looks like.' Just at that moment, Safwaan groaned and moved awkwardly, trying to shift his position. I don't know how much of our talk he'd heard, or paid attention to, if any, but his timing was good nonetheless. 'See,' I said, 'he is in pain. He needs a soft bed on which to lie.'

Abdi bent and spoke to him in Somali. Safwaan nodded faintly without replying and Abdi straightened up, spat, and without looking at me walked quickly back to the others. He snapped at them and with much whingeing and wasting of time they got themselves together, found an axe and a couple of pangas, hitched up their *kikois* repeatedly, blew their noses, coughed, spat and bickered before shouldering their rifles and shambling off up the side of the ravine. I was pleased enough at having stuffed up their quiet morning, but was then overjoyed to see that they *all* went off, quite forgetting to leave someone to guard me. I knew it couldn't last, so I just stood there, hands on my hips, looking after them. Sure enough, as they started clambering over the rocks Abdi suddenly stopped and yelled at them in Somali. He really screamed, as one whose fault it is screams at someone he hopes to blame, and Sufi wordlessly detached himself from the others and wandered back to camp. I laughed as loudly as I could and Ahmed, the man who'd been left to look after Safwaan during my abduction, and Bashir glanced back. Ahmed made the mistake of sniggering whereupon Abdi, dying to vent his rage on someone or something, whacked him viciously with the muzzle of his rifle, cursing. I laughed again and stood and watched as they disappeared into the rocks. I smirked at Sufi, but he was commendably impassive and managed to act as if he couldn't see me at all.

I spent a peaceful few hours in the shade occasionally getting up to make Safwaan drink some water. I'd given him a lot of sulpha pills, thereby running the risk of collapsing his kidneys if he didn't seriously rehydrate over the next few hours. Not surprisingly, he began to find that he quite liked a regular drink of water and it became easier to get it into him sip by sip. The fact that he was feeling thirsty was a good sign, though he was otherwise still very weak, emaciated and feverish. The drip emptied and I made a fresh bottle.

The woodcutters of course managed to stay out for the rest of the day and it was evening before I could get a rough bed made for Safwaan. I didn't really care where the bastard lay, but, as I didn't have to think of ways of making him uncomfortable – I could hardly better his situation in that respect – I might just as well concentrate on getting him to recover. As it was extremely difficult for him to move at all I didn't want bedsores to develop and complicate things. So the softer the surface he lay on the better. A bed would also help keep the ants at bay and for all that I used it to give Abdi a hard time I knew that all the fuss I made would contribute to the air of medical authority that I needed to create and maintain.

I'd told Abdi to strip plenty of acacia bark, like elephants did, so that we could lace a flexible support of bark strips between the longitudinal poles of the bed frame. They knew what to do and it didn't take long to botch up a bed frame and support it on rocks at the corners. There was no such thing as grass anywhere nearby, but they'd collected enough leaves to make a semblance of a mattress and in due course Safwaan was installed in his hospital bed, drip by his bedside, flies frustrated by the wound dressing, consultant medic on hand – in short all that a wounded *warenleh*[75] could wish for. I couldn't help feeling what a surreal, ridiculous scene it made. If Dad, Leila and Hutcheon could see me now they'd be hysterical with laughter.

I went to sleep that night quite relaxed. Safwaan wasn't I reckoned going to die before morning, so I figured to get as good a sleep as I could, given that I wasn't exactly in a top-of-the-range room at Torr's Hotel. I told Abdi that I didn't want to be disturbed unless Safwaan asked for me, and he

[75] Warrior (Somali)

suffered that order in silence. Wearing him down, am I, I thought to myself? Though I knew that to be very far from the case in reality. He was about as well disposed towards me as a cornered mamba, and I mentally told myself to watch my step. If he thought he could get away with anything to hurt me he wouldn't hesitate. Bashir's desire to add me to the macabre gnawings on his rifle stock was child's play compared with the pure hatred Abdi undoubtedly felt. No – Abdi was a far more dangerous hazard in my present life and I would be well advised to tread warily. So I contented myself with instructing him to ensure that someone gave Safwaan a drink every two hours throughout the night.

In the morning Safwaan was not perceptibly changed, except that his face was a little less sunken and gaunt, evidence that my efforts at rehydration were paying off. But he was still running a high fever, and very weak. On the other hand, he wasn't worse – but then worse would really be another way of saying dead: he wasn't far from the Big Hideout in the Sky. After the elation of the day before when I felt I was gaining ground I was now depressed and disillusioned again. A fistful of sulphonamide and some water – that was really all I had with which to save our two lives. He had blood poisoning, he had no fat reserves before he began, let alone now, and his immune system, well, I just couldn't imagine the war being waged inside his scrawny, emaciated carcass. Hard-arsed sod though he was, even the Alexander the Greats of the world fall sick and curl their toes up easily enough. I remembered the line from *Peter Pan* or some like baloney, *to die will be an awfully big adventure*, and thought what crap that bloke Barrie talks. Only someone who hasn't stood outside the Pearly Gates could possibly come up with such *twak*, I thought. I dug out another handful of sulpha pills and set about getting them into Safwaan's system. At least he was drinking more easily now and this time he didn't start retching as soon as he'd swallowed them. But his eyes, sunk deep in their sockets, still had the dull, dry look of a dead animal's eyes and he was wretchedly weak.

After reloading his drip and checking his wounds, which at least seemed no worse, I wandered off and found a shady spot. I'd no appetite and had to force myself to eat some of the *ugali* the *shifta* cooked. I noticed how they all avoided me and tried not to catch my eye – that at least bucked me up a little. Nothing like a little mutual loathing to dispel the blues. I made a mental note to keep the level of hatred as high as it presently was by not making even the slightest move towards general conversation or common interest of any sort other than the welfare of Safwaan. I decided to combat depression and keep myself going by mentally reviewing and memorising every detail of the lie of the land and of the men and their weapons. Each had a rifle and Abdi also kept with him my revolver and its belt holding twenty cartridges, plus another rifle I took to be Safwaan's. It wasn't too difficult to figure out how much ammunition there was in the hideout, because the men loved to idle away the time by going through their cartridge clips, emptying and refilling them, inserting them into their guns and levering the rounds into and out of the breeches, over and over again. They hadn't much; an average, I reckoned, of fourteen rounds each, variously distributed.

At the forefront of my mind was the matter of my ultimate escape. If ever there was a setting for a replay of the legendary tableau of the lion with a thorn in its foot, this was it – except that I was thinking of Hutcheon's version of the old Roman tale. The story goes that the runaway slave, Androcles, chances upon a lion incapacitated by a thorn in its foot. Setting aside their traditional enmity, Androcles high-mindedly removes the thorn from the foot of the suffering lion and the two go their separate ways. Years later both Androcles and the lion are captured and

305

meet again, this time in the arena. But the lion recognises Androcles and declines to harm him. The emperor Tiberius on hearing why the lion spared Androcles frees them both. It seems, though, that Hutcheon had one day chanced on a *Punch* cartoon in which the fabled lion, recovering rapidly once the thorn is pulled, thinks to himself, what the hell, why pass up a chance like this and kills and eats Androcles. Hutcheon had laughed himself to tears and had the cartoon framed and hung up in the mess tent. 'The *oke* that drew that had your dad to a T, ay! Just can't help pulling thorns out of lions' feet, however often they turn round and *moera* him. It's his destiny, ay.' Well, my destiny was beginning to shape up pretty clearly. If Safwaan recovered, was he, a *shifta*, a plundering murderer, magically going to express a depth of conscience never before displayed by one of his ilk? Was he, hell. Towards me, a *káfir*, and moreover a *faranji káfir* who had systematically insulted and abused his comrades? Even if he were willing to consider turning me loose Abdi and the other ruffians absolutely never would let it happen. Whether Safwaan lived or died I was a dead man walking, no doubt about it.

Much as I wished I could think of a plan that would allow me to gain the upper hand by knocking out all five of them I knew my chances of ever achieving that were slim indeed. I was outnumbered by adversaries who were far more attuned than I would ever be to defending themselves from attack, who would not be cowards and who would love above all things to kill me. The more I thought about it the more I realised that the only plan that could hope to succeed would be to escape unseen and make a desperate attempt to get far enough away quickly enough that trying to find me would become too boring for them. Except that I knew where their hideout was. Or at least they would think that I did, though, in truth, I had only a hazy idea as to its general location. Escape at night was never much of a proposition. The *shifta* were too wary of lions not to keep someone on watch throughout the night. While sentries were apt to fall asleep, it actually wasn't so difficult for them to stay awake at night because they spent so much of the day asleep. Presumably, they were going to skulk around their hideout until Safwaan recovered – or died, perish the thought – so I could assume that the status quo would prevail for the foreseeable future. Escape, if I was going to achieve it, would have to be during the day. The circumstance that offered the best chance was when I was alone with only one guard. These conditions applied only when I went for a shit or to wallow in the pool. I began to think more about the latter. If I went during the heat of the day I would have the best chance of my guard dozing off – it was, after all, their favourite time to sleep. I decided to make that my plan in the absence of any better strategy and when the sun was at its hottest made for the water. I wallowed about for an hour or more and was encouraged to see that my guard of the day, Ahmed, did indeed doze off in the shade of the boulder he was sprawled in. Not enough to enable an escape – if I'd done anything out of the ordinary he'd have come to, like as not; but I reckoned that after a couple of days they might well get a lot slacker.

By the end of the day, Safwaan was perceptibly improved. He'd drunk a lot all afternoon, had been moving on his bed more, and in the evening he spoke to me. He asked how I thought he was and told me he felt a little stronger. The following morning he was definitely improved, much stronger and though still feverish I reckoned his temperature had fallen considerably. He still lacked the will to converse much, saying only a few words to me and to Abdi. I spent the rest of the day worrying. I was confident now that barring a severe relapse he would likely recover. That, ironically, meant that I would not therefore get the bullet for failing to save their Glorious Leader's life, but for becoming redundant. Damnation's damnable double whammy. And why? Because that day-dreaming *dikkop* of a father of mine couldn't stop chasing around after some old Hebrew chieftain's mythical gold mines. I looked around me at the dull black basalt boulders. I thought of all the lava fields that bestrew this hell's waiting room of a desert and thought to myself, as I had so many times before, that there was about as much chance of finding gold in this abomination of desolation as there was of finding pubic hairs on a naked mole rat. I would never have got into this mess if Dad hadn't sent me up here looking for gold. Bloody gold. I paced around, racking my brains and coming up with nothing. That night I slept only fitfully and got up as dawn was breaking with a crushing headache.

Safwaan on the other hand woke up greatly improved. No doubt about it, the bastard was on top of the infection of his wounds and gathering strength by the hour. Around midday, when the others had spread themselves around the shady spots and were either talking quietly or dozing, Safwaan beckoned to me. I walked over to him and he indicated that I should sit down.

He mumbled a couple of platitudes and then said, 'You saved my life. I am grateful.' He paused and before I could say anything he added, 'I will not forget.'

I replied to the effect that I was glad he was recovering and, then, decided not to pussyfoot around the matter – much more pressing in my mind of course – of how now to save my own life, notwithstanding that I was in excellent health.

'Safwaan,' I said, 'you now will live with only some scars to remind you of how close to death you were. Now it is I who face death, as I'm sure you understand.'

He moved his position a bit, the better to look straight at me. For a long while he said nothing, just stared hard into my eyes. 'It is not certain,' he said.

22

A Proposition from Hell

'You see,' said Safwaan, I have a proposition to make to you.'

I looked at him and I must say I got the cold shivers, notwithstanding the heat of the day that was approaching its peak. Something in me didn't want to hear what he had to say. I began to feel my headache again, just when I thought it was fizzling out. I felt a powerful urge to change the subject, get away from whatever it was he had in mind. I definitely didn't want to know.

'Safwaan,' I said, 'how did you come to get these wounds? Abdi said you had been attacked by a leopard.'

'Ah,' he said, 'the *shabeel*,' and looked over to the piles of leopard skins and wire snares tucked under the overhang. 'There are some Gabbra near here who obtain leopard skins for me. In return we do not molest them.'

He paused and grinned. 'You understand we are *shufto* and we must live. But there are many leopard in this area and the people are clever at trapping them, so they pay us in that way.'

One step better than bloody murder, I thought to myself, good old neighbourhood extortion.

'But one of us – that young man, Ahmed – is himself a good leopard hunter. The people did not bring many skins this month – we do not stay here long, you understand? We *kurra-jog* move all the time . . . *shufto* cannot stay for long in one place.'

'So, I told Ahmed to set some snares to try to get some more skins before we moved away. He put out many traps and after two days we went to see if any leopard were caught. He did not put all the wires in one place and we separated, each man to check a certain number of traps.

'I came near one trap and I heard a leopard growl. I was pleased, as I knew we had caught one. I approached carefully – I think you understand how dangerous leopards are?'

I raised my eyebrows and nodded, looking at his wounds.

'Sure enough, I came upon a leopard and saw that the wire was around its shoulders so that it remained alive. The animal was frightened and jumped away from me. Each time it jumped the wire stopped it and it fell back to the ground. It became frantic and jumped with great power. It was difficult for me to aim my rifle. Eventually I fired at its head and it fell to the ground and lay still. I thought it was dead whereas in fact the bullet had only knocked it senseless. As I approached, the animal woke up and seeing me much closer it jumped at me as if to attack. But I stood still, trying to get a good aim with my rifle, as I knew the animal could not reach me. But – I was wrong, as you know, and before I could shoot, the animal was upon me and – well, you can see the consequence of my carelessness. It might have killed me there and then, but Abdi and Sufi heard the noise and came to help. They killed the animal as it was savaging me – that is the skin . . . that one, there.

'Only then did we see that when it was jumping so strongly to escape the wire had broken. You know how if you bend wire many times eventually it breaks. Even the leopard did not know it had broken the wire. The last bits of wire must have parted when it made the final jump towards me.'

Safwaan was not the first person to make such mistakes with leopards, nor would he be the last.

I mumbled something to the effect that he was lucky to

310

have survived – many others had died in similar circumstances.

'Then,' he continued, 'I fell ill from the wounds. We knew where you were camped – we always know where you and your father are, and that other white man who is his friend.'

He saw my expression and chuckled. 'You should understand that it is my business to know what goes on in this country. As *shufto* we keep a watch on everyone's activities.

'Anyway,' he continued, 'I discussed with Abdi what to do and we agreed that you should be brought here to make me well. We had heard many stories from the people of how your father was a great doctor and had cured many people of bad illnesses. So I sent Abdi and the others to capture you.'

Just like that, I thought. How nice. We need that white man – simply go and abduct him, as in go down to the *dukas*,[76] and buy a tin of sardines. We had always assumed that any *shifta* in the part of the N.F.D. we operated in would know something about us, but I hadn't realised just how matter-of-factly we fitted into their scheme of things. We were, the way Safwaan put it, little more than *maridadi*[77] in this part of the world.

He saw my discomfiture and chuckled again. 'There are many secrets in the bush,' he said, 'but you are not one of them.'

I had to laugh. I suppose that to him, in what to us is the vastness of the N.F.D., we stood out like luminous unicorns.

'Then we nearly missed you,' he said.

'Oh,' I said, 'what do you mean?'

'That night you were captured was lucky for us. Abdi was watching you from that hill south of your camp on the wadi.

---

[76] Shops (Swahili)
[77] Decoration (Swahili)

He planned to surprise you asleep in your camp. But then he saw you drive away and thought he had failed. Then he saw you stop – perhaps because of a puncture – and realised that if he was quick he might be able to ambush you further down the track. As you know, the track first goes east then returns west and passes a few miles south of the hill he was on. So they marched really fast to cut the track south of the hill while you repaired your *gharry*.'

'They reached the track before you passed and waited in ambush. But you never came. So they walked back up the road and saw that you had camped for the night.'

Safwaan delivered this intelligence laconically as one would describe some mundane exercise to collect a goat from someone over the way. That and the revelation that he kept track of Dad's movements as a matter of course was somewhat chilling. He made it all sound quite ordinary, except that these were *shifta* we were talking about, not neighbours. If we were an open book then an obvious consequence was that at any time they could choose to set upon us and kill us. A thought occurred to me.

'If, as you say, Abdi walked back up the road and saw that I had stopped for the night . . . that would've been the early evening. But he did not attack me until midnight – at least six hours later. Why? Why did he wait so long?'

Safwaan smiled and laughed his quiet laugh. 'You are correct,' he said, 'Abdi came upon you as the sun was setting. When he realised you were going to sleep there he decided to rest before capturing you. You see, he and the others were very tired. They had not slept since leaving here, and also they had moved swiftly from the hill down to the road to ambush you – a distance of many miles.' He paused and added, 'Abdi is very experienced in such matters – I depend upon him for many things.'

I stared at Safwaan. 'You mean he just rested there, close to where I was?'

'Yes. They all slept in turn, with one man on guard for a couple of hours, then another. It is more complicated if you have a prisoner to control as well.' He laughed again and went on. 'They told me when they came up to you that you were sleeping very deeply, that it took some time to wake you up. Abdi had made a good decision – you will agree?'

The cold-blooded bastards. It gave me gooseflesh to think back on what had actually taken place a few days ago with these anointed scoundrels casually catching up on their beauty sleep while I slept a couple of hundred yards away in total ignorance of their presence and what they were about to do.

'Yes, I agree that Abdi made a good decision. I can see, too, that he is wise in the ways of the bush and of men. That is one reason why I know that he will kill me as soon as he knows that you will not die. For what possible reason would he let me go free? Moreover, that accursed man, Bashir – he is a *shaytaan*, a shameless *shufto* with no respect for any person on earth, except, it seems, you. He would cut my throat as casually as he would squeeze a tsetse fly.'

'These men obey me,' said Safwaan. 'Your life is not for them to decide. Do not forget there is *diya* they must pay or their own lives will be forfeit.'

'You cannot control everything they do. If they really want to kill me, they will not do it in your presence. They will follow me in the bush like hyenas, and as with hyenas I will not be able to hide my tracks from them. Even a *shufto* could not outwit a hyena if it chose to follow him.'

I decided to push him a bit to see how he reacted. 'How do I know that they will in fact obey you in the matter of my life? I am not a Somali – I am a *káfir*. They will not regard my life as having any part of whatever *diya* it is that binds them in allegiance to you. If they killed me what power do you have that could make them pay for such an action, make them pay so much that they might fear to do it? They would think that whatever you said about a mere *káfir* would soon be forgotten – that all they would have to deal with is your anger. And they are not afraid of another's mere anger – not even yours.'

His reaction did not encourage me. He did not look at me, but rather chose to look away, and scratch himself. Not good signs. I had touched the truth or something close enough to it.

'They will do as I say,' he repeated, rather lamely I thought, though I realised that my pessimism could just as easily be doing the judging for me. But at least I felt I had ascertained that Safwaan himself was not planning to kill me. I had the strong feeling that rubbing me out was not on his mind, at least not at the moment.

Safwaan then asked me, very politely, for some water, which I fetched. He drank and settled himself in a more comfortable position. 'Mr Alan,' he said, looking me directly in the eye now. 'Mr Alan, I have a proposition to make to you and your father. I think you will see that I do not wish to threaten your life.' He paused and drank some more water. 'When I first came to know about your father I thought he was only interested in cattle and ivory. I did not like to see another buying ivory, which I considered my business, but he had a lot of money and he did his business always with money. I had no money so really we were not competing one with another. He had his business, I had mine.' He paused again, then added, 'Also . . . he was well armed and wise in the ways of this land. I knew that to plunder him would be difficult and that we *shufto* would perhaps suffer if we tried.' He laughed his quiet laugh. 'I myself did not want to die fighting your father.'

He paused for a while before continuing. 'Sometimes these useless people of mine urge me to raid your father's kraal because they believe he has a vast amount of money hidden there. And many fine guns. At such times I remind them of what happened to Hassan Asaf when he thought he would become rich by raiding your father.'

'Who is Hassan Asaf?' I asked.

'He is the *shufto* you and your father killed that day four years ago. I think you remember? You killed many *shufto* that day and one other nearly died from his wounds.'

Safwaan was grinning as he recounted this. 'Hassan Asaf was a man of no account – you did a good thing that day. We Somalis say that Somali lives are cheap as dust and that man and his followers were nothing more than dust. But I knew then what I had long suspected – that only stupid men attack your father.'

He paused again for quite a while before adding, 'I know, though, that many *shufto* are stupid men.' Again, he paused. 'Fire with honour – you know that Somali saying?'

'No – what does it mean?'

'A Somali knows he will probably go to hell, considering the life he has led. Certainly, all *shufto* know that. But they say it doesn't matter, as long as they die with honour. Hassan Asaf was the sort of Somali who, when your bullets hit him, believed he would go to hell – but with honour.'

I thought it best at this juncture to say nothing to all that.

After a while, Safwaan went on. 'But then I learnt that your father is not really so interested in cattle, or even ivory. I began to hear stories that his real purpose is to look for gold. I have even heard that he seeks some old gold mine from the days of the ancestor Ibrahim. Tell me – is that true? Somalis tell so many lies – as do the Rendille and the Gabbra – that sometimes it is hard to recognise the truth, especially when they do not know what they are talking about and do not even know themselves if what they say is lies.'

I laughed as he said this and thought, as I had already, that there was a lot more to this ruffian Safwaan than would

315

normally be expected from a *shifta*. I marvelled yet again at the extent of his intelligence regarding Dad. Now it was my turn to avoid his eye, look away and scratch thoughtfully. No point in being evasive, I thought, he knows so much he'll spot it straightaway if I start dissembling.

'What you heard is the truth,' I said, 'except for one thing. The mines my father dreams about are not from the days of the father, Ibrahim, whom we call Abraham. Long after the time of Ibrahim, many generations later, there was a great prophet Suleiman, Solomon we call him, who was descended from Ibrahim. This Suleiman, the son of David and Bathsheba, is written of in both the Koran and the Christian Bible. He lived in Jerusalem – the holy city of both the Arabs and the Jews, as you know – and was a mighty king.

'Long before you *shufto* started plundering this land King Suleiman was raiding here. He was very powerful and he controlled all business from Jerusalem as far south as here. Slaves, ivory, incense, leopard skins, and – gold. In particular, gold. The Christian Bible says that Solomon obtained great quantities of very fine gold from somewhere in the Ogaden – it does not say exactly where. They called the place Ophir, but today there is nowhere by that name. Eventually Solomon died, but his sons were useless boys who wasted his wealth and lost the business he had made. The location of the gold mines was also forgotten – to this day.

'My father – indeed his father and his grandfather too – have always had the dream of one day finding the lost gold mines of King Solomon. My great-grandfather is buried somewhere in the Ogaden. Before you or I were born, about fifty-five or sixty years ago, he came here with two other white men and searched for these mines. He was killed by the Rendille or the Borana or the Gabbra some-

316

where in this country – I do not know exactly where. His grave is forgotten, I think.'

'You say your great-grandfather came here – what of your grandfather? Is he still alive?'

'No. My grandfather died as a very young man, in the year of his marriage. My father never knew his father.'

Safwaan nodded and looked away. He sat for quite a time without saying anything then he turned to me again. 'I too have heard of ancient gold mines in this part of the Ogaden,' he said. 'The Gabbra say that gold was found here long ago, but they themselves know nothing of it. There is some gold mined today in the south of Ethiopia, in the area of Negele – Borana country. However, the people say the Negele mines are new, that in the time of their fathers and grandfathers gold was unknown there. They say the old gold mines were south of Negele at a place that has been forgotten.'

Now he had my undivided attention. For the next half hour we talked of the stories Safwaan said he'd heard – whom from, where, when, and so on. I couldn't tell if he was just humbugging me or on the level – he was far too inscrutable a man for someone as naïve as I to deconstruct. On the whole, though, I was inclined to believe him with the one proviso that kept recurring; namely, that Dad had never heard these stories. On the other hand, Dad had not spent much time in this part of Solomon's Triangle and certainly had not talked to all the families that grazed this part of the world. Safwaan lived infinitely closer to the land and the people than we did. It was possible he was not making it all up. In any event, what was more to the point was what Safwaan was leading up to. It was clear to me by now that he had more on his mind than he had divulged so far.

Once again, he paused and reflected for quite some time,

while I sat and concentrated on killing some of the more persistent flies that attended us. Two Ruppell's vultures glided overhead and examined our camp as they always did when they had nothing better to do, which was most of the time. Sometimes one or two of them would plane down and sit on the crest of the highest boulder slightly upstream of camp, the better to watch and see if by any lucky chance something edible might be forthcoming from our establishment. After a couple of hours or so they would get bored and catch a thermal to take them back up to the cooler air a couple of thousand feet above ground.

Safwaan interrupted my reverie by saying, 'You see, Mr Alan, when I discovered that your father was interested in gold rather than the things we *shufto* deal in I thought differently. I asked myself why should I interfere with this man now – and maybe feel a hot bullet for my trouble – when I could wait until he found this gold.' Once again, he laughed sardonically when he saw my reaction to this revelation. Bloody hell, I thought, there is no bottom to the well of iniquity these *shifta* will draw from. So, he planned to sit there like some *nyangau*[78] while the sweating lion risked its hide wrestling the sharp-horned kicking beast to the ground; then, when all the hard work was done swagger up and pirate the booty.

All the same, I had to laugh. 'Safwaan,' I said, 'you are a rascal, a shameless rascal. Even the Mad Mullah would have wagged his finger at you.'

'Not him,' said Safwaan, chuckling. 'Compared to him, we *shufto* are like innocent children.'

'So you planned to wait until my father found the gold mines and then steal them from him?' I said. 'What do you think my father will say when I tell him I saved your life when I had it in my power to consign you to hell?'

---

[78] Slang for a marauding wild beast (Swahili)

'*Shufto* understand one another,' Safwaan replied, 'your father in his way is a *shufto* too.'

'Shit . . .' I began, but Safwaan put his hand up quickly and interrupted me. 'Wait, Mr Alan, wait. I have other things to say.' He smiled and added, 'But you must agree my plan was a sensible one?'

'Safwaan – I believe you would sell your grandmother into slavery if the price was good.' He just laughed his sardonic little laugh, of course, and said, 'Nobody would buy her. She is too lazy and bad tempered.

'Mr Alan,' he then said, 'I cannot easily move. Bring my possessions – those over there.' He indicated a dirty bundle made of a *shuka* knotted together to contain what presumably passed for his personal effects. I got up and brought the bundle to him, surprised at its weight. I sat down again and watched, with some curiosity I must say, to see what a *shifta*'s luggage contained. A shirt, no less, worn so thin it could not even hold much dirt. It might possibly at one time have been coloured blue. A curved knife in a sheath (I thought briefly, very briefly, of the blood that knife must have let in its time). Some rounds of 6.5 mm ammo for his gun. My revolver in its holster: that was interesting – I had not seen him divest Abdi of this bit of loot. I chose to ignore it for the time being. A small, tatty book that I assumed was a Koran. A bundle of the tiny leather pouches not more than an inch and a half square that most Moslems carry in the bush. Passages from the Koran, minutely printed, are sewn into them as talismans against outrageous fortune. What looked like, from its shape, a razor blade wrapped in a scrap of paper. A little silver earwax excavator of the kind popular in Ethiopia. A small, tight roll of banknotes contained by a piece of dirty string. Two boxes of matches. Several giraffe hair bracelets. Plus two or three other shapeless cloth wrappings containing the devil knew not what unspeakable little objects. His entire wardrobe

consisted of the shirt, the *kikoi* he was wearing, a *shuka* and
the backup *shuka* that doubled as his suitcase. I asked if I
could look at the book that I assumed was a Koran. He
nodded and I picked it up and opened it. It was not a
Koran – it was a volume of Somali poetry as far as I could
judge from the way the words were set out on the pages. I
asked him if in point of fact he could read and he replied
that he could. As usual, he smiled at my doubtful
expression. I opened the book at random and asked him to
read what was written there. He did so easily – as far as I
could tell – and so I asked him to translate into Oromo.

> *You know nothing young man, you are a fool.*
> *Your head is choked up with stupidity*
> *Else you surely would not be so useless.*
> *You will be lost; but I take refuge from these matters*
> *With the Everlasting One.*

'Do you know whose words those are?'
I shook my head.
'The one you spoke of not long ago, the *wadad wal*, the
Mad Mullah. He was much admired by us Somalis for his
poetry as well as for his bravery and his scornful defiance of
the British.'
Once again, I had occasion to marvel at this man: on the
one hand a barbaric ruffian living on the bones of his arse,
permanently on the lam; on the other a literate in a land
whose people are almost universally illiterate.
'You are surprised that I can read,' he said. 'I can write,
too, though not easily.'
'Then why are you nothing but a *shufto*?' I asked. 'You
cannot pretend it is an honourable occupation for an
educated man.' I added for good measure, 'Or for an
uneducated man, either.'
He laughed at this, and allowed only that it was a long

story. 'You do not want to hear my story,' he said. 'You are right to say that my life has not always been an honourable one. Do you know what my name means?'

'No.'

'It means "stony ground". It is really an Arabic name and is not the name my mother and father chose for me when I was born. My mother wanted to call me Nadif and at first my father agreed. However, when I was still quite a young boy I started to be very troublesome and caused my mother much sadness. Eventually my father started to call me Safwaan, the name I came to be known by. He said that when I was conceived his seed had obviously fallen on stony ground.'

He began unwrapping one of the bundles, larger than the rest, undoing several layers of rag before revealing the contents: two stones, a larger and a smaller. He handed me the larger, saying nothing. I took it and immediately noticed its heaviness. As I held it up to the light, I realised straightaway what it was. It was a piece of greenstone through which wound several ribbony dark seams – but that was not what I was looking at. The seams positively glinted with gold, and not fool's gold; but the genuine article, as the weight of the object attested. The quantity and size of the flecks of gold in the seams was mind-boggling. The jagged lump of greenish stone looked just like the pictures Dolores had shown me in one of her geology books of exceptionally rich veins of gold in pieces of greenstone that reside in museum showcases, never to be seen in real life except so rarely as to be almost unbelievable.

I looked at Safwaan, my mouth slack with amazement. He was watching me closely and when he saw my expression, he laughed and held his hand out for the lump of greenstone. I returned it to him, still speechless. My mind was as loose as my face and all I could do was gasp, 'Weh!'

He looked at me quizzically. '*Dhahab?*'

Before I could confirm that it was indeed gold he interrupted me. 'Where, is what you were going to ask next, I think?'

I could only nod.

'Well,' said Safwaan, still smiling, 'Not so very far from here.'

I got my wits together and began peppering him with questions. How long had he had it, how did he come by it, did he find it himself or did he get it from someone? There was so much I needed to know to put the astonishing piece of greenstone into perspective. But Safwaan was too crafty for that.

All these questions, he said, had answers; but he was sure I would understand that a man does not divulge the number of camels he owns to a stranger, because that is the first step towards losing your camels. I allowed that I understood.

'Mr Alan, it is I whose turn it is to ask questions. My question is this. Will you promise me to tell all that you know to your father?' I promised that I would – not a difficult undertaking given that I would do so regardless of anything Safwaan might say. But that of course was not what Safwaan was after.

'Alan, will you further promise me that you will tell him that Safwaan Ali Hassan wishes to exchange the information he has about the gold that he has shown to his son for an agreement to share in the wealth of that gold when he, your father, finds the source of the gold and sells it.'

Something was missing here. 'Safwaan – why do you bring my father into this? Why don't you sell the gold yourself?'

'Ah . . . you are moving ahead too fast. Will you promise me those two things?'

I shifted uncomfortably where I squatted, and scratched a couple of itches that suddenly became very pressing.

'Come, Alan, I am only asking you to be the messenger. It is not much to ask, surely?'

'Safwaan, you must know that in the old days messengers were often killed after delivering their messages?'

'Your father will not kill you.'

'All right,' I said, 'of course I can tell my father what you say, but he will not be pleased to learn that his son has been negotiating business with a *shufto*. He would expect me to refuse to do such a thing.'

Safwaan laughed. 'I see what you mean,' he said, 'but surely you will explain to your father that you were not really in a position to choose. As my captive you were compromised, were you not? More than that. For me to release you unharmed puts you in my debt, I think. A small *godoh*, shall we say? Your father will understand such things.'

'Sounds more like a *jizya*,[79] Safwaan,' I snapped, getting angry. Naturally, he just chuckled at that.

'Safwaan, you are forgetting something. It is you who caused the first *godoh* by abducting me.'

'Ah – now you begin to talk like a Somali. But you are wrong. You created the first *godoh* by invading this country that belongs to the Somali and the Boran. Since my father's day you British have been trying to claim this land as far as the Juba River for that fat queen of yours, and still this border matter has not been settled. It is I who is the aggrieved one. Furthermore, your abduction was conceived out of necessity, not plunder. There is no *godoh*.'

'No wonder the British never wanted to rule Somaliland,' I said. 'It's simply impossible. Neither Somalis nor anyone else could rule Somaliland. You people could twist a snake in such a way that it would forget how to unravel itself. And the fat queen died many years ago.'

---

[79] Tax extorted from infidels by Moslem rulers (Somali)

'So. You will tell him, then?' Safwaan looked at me enquiringly, the slightest of smiles at the edges of his eyes and mouth.

I slumped and exhaled loudly. 'Phew . . . yes, I will tell him. But immediately he will ask the same question I asked. Why include me?'

'Of course,' said Safwaan, 'of course. But I hardly need explain, surely?'

I looked at him for a moment or two, but he was expressionless.

'You don't actually know where it is, do you?'

'Exactly, Alan, exactly.' He laughed and so did I. Scoundrel that he was he had a droll view of things that I couldn't but empathise with. 'When your time comes, Safwaan, even the devil will turn you away, you know.'

'He cannot,' said Safwaan. 'It is his trade.'

'So,' I said, 'you say that rock came from a place near here, but you don't really know? Maybe it came from the moon. Why should my father believe you?'

'It came from near here, of that I am certain. However, I do not know the exact location. Nor do I know how to look for such things. I can read, but what am I, a *shufto*, going to read? Am I going to read books that teach me how to find the rocks from which gold is extracted? I have walked many, many miles in this country looking for some sign of this rock of which I have a piece. There are plenty of stones in this region – in fact, there is little else beside stones. My feet are sore from treading those stones. But I have never found a stone that resembles that which I showed you. If it was easy to find there would be no mystery as to its whereabouts, would there?

'Yet, when I showed you that rock I saw from your face that you knew immediately what it was. When I first saw it, I did not know what I was looking at. I know, therefore, that you have a knowledge I lack. In the same way that I know you have a knowledge about medicine. But you are a young man, too young to be so very experienced. So I know that your father must have a much greater knowledge than you about such things. For that reason I am certain that your father can find the exact place this little rock came from.

'And,' he added, 'I think it must be the same place he has been looking for, and his grandfather before him – King Suleiman's gold mines.'

He paused for a while and rummaged again in his bundle, looking for the second, smaller, stone. He found it and handed it to me. It was a smaller fragment of the same gold-bearing greenstone he'd showed me originally. 'Take this piece with you and give it to your father. Tell him what I have told you. He will want to tell me to go to hell – most people I know are of such a mind. But, he will find it difficult – I think impossible – to turn his back on my proposition. In all of us there is something to which we are susceptible.'

I sat for a while, thinking over what he had said. Whether I liked it or not I was becoming embroiled in devilry the like of which I had never imagined I could ever be part of. Only hours ago it was staying alive that occupied my entire mind, making me depressed and angry because I believed that I really was looking death in the face. Now it seemed that my life, though hardly secure, was not what was on the chopping block at all. Or rather, my life was simply one element in a much more elaborate pattern of events that was only just beginning to take shape. There was too much to ponder for me to see clearly what was going to happen next as a result of the conversation with Safwaan. However, one thing I was already sure about. Safwaan had introduced something into our lives that was going to strongly influence them – of that I was certain. Just how that influence would exert itself – no, I couldn't see that yet.

Meanwhile Safwaan had lain down, looking very tired and

listless. He had been concentrating hard for a span of time that in his weakened state had inevitably taken a lot out of him. Without turning his head, he asked me to leave him to sleep for a while, but to return towards sundown so we could talk again. I said I would and wandered off to think over all that had transpired. Thoughts were flying about my mind all over the place like sandgrouse uncertain about where to settle. After a bit I managed to put all of it away for the time being and forced myself to return to the most pressing matter of the moment – how I was going to depart from this den of thieves intact.

Towards dusk I saw Safwaan sit up and beckon to me. I walked over and found him much recovered. Once again, I marvelled at his powers of recuperation, at how his slight, skinny body could restore itself after the enormous demands made of it by the infection that any normal person just could not have endured.

'I've been thinking,' he said without preamble, 'about what you said in regard to those *shufto*,' indicating with a slight chuck of his chin the gang of verminous bandits sprawled about the ground forty or so yards away. 'It is true that they are not to be trusted, and it is also true that you have insulted them on many occasions.' He grinned and added, 'I commend you for that – I too find it necessary to insult them regularly. But it would have been better, perhaps, if you had locked your tongue.'

'If I had locked my tongue,' I said, 'they would have taken my silence for subservience or fear. It would not have made me seem any better – in fact, probably worse. However I behaved, they would enjoy killing me. A dog they would merely stone; but a white *káfir* – that is worth spending even a bullet on if the knife cannot be employed instead.'

'I can order them on pain of death to escort you to

safety,' he said. 'You may think they are not afraid to die, but they are. Even *shufto* are afraid to die.'

I shook my head emphatically. Like most leaders, I thought, Safwaan had an inflated view of his own authority. 'They just will not believe that you really mean to set me free. They believe that in the end you will not care if they kill me somewhere out in the bush, where you will never know for certain what happened. If you hear that I never returned to my home they will simply say they know nothing about that, I was alive when they parted company with me. They will know that you think they are lying, but that in the end you will let the matter pass.'

Safwaan regarded me quizzically for a while, then seemed to make up his mind. 'Then you will have to leave here alone and find your way back without assistance.'

'I can do that,' I said, 'provided I have my gun. Without it, the lions may get me, as you know. Last night, and the night before, I heard them over towards the east. But who knows where they will be tomorrow?'

'The lion roars to remind the zebra that he is afraid,' Safwaan said, his sardonic smile just perceptible on his otherwise inscrutable face.

'The lion does not inform the zebra where he is to die,' I said. 'For that reason I need my gun. I cannot reach North Horr in one day. I will have to pass one night in the bush. I might be lucky – or I might not. With my gun I know that I can defend myself from a lion.'

'So you plan to go to North Horr?'

'Yes – it is closer than my camp – or am I wrong about that?'

'You are not wrong. It is closer. But there are police there.'

'I will not tell the police anything; only that my *gharry* is broken near the Ethiopian border and that they must send

327

a signal to my father at Rumuruti. The police will not be interested. They know us and we take care not to annoy them. Also, they know that we know to whom they sell the ivory and the leopard skins that they confiscate from the people.'

Safwaan smiled and asked, 'Who is it they sell government property to under the counter?'

'A Somali trader in Marsabit – Abdulrahman Barr. Probably you know him?'

'You know this man?' asked Safwaan, with some interest.

'Of course. Everybody knows him. He is a rogue who, if it were not for the British, would be dealing in slaves. He should be in prison except that he has corrupted so many officials that he is safe because they know he will expose them if they try to put their hands on him. It is possible he would even offer you a price for your grandmother.'

'It is good that you know him,' said Safwaan, somewhat enigmatically, and then went on. 'Well then, this is what I propose. Tomorrow morning at first light all my men will go to hunt an animal to eat. I will tell them that you ordered it, that you said I must have fresh meat – for my health!' He laughed. 'Yes, they will go in anger, resenting the orders of the *káfir* . . . one last insult before you depart! I will also tell them that your order is that it must be a large animal – that a small *ghazeela* such as a dibatag or gerenuk will not do. That means it will take them a long time.

'As soon as they are gone you will leave, so that by the time they return you will be many miles away. Is that not a good plan?'

I agreed that it was an excellent plan. We discussed details and Safwaan explained the route I should take out of the ravine and thereafter. As best I could figure it, I would have to walk about sixty miles to reach North Horr. By heading south-west, I would strike either the Bullul or Wata luggas that ran south from the Abyssinian highlands to end in the large salt-pans near North Horr. They'd be dry, of course, but would make navigation easy. It would take me two hot, rough days if all went well. My two water bottles would be enough to get me there, though I would be finding the thirst hard going on the second day. Only the certainty of water at the end of that day would enable me to walk that far with only the water I carried.

There remained one other thing to arrange. 'Safwaan,' I said, 'how will my father reply to you?'

'That will be easy,' said Safwaan. 'Leave a letter with this disreputable Somali in Marsabit that you spoke of. He will know what to do with it. But – tell your father to write in simple words, and to make the characters large. Like the teachers do for the small children. It is true that I can read, but . . . well, a *shufto* does not get the *Government Gazette* sent to him to read every week.'

23

Eldorado and How to Get There

Just as the sky was beginning to lighten and the stars to fade I woke with a slight start. It was still and quiet, the wind that had blown for much of the night having died down completely. The robin chat whose songs I'd got to know so well was just starting his early morning mimicry of the birds in his neighbourhood, perched low in one of his favourite spots in a scraggly acacia at the end of the overhang. Don't get too friendly, I mentally warned him, or you'll get your throat cut. A lion was roaring, a long way off, maybe two miles. Hard to tell the direction from down in a ravine, but I reckoned to the east, as before. I would be travelling south, out of their way – maybe. If Hutcheon had been there he'd have said 'straight towards the ones that aren't shouting.' The *shifta* were just rising, wandering off to pee, then returning to fiddle with the fire and make tea. Safwaan had been as good as his word for they quite soon got their things together and after a brief word or two with their leader made off up the rocks to the south-east, the way we'd come in. Safwaan had ostentatiously picked up his rifle as they departed to indicate that he was ready to guard me while they were away hunting. They ignored me and I pretended not to notice what they were up to, having stayed put where I'd been sleeping.

I waited a quarter of an hour or so in case one of them came back for some forgotten item then got up and went over to Safwaan. He told me to go to the men's fire and get the tea and *ugali* they said they'd cooked for him and urged me to drink as much sweet tea as I could, which I did. We ate together, I tied my blanket to my water bottles and stuck a ball of *ugali* into a pocket of my shorts. There was nothing else I could carry it in and though it would travel very badly in my shorts, I knew that by evening I would eat it without a twinge. I put on my hat and was ready to go. Safwaan gave me back my beloved pistol, Dad's old Beaumont-Adams .49 that he'd given me for my fourteenth birthday. I was very attached to the gun, and had spent hours with Dad and Hutcheon learning to shoot it reasonably accurately. At close range it was a lethal weapon against lions, anything in fact that might attack a human except for a rhino or an elephant – and they were easily avoidable beasts anyway and most unlikely to pose a problem for me. I felt a great deal more relaxed as I buckled the belt, for all that by tomorrow afternoon the gun would seem to have doubled or trebled its already considerable weight.

Time to go. Safwaan slowly and stiffly sat up and got his marabout-stork legs over the edge of his bed onto the ground. He was smiling his slight, sardonic smile as he watched my final preparations. I crouched down and we looked into one another's eyes.

'*Tag, káfir, tag.* Go – and travel warily, like the *kurra-jog.* Your fat thighs will delight the lions.'

'Before I go,' I said, 'would you like me to teach you how to hunt leopards? It will not take long to . . .'

He interrupted me with a snort. 'Don't forget, my rifle is loaded. It will not take long to shoot you.'

We shook hands and I stood up.

'*Inshallah.*'

'*Inshallah.*'

I turned and went. As I passed through the defile to where the water was I paused and looked back one last time.

He was watching me and when I turned, he shouted, 'Remember, *káfir* to hell – with honour!'

'With honour!'

The last thing I heard was his short, sardonic laugh as I rounded the edge of the boulder. In seconds, I was up and over and around the rocks like a *dassie* with a caracal behind. The elation was head-spinning and I had to make a real effort to slow down and watch my step. A sprained ankle at this point in time was not to be contemplated. The euphoria would soon be well and truly cooked out of me by the sun, plus the sheer monotony of slogging on and on and on through the stiff, thorny scrub, stumbling on the hot, sharp stones, constantly warding off flies, trying not to think about thirst, about lions, hunger, *shifta* and all the other demons that would haunt me by the hour.

Once out of the ravine I steadied my pace and headed south-west. Behind me, to the north, were the mountains of the Abyssinian swell. To the south-east I could see some volcano-shaped hills that I took to be the Huri Hills. All these landmarks made navigation easy and I knew that any luggas I encountered would all eventually join to flow into the pans at North Horr. So, I settled down to threading my way through the scrub as efficiently as possible, as to begin with there were no tracks to follow. For the most part the vegetation was not too dense except for occasional thickets that forced unwelcome detours, and I kept up a good pace. Towards midday, I struck a well-defined lugga running south-west that I decided to follow as I was certain it would lead me to my destination. The going was easier in and around the lugga as there were many animal tracks running along it. The day passed uneventfully and by late afternoon I was far out on the increasingly flat and open plain of the desert, the mountains of Abyssinia receding into the dis-

332

tance behind me. In the last two hours or so of daylight I started looking for a bird to shoot to supplement the unappetising *ugali* in my pocket. I'd disturbed lots of dik-dik and several gerenuk during the day but came across nothing that waited to be shot, which was why I'd opted for easier meat. Thinking that I would have to settle for the tiny carcass of a dove, I was lucky to shoot a slightly larger go-'way bird just as I was about to give up and make camp. I easily enough found a suitable place to stop with two thorny bushes growing close to each other, their lower branches touching the ground. I reckoned to wriggle under the branches to sleep between the stems with a fire that would give me at least some light to help see any lion that might fancy making a meal of me. It was going to be a dark night with no moon. I collected a lot of firewood and found enough bits of wood to close up the space between the two tree trunks, to protect my head while I slept. I made two small fires on either side of my feet, about a yard distant. I gathered as many dead sticks as I could find and spread these around in the spaces between the branches to make it difficult for an animal to approach without making at least some noise.

As my knife had been stolen when I was captured I had no blade with which to butcher the go-'way bird. The bullet, though, had opened it up and it didn't take long to char and eat such bits as were halfway edible, hunger overcoming the gustatory hesitation that would normally accompany such a discouraging meal. I fell asleep quickly enough, lying on my back with my pistol clasped over my belly. The ground was hard and I knew that it and nervousness would guarantee a fitful sleep – deep sleep was not recommended if anti-lion measures were to be taken seriously. As expected, I woke frequently and each time I got the fires burning again. There were plenty of alarming rustles all night, but nothing more than that and sometime before dawn I got going again, tired and hungry, but glad to be putting more distance between me and the *shifta*'s lair. I thought happily of their disappointment at losing out on the chance to torture and murder me, and felt a surge of energy and enthusiasm for making sure they had in fact lost out. I didn't actually look back behind me, but I certainly felt the urge to.

The rest of my journey home was equally uneventful, just a hard, hot, thirsty foot slog made easily bearable by the relief at having, in the end, escaped what for a while had seemed to me an insoluble predicament. I found the luggas leading south to North Horr and got there well before dark on that second day. The police detachment stationed there was out on a camel patrol and the two men holding the post were visibly relieved when they realised that I wasn't going to ask them to do anything for me other than send a signal to Rumuruti to be forwarded to Dad. He got it very quickly a day after it was sent and he, Hutcheon and Leila immediately drove non-stop through the night and into the next day, arriving at North Horr in the evening of the second day after I got there. We then drove directly to my camp on the lugga that I had been abducted from ten days previously. The men were amazed to hear what had transpired, having had no inkling of what had taken place the day I left. They'd been told not to separate and to wait until I showed up again. Though worried by my taking so long to return they assumed that whatever had gone wrong would in due course be resolved. Ali had not returned to camp and we gave him up for lost. Either he had died out in the bush somewhere – perhaps the *shifta*'s shot had mortally wounded him – or, more likely, the lions got him. Maybe he survived and decided to split, uneasy perhaps at having got away, when, as far as he knew, I was done for. Whatever his fate, he left no trace. Something over a year later we heard that he had been seen in Laisamis, a rumour we were never able to confirm or deny. My car was where we'd left it and eventually we got back to Rumuruti without further incident.

As you might imagine we talked endlessly for the next few days about my abduction and everything surrounding it. Dad and Hutcheon, as do all people of the bush, had to know the exact details of everything recounted in their chronological order, complete with the weather and anything else that might have coloured what took place. It's how hunters and other adventurers learn their trade – by absorbing the experiences of fellow hunters, which, by detailed verbal recounting and rehearsing, gradually becomes part of their own experience. The way I described things was the way these two men had taught me to as I grew up so that it was easy for them to picture all that had happened. Before long they would have been capable of accurately describing what transpired as if it had happened to one of them rather than me.

Once the events themselves were clear in their minds they began discussing at great length the significance of the piece of greenstone I had brought home. Hutcheon for once was as absorbed as Dad. As long as Dad was talking of merely legendary gold Hutcheon was inclined to be scornful and dismissive for all that he had to admit that there was something fascinating about it all. But now that he could actually heft a chunk of rock full of gold, knowing that it came from Solomon's Triangle, his interest was intense. We could forget about looking for our own greenstone now that we had the real McCoy in our hands. It really was very exciting after all that The Geologist had told us about greenstone and its common link with gold.

Dad of course couldn't wait to extract the gold and get it sent off to Europe for assay. In the meantime, what we all discussed from every conceivable angle was the matter of its true provenance. Was Safwaan humbugging us on that score, or was he on the level?

'You say,' said Dad, as he had so many times already, 'that you felt this *oke* Safwaan was telling the truth?'

'I'm sure of it.'

'What makes you so sure? He could've got it anywhere and is using it to lure us into some sort of trap.'

'What trap, though? He doesn't need to trap us. If he wanted to jump us, he could at any time. From what he said it's obvious he'd thought of doing so years ago.'

'Yeah – but he's windy of jumping us. You said he knew very well that he might come off second best. Maybe he reckons to lull us into dropping our guard so's he can make a really big hit and get everything we have. He's just a marauding *shifta* – don't forget that.'

'But that's the point – he's not your average *shifta*, with no more ambition than tomorrow's opportunity for murder and pillage and to hell with the consequences. There was something else about him, some sort of imagination that puts him above mere barbarity.'

'You were too close to him for too long. Wanting always to escape stuffs up your judgement. Instinctively you will take sides with anything that even halfway smacks of a way out. Nobody can help it.'

'Yeah, well, maybe. All that's perfectly true, of course. I kept telling myself those things all the time. But, he didn't behave like the others at all. They were everything you've come to believe about Somali *shifta* – cold, humourless bastards who watch you the way a leopard does, figuring always the best way of getting the drop on you. But Safwaan was never like that. He had a sharp sense of humour and . . . well, the book of poetry. True, Somalis are known for their love of poetry, but you must admit that poets are as rare among them as they are among us. It sets him apart from the rest.'

'Plenty of bloodthirsty poets. The Mad Mullah was a greatly revered poet. Just because this Safwaan toerag likes poetry doesn't change his spots. He's still a *shifta*, for *krar's* sakes – still a *shifta*.'

'The only sensible thing to do,' said Hutcheon, 'is head back to that place and shoot the lot of them before they disappear. Doesn't sound to me as if that bloke Safwaan is going to be very mobile just yet. They're probably squatting there as we speak.'

'You're right, of course,' said Dad, 'but could you really do that? Just shoot 'em in cold blood? No way, man, not even a Class A *mokora* like you.'

'Piece of piss,' said Hutcheon, but the truth was that none of us could pretend to be that sanguinary. Until they actually threatened us – and from what Safwaan had said they seemed to have actively avoided us hitherto – we hadn't in us what it would take to deliberately set out to kill them. If you lived in the N.F.D. up near the Somali and Ethiopian borders you had to be ready at all times to fight for your life, no question about that, no question whatever. But to set out yourself to murder someone in cold blood, however shameless a desperado that person might be, called for something quite foreign to the likes of us. We all knew that and the subject was soon forgotten.

'What really bothers me,' said Dad, 'is the idea of doing a deal with this god-awful bandit. It's one thing to poach the king's leopards – I would be ashamed of myself if I didn't, really – but going into business with the *shifta* . . . *krar's*, man, I never would've thought I would one day find myself considering just such a thing.'

'He called you a *shifta* yourself,' I reminded Dad, just to enjoy his reaction.

'Bloody hell, that's just it, that's exactly the point,' said Dad. 'The day I deal with this conscienceless rogue is the day I sell out to the devil. And he knows it.'

'C'mon, Rider,' said Hutcheon, 'there's no halo shimmering round your ugly swede. When the day comes you can try knocking on the Pearly Gates; but no one's going to answer the door when they see it's you.'

'He's not proposing murder and pillage,' I said. 'Sounds fair to me, what he's got in mind.'

'It's not what he's proposing as such, it's who's proposing it – as both you toerags well know.'

'Who gives a shit?' said Hutcheon. 'You've been waiting for a break like this all your life and now you're thinking of letting it slip through your fingers because your conscience, that romantic conscience you've told me about so many times, is bothering you. Get a grip, *kêrel*; he's just a toeraggy *shifta*. It's not as if you're plotting to overthrow the government, ay.'

Dad was silent for a while and after a bit he wandered off without saying anything more. It wasn't at all an easy situation he found himself in. One part of him was excited as hell by the truly extraordinary piece of greenstone Safwaan had given him. But another part of him balked strongly at the notion of getting into bed with such an unprincipled rogue. But was he really so unprincipled? Of course he was. By his own admission he was simply a *shifta*, and a principled *shifta* was an oxymoron. But that was as it related to his pursuit of banditry. For all that it amused him to call Dad a *shifta* he probably knew as well as anyone that Dad was far from that. What he was alluding to was something else in Dad's make-up; the anathema for authority, the living by his own wits, by his own set of rules, the helping himself to what he considered to be fair game. That's what Safwaan had rightly surmised about Dad when he called him a *shifta*. Moreover, if he and Dad were to deal together in the matter of gold it wouldn't surprise me if Safwaan did so in a principled way. After all, he'd dealt with me in a remarkably civilised way. Or was that only because he already had this deal in mind? None of it could be thought through to a logical, clear conclusion. Far too many ifs and buts and maybes. The simple truth was that we could only guess at what would happen next if Dad agreed to Safwaan's proposal.

And – as Hutcheon said – what the hell? Why not? What really would the moral price be? Would any of us really go around stricken with guilt at the awful depths of depravity into which we'd let our venality drag us? Would we hell.

The other thing was the apparent origin of the green-stone. Dad must've desperately wanted to believe Safwaan was telling the truth when he said it came from Solomon's Triangle, the very place Dad had reckoned the ancient gold of Suleiman had come from. But he clearly thought it was just too good to be true. I pointed out that Safwaan couldn't have known about Dad's concept of Solomon's Triangle.

'Maybe not,' said Dad, 'but he knew damn well we were interested in that area. He's crafty enough to have figured out that if he wanted to engage my attention he had only to say he'd found it where he knew I wanted to find it. It's too bloody obvious.'

'I don't agree,' I said. 'What does it matter where it came from? He's an Ogaden *shifta*, he could only have got it from somewhere in the southern Ogaden.'

'It's not certain,' said Dad, 'he might've come by it in a hundred different ways. We can't take his word for it.'

'But what do we lose by assuming he's levelling with us and going to look?'

'Our lives?' said Dad.

'We don't have to walk into a simple ambush,' I said. 'I don't believe that's what he's up to.'

'Why not?' said Dad. 'Kill the three of us then race down

here and clean out our headquarters where he probably thinks we've got a huge fortune in hard cash stashed away. The man's a bandit, nothing more. It's the sort of convoluted trick he'd adore to play.'

'He could kill us anytime if he really put his mind to it.'

'Not so. There's very few occasions when all three of us are together and he's in a position to surprise us out in the bush. His intelligence can never be that good. We move around too much. He knows that to be certain of getting rid of us and having time to raid our headquarters, he has to arrange for us to be at a place and at a time of his choosing. He's not an amateur.'

'If he wanted to kill and raid us there's never been anything to stop him simply attacking us at home. But he never has. That can only mean he doesn't plan to. Sure he'd like to, but for whatever reason he's not done that.'

'Could be he just believes we're too well guarded at home, that he hasn't the capacity to wipe us out.'

We went over all this and much more for days. At first Dad seemed increasingly disinclined to go along with the proposal. He stopped talking about it and when I raised the subject, he avoided it. We all knew, though, that it was bothering him, because he was noticeably irritable – something he never was unless there was an unusually difficult issue he had to deal with. It was rare for him to let anything make him short-tempered with those of us not involved in whatever he had to cope with at the time. 'It's his bloody conscience,' said Hutcheon. 'He wants to jump in there and get stuck into his dream but his bloody romantic conscience tells him he shouldn't truck with murderers and thieves. He's incurable.'

Then one day Hutcheon, who was really only having a dig, remarked that if Dad 'didn't get a rift on those *shifta* would give up on him and end up finding the gold source themselves, ay. You have to remember that Alan's good friend Safwaan didn't really know for sure what he had. It wasn't until he showed it to Alan and saw his reaction that he knew for certain that he was onto a *lekker* thing. Moreover, Alan's reaction to his proposal would've further strengthened his conviction that what he had was serious gold, man. Now he knows, he's really going to look hard. Could be he was bullshitting when he said he'd already searched all over the place. Probably just had a quick shufti and gave up. After all, he admitted he had no idea what he was looking for.'

'Hutcheon,' said Dad tartly, 'all these long years you've scoffed at my obsession with the idea that there's a lost gold mine somewhere in the N.F.D. or thereabouts, and now a skellum of a *shifta* has you panting to be off after it. As long as something's got a strong element of knavery in it you'll be interested.'

Later, when Dad had gone, Hutcheon said, grinning, 'You wait, Alan, he's going to crack any time now. I can tell, I know him too well, ay.'

I'm certain that if Dad had left the matter entirely up to his conscience to decide he'd never have accepted Safwaan's proposal. The way I see it, he talked his conscience out of it. He weighed up the ethics of dealing with a bandit *per se* against the wider ethic of what was being proposed. While he could not approve of brigandry in so far as it subjected people to terror – the terror of murder, mutilation, pillage, rape and so on – he wasn't convinced that Safwaan's proposal embodied any relaxation of his principles regarding terrorism. True, the government would say that he was duty bound to do anything he could to prevent bandits from going about the business of brigandry. But no one could expect him to actually intervene – indeed the government would always say that only the government was empowered to intervene. They'd taken a dim official view of Dad's defence of his establishment when raided by the *shifta* back in 1935, muttering about excessive violence, can't have people taking matters into their own hands, and so on. Everyone knew that at any time there was a high probability that somewhere in the N.F.D. there was a gang of Somali *shifta* who might strike at any one any time. It could be said that if someone such as Dad came by the knowledge of the whereabouts of a *shifta* group he ought to provide that information to the government. But the reality was that he would do no such thing. The government was highly unlikely to make good use of that information; more likely in point of fact to disregard it altogether.

But the more we did the more I saw that Dad was leaning towards accepting Safwaan's proposal. I guess it was inevitable, really. Nothing had happened for years to stoke his imagination as vigorously as that little piece of greenstone. So none of us was surprised when finally Dad announced that he was going to give it a go. By then even Hutcheon was getting quite keen. Leila was always against the idea – just the sort of idiocy she had come to expect from the men in her family. She usually had a poor opinion of men's ideas of how to do things sensibly and we all had to admit that we'd set some sound precedents for her views. Yet no one could deny that it was a most romantic scheme – to set out to find the legendary King Solomon's mines in the company of a band of shameless bandits. So Dad wrote the letter that was to start the ball rolling and left it with Abdulrahman Barr in Marsabit – who'd grinned wickedly when he heard who he was to give the letter to.

It was late 1939, though, and the war soon put paid to any plans we might have made to look for King Solomon's mines. The Director of Manpower in Kenya, Lord Erroll, assigned Dad and Hutcheon to the intelligence section of the campaigns against the Italians in Abyssinia and Somaliland as a consequence of their experience with those countries and skill in obtaining information. When those campaigns were over, they were assigned to other duties that kept them busy right through to 1945.

I turned 18 in 1939 and in September was called up into the Kenya Regiment that had been formed in 1937. With help from Dad and his contacts, I managed to get myself seconded to the Kenya Auxiliary Air Unit under Bob Love more and was sent to Kumalo in Rhodesia to train as a pilot. Not long after, the KAAU was absorbed into the RAF and I served in various hot and sweaty places such as Habbaniyah and Ismailia. I loved the flying and, I'd have to admit, the uninhibited destruction of property that went with aerial warfare. I let some blood, both the other bugger's and my own and was sent back to Kenya as unfit for further active service following a skirmish that I was lucky enough to come out of alive, albeit a bit bent. My legs were partly paralysed and for a long time I was considered untreatable and shunted off into the human equivalent of the damaged goods department. It turned out that the problem was caused by a small chunk of shrapnel lodged inside a vertebra that no one knew was there. A surgeon in Mombasa military hospital, who was probably trying something he didn't know much about, managed to pry it out. After that, the paralysis slowly remitted and I was eventually discharged with nothing but a few scars to remind me of what had happened.

24

On the Hollowness of Baobabs

I didn't get back to Luoniek until the end of 1945 after demobilisation from the Air Force, glad as all of us who hadn't been despatched on the Great Airlift to the Sky were to say goodbye to all that. It was a marvellous time, that reunion of my family – Dad, Leila, Hutcheon, Abdullahi and Hawa, Ndaragus, Osman and many of the other people I'd grown up amongst. We spent many long hours catching up with each other's news, adjusting to the changes in everyone's appearance and manner and generally trying to put life back to the closest match we could achieve to the world we'd had to abandon in 1939. In many ways, not much had changed. The country was the same, the Samburu and Boran were the same – in fact, it was only that we'd all aged a bit that seemed to have really changed. Abdullahi and Ndaragus were both now in their sixties – they couldn't say to better than the nearest decade – and showing a good deal of grey hair. Abdullahi was still the same acerbic, aloof man I remembered so well, though readier now to risk an occasional dry chuckle. Ndaragus was if anything even skinnier, but upright and alert with eyes still as sharp as a vulture's. I was glad to find Hawa as warm and cheerful as ever, though slowed down considerably by arthritis. Dad and Hutcheon in their late fifties were looking somewhat weather-beaten. Deeply tanned, eyes narrowed even more against the sun; but *mokoras* yet, with Hutcheon's black eyes flashing as of old, the gold earring glinting through greying hair still as long and unbrushed as ever. Leila at twenty-two was ravishing and seemed to get a great many handwritten letters not always penned, I noticed, by the same hand. Poor bastards, I thought, she's not about to do the swoon at any of you toerags' feet, I don't reckon. Dad was enormously happy to have all his family back together again and for the first time I could remember would speak comfortably about my mother. Leila, he said, was so like her in looks and manner and Hutcheon confirmed it, commenting, inevitably, *nou dars 'n ding* whenever Leila did or said something that he and Dad thought was just like her mother.

'Not as good-looking,' Dad would say, 'but you do your best with what you've got, Poppit.'

'At least I don't have to be fettered in case I run away,' Leila would say in answer to remarks like that, and Dad would simply retort, 'Piss off, you cheeky bint.'

That was new. Nobody in the old days would ever even refer to my mother, let alone make slave-girl jokes about her. Mind you, it was only Leila, Daddy's darling, who could chance her arm with stuff like that. For the most part the memory of my mother was still largely off limits unless Dad chose to bring it up. When he did, though, both Leila and I would seize the chance to pepper him with questions about her and we learnt more about our mother in those few heady post-war days than we'd known in our entire lives before. Of course, we'd pumped a great deal out of Hutcheon, but it seemed very different coming from Dad.

Then I managed to interrupt the smooth flow of things by shlooping the buffalo horn. Thinking back over it I suppose that as much as anything I was totally out of practice. I'd scored well in gunnery training during the War and learnt all sorts of things about fighting and keeping alive. None of that, though, had much bearing on hunting buffalo in really thick stuff. On top of which, I'd spent a long period in the latter half of the War doing very little until my wound was sorted out. While I felt fit, I probably wasn't yet quite on form. Whatever, I had to spend several weeks away from the plaas and several more after I returned to get back into kilter.

It was while we were still all of us savouring the pleasure of being together again with no buffalo or anything else looming to spoil the moment that Abdullahi came up one morning while we were at breakfast and said that there was someone who wanted to speak with me.

'He is not a good man,' said Abdullahi, looking as if someone had just offered him a dead snake. 'I told him you would not want to see him. But he says you know him. He is lying, I think – he is a Somali and you cannot trust them.'

Nice one, Abdullahi, I thought to myself, considering that you are half Somali yourself. At least you haven't changed while I've been away. 'Tell him I will see him after breakfast,' I said and Abdullahi stalked off muttering and frowning. In due course, I went over to where the visitor would be and saw a small, slight man sitting alone under a thorn tree where he'd presumably been shunted off to wait. He got slowly to his feet as I came up, adjusting his *shuka* over his shoulder, and took a couple of very stiff steps towards me. There was something familiar about him though I couldn't place him.

'*Salaan,*' he greeted me in Somali, then reverted to Oromo, speaking very softly so no one else could hear. 'Remember me, *káfir?*'

For a moment, I just stared, then suddenly I realised who it was. 'Safwaan,' I said, 'Is it you?'

He said nothing, just stood there with the faint sardonic smile that I now remembered so well. 'I'll be damned,' I said, 'I thought you were safely in hell.'

He chuckled. 'Not yet, not yet, Mr Alan. There are things still waiting to be done. Then maybe we shall all go together.'

I looked him over, all sorts of mixed memories flooding back. I'd never seen him on his feet before, but he looked as small and gaunt as he had all those years ago lying on his makeshift bed in the hideout in the ravine. The same deeply lined face with the sunken eyes like a burrowing viper's, the scornful, sour expression. We asked after each other's health and exchanged the usual platitudes and I took him to meet Dad and Hutcheon and gave him what was obviously a very welcome meal. Then, over several cups of tea, he told us that he had received Dad's letter all those years ago and realised as war broke out in Europe that we would be engaged on other business for the time being.

'I knew that the letter meant nothing now, that you white men would be busy fighting each other with no time for such as me. Your war is finished now, I hear, so perhaps we can consider my proposition again?'

We were all a bit nonplussed by this sudden turn of events. None of us had brought up the subject of Safwaan's gold and while it wasn't that it was forgotten altogether it just wasn't something that came up naturally in the context of what was happening now. Therefore, Safwaan's sudden appearance took a bit of adjusting to.

'What have you been doing, Safwaan, since that day I left you in the rocks? Plundering the Gabbra as usual?'

He chuckled his quiet, dry laugh. 'That leopard had sharp teeth,' he said, 'too sharp for an old man like me. Thanks to you, I am still alive; but since that time, it has been difficult for me to walk, too difficult to keep up with the other *shufto*. I had to leave the *kurra-jog* and join the scum of Marsabit town. The Galla will not suffer by my hand again.'

'So you are no longer a *shufto*?'

'That life is a thing of the past. I can never again be one of the *kurra-jog*. Nowadays, I live among dogs and whores and shopkeepers and beggars – even the young *shufto* do not speak with me.'

What struck us all was the wistfulness in this ageing ruffian's voice – he really was nostalgic about his former existence as an outlaw. I was reminded of the fact that a particular emotion cannot have a precise circumstance associated with it, because there are infinitely more circumstances than emotions. We all have the same limited range of emotions, but each of us is likely to experience widely differing circumstances. We should not therefore be surprised if we do not always equate emotion and circumstance in the same way as the other person. All the same, it took a bit of getting used to, that this old, limping bandit so missed his brigandry.

Looking at Dad's face I realised, too, that Safwaan's retirement from active rapine and slaughter meant that the doubts he'd had back in 1939 about the ethics of going into cahoots with a bandit were now redundant. Things could be considered in an altogether rosier light from here on. We talked for hours and by late afternoon I could see that Dad was all fired up again, ready to pick up the spoor of King Solomon's mines where he'd left off before the war. He went and got Safwaan's piece of greenstone and showed it to him, saying that he remembered that Safwaan at the time had another, bigger chunk.

'Yes,' Safwaan said, 'I still have it.'

'Where?'

'In Marsabit.'

'If I take you back to Marsabit you will show me this other rock?'

'Of course.'

*

The next day we all drove to Marsabit and dropped Safwaan off at the edge of town.

'Leave me here,' he said, 'I do not want the robbers of this place to see me with you. Meet me here after dark and I will show you the other stone.'

He was as good as his word. By now, Dad was totally hooked and it was a foregone conclusion that we would work out some deal with Safwaan. It was simple enough. He had nothing much more to offer other than to take us to where he'd found the pieces of greenstone – but, as Dad kept saying, that was already a great deal.

Thinking back on it all I see now quite clearly what I vaguely suspected at the time: that Safwaan wasn't telling us all he knew. On the one hand, it was natural for him, considering the life he'd led, never to reveal more than he absolutely had to. Secrecy and deception were after all tools of his trade. As the Somali say, he would from force of habit always show his right ear with his left hand. On the other, he was intelligent and a good judge of character. He saw that Dad was interested and while he didn't as it turned out have that much information he spun us along with what little he had simply by being vague, knowing that we would think he knew more than he was divulging. However much Dad pumped him for detail he acted as if he'd just come by the bits of greenstone by chance, lying on the ground with nothing else of interest associated with them. That wasn't quite true, but he rightly figured his vagueness would simply make Dad even more curious and keen to see for himself where the find had been made. Therefore, we arranged to meet again in Marsabit in about a month's time and head off up to the Abyssinian border country to the place where I'd been abducted back in 1939.

*

349

As it wasn't practical to try to reach the south-west corner of Solomon's Triangle by vehicle we opted to drive as far as North Horr, leave our vehicles at the police post and continue on from there with camels. Dad sent a couple of men on ahead of us to buy camels from the Rendille and assemble them at North Horr, and signal us when they had enough. All these arrangements took some time, complicated by Safwaan's insistence on travelling incognito in that part of the world. No doubt he had very good reason, having been in his day a much-wanted man by the police and King's African Rifles. Dressed in shirt and shorts, tackies, a hat and dark glasses – a sight that made us laugh about as much as it made him scowl – we passed him off as one of our men and in reality there would've been few people who could have identified him in such garb and surroundings.

Eventually, in early February 1946, we loaded up our camels and set off from North Horr. On the second day out we got on to the Bullul lugga that descends from the Abyssinian highlands some sixty miles to the north and runs for its entire length almost due south to where it debouches into the pan at North Horr. This was the same lugga I had descended back in 1939 on my way out of Safwaan's hide-out, though I hardly remembered it. By the time I'd got this far south on the previous occasion I was so tired and thirsty I was really only looking at the ground just in front of me; my surroundings interested me not in the least. On the fourth day we passed a tributary lugga coming in from the north-east that Safwaan said was the lower end of the watercourse on which his old hideout had been located. Shortly after that, we left the Bullul to follow another tributary lugga that came in from the north-west. The sandy lugga soon became rocky and rough as it started to rise up the foothills of the great Abyssinian escarpment now looming over our northern horizon. Safwaan insisted that no *shifta* had been in this area for years, the band he'd led having dispersed soon after he'd recovered from his wounds. Not long after we'd worked our way up the first rise of the highlands Safwaan said that there was a hidden well a little to the west side of the lugga in a dense thicket. We spent the better part of a day looking for this well as Safwaan had not been to it for many years and had some difficulty locating it. Late in the afternoon we investigated what must have been the fifth or sixth likely looking thicket and found the well, well concealed under a covering of poles and rocks. He advised us to camp at this spot, as there was no other water for miles around. There were no Gabbra there at the time, which was not surprising as there was no grazing and very little browse in the vicinity. It was an exposed campsite, with no trees high enough to make shade; but the water was good and we'd brought tarpaulins for shelter and grain to supplement the camels' food.

It was a strange feeling to be back in the area where I'd passed such a nerve-racking time, wondering day after day if I'd get out alive. The country was as I remembered it: devastation, desolation and damnation. Those were Kitchener's words to describe Nubia; he'd have said the same, I felt, had he been here. If it wasn't such a grind getting to this remote corner of Solomon's Triangle one might disparage it less, I suppose, though I'm not certain about that.

I will always remember that hot, muggy morning as we prepared to set off to where Safwaan said he'd found the gold-bearing rocks. We'd got up well before dawn and eaten a good breakfast as Safwaan said it would be a hard day's walking. At first light, before the sun was up, we started off, heading north-north-west through the bush that got thicker and harder to work through the closer we got to the foot of the escarpment. To our north, the mountains rose incredibly steeply and we knew from the map that they were over seven thousand thousand feet only a few miles from where we were, less than two thousand feet above sea level. Everywhere we looked we saw towering cliffs, rent by deep gorges sometimes sheer sided, sometimes collapsed in an enormous jumble of huge, reddish-black basalt boulders. The rocks were mostly bare of vegetation but in the ravines where some moisture accumulated there were dense thickets of low vegetation. Safwaan said there were no springs anywhere in the vicinity and wells were rare. Even the Gabbra avoid this place, he said, because there is little water, nothing much for their livestock to eat and no chance of cultivation. Besides, he said, the Gabbra say many people died here long ago and nowadays if you bring your stock nearby many will die. So everyone avoids this area.

Well, that first day got us nowhere. For a start, Safwaan made heavy weather of the walking. He was terribly scarred from the chewing the leopard had given him and while he said that that was what was giving him gyp, it was probably arthritis that was more to blame. Whatever the reason, he had to go very slowly and though he was mentally the hard-arsed bastard he'd always been, and never complained, he just couldn't do anything about his stiffness and pain. By midday, he admitted he had no more clue about where the place we were looking for was than when we started. We returned to camp and made another early start the following day. This went on for the next three days with Safwaan gradually realising he was definitely way off track. We couldn't blame him. The country was so broken and there were so many ravines cutting through the cliffs that appeared almost identical that even if you lived here you could easily enough get lost. We'd come prepared for a *tabu* safari and had plenty of food. We had three men herding the camels all day so that they could browse and while there wasn't much, it was enough if they didn't have to trek with loads. Therefore, we told Safwaan not to lose heart but rather keep at it, trying a new route each day. Sooner or later, we assured him, he'd be bound to come across some feature he remembered. We didn't doubt his story, as there didn't seem to be any other reason why he would put himself through such a hard time in such a wasteland.

On the fifth day, Safwaan headed east first, almost to the Bullul, and then turned north to hit the escarpment at a point he said he had thought up until then was much too far north and east. It proved a good move and late in the morning he suddenly stopped and said he recognised this spot. From then on he travelled confidently, leading us up a steep slope onto a poorly defined step that ran round the foot of the cliffs above us. We picked our way along this step through the boulders and scree and came to where the cliff started to overhang the step. A little further and the step narrowed to a ledge and finally petered out under a deeply undercut overhang, almost a cave.

'This is the place,' said Safwaan with more excitement in his voice than I'd ever heard, 'back there where the rock is low.'

The floor of the overhang extended back some twenty feet or so and was dry but quite hard sandy dirt with lots of bits of basalt rock. Safwaan said he'd found the bits of greenstone right at the back where some animal had been digging in the ground. We had to crouch down to get there, but it wasn't dark, as the overhang was not enclosed on the sides. We all spent some time rummaging around in various old animal excavations and it was not long before Dad gave a loud exclamation and went back out to the front of the overhang with something in his hand. It was an obsidian flake, a typical Stone-Age artefact that looked like an arrow or spearhead with a chunk missing out of one side. There are innumerable such objects strewn all along the Rift Valley and its environs, relics of the glory days of the many Gardens of Eden of the Rift Valley that palaeolithic man inhabited in past millennia.

Well, we spent the next hour talking and examining the floor of the overhang, musing over what we were sitting in. The obsidian had undoubtedly been dropped here long before the bits of gold-bearing rock, probably many thousands of years before. We had no doubt that if we carried out a diligent archaeological study of this place we'd find evidence of its use by man stretching back from the present day to, quite possibly, the early Stone Age, fifty thousand years ago. Neither the obsidian nor the green-stone originated at this spot; both had been brought here. The spoor was hotter than it had ever been, but for all we knew it might still only be lukewarm. However, it did considerably encourage us when Hutcheon found a small piece of greenish rock that matched Safwaan's pieces. While we'd accepted his claim to have found them here, it was all the same reassuring to corroborate his story. It is a strange sensation, to sit in the shade in one of these enduring spots looking out over the vastness of the yellowy-green plain below, the wind much cooler than on the hot, scrubby savannah, and know that you are on exactly the spot that a thousand generations of people have sat on before you, seeing the same things and feeling the same sensations. Eerie, very eerie.

We got back to camp very late that day and spent the next day resting and discussing what our next move should be. Safwaan was severely creased from his considerable effort to keep up the search until he found what he'd promised to show us, and was really not fit to continue such hard walking as we'd been doing on a daily basis. Our food had practically run out as well so we decided to leave and refit for a return journey. The way Dad interpreted what we now knew was this. As it appeared that the gold-bearing

354

rocks had been buried in the floor of the overhang before Safwaan found them unearthed by an animal he figured they'd been left there a long, long time ago, long enough to have been gradually covered by successive layers of debris. Someone may deliberately have buried them, yes, but even so, it was probably long ago. Safwaan said he'd found them many years before when he'd first come to this country. The reason he'd come to the shelter in the first place was because he'd climbed up the foot of the mountain above us to find a place from which he could sit for a few hours and watch the plain below to see if he could see any sign of Gabbra livestock. He never returned, he said, and was sure no one else ever came here, because once he got to know the country he found out that the Gabbra themselves avoided this place.

Dad was sure that when people had used the shelter there would have been water nearby. The well we were on was many miles away – too far for convenience. He pointed out that the well also told an interesting story in itself. It was not a simple affair, but actually an impressive structure for its age, which he put at more than a century, possibly many centuries. It was very deep, about sixty feet, cut all the way down through sandstone. It sloped at a steep angle, allowing rough, extremely well worn steps to have been cut into the floor. By placing a man at the bottom and a couple of others on the way up bags of water on ropes could be brought quite quickly to the surface. The presence of a clearly old well in the vicinity suggested that surface water had not been available for centuries and also that there must have been a lot of comparatively well-organised people living here long before the present-day Gabbra, who said they'd no idea who'd made the wells in their area. They'd found them already there when they first came. What Dad was driving at of course was his conviction that there had been big changes in the occupation of this area almost certainly aligned with strong climatic changes and the availability of water. Such changes could have mediated protracted depopulation – perhaps on several occasions – of a severity and duration sufficient to break the collective memory of such things as the location of gold mines. For Dad was of course always assuming that the gold-bearing rock we had in our hands originated from a mine or mines in the area, and, further, that the mines were the fabled mines of Ophir, King Solomon's mines. He felt that he might be seeing the evidence for a chain of events that fitted this hypothesis – not a certain proof of it, far from it – but enough to encourage him to now look hard for the source of the greenstone in this rugged, mysterious corner of the world. For, as he said, you had to admit it could very well have come from a fabulous ancient mine. We all agreed there was no denying that; however wishful such an interpretation might be it was undeniably plausible.

There was one nagging problem with this hypothesis, though. While it was easy enough to imagine people disappearing for long enough to forget where something as small and narrowly located as a mine was, the area, while harsh and forbidding and remote, was not uninhabited now. The Gabbra, as part of the Galla nation, had been here for quite some time, at least as long as the great Galla expansion of the sixteenth century that saw them almost overwhelm the Abyssinian highlanders. They must surely have stumbled upon the postulated 'lost' mines; it seemed inconceivable that they could have been overlooked for so long.

Dad had always countered this argument by agreeing that the Gabbra and their predecessors must have come across the forgotten mines, but either made nothing of them or kept their lips well buttoned. Even if they understood what they were looking at – and the Gabbra have no cultural knowledge of gold mining – they must have foreseen that if the knowledge reached the Abyssinians they would suffer

ON THE HOLLOWNESS OF BAOBABS

even more depredations at the hands of the *tigre* and the official authorities than they already did. Arnold Hodson had told them how when he trekked the border back in September 1915, probably using the same well we camped on, he came across a Gabbra village near El Adi, not far from where we were, strewn with the remains of the inhabitants – men, women and children – who'd recently been slaughtered by Abyssinian *tigre* from the Mega highlands. Those who hadn't been killed would have been abducted as slaves. Life for the Gabbra was hellish enough without introducing something like gold. If the *tigre* knew there was gold there they would force the Gabbra to extract it for them – as the Gabbra well knew.

But Hutcheon never could swallow that story. '*Krars*, man, nobody keeps a secret for years on end, ay. Eventually some *oke* will spill his guts either to score a point for himself or to fuck it up for some bastard he's got it in for. 'S'uman nature, ay?'

It was only after our recent experience that Dad felt absolutely sure he had the answer to Hutcheon's scepticism. When they'd argued this point before Dad would dodge it by saying he hadn't enough information, too many pieces were missing from the jigsaw. Hutcheon would accuse him of getting off the subject and they would bicker on about it without ever reaching any conclusion. Now he was sure he knew why no one had apparently rediscovered the source of the bits of gold ore Safwaan had found. The clue he said was in the absence of good surface water anywhere in the vicinity. Lack of water was the reason why this patch of country was nowadays devoid of people yet had obviously in the past been occupied by people for whom the rocky overhang was a comfortable spot. It would only have been a comfortable spot if there was good water nearby.

'Something happened to the water here,' Dad said, 'there must've been a spring and it dried up. We're right near the edge of the Rift Valley, only fifty miles in a straight line. These mountains to the north are the mountains that pile up all along the edges of the valley where the ancient shield rocks split and pulled apart to let the hot magma squeeze up through all the faults. This is geologically active ground. It's common all along the edges of the Rift for springs to start and stop, lakes to rise and fall; bound to happen where there's so much seismic activity.

'And there's something else about this spot as well,' he continued, 'something very significant. We're at the edge of the vast basalt mantle of the Ethiopian highlands as well as being on the main fault line of the Rift Valley. All Ethiopian gold is near the edge of the swell – none's been found far in towards the middle. The edges are where the rivers that rise in the middle erode through the basalt down to the older rocks beneath. Gold, as you know, only accumulates in the vicinity of really big faults and shear lines where there were violent movements of the earth's crust combined with huge flows of hot gas and chemical solutions that transported and then deposited gold dissolved out of the base rocks. Geographically, this spot could easily be one such place where conditions allowed gold to accumulate. The parent rock is highly metamorphosed, which means it was formed under enormous pressures and high tempera-tures. The greenstones that were probably here from bil-lions of years ago were subsequently faulted by yet more earth movements. Dissolved gold then crystallised in the cracks in the greenstone.'

'So – some sort of geological movement cut off the spring you think used to be near here, ay,' said Hutcheon, 'but so what? Stopped people living here, but didn't stop them moving through. Could still've stubbed their toes on these bits of rock lying around the entrance, ay?'

'The reason that didn't happen,' said Dad, 'is because what stopped the spring also hid the mine.'

Hutcheon stared at Dad in disbelief. 'That's very wonderful to hear, Rider. After all this crashing about the veld you tell us there was a huge earthquake that caused a landslide, which buggered up the spring and buried old Suleiman's gold – is that what you're trying to say, man?'

'Landslide, ay?' said Dad. 'Mmm, I hadn't thought of that. Bet you're right, though.' He looked towards the escarpment ten miles to our north. 'Yeah, that's it. We must look for a landslide. Could be as simple as that.'

'Simple, hell,' said Hutcheon. 'So what if we find a landslide? What use is that? Could be a *moer-on* great heap of pure gold there – buried under a hundred thousand tons of rocks, ay. *Magtig*, man, you can talk *kak* sometimes, Rider.'

The camel flies were bad in our camp and they seemed to be ganging up on Hutcheon. He swatted irritably at them.

'Not necessarily, Hutcheon. Sure, a big landslide would be bad news. But we never saw any sign of a big landslide. Maybe we're talking about a *tinish*[80] landslide, just enough to make it hard to see what was there. But Alan here, our geologist, will tell us if that unusual type of metamorphic rock is in the vicinity and then we'll know we're on the spoor.'

'You're dreaming again, Rider,' said Hutcheon, 'your paws are twitching and your eyes are rolling like a dog imagining he's about to catch up with a springhare.'

Safwaan took no part in this conversation – in point of fact, he was asleep most of the time – and it ended with Hutcheon saying that he was tired of talking about kings and gold mines and landslides and 'all that *twak*' and wandering off to see if he could shoot a greater bustard for the pot. The following morning Safwaan was ill with a fever

---

[80] Small (Amharic)

and considerable muscle and joint pain. Therefore, we decided to stay put for another day at least and let him rest some more before starting off on the rough ride back to North Horr. Dad was quite pleased, really, and had us all up and away back to the escarpment to see what we could find. Unencumbered by Safwaan, we were back near the overhang quite early on and decided to continue north-east round the foot of the krans. We passed a small ravine, and another, without bothering to go up them, as there was no sign of any old watercourses. Then, probably not more than a mile from the overhang, we came to a much bigger ravine that descended steeply out of the escarpment. Looking up it, we saw that it turned sharply to the west a few hundred yards in. But what we all immediately remarked on was that the boulders in the floor of the ravine were rounded and polished by water – in fact, there was a distinct waterline on the rocks on either side. It was clear to all of us that when this watercourse had flowed it ran hard with a considerable volume of water. The bedrock was extremely well worn, with one or two deep potholes where the stream had whirlpooled over the years. We weren't surprised that it was completely dry – it was after all the height of the dry season – but then Dad said something that gave me gooseflesh the moment he spoke the words.

'I don't see any debris from the last time it flowed.'

The rest of us were quiet and the more we looked the more it struck us as it did Dad – there were no branches caught up at the waterline, or bunches of twigs and rubbish such as you invariably see after a flood has passed down a watercourse. We scouted around a bit and, primed no doubt by what we wanted to think as a result of what we had recently been discussing, confirmed to each other the fact that no water appeared to have run down this river bed in the recent past.

Well, we lost no time clambering up that old riverbed. We got to where it turned sharply to the west and here it ran more or less level for a hundred yards or so before it again changed direction, to the north. Some gravel had accumulated on the level section and, once again, we all stopped and gaped, each of us seeing the same thing: several scrubby trees growing in the patches of gravel. Not young trees, but old and gnarled. Serious water had not flowed down this watercourse for decades at least. We just looked at one another, silently. It was as if we dared not break a spell. Rounding the next bend, we worked our way for some distance upstream to where it swung around again to the west. Then as we rounded the third bend we came to what I will certainly never forget: a landslide that had tumbled down from the east side of the valley across the river bed. The ravine, probably not more than seventy yards wide at this point was blocked by rocks and rubble up to a height of twenty or so feet from the lowest point. Over the top of the blockage, just beyond it, we could see a sheer, vertical cliff-face that rose at least two hundred feet above us so that our horizon was made up of the top of the cliff as far as we could see on either side.

'*Yurruh magtig*,' said Hutcheon, '*nou dars 'n ding*, ay.'

Dad was simply staring slack-faced, as was I. Hutcheon looked at Dad and laughed. 'I'm only glad,' he said, 'that I didn't promise to eat my hat, ay.'

It was rough going over the sharp rocks and scree, but a bunch of babs wouldn't have made it any faster than we did up that wall of debris. We got to the top and saw that the ravine indeed ended abruptly only seventy yards or so beyond the bottom of the landslide at the foot of the sheer cliff. Then we saw that the stream had originally tumbled down the cliffs, leaving paler vertical streaks on the reddish-black rock. At the bottom the water had gouged out a pool, long since dry now of course, and choked with a thicket of the same low scrubby trees we'd seen downstream. However, the most striking feature and one that had us all pointing and wondering was that on the eastern side of the ravine, in a small flattish widening of the valley floor, there was a clump of three large baobabs. You may think that unsurprising – baobabs grow all over the low, dry country of sub-Saharan Africa. But their distribution is not continuous and up in the north-west corner of the N.F.D., for example, they are generally absent so that these three specimens stood out like polar bears. They were huge; we later paced their circumferences: the smallest was seventeen yards, the largest nineteen. The latter would have been six yards in diameter. Otherwise, the ravine was unremarkable with scarcely any vegetation except for the thicket at the base of the now defunct waterfall, and the baobabs.

We wandered around for a while, looking at the base of the waterfall and around the baobabs. Dad and I sat down on the rocks a little way up the west side of the ravine and tried to work out the geological structure of the place. Although it didn't look like much at first sight, after a bit it was clear to us that we were sitting astride a massive fault that had split the mountain along the axis of the cliff-face – more or less parallel with the throw of the Rift Valley – which had been created when the mountain on the northern side of the fault had been pushed upwards a couple of hundred feet or so. Then we saw that another, much less well-defined fault line ran parallel to the first. Where this intersected the ravine it was marked by a fissure extending a short distance from the valley floor before becoming choked with rocks and rubble that had fallen into it. The ravine itself had evidently been eroded by the old, long-dry river that had run along another fault that ran at right angles to the other two fault lines. Each change of direction downstream probably marked other, similar fault lines.

The fissure running off the ravine was where the baobabs

grew. Then we saw that the landslide consisted of rocks that had fallen out of another fault line parallel to the one just north of it at the mouth of which grew the baobabs. Clearly, we were sitting on a spot that had been subjected to massive faulting associated with the main Rift Valley lines of weakness. The faults running parallel to the Rift Valley axis – north-east–south-west – were the really massive ones where the Horn of Africa was separating from the African continental plate. The immense pressure from the molten magma below pushed up the huge mountains that bordered the Rift from here to Harar. It was easy to visualise how this same force pushing up from below would also split the mountains at right angles to the main valley cracks to relieve the pressure.

Although the small landslide had blocked the ravine, probably set off by an earthquake generated by further rupturing of the faults, it obviously wasn't what had stopped the river. That had dried up above us, perhaps a long way off, as the result of underground earth movements some distance away; though in all likelihood they all occurred at the same time.

We then spent some time looking around the baobabs, puzzled by their presence and awed by their size. 'Got to have been planted by people,' said Dad, 'long ago when this river still flowed. You know how the *watu* make flour from the fruits. A sour, unpleasant flour that they only bother with when they can't get millet in really dry years. Reckon they brought the seeds here for that reason and some germinated and grew into these trees. But – *krars*, man, they're *stokond*, ay? You know how long these trees can live?'

Everybody wonders how long baobabs can live and like the size and speed of black mambas on a hot day, some opinions are apt to draw more from imagination than observation. That they live for centuries is, however, well attested. In 1868, the explorer Thomas Baines came across a baobab that had been pushed over by an elephant on the edge of the Makgadikgadi Pans in Bechuanaland. He was struck by the fact that despite lying on its side it was still growing, so made a drawing of it. You can still see that tree, still lying on its side and still growing. Sixteenth century cannon balls were found in a baobab, still alive and healthy, that was bulldozed aside for a block of flats near the entrance to Mombasa harbour. Scientists, extrapolating from the measured growth of baobabs, opine that they could live for two thousand years. There's nothing, they say, to rule out such an age. It is also a plant that, while it stops growing upwards, never stops growing in girth so that its waistline reflects its age.

'A thousand years, easy,' continued Dad, 'to grow this fat we're talking many, many centuries.' We all agreed that without doubt we were looking at something that had been here for a long, long time. But of the hand of man, we at first saw nothing. Then, at the base of one of the trees, I found some pottery shards, evidently old and weathered. But that was it – at least for a while. It was Hutcheon who remarked that there were several boulders lying in the old watercourse that were not water-worn, but which had pre-sumably rolled down at the time of the landslide. Then he pointed to the baobab furthest away from the riverbed, the one we couldn't pace because it was growing partly on top of the bedrock. 'Look – I think there's a stone that's rolled down and broken right through it. We clambered up the rocks around the base of the tree and, sure enough, there was a rock sticking out of the trunk on the uphill side. When we got round to look closer we saw that a huge boulder had rolled down the side of the ravine, hit the tree and broken through and come to rest inside the hollow trunk. Although it half filled the interior there was still space enough around it for a man to get into. I don't know why, but one is always drawn to look inside a hollow tree or a cave and we were curious to look inside this one. As it was a good place for a leopard to park her cubs we were circumspect and took care not to end up looking like Safwaan. But there were no hostile residents and we squeezed in past the rock quite easily.

Well, I can't do justice to describing our feelings at what we saw next. Over the years – over the centuries I should rather say – the trunk of the baobab had widened and widened until it entirely surrounded the entrance to a cave. Only it wasn't a cave. It was really dark inside the baobab owing to the rock that blocked most of the hole knocked in the tree's side, so we got out and put together a torch of dried sticks and went back in after we got it burning. We soon saw that the cave had in point of fact been made by people chipping away the rock. And the rock they'd chipped away was the same stuff as the gold-bearing rocks Safwaan had found, that much we could easily see. There'd been a whole seam of greenstone running through the parent rock, which they'd presumably removed as they burrowed in. Moreover, they'd gone a long way in – I've no idea how far as we weren't game to go in any distance, not knowing how stable it was.

'It's a mineshaft,' said Dad, 'a bloody great mineshaft. Now, Hutcheon, what've you got to say, ay?'

'Nou dars 'n ding. God, jong, the ancient eldorado of all the old fools . . . We're standing right in it . . . here where the lammergeyers and the klipspringers play. Oom Quatermain never loses the spoor, ay? Magtig, Rider, the spoor ends right here, man. Probably find old Suleiman himself at the end of the tunnel, counting shekels, ay.'

We got out to let the smoke from the torch disperse and decided to make a new one and have one more look. It was on the second sortie inside the baobab that I saw on a particularly flat patch of rock near the entrance what looked like some markings. We had a closer look and sure enough there were four characters deeply gouged into the rock. Large, bulbous, squiggly characters with some dots – they vaguely reminded me of Arabic characters although I'd no idea what they were. We asked Dad what they were, but he, too, didn't know. Then he remembered his camera, which he sometimes carried but rarely used, because most of the films got forgotten, or ruined by the heat or left too long before processing. We held the torch right below the marks and he took a shot. It was a long time before he got that film developed and an even longer time before he got his old friend Sir Wallis Budge, the famous Egyptologist at the British Museum, to decipher it. As Wallis remarked, for all that the engraver wasn't one of Michelangelo's ancestors it was easy to see that what he'd carved into the rock-face was the Hebrew word שְׁלֹמֹה that spells the name Solomon.

25

Do Not Remove Thorns from Lions' Feet

It's been more than a year now since we found the mine and I haven't been back. I'm not at all sure that I ever will go back. Things aren't the same, can't ever be the same and the changes are going to take a fair bit of getting used to. You see, the mystery of the mine was always Dad's thing, his obsession, his dream. For sure I got caught up in it, am still snarled up in it in many ways, and the next generation of Quatermains – if there is one – may well embroil itself in it; but I never had quite the same drug-like dependency on it that Dad had. I just haven't been around long enough, I guess. If I get to spend as long as he did pondering the whole mystery perhaps I will become as hooked. But I don't think so, because one of the main things that's changed is that the whereabouts of King Solomon's mines is no longer forgotten – at least I'm pretty sure of that, for all that a lot of questions remain unanswered. You see, finding the wretched thing constituted an arrival in Stevenson's sense. I don't know how many times I heard Dad quote the man's maxim, but I do know that for him it summed up a fundamental truism – as it does for so much of mankind's affairs, particularly those that are more wishful than real. But of course there's something else that's changed that has a far greater effect on my attitude towards King Solomon's mines than any of that.

After we got back to Luoniek, having dropped Safwaan

off in Marsabit with an arrangement to meet again in the near future to discuss our next move, Dad seemed strangely reluctant to pursue the matter. Or at least I found it strange, as I'd expected him to be all fired up about getting back to the place and delving a bit deeper into what exactly we'd discovered, find out more about what that old mineshaft meant.

There was – still is and always will be – no doubt in my mind that what we'd found was one of King Solomon's legendary gold mines. Although the evidence is circumstantial it's too much and too compelling not to conclude that this mine fed the legends of Ophir and King Solomon's mines. Geologically, it's in the right place, on the edge of the great Ethiopian highland swell. What we saw had all the features of something that came to an abrupt halt many centuries ago. A gold mining enterprise on a geologically active site – the ever-widening Rift Valley – experienced a sudden cut-off of its indispensable water supply and probably devastating collapses of the surrounding country as the result of an earthquake. For all we know the mineshaft we found has collapsed somewhere along its length – we haven't looked yet. There may well have been – almost certainly were – several mines there, now buried under the landslide. In any event, the place was abandoned and its whereabouts forgotten, possibly as the result of a depopulation of the area following prolonged droughts. Rediscovery was prevented by the simple fact of a baobab tree – ironically planted fortuitously by the miners themselves – growing in and eventually over the entrance to the only remaining mineshaft. The great age of the baobab shows that all this happened centuries ago – possibly a thousand years ago. Or more. The baobabs there now may be second or third generation trees for all that anyone knows. We have nothing else by which to date the place, except of course the Hebrew inscriptions.

But Dad busied himself with mundane things, cattle and safari bookings and such like, saying we'd talk about it all 'later'. Hutcheon said he wasn't at all surprised; that he'd always suspected Dad would be far happier searching than finding. At first, I was really disappointed; for me the discovery was enormously exciting and I couldn't understand why Dad was so evasive and seemingly uninterested. I didn't pay much heed to the obvious practical difficulties of doing anything, like the simple fact that the place was quite possibly in Ethiopia rather than Kenya. The actual location of the border between the two countries had not, in 1946, been settled yet. And even if it had, we didn't know except roughly where we'd been. The map itself was far from accurate so that even if we'd tried to plot our movements the result would only have been an approximation. It would take a couple of astro-fixes (assuming we were equipped and able to make them, which we weren't) to accurately determine the latitude and longitude of the mine. Moreover, how would we investigate such a thing without people getting to know about it – something we certainly didn't want to happen. If it was in Ethiopia and the Ethiopians got wind of a possible gold mine in their country we could be absolutely sure we'd be the last to retain any interest in it. But before I got around to thinking through such imponderables, destiny stepped in with a much bigger imponderable.

It all happened while Dad was on a recce for a big safari that an old client had booked. This man, a Texean as he liked to call himself, had hunted with Dad in the thirties and was anxious to make another safari now that the war was over. Dad liked him and wanted to make sure he laid on a good safari; so he decided to recce some of the areas he hadn't been in since the War began to make sure he didn't waste the client's time. Dad had asked me to accompany him up in the north in Boran country in an area that had in years past been good for greater kudu, which in East Africa are never that easy to come by, though in Southern Africa they are common. It was also a place where past clients had taken very good rhinos and Dad was keen to find out if there was still a chance of one. We made camp near some Boran whom we knew well and on the first day Dad told me to take Ndaragus and another man who was good in the bush and head off with a couple of Boran who claimed to know where we could find kudu. He said he wanted to talk to the old men for a couple of hours and catch up on the local gossip. I was to return around midday and we would then go out again together in the afternoon depending on what Dad had learnt from the Boran *wazee*.[81]

From the moment we'd set up camp Dad had been depressed, the first such episode since we'd all got back together after the War. It reminded me of the old days before the War when he had many times gone through long episodes of melancholia that none of us had ever been able to do much about. That's the problem with depression – and I knew well enough having inherited the trait – you're on your own. Regardless of how genuinely sympathetic other people may be there's absolutely nothing they can say or do that helps. Once it settles on you like an evening shadow, it's immovable. You just have to wait and see it out. Knowing all this I knew there was no point in hanging about or making worn-out remarks that had never been any help before; so I got on with my business and left Dad to his. I hated to see him like this, specially since he'd been so elated in recent weeks; but I could think of nothing I could help him with.

I didn't know it at the time because Dad had never ever discussed it with either Leila or me, but where we were camped was not very far from where they'd been camped the night my mother was killed. Had I been aware of this his depression would of course have presented in quite a different light. But I didn't know. I left camp that day before dawn and didn't get back until after midday. I therefore was unaware that only minutes after I'd gone some Boran from a neighbouring kraal came into camp to tell Dad that there was an injured rhino near their kraal. It wasn't far away so Dad said he'd go and investigate. He chose one local man to guide him to the animal and the two of them set off. I had the only two men who were any good at hunting with me, so Dad had only his Gibbs .505 with him, there being no one else he would trust to accompany him with a gun.

The rhino turned out to be something like eight or nine miles from camp. Dad drove his hunting car most of the way, slow going through the bush, but with no real difficulty. When his guide said they were within a mile or two Dad stopped the car and walked the rest of the way. There was a steady easterly blowing and they were heading upwind so that approaching the animal was straightforward. Rhino are exceptionally easy to hunt because, like elephants, they don't maintain a high level of vigilance with their eyes, which they keep focused on their immediate surroundings most of the time. They have extremely keen noses and ears, but if you stay downwind you can if you know what you're about approach them closely with remarkable ease compared to any other wild animal.

It seems they got up to the beast without incident and found it standing in the shade of a tall anthill out of the base of which grew a large *hadama*[82] tree. They saw this from sixty or seventy yards away as they crouched down to peer through the stems of the scattered bushes between them and the rhino. As the morning sun was still low the

---

[82] Candelabra tree, *Euphorbia robecchii* (Oromo)

combination of the tree and anthill made for a large patch of shade that would last for several hours. Dad no doubt quickly saw what the animal's problem was. A thick wire snare made from a length of cable was round its right rear leg. There was about three or four yards of cable trailing behind the leg attached to a short, but very thick tree stump, designed to hamper the victim's movements and make it easier to catch up with and despatch. But whoever had set the snare had for whatever reason not followed up his catch as the snare had evidently been in place for quite some time. It had worn a huge open wound on the rhino's leg and would almost certainly lead to the animal's death in the next few weeks or sooner. All this I learnt from the Boran man who was with him.

What happened next is that Dad, good old soft-hearted Dad, felt compelled yet again, for the umpteenth time in his life, to pull the thorn from the unfortunate lion's foot. He whispered to the man with him to stay put and get ready to bolt if need be. He, Dad, was going to ease up closer to the rhino and try to shoot the snare off the animal's leg. It was the sort of stunt that Dad could pull off. As I've mentioned before, he was a natural-born marksman who really could get a second bullet to touch the first at close range. He'd sighted the .505 to shoot dead on at around twenty-five yards and what he set out to do was quite feasible if he could get himself suitably positioned. The rhino was sick and exhausted and even less alert than it would normally be, allowing Dad to get within the distance he wanted without difficulty. The Boran man, watching from a distance, said that Dad waited in position for a long time while the rhino shifted its weight occasionally, but keeping in the shade of the anthill. The noose of the snare had been crudely made by tying a large, clumsy knot at the cable's end, through which the cable ran. This resulted in a large bundle of wire, pulled up tight against the back of the animal's leg. If Dad could get the heavy .505 bullet – with its striking energy of around two tons – into the middle of the knot there was every chance it would shatter enough of the wire for the animal to free its leg. Dad waited until he had a perfect line of sight to the knot, with the rhino's left rear leg forward and out of the way, and squeezed off a shot.

Exactly what happened next will bother me for the rest of my life – of that I am quite certain. Because sometimes I think I do know exactly what happened and I don't much care for it. At other times I think that nothing happened other than what Dad told me took place, though he didn't explain it very clearly and sometimes I wonder if I actually remember what he told me, or only think I remember. You see, his shot was good and the rhino did shed the snare within fifty yards of where it'd been standing and eventually took off into the *porini* for good. But it's what happened in the moments after Dad so skilfully drew the thorn from this particular lion's foot that plagues me: because the rhino didn't just split when the gun went off.

All this took place as far as I can determine at about ten-thirty in the morning. I got back to camp a little after noon to find that the Boran who'd been with Dad had got there just before me, having legged it the nine miles or so in quick order. As I pulled up, people converged on me like tsetse flies, shouting and gesticulating. And wailing. That's what got me – someone wailing. I seized up, apprehension creeping over me like *siafu*,[83] cold and prickly in the midday sun. Something awful was afoot, but for a time I couldn't get the gist of it, everybody was so worked up, all yelling at once. But of course, I soon did get the news. Dad. Dad was hurt. Was dead according to someone; no – alive, but seriously injured according to another. Angrily, I told them

---

[83] A predatory, swarming ant (Swahili)

all to shut up and tell me where. Could I drive there? Yes, yes. The throng piled into the *gharry* and I got the Boran who'd been with Dad to stand up in the back next to Ndaragus. He was to lean over the cab and wave a stick that I could see through the windscreen to indicate which way to turn. We followed Dad's wheel tracks to his car and continued on the remaining mile and a half to where the Boran of necessity had left Dad. 'There, there,' he shouted, Ndaragus pounding on the cab for me to stop, 'by that bush.'

I can see him now, lying on his left side in the sun, awfully still, with flies crawling unswatted over his skin. His rifle was beside him, his right hand resting on the breech. There was blood on the ground, not that much, churned up in the sand where he'd evidently moved before I got there; but I saw none on him at first. As I raced round to his front, he moved his head to look at me, his mouth moving though I couldn't hear anything. His sunburnt complexion was a dreadful browny-grey. I sent everyone except Ndaragus to cut the ends of the scrubby branches of the trees and bushes around to get as much leafy material as possible to make a base for him to lie on in the back of the truck. Then I knelt down and bent my head close to his. He spoke slowly in a shallow, grating sort of whisper.

'Listen carefully, Alan, there's something you must please, please do. You'll think I'm delirious, but I swear to you I'm not. What I want you to do is something I decided long ago when Amina . . . your mother . . . when she died.' He paused and shut his eyes for a while – clearly, it was a great effort to talk. Of course, I wanted to ask him what the hell had happened so I could better decide what to do next; but somehow he conveyed an urgency that made me wait to hear him out.

'Go ahead, Dad, of course I'll do whatever you say.'

'Promise me, Alan, and promise me that you'll get Leila to promise as well?'

'I promise.'

I took his hand where it rested on the rifle. The steel of the gun was hot in the sun; his hand was cold and dry. His shirt was pulled up a bit, exposing his abdomen. Dad was a hard, muscular man who'd never carried any extra weight, so when I saw his belly bulging where his shirt had pulled away I knew immediately what it meant. I already knew from his limpness, from his pallor and faint voice that he was very badly injured. I took his forearm and gripped it in my left hand, then let go. The indentation of my fingers slowly, oh so slowly filled out again. His blood pressure was very, very low and I knew – God how I hated the knowing – that he was bleeding internally, and had been so for quite some time now. That was why there was so little blood on the ground or on him; his injuries were internal. I looked at Ndaragus, who'd positioned himself to shade Dad as best he could, and our eyes met. He said nothing; but he was crying, the tears muddying the grey dust on his face, that was all of a sudden the face of an old, old man. Ndaragus had seen too many animals die, and men too, not to know as surely as I did what was soon to happen. I moved to try to investigate Dad's injuries, but he started to speak again.

'Alan, there is a letter for you and Leila at Luonlek. It explains what I hope you will do for me. I want you to take me back to Amina. Abdullahi knows the place, and Ndaragus and Hutcheon. You must leave us together there. Mustn't bury me, can't stand that, as you know. Just leave me where the lions left her . . . we just want to be together again. Leila must come with you. Promise me you'll make Leila come. I want you and her to know where your mother is. She loved you both so very dearly . . .' His voice trailed off. If he'd had the fluid for tears he'd have wept then, I think. He spoke again.

375

'She's not far from here. Ask Ndaragus – he knows. Sorry I never showed you before, but I . . . I couldn't. Don't know why. But I missed her so much, I loved her so . . . I couldn't ever find the courage to go back there . . . But I always planned to join her when I died.'

He seemed to fade for a long time, just lay there in the sun, eyes shut, breathing slowly, just perceptibly. Then his lips started moving again, and he opened his eyes.

'Waited until you and Leila were grown up . . . she would've expected that of me.'

He paused for a while, then said, 'But I can go now . . . you'll be okay.'

His eyes shut again and his hand went limp in mine. My father on the ground beside me was dying and for Ndaragus and I there was really only a short wait now during which the only thing we could usefully do was brush the flies off Dad's face. I didn't expect to ever hear Dad speak again – but I was wrong, though not by much. His eyes opened and he was able to look at me one last time. I took Ndaragus's hand and got him to clasp Dad's. Dad looked away from me and caught Ndaragus's gaze.

'*Salaam, mzee, salaam.*'

Poor old Ndaragus, he couldn't speak. Just cried, soundlessly, without any visible movement.

'Alan, tell Leila I love her . . . and Hutcheon and . . . and . . . Abdullahi . . . Hawa . . .'

That was it. Some little time later he drew a couple of deep breaths; his limbs twitched slightly as if in sleep and he was gone. We knelt there, Ndaragus and I, sobbing, for I don't know how long. The voices of the men returning with the brush they'd cut broke the silence and our sorrow and we got to our feet and began to do what we had to do to move on.

I told Ndaragus what Dad had made me promise and asked him where the place was where they had killed the

lions that took my mother. I explained that Dad wanted to be taken there in the company of certain specific people.
'It is very close to here,' he said and indicated the direction. 'Beyond the kraal that is close by.'
'Can you find it again?' I asked.
'Yes. I cannot forget that place.'
'How long would it take to reach it?'
'In the *gharry* . . . if we start in the morning . . . we can be there by midday.'
I was going to have to get a rift on. But before moving I had to know what had happened a few hours earlier, just how Dad had come by his injuries. I asked the Boran who'd witnessed it all. He told me the story of the wire snare and how Dad had said he was going to shoot it off. When Dad fired, he said, the rhino moved very quickly, turning away from the anthill to run towards Dad. But not directly, he said. It looked as if it was going to pass some distance in front of him; but suddenly it saw Dad when it was only a few yards away. At that point, it wheeled and charged straight at him. Dad fired a second shot high over the animal, but it didn't pause and was upon him. It stopped in front of him, head down, and hooked its horn under Dad, throwing him high in the sky. Dad fell and the rhino hooked him a second time, throwing him some yards to the side. Then it ran off. I looked at Dad's body, at his right side that he had been lying on and saw the bruised and torn flesh where the horn had hit in the abdomen. The kidneys were also massively bruised and battered. His liver and other internal organs must have been pulverised. Ndaragus, who had been walking from where Dad was to where the rhino had been, looking carefully at the tracks and positions then said to me that it was clear that the rhino had not initially attacked Dad. In Ndaragus's opinion the gunshot had echoed off the anthill causing the animal to think that was where the shot had come from. It was trying

to escape, he thought, and mistakenly ran towards rather than away from Dad. Only when it saw Dad from very close range did it turn to attack him.

But why, wondered Ndaragus, had Dad not killed it with his second barrel? For Dad it would have been an easy shot. Firing a warning shot at close range like that was never going to have much chance of success and, moreover, leave no time to reload. I too wondered at that. It wasn't until long afterwards that I came to accept that Dad had never intended to protect himself. At the time, too much was going on, too many confusing thoughts made all the murkier by the awful sense of loneliness, of loss. Something Dad had said just before he died flashed back into my mind. *Waited until you and Leila were grown up . . . she would've expected that of me. But I can go now, you'll be okay.* But I can go now . . . but I can go now. She, meaning our mother . . . but I can go now. What did he mean by that, what was he saying? I skirted around the really very simple implication of those words for ages, not wanting to accept their likeliest meaning.

I found myself standing – staring at nothing. I sensed I'd stood like that for quite a while because I noticed that Ndaragus and the others were looking anxiously at me, obviously wondering what I was up to. I made an effort to snap out of it, put aside those frightening thoughts and concentrate instead on the practicalities of what I now had to do.

We took Dad's body to our camp, left Ndaragus there and drove back to Luoniek to fetch the others. I got there sometime during the night and broke the news to Leila and Hutcheon and to Abdullahi and Hawa. What an awful time that was, so many tears, so much anguish. Leila and Hawa huddled together, weeping. Us men spare and awkward and mostly silent, as many men are at such times, wrapped up in jumbled, confusing thoughts. We found the letter Dad had told me about. He'd written it ages ago – that was a rather chilling thing – having decided as Hutcheon had rightly figured before ever leaving the baobab tree back in 1926 what he was going to do. The letter reiterated his wish to be taken to the tree and left where he'd left Amina, and the rest was in effect a will. There was, however, one other thing in it, which, as Hutcheon said was so very typical of Dad. Scrawled at the end of the letter, obviously quite recently, was a note to the effect that a small stipend was to be deposited in the bank in Marsabit for Safwaan, for him to draw until he died. It ended as follows: *Tell Safwaan that there is one condition. He is not to spend it all, but to keep enough that when he dies he can bribe the guards at the gates of shifta paradise to let him through.*

'He was something else, ay, your dad,' said Hutcheon. 'His romantic conscience refused to let him deal with a *shifta*. Then, when circumstances changed, that same conscience compelled him to pull thorns from the *shifta* lion's feet – even after he's dead and gone, ay. He was a cut above the rest of us, on a different plane. One of those people who unconsciously determines the lives of those around him, though they themselves may never know it.'

We were all silent for a while, then Hutcheon went on. 'Think I can speak for all of us when I say that we all tried to do things in such a way as to justify your dad's faith in us. He never asked us to. He wouldn't have known that we were trying to. We ourselves may never have realised that we were doing it. But I know now that I always was; and I think we all were.'

He was right, of course; Hutcheon usually was.

We got in the car – except Hawa, too arthritic and too distressed to cope with such an expedition – as soon as we could get ready, and drove back, arriving in camp I suppose about mid-morning; I wasn't keeping track of time at this stage. We loaded Dad's body and set off for the spot where, twenty years ago, Nature had determined that my mother's remains should come to rest. For Hutcheon, Abdullahi and Ndaragus it was not difficult to find the place. As Ndaragus had said, none of them would ever forget it. It was slow driving through the bush, but we made steady progress as there were no impassable places. Rather than try to retrace the direct route the lions had taken all those years ago, which would've been guesswork, we took the longer but more certain alternative of following the lugga southwards to where it descended the slight escarpment. From there we went west along the escarpment to the little group of baobabs that they told me were about half a mile or so from the baobab where they'd caught up with the lions. We got there about four o'clock in the afternoon.

Tired, very tired, dejected, hot and thirsty, we got out of the car and assembled dispiritedly and not a little uncertainly. Leila took my hand and pressed herself against me. We hugged each other and stood there forlornly, gazing wordlessly at the baobab tree where our mother lay, such dust as might still represent her. Hutcheon showed us what they had done that day in 1926, how Dad had got them to drag the bodies of the lions up to the base of the tree and pile them together.

'Where,' asked Hutcheon, gently and oh so softly, 'where shall we lay your dad?'

I looked at Leila. 'Exactly where the lions were?'

'Yes,' she said, 'they just want to be together. It's what we must do.'

We cried then, Leila and I, cried and ached as the three men took Dad's body and laid it down at the base of the tree in the dried leaves and twigs that lay scattered over the sandy ground. There was of course no remaining sign of the lions that had once lain there. The baobab was in flower and several fallen blossoms lay among the debris on the ground. Leila gathered as many as she could find and dropped them over Dad's body. Although we had already explained to Abdullahi and Ndaragus that Dad had insisted he not be buried I went through it all again for them, as they found that extremely difficult to come to terms with. For them, the dead should be buried; it was wrong to leave a body exposed for the hyenas to desecrate. But they understood perfectly that Amina had not been buried and that Dad wished to lie where she had lain, to share her fate. That they could accommodate and so, reluctantly, they went along with what we were doing; but with one proviso that they felt strongly about. His body must at least be covered with branches, like the elephants do, they said. They were sure that Dad would agree with that. So we cut branches – in point of fact, it was a welcome diversion that stopped us feeling so bad for a bit – and arranged them over Dad until the two of them, Abdullahi and Ndaragus, were satisfied.

All this time none of us had noticed what Ndaragus suddenly saw, drawing back nervously from placing a branch with a loud exclamation: 'Uh, uh!' He was pointing at the branches on Dad's body, I thought at first; but no, he said, the tree. I looked and looked back at Ndaragus, seeing nothing. He then leant over the branches on the body and moved one aside to reveal the tree trunk low down. Then I saw it. There were marks on the tree – writing – gouged into the bark and long since healed over, almost grown together. Nevertheless, it was easy enough to read once you knew it was there.

> *Of shadows on the ground*
> *The long grass spoke.*
> *But not of the thing that lay*
> *More softly than the shadows.*

I read them out aloud and translated them for Abdullahi and Ndaragus who recited them quietly two or three times.

I told them that they were from a poem by Dad's favourite poet[84] and they asked me to write them down in Oromo. 'So *that's* what he was doing!' exclaimed Hutcheon suddenly. He spoke rapidly to Abdullahi and Ndaragus, recalling what Dad had done on that day twenty years ago when, at his request, they had left him alone at the tree just as they were leaving. 'He was carving these words into the bark, ay. I wondered at the time why he'd hidden his knife. He'd foreseen that I would disarm him if he went off alone, so he . . .'

He paused, frowning and mouthing something to himself. Then he spoke again, still softly and gently.

'He had it all worked out, even then, ay! He'd already decided what he was going to do – be brought back here when he died. All these years he was really only waiting for this moment, ay. There's no way he was ever going to accept being parted from her. He was just waiting until you two grew up.'

He shook his head and looked at us all. Leila had tears in her eyes again; she looked so sad. But she smiled through her tears as she said to me, 'He loved her so, didn't he? I'm glad for them, that they are together again. Now they can travel forever on their eternal journey.'

One other thing happened before we left my mother and father that afternoon, the shadows long now, the grass that had been yellow in the sun turning grey. Ndaragus, sharp-eyed Ndaragus, suddenly stooped and picked something up, showing it to Abdullahi. Immediately the two of them cast around the ground under the branches of the baobab. They soon showed us what they'd been looking for: two small stones. I didn't get it at first, my mind being elsewhere.

'These are the stones we threw there long ago,' Ndaragus

---

[84] From the poem *Veld Secret* by Herman Charles Bosman

said, a slight smile on his face now. Leila and I remembered then how Hutcheon had described each of them tossing a stone onto the dead lions, onto our mother's resting place. Maybe they were the same stones, maybe they weren't; but we each of us searched until we found one and dropped it on the branches covering my parents' remains.

In keeping with Dad's wishes, I won't say where he and my mother are. It's a private spot where two lovers lie who deserve what tranquillity they can negotiate with Nature, now that the Old Vixen's finished messing them about. The N.F.D.'s a big place; much of it looks like the rest and even if I did describe where that baobab tree is, and how to get to it up there in the northern part of the district, you'd be hard pressed to make your way there.

On that subject you may wonder why I was apparently more forthcoming about the location of old Suleiman's gold, given that there could very well be an abundance of the sweat of the sun still there. By all means – go for it! But don't be surprised if, having fended off any *tigre* or *shifta* you could so easily bump into up there, and denied the lions a meal, and survived all the other pitfalls of trekking that part of the world, you find my directions confusing. It's rugged country up there, the maps are hopeless and men's memories being what they are it's always possible I meant turn left when I said turn right; no – not *that* lugga: *this* one. As Safwaan once remarked, 'There are many secrets in the bush.' Veld Secrets . . . oh yes . . . there's a few I'm privy to and sometimes I think they're best kept right where they are: next to my heart. Like Dad, I hate it when romance is demystified. Life's prosaic enough without blowing away the little luminous wisps of secrecy and romance that occasionally – and it is only occasionally – adorn it.